STRANDED
IN EXILE

A.L. MCDONNELL

Published in Australia by Thestel Books
ABN: 71 163 373 402
First published in Australia 2020
This edition published 2020

ISBN: 978-0-6450296-6-6

Cover design, typesetting: WorkingType (www.workingtype.com.au)

McDonnell, A.L.
Stranded: In Exile
pp430

almcdonnell.com

ABOUT THE AUTHOR

The author, **A.L. McDonnell** is a medical practitioner and psychologist who lives in Queensland's Lockyer Valley. She has written many scientific pieces and articles for lifestyle magazines and, as a medical practitioner, has worked extensively throughout the outback which is home to some of life's most colourful characters. Odd experiences are often the norm in the remote far west, and she was fascinated by the way individuals could spin their yarns, in pubs or around the campfire, turning ordinary events into something beyond this world and, even more, the many methods they claimed to have used to confront their bizarre encounters. Abandoned grew from such a tale when she was asked what she would do if a spaceship landed in one of her own paddocks …

For more **https://almcdonnell.com**

To Barry
For believing in me

ACKNOWLEDGMENTS

Without Barry, this novel would still be gathering dust in the bottom drawer of my desk.

My thanks to my lovely writers' group for all their help and encouragement – Jill, Kate, Jan, Danae, Bryce, Ruth, Barbara, Claire and Jo– and all the editors and instructors who helped with early drafts.

Thanks to Mark Griffiths for his military knowledge, and my apologies to Mark for the number of times I ignored his sound advice for the sake of a good story.

CHAPTER 1: 2020

Inter-Planetary League Command Ship

Earth Date: Saturday, August 15, 2020

Bile rose into Jemma's throat and she gagged at a foul smell, like meat going off in the sun, but she refused to give in to the pain that seared through her body or the fog that mired her brain. If she could get to her room, she'd be alright, like she had each other time this had happened. She firmed her grip on the rail and stared helplessly at all the identical doors in the never-ending spaceship corridor, her vision now so blurred she couldn't see the familiar landmarks she'd normally have used to find her cabin. Her apartment, like all the others, was secured by a tiny bead-like structure set into the architrave, essentially a microscopic computer. It assessed twenty-five personal identification points, all of which had to match for the door to open. She'd have to stand in each doorway in turn until she found the one that opened. Not particularly efficient, but it was her best hope. First, she had to get across the corridor to reach the doors.

The pain shot through her again, and she cried out as she dropped to the floor. She kept one hand on the rail, afraid to let go in case she couldn't get up again and clutched her stomach with the other. It'd be so easy to curl up on the soft, cushioned floor and wait to be found.

She'd almost given up when she heard someone running towards her along the corridor. She did her best to stand, but her legs buckled beneath her. 'Help,' she whispered when the man reached her. He knelt beside her, and she was grateful for the arm that came around her waist to balance her.

'Lean on me now,' he said, and he sounded quite alarmed.

'Thank you.' She accepted his assistance without looking up but, when she raised her head, she found herself staring into the face of the man who, just two weeks ago, on the orders of his boss, Fredrick Pritchard, had ambushed her military protectors and attempted to kill her. Thanks to the intensive training she'd been subjected to for months by General Hunt prior to the attack, who'd sworn to protect her, she'd survived. Others hadn't. The General himself had been seriously injured.

The scars on the man's face stood out as he stared back at her, but his smile failed to reach his eyes and, when she tried to pull away, he dropped the pretence. 'Come with me,' he said, clasping her arm harder.

'No,' she screamed. She knew how rigidly the aliens had screened everyone who came on board. There was no way anyone could have slipped through, but it was pointless worrying about how he'd got there. He wasn't taking her again.

She forced herself to straighten up to her full height. Even though she was just shy of 180 centimetres, he towered above her. 'Get your hands off me.' She reefed her arm away from him, so shocked by his presence that her brain seemed to slip into automatic.

Centring and focussing as Hunt had drummed into her, she rammed her knee into his groin, smashed her fist under his jaw, then jabbed a finger into one of his eyes. Pumped with adrenaline, she ignored her pain as she staggered across the corridor to the nearest door and stood under its bead. It didn't recognise her, so she dragged herself to the next one, terrified that he might be following. Two more doors failed, and then one opened. Letting out the breath she didn't realise she'd been holding in, she stepped through, but she couldn't let down her guard yet. Grasping her stomach and trying to ignore her agony, she turned back to face the corridor until she was sure the door was securely shut, and she was alone.

Heaving for air, she staggered across the small apartment to the end of the bed, and half fell, half dragged herself onto it. Pulling her knees up to her chest didn't relieve the pain, so she rolled forward and, resting her head on her legs, allowed her face to nestle into the soft fabric of the alien-provided maroon uniform which identified her as a member of the security force. It felt damp. Any resolve she had left vanished when she saw rivulets of blood streaming down the pale grey bedspread. Her cries were now little more than whimpers. Sweat covered her face, even as she shivered, and stars swirled in front of her eyes. Her hands were so cold she couldn't coordinate them to pick up the personal communicator on her belt. She started to fall forward and, reaching out to steady herself, touched the strange screen that covered most of the wall at the foot of the bed. It lit up, and she reeled back, which triggered another barrage of pain. The sight of the bright light and the figure standing in the centre of the screen made her wonder if she'd become delirious. Sean, her husband, had accessed the screen when they'd first arrived, and it had been so rude, they hadn't used it again. But it was there now, and a haughty Sidlown male stared down at her. Like all the aliens she'd met from the planet Sidlow, he was well over two metres tall, with strangely large hands and head, but otherwise mostly human features.

'The man,' she whispered, and slumped back on the bed. 'The man …' She couldn't form the words to explain her predicament. 'I need help.'

'What sort of help?' The arrogant voice changed abruptly when she didn't answer. 'Your vitals are low. Rest back on the bed to stop the syncope.'

'What?'

The voice was now firm, no further sarcasm. 'It will stop you from fainting. Now, move back onto the bed. An emergency team is on its way.'

'I'll have to open the door.'

'No, they will bring an override key.'

Too weak to resist, she put all her effort into wriggling back, her body so cold she doubted she'd ever feel warm again. Something crawled inside her head and a veiled shadow seemed to fall across her eyes. Everything seemed dark. So far away. She couldn't hold herself up any longer and, falling backwards, she slipped into unconsciousness.

Someone touched her arm as she stirred. She screamed, and tried to pull away. No one could have got in, although that man had evaded the alien security to get on the spaceship, so, getting through an apartment door, no matter how secure, would be child's play. She kicked, did her best to throw a punch, but everything was so blurred she couldn't see her target. Someone pinned down her hands. Big hands encompassed her face, and someone else leaned over her, stroking her hair. A gentle female voice whispered, 'You are safe now.'

Tears ran down her face when she realised it was Werrimen, Supreme Commander in Chief of the Inter-Planetary League, the IPL. She didn't really understand the IPL, but she trusted them. They were essentially the guardians of the universe who intervened when other planets were in trouble.

'She's pregnant,' said the man on the wall.

Jemma formed the word, 'No,' in her mind, but nothing came out and the blackness again consumed her brain.

When she regained consciousness, she was in the medical centre. Sean, her husband, sat beside her bed, holding her hand, and a cloudy, yellow fluid pumped into her arm through a thin metallic bar, the size of a lead pencil.

Werrimen eased out from behind the bed. 'Good, you are awake. How far along is your pregnancy?'

'I'm not pregnant.'

'I'm afraid you are, my dear. I would say three to four months. You have a severe infection and are now bleeding heavily. The fluid I am giving you is to replace the blood you have lost.'

'That's not possible. Sean, tell her it's not true.'

He hesitated before he answered. 'You know, you've been complaining of feeling sick, off and on, for a few weeks. Pregnancy didn't occur to me, but maybe …'

Werrimen nodded. 'We must stop the bleeding.'

Jemma looked at the small scar on her arm where a hormone implant had been. It had stopped her from cycling for four or five years, and even after it was removed, she hadn't returned to normal, so she hadn't thought pregnancy possible. Werrimen fiddled with one of the bars and, unable to keep her eyes open, Jemma surrendered to a deep, and this time, relaxed sleep.

Next time she woke, Sean sat in a lounge chair beside her bed. His normally ramrod straight back was slumped forward and red, puffy eyes marred his handsome face. The dark hair that usually fell softly forward was slicked back where he'd been rubbing his hands. Erin, his mother, sat beside him, cradling his head against her chest.

'Hello.' General Hunt leaned forward from the other side of the bed.

Her mouth was too dry to respond. Jemma watched him wriggle towards her, past the moulded structures the aliens had applied to treat his shoulder and knee wounds where he'd been shot when Pritchard's people had tried to hurt her.

'Sean,' he said softly.

Erin swung around and gently shook Sean's shoulder. He rubbed his eyes for a few seconds and looked as though he couldn't work out what was happening, then jumped up and pulled his chair closer to her.

She gripped his hand as he leaned over to kiss her on the forehead. 'Was I pregnant?'

'Yeah, but there was no heartbeat, and your body was trying to expel it. Werrimen has cleaned everything out and stopped the bleeding, so you'll be fine. She asked me if you'd had any recent trauma to your abdomen. I couldn't remember anything, but I wondered about when you overpowered that terrorist back on Earth.'

'He punched me before he went down. Was that what killed the baby?'

'I don't know, sweetheart. I doubt we ever will.'

'He was there. The man who punched me. He was there, in the corridor, before I got to our room. Before the man on the screen called for help.'

'Are you sure honey? You were in a pretty bad way.' Sean exchanged a look with Hunt.

She glared at each of the men in turn. 'I bloody well am sure. It was him.' How strange it all felt. She'd lost a baby she hadn't known she was carrying, and all she could think about was that Pritchard's people had somehow found their way onto the spaceship. She buried her head into Sean's shoulder and, when he circled his arms around her, she sobbed. He stroked her face, and she could feel the tears that flowed down his cheeks too.

Erin stood beside Sean, doing her best to comfort them both.

'Jemma, central control reported what you said about that man before you passed out,' said Werrimen. 'Are you certain he was one of Pritchard's people?'

'It was him. I'd recognise his face anywhere. The one who shot General Hunt. The one who killed Tom.'

'I will commence a search immediately,' said Werrimen. 'Do not worry now. You have lost a lot of blood my dear, and you must rest.'

'Why did I lose the baby?'

'You had a severe infection which caused the bleeding. When you become pregnant again, we will aim for total rest.'

'I don't think I'll ever risk that again.'

Werrimen laughed. 'You will. But I feel that should not happen for a while. You must allow several months for your recovery. Rest now. There will be much to do once you have recovered.'

After Werrimen, and everyone else, had left, one of the Sidlown medical staff came forward to check on her. 'Who is Pritchard?'

'Oh God,' she sighed. 'Now that's a long story.'

The woman smiled as she shrugged. 'You're not going anywhere for a while, so why don't you tell me? I need to know if you are at risk here.'

'I suppose I might be. Pritchard has pursued me for months, nearly killed me once. I didn't know why until a few weeks ago. You see, I'd always accepted that I was born on

Earth. It never occurred to me otherwise, but it seems we moved there just after I was born. We were refugees from a planet called Anders Major, from a war I knew nothing about.'

'Yes, I am familiar with Anders. It is in this galaxy but on another arm of the helix. There is still unrest there. It is very unsafe.'

'That's why we're here. Earth has rejected us, and Werrimen told me we can't go to Anders. I'm not sure if we'd want to anyway. We've never been there. How would we fit in?'

'So why is he after you, particularly?'

'That's the weird part. It seems that my grandfather was the Supreme Ruler of Anders Major although, if that's true, I can't understand why no one had ever told me. Pritchard killed him. My mother was to go back to take over, but he killed her too, along with my father, to stop them from returning. I always thought they'd died in an accident, but he admitted to me that they were murdered.' She turned away from the woman as the horror of her parents' deaths resurfaced.

'If it is too much, we can talk again later,' said the woman.

'No, I'm okay.' Jemma turned back. 'It appears I'm now the heir apparent, and Pritchard's determined to stop me from claiming my heritage.'

'By the stars, this is a heavy burden for you.'

'For all of us. So many people are doing their best to protect me, but Pritchard always seems to find his way through.'

'Are the others also from Anders?'

'Yeah, they are. Pritchard killed Sean's father, and almost

destroyed his mother. His brother, Dan, was raised by an uncle and aunt. Pritchard killed them too, and General Hunt's parents and my cousin Nik's guardians. Sean and Dan were destined for some security group.'

'Ah, that makes sense. They are both very large and strong for humans.'

Jemma laughed. 'Yep, they tower above everyone. They're even a bit bigger than their boss, the General. Mind you, neither of them can take him down.'

'Take him down?'

'Sorry, beat him in a fight.'

'Oh, I see. They are a good protection team for you and, while you are here, we will ensure your safety.'

'Thank you.'

'Sleep now. It is the best way to regain your strength.'

Jemma remained in the medical centre for a week, even though physically, she'd recovered well. Her fear of seeing the man with the scarred face, or worse Pritchard, had her jumping every time someone moved. On the last morning, Werrimen came into her room, spoke to one of the attendants, then sat on the end of Jemma's bed. 'My dear, I know you still feel weak, but you have healed well. It is just a matter of time now to redevelop your strength. I feel you're ready to re-join your team.'

'No,' Jemma whispered. 'No. That man might still be there.'

'We have searched, my dear. He has not been found. You were very ill when you thought you saw him. You may have been mistaken.'

'I wasn't hallucinating.' Jemma sat forward, her hand on Werrimen's arm. 'I wasn't. It was him.'

'I know you believe you saw him, and I'm not discounting the possibility that you did, but, if he is here, he's found an effective way to hide from our detection systems. Your best protection is to regain your capacity to fight back, and you will do that by becoming an integral part of your team again. Remember that you were in a seriously weakened state when you saw him, and yet you managed to fight him off. Now, come with me. Zadrus wants to speak to you.'

Zadrus, the ship's commander, was also Werrimen's life partner. Both held the highest rank of Supreme Trustee of the IPL, and she trusted them implicitly, but, right now, her fear outweighed her capacity to accept anyone's reassurances. Jemma grabbed her uniform and walked behind a small screen where she slowly dressed. She stared at herself in the mirror. Her dark brown hair fell in limp strands beside her face, her normally fair skin now pale, and her cheeks colourless. How could anyone think she'd recovered. With a sigh, Jemma pushed the screen aside hoping Werrimen might have thought her too slow and left, but she stood near the door, smiling.

'I do understand, my dear, but the worst thing I could do for you is to allow you to remain here, wallowing in self-pity.'

'I'm not wallowing,' muttered Jemma.

'You are, and it is time to move on. Come with me. Zadrus is waiting.'

Jemma kept her eyes on Werrimen, terrified she might leave her alone in the corridor, as they walked down to the disc, a circle on the floor, slightly darker in colour than the rest of the floor, and set into a small alcove at the side. Although still uncomfortable with it, she followed Werrimen and stood beside her.

'Level ten,' said Werrimen. The surrounds faded and Jemma had to summon every bit of self-control she could muster as she stood in the total blackness, unable to see Werrimen even though she stood directly beside her. It was only seconds until it cleared, although it felt much longer.

She shook her head as she walked off the disc. 'What would happen if someone wanted to use the disc from another floor while we were in it?'

'Nothing.' Werrimen laughed. 'It is managed by central control. We came down from level seventeen. If someone had stood on the disc at say, level fifteen, as we were moving, control would have held them there until we were finished. We cannot crash on the way.'

'Oh.' It was still such a strange world to Jemma. Control was some kind of artificial intelligence, although it claimed to be far superior. Zadrus had told her that it was built into the fabric of the walls, and the best description she could get was that it was *sort of a computer, but sort of not.*

She stiffened as Werrimen stood under the bead of Zadrus's door and it slowly slid open. He looked up and smiled as they walked in, waving Jemma to a chair. His office was quite basic, none of the fancy technological whizz bangs that Jemma had expected. He had good quality wooden and leather furniture, much like her own had been on Earth. It was set up comfortably but not extravagantly.

'I must go,' said Werrimen.

Jemma jumped up. 'But how will I get back?'

Werrimen smiled. 'You must trust us, my dear.'

'I do. You know I do.'

'Perhaps not enough,' said Zadrus. 'We will talk about that. Thank you Werrimen.' He stood and walked with her to the door, then sat beside Jemma. 'Put your hands in mine.'

She did as he asked and immediately felt a warm, calming sensation flow through her body. They called it transferring energy, which she didn't understand, but she didn't resist, it felt so good. 'I do trust you,' she murmured again.

'Your fear is interfering with that trust.'

'I can't stop thinking about that man. If he's here, then so is Pritchard.'

'Yes, that is likely.' Zadrus sat back in his chair. 'There are two possible scenarios. One is that you were delirious and hallucinated the whole thing. I cannot dismiss that possibility. The other is that he was genuinely there. We have mounted an extensive search and will continue. All our people, and control, have his image and Pritchard's image.'

'What if he has the technology to slip through all that?'

'If he has found a way onto the ship, then it is most likely that he does have the technology.'

'Dear God, this is a nightmare.'

'Yes, and it is time to put it into perspective. We must move on regardless. Someone will be available to escort you at all times. I have already spoken to Sean, Liam, who was your physical trainer at SCARF, and Mary, your guardian.'

SCARF had been a hidden alien facility on Springbrook Mountain in Australia's Gold Coast hinterland where Jemma had been taken after she was rescued from Pritchard, but it was the mention of Mary which made her cringe. Mary had been appointed, at the time of Jemma's birth, to protect and guard her and, as a result had been caught up in the turmoil on Earth that had forced Jemma and Sean to seek refuge with the aliens.

'Pritchard wants me dead. He's already killed most of my family.'

'Yes, and now we will ensure your safety, but you must work with me to build up your confidence.'

A small sound, something like the ring of a very early telephone, interrupted them. Jemma looked up to the screen next to his door, the same as the one in her room that had called for help that day. Mary stood patiently outside. She wore the black uniform of a Supreme Trustee, like the ones worn by Zadrus and Werrimen, although she only had five stars compared to Zadrus's ten and Werrimen's eighteen. Still, given that each star meant she'd led a major operation and had shown outstanding valour, five was impressive.

Zadrus touched a spot on a smaller screen that sat on his desk and the door opened. 'Good morning, Mary.'

She smiled, her hands clasped in front of her chest in the Trustee greeting. 'Your servant, sir.'

Jemma had always been close to Mary and had naturally turned to her when her parents died, but hadn't had any idea of the depth of their relationship at the time.

'Mary will escort you this morning,' said Zadrus. 'Mary, I

will leave you to converse with Sean. One of you should bring Jemma back here at the same time tomorrow morning.'

'I will ensure that happens,' said Mary, turning back to face Jemma. 'We should go. Zadrus is busy.'

Jemma stood and followed Mary, too numb to argue. 'Are you taking me back to my room?'

'I thought we'd go to the lounge first and join some of the others for morning tea.'

'I'm too tired. I need to go and lie down.'

'Not yet, honey. Soon. A nice cuppa first.'

'I'm not up to it.'

'Yes, you are.' Mary put her arm around Jemma's shoulder. 'Honey, I knew Drick, the man you know as Fredrick Pritchard, on Anders Major, before we sought refuge on Earth. Before you were born. He'd tried to kill your grandfather, and it was my job to catch him, which I did, but some fool decided he was rehabilitated and let him go. Men like Drick are never rehabilitated, so he finished the job and killed your grandfather. Then he went after your parents. I give you my pledge that he is not going to get you.'

'Was that where you got one of those stars?'

'It was.'

'I know I've said this before,' said Jemma, 'but, what if I renounced my heritage, if I publicly stated I would never be Supreme Ruler of Anders Major? Would that stop him?'

'I don't think so. While you're alive, the royalists on Anders would hold out hope that you'd return. He is determined to squash that.'

So engrossed in their conversation, Jemma didn't realise they'd reached the lounge until they walked through the door where Sean, his brother Dan, and their mother, Erin, all stood to greet her. She had to laugh. Clearly, Mary had set this up. Tears rolling down her cheeks, she gladly accepted Mary's embrace, and they stood together for several minutes. It took her right back to the terrible time just after her parents died when she'd felt so lost. Mary had kept her on an even keel, steering her through those dark days. She hated to admit that she was going to need the same again.

'I love you,' whispered Jemma, easing back.

'I know,' replied Mary. 'So, now you need to believe in me, too. I've protected you all your life. I'm not going to fail you now.'

Mary's arms were replaced by Sean's, then Dan's and Erin's and, as they sat down, Eric, Mary's husband, steered Anthony, their son, into the room on an alien PTD, or personal transportation device. Anthony had also been the victim of the terrorists, succumbing to a virus that Pritchard had developed. His recovery had been slower than Jemma's, and he could only manage a few steps on his feet.

They sat together as a family for nearly an hour until Jemma felt herself nodding off. Mary must have noticed because she stood and held out her hand. 'Come on. Time for you to have a sleep.'

'You'll call me if you need anything,' said Sean.

'Of course. I'm not allowed to go out without an escort.' She shuddered. 'I wouldn't anyway.'

'Oh sweetheart.' Sean stroked her hair. 'It'll get better. Give it time.'

But over the next few days, it didn't get better, and she slipped into a deep depression. Each morning, she followed Mary to Zadrus's office because Mary wouldn't take no for an answer, but she convinced Sean to bring her meals in to her.

She knew he was worried, but she couldn't lift herself out of it, even for him, which sent her depression even deeper. It worried her that she was letting him down, but she couldn't do anything about it, no matter how hard she tried.

Almost a week after Werrimen had first escorted her from the medical centre, her mood had slipped so far that, as she sat in Zadrus's office, the tears which had become a feature of her daily existence burst out with loud sobs that she couldn't control. Zadrus had to be disappointed in her. She expected a stern lecture, but his kindness was, in a way, even more difficult to deal with.

'Jemma, we are still looking for that man, but so far, we have not found him.'

'He's there. I know you all think I imagined it. But I didn't.'

'We will keep looking. I believe we have your safety covered, and I am now more concerned about your state of mind than your physical wellbeing.'

'So am I,' said Jemma. 'But I can't seem to change it.'

'When we first met you, you had been severely injured in a bushfire that had been set by Pritchard. Do you remember how depressed and angry you were then?'

'I do. With good reason, I think.'

Zadrus nodded. 'There is no question you had very good reason. Do you remember what you did to change it?'

'I … um … just settled down, I think.'

'No,' said Zadrus. 'You worked hard with General Hunt, and you learned to believe in yourself again, and your capacity to fight back.'

'That's true, I suppose, but I can't do that now.'

'Why not?'

'I'm weak.'

'You were weak then.'

'General Hunt's injured,' snapped Jemma. 'He can't help me.'

'There are others who aren't injured,' said Zadrus, kindly. 'Think about it, my dear.'

She stared at him, fighting back the tears that threatened her composure again. Why couldn't they understand how badly she was hurting, or how much she wanted to get better? Ever since she'd learned about her heritage, her life had changed. Her guardians had talked to her about going back to Anders to have a look and decide if she wanted to take up her birthright. Supreme Ruler for goodness sake, how could she be that? She'd grown up in the suburbs of the Gold Coast, an ordinary girl who'd attended ordinary schools and worked hard to become a scientist, and that was all she wanted from life. None of this royalty rubbish.

Pritchard, and his cronies, were obsessed with stopping her from returning to Anders even though she'd made it clear she had no interest in going back. Now Zadrus demanded she fight back. How was she supposed to do that? She couldn't even understand what it was she was supposed to be fighting.

CHAPTER 2

Sean endured constant jibes from Hunt and thinly veiled pressure from Zadrus because he refused to push Jemma, determined she would have whatever time she needed to recover. Now though, almost a month since her miscarriage, he felt as helpless as he had when he'd rescued her from the bushfire that nearly took her life. She fought against leaving their room, although she gave in when Zadrus and Mary insisted, but he had to bring meals to her. Both his mother and Mary spent time with her every day, trying to lift her out of her depression, but neither of them had been able to bring her around.

He'd have spent every moment of every day helping her face her fear, if Zadrus hadn't made him responsible to manage security for all the humans on board. Hunt would take over eventually but, at present, it took most of his time which was probably what Zadrus had intended, to stop him from mollycoddling Jemma.

Both Zadrus and Werrimen had dropped hints that he should encourage her to get out and about so, when Werrimen summoned him to her office, he expected another onslaught, rehearsing in his mind how he'd answer. *Jemma was too weak;*

she wasn't ready; they had to find Pritchard before she'd feel safe. He sighed. How many times did she have to go through life-threatening injuries and then sort herself out and act as if nothing had happened? She was his wife, his responsibility, and he planned to do everything in his power to protect her, not just from Pritchard, but from everyone who was supposed to be on her side and should be more understanding.

He stepped onto the disc that would take him down to the tenth floor. Although he'd used it many times now, he stiffened when the surrounds faded and, when he reached the new level, he punched his fist against the wall. How could life have turned so sour? It wasn't just Jemma. Two of his men, both mates, were dead. His boss, along with his adjutant, Nik, had only survived through the advanced treatment offered by the aliens. None of them could laugh it off and move on, but that was, essentially, what they had to do. They had nowhere to go other than the spaceship and they'd have to find a way to make the most of it.

'Good morning, Sean,' said Werrimen as he entered her office. 'How is Jemma?'

He wasn't sure if it was her cheeriness, or the care and concern in her voice, that cut through his control, but he had to grab the back of a chair to steady himself. He couldn't answer. Somehow, the events of the last few weeks all seemed to crush in on him at once.

Werrimen eased him into the chair, then dragged another close to his. 'Put your hands in mine.'

It was a command, and he obeyed. As she encircled his

hands with hers, the familiar surge of calming energy flowed through his body. He didn't know how the aliens did it, but it felt good and, even though he readily gave in to the transfer, it took several minutes for his breathing to slow. When it did, he looked up. Werrimen was the only person he'd ever met who could, with a few words and a gentle touch, peel away the complicated layers he'd built around himself to deal with all the trauma he'd faced in his life.

'That's better,' she said, softly. "You have put all your strength into helping Jemma, which I understand, given the threat to her life. But she is recovering, and I do not believe you have allowed yourself to consider how you feel. It was your baby, too.'

My baby. He stared at her. Looking after Jemma was all that mattered. She was terrified that Pritchard was out there looking for her. He couldn't worry about his own feelings. He had to protect her. Werrimen firmed her grip on his hands to stop him from pulling away. Then her arms circled around him, drawing him in until his head rested on her chest. Her size made him feel like he was nestled into his mother's shoulder just like he had when he was a little boy and skinned his knee, but now his body was wracked with sobs that flowed from somewhere deep within his soul.

When his trembling stopped, Werrimen eased him back onto his chair, then took his hands back in hers. 'I thought so. It will take a while for both of you to get through this. It is important for you to think about it and talk about it. I understand that you don't want to let Jemma see your distress, and you feel you must be in control in front of your staff. But I think that control has been so important to you, that you have forgotten how to address your own feelings. As we start your Trustee training, I will focus on that. You must look deep inside and address all those ghosts that hold you back.'

Despite her smile when she let his hands go, he had no doubt she meant what she said. She'd been clear before they left Earth that she planned to induct him as a Trustee. He'd have to deal with whatever she had in mind. Zadrus had already inducted Jemma although he'd backed off since the miscarriage. Sean didn't really understand what it would mean to be a Trustee, although they were clearly the most revered members of the IPL. He guessed in time he'd figure it out.

Werrimen walked around her desk, sat down, and in her calm controlled manner, continued. 'There is something else we must discuss, if you feel able.'

Sean nodded, too numb to argue.

'I have not been able to find anyone matching Jemma's description of Pritchard's man. We have less than a hundred humans on board at this stage, so he should not be too hard to find if he is here. I have to lean towards the probability that she was mistaken; she was so ill.'

'Understood,' replied Sean, but he shook his head. 'Jemma's certain it was him, and I don't think that's a mistake she'd make.'

'We have been careful about who we have brought on board. Every person is checked thoroughly.'

Jemma had been so definite about the man, that Sean believed her. 'Would it be possible for someone to stow away?'

'It may be, but it would take a lot of planning, and knowledge of our process to enable him to keep on hiding.' Werrimen sighed. 'But I agree, my instinct tells me we must not reject Jemma's belief entirely, which leaves me with another problem. We must bring her back up to peak fitness. She must regain her confidence and again be ready to defend herself.'

Sean leaned forward. 'No. Please. Give her time to recover. You can't do that to her again.' After the bushfire, it had taken months for Jemma to recover and it was a tribute to her strength of character that she'd persevered through Hunt's intensive self-protection training. 'I'll ensure she's never alone. She'll listen to me.'

'Yes, I know she will listen, but we cannot wait too long.' She stood and headed for the door. 'General Hunt took charge of her before because you were too close. I will give you a little more time, but soon Zadrus and I will take charge of her, if she does not respond.'

'She's not ready. Forcing her now could break her.'

'She is stronger than you recognise. Much of your fear for her arises from your own pain.' She stood and pointed to the door. 'We must join Zadrus now. He has something he wishes to discuss with us.'

His mind in tatters, he followed Werrimen to the spaceship's control room. Waiting for the bead to recognise her, so she could enter the control room, gave him a moment to collect himself. Security was particularly strong here, so once the bead had accepted her, someone on the other side was required to confirm her identity, through visual recognition, before the door opened. Even though he'd been in the control room many times before, and knew what to expect, he had to stop to orient himself. It felt like he was standing out, unprotected, in the middle of space. The entire front of the semi-circular room appeared to be open to the stars. In fact, it was an image projected against the solid front wall, but it was more than a screen image, or even a hologram. It felt real.

Zadrus stood at the control desk, a long narrow bench curved to reflect the shape of the front wall. Three screens that didn't appear to be attached to anything hovered above the bench and each was closely monitored by a Sidlown crew member.

'Good morning,' said Zadrus, when he spotted Sean. 'We are ahead of schedule.'

'Okay,' murmured Sean, his eyes drawn to the screen, which appeared to be monitoring the landing bay and twenty transporters lined up and ready to leave, far more than he'd ever seen mobilising before. The transporters, each fifteen metres in diameters, looked like spheres that had been squashed down from the top and up from the bottom. A central section for passengers projected out about a metre from the middle. 'Ahead of what schedule?'

'My apologies,' said Zadrus. 'Do you remember when we told you we plan to move forward in time?'

Sean laughed. 'Not really something I could forget.'

'We have seen no evidence that Earth has changed its

ways. We could have helped them handle the pandemic virus that shattered so many lives earlier this year, but they wouldn't communicate with us, so we are proceeding with our plans.'

'Why wouldn't they talk to you?'

'Earth's governments have maintained for so long that we do not exist that they have begun to believe their own rhetoric. It does not bode well for the future.'

'No, I guess not,' murmured Sean.

'The portal here will move us forward about eighty years. The IPL remains convinced that Earth will continue on its path to self-destruction. Hopefully we are wrong, but if not, we will aim to start again provided we can find enough land surface. That is the only way we can ensure the survival of Earth's human species. If there are still people alive, we will help them but, if not, those who come with us will form the basis of a new civilisation. You have all agreed to join us, but I must reiterate that we have never found a portal that will take us back in time, so you must all think hard about your decisions. Please make sure your people understand that. We can find other options for them if they wish.'

'Okay, I'll do that, but are you really intending to search for people to join us?'

'Oh yes,' replied Zadrus. 'And we will find them, I assure you.'

'No one will join you by choice, particularly when you say you plan to travel eighty years into the future.'

Zadrus smiled. 'They will.'

'What if the transporters are seen?'

'Unlikely,' said Werrimen. 'They have all activated their cloaking mechanism which will change the outline of the craft to look like a cloud. Astute observers might notice the cloud moving in a direction that is different from other clouds, or that it doesn't change shape as it moves beside clouds that are shifted by the wind, but most people won't.'

Sean shook his head. What could he say? It was only months since he'd had no idea that there were aliens on Earth. Now he was in a spaceship hurtling through space and preparing to travel in time.

'I must inform you,' said Zadrus, looking up, 'I intend to commence our introductory chats tonight. I would like you to attend.'

'Introductory chats?'

'I will address the people we bring on board and offer them the opportunity to join our mission.'

'Sir,' said Sean. 'I know your intentions are honourable, but you intend to kidnap people. No one in their right mind will be prepared to stay here.'

'I understand your concerns,' replied Zadrus. 'But I expect you will be surprised. The way in which we bring people to us will convince them that we are who we say we are. Our technology will show them we can do what we propose. Please do not feel that you are required to convince anyone although, if you want to tell your story, or confirm that we are genuine, you are welcome to do so.'

'Okay.'

'I'd suggest you rest now,' said Werrimen. 'We need you to be alert tonight.'

Sean looked at each of them in turn, then walked away, shaking his head. All he could do was wait for nightfall and see what happened. Although night and day didn't exist in space, climate control on the ship mimicked a typical day on Earth so that when they returned to Earth, their systems would cope.

Heading back to the seventeenth floor, his mind buzzed with Werrimen's words before they'd met with Zadrus. Perhaps she was right, and his own grief had interfered with how he'd dealt with Jemma, but when he entered the apartment and found her sitting on the bed with her head bowed forward, his heart almost broke.

'Come on, Jem. Let's go have some lunch.'

'Have they found that man?' she said, looking up at him, her eyes red and swollen.

'No, not yet. Werrimen's going all out with her search. They will find him.'

'I'd rather stay here then.'

'Yeah.' He couldn't afford to acquiesce. She was deteriorating and he wasn't about to let her curl up and die when there was nothing physically wrong. 'Come on. Wash your face. I'd like you to come with me. I won't leave your side.' He pushed her into the bathroom as gently as he could, shattered by the slump in her body and her obvious difficulty in complying with his simple request to wash her face.

'I'm ready,' she whispered.

'Excellent,' he replied, forcing himself to sound cheerful.

Each floor had its own dining room and it was less than two hundred metres from their apartment, but she clung to him as though afraid he might disintegrate. As they approached the table where Hunt sat with Erin and Mary, a hush came over the room. He'd expected people to at least say, 'Hello,' but nobody spoke and, when he looked at Jemma, he could see why. Her face was drawn tight, her eyes rigidly focussed on the chair that Hunt held out for her. People were clearly as nervous dealing with her as she was with them, and that had to change.

Hunt tried to include her in the conversation, but her answers to all his questions were monosyllabic. Mary fussed over her which made her sink even further into her shell. He decided there and then to sit everyone down later and lay out some rules for interacting with her. It distressed him he'd have to do that, but this couldn't go on. By the time they got back to their apartment, Jemma was so exhausted she had to lie down.

He sat with her for a while, stroking her hair until, an hour before the meeting was scheduled to start, Werrimen called him to join her so she could give him final instructions. He kissed Jemma on the forehead and headed for the door. He'd already arranged with Mary to bring her some dinner, and to sit with her for a while.

Werrimen greeted him but didn't waste time chatting. She expected people would come from a wide range of countries, and many would not speak English, so she checked his translator, then led him to a small room. A screen at the front enabled them to see into a larger room which was set up like a modern university lecture theatre, although the seats were larger and looked more comfortable. Every few minutes, a Sidlown would lead two or three people in and settle them into seats. Most looked confused, staring around at other people who were already seated. A few tried to shake off their Sidlown escorts. Sean wasn't sure how, but the people all settled when the escorts touched them lightly on their necks. A few whispered to the person sitting next to them but mostly, they were quiet. There were no stairs in the room, and the corridor that ran between rows of seats seemed flat, but as each row was filled, it seemed to rise above the one in front of it.

Sean nodded to each of the Sidlowns who joined them in the small room, but he was surprised to hear individual crew members muttering in the background.

'All the humans have arrived Commander,' said one of the Sidlowns.

'Thank you.' Zadrus turned to his crew. 'Listen to me now. This is an ambitious plan. Without it, I, and our Sidlown commanders, believe that the population of Earth will not survive. If you have any doubts, cast them aside. You know we can do this. We have done it before. The people in there have no reason to trust us, but we must convince them to do so. Each of you must work on assuring them we are friends. Are you all clear?'

'These humans are so primitive,' growled a Sidlown who

sported a slowly spreading black eye and pointed to a man sitting in the front row. 'Look at them. Most are panicking, irrational, aggressive. Do we really want them with us?'

'You have all met the humans we have on board.' Zadrus looked at Sean. 'Many of you have commented on how well they have coped. Put yourself in the position of the people in the next room. Would you not respond much the same way? You have your orders. Follow them. We will go in there now, and you will leave your anger and negativity behind.' Zadrus strode into the larger room, followed by his crew.

Werrimen held Sean back when he went to follow. He wanted to run in and reassure the people as they gasped at the sight of Zadrus and demanded an explanation. When Werrimen finally let him go in, he was shocked that someone yelled at him, calling him a traitor, and demanding that he do something to help them escape from the aliens. He felt Werrimen's hand on his shoulder and said nothing, presuming that he'd have reacted much the same if he'd been sucked up by a spaceship, without warning, and left sitting in a room until the aliens chose to show themselves. Werrimen whispered to him to wait as Zadrus raised his hand. To Sean's surprise, silence fell, and most people looked expectantly at Zadrus, waiting for him to speak.

'Ladies and gentlemen.' Zadrus's soft, melodic voice resonated across the room. 'Please be seated and make yourselves comfortable. I understand we have intruded on you this evening, and that you are upset and frightened. Be assured we will not do you any harm.'

'Who the hell are you?' yelled someone at the front. 'What do you want?'

'Let me explain.' Zadrus calmly detailed their plan, in the same way he and Werrimen had explained it to Sean and his people a few weeks earlier. But they already knew and trusted Zadrus. These people were in an entirely different situation, and Sean stood by his belief that they'd reject the plan.

Zadrus went on to assure his audience they could leave if they wished but asked them to listen before making their decision. He explained the IPL's fears for Earth, and the nature of their mission to travel forward in time, then he opened the floor to questions.

A light murmur broke the silence before someone shouted, 'Is this a joke?'

Someone else demanded, 'Yeah, where the hell are we?'

Zadrus stood patiently at the front, his hands clasped in front of him, and made no attempt to respond to the angrily hurled questions. Sean, thinking they should intervene before the whole thing got out of hand, looked to Werrimen, but she stood in much the same way as Zadrus, and indicated to him to do the same, which he did, although he doubted he could hold back much longer.

Suddenly, someone at the back called for order. 'I have no idea where we are, but I don't think this is a joke. I've read about these abductions. I always thought they were rubbish, but I think we're in one.' He stared directly at Zadrus. 'Am I correct?'

'You are,' he replied. 'Again, I apologise for frightening you.'

'We need to stop the panic, and start thinking,' said someone in the front row. 'My question is can you do what you propose? How do we know Earth won't wipe itself out all together? Where would we be then?'

'I do understand your fear,' replied Zadrus. 'We can show you evidence of similar interventions on other planets. You are of course right. There is a slim chance the people of Earth may destroy the planet before we can stop them. If that were to happen, there are other planets that would welcome you, which would be our responsibility to organise. But please understand we will do everything within our power to prevent that.' Zadrus motioned Sean forward and asked him to mingle with the crowd.

Sean chatted to people, impressed by how focussed most of the discussions seemed to be. He reassured a few of them that the aliens were real, and that he trusted them, but mostly people seemed to be genuinely deciding whether they should consider staying. He continued chatting for around an hour until Werrimen beckoned to him to return to her. Zadrus resumed his position at the front of the room and quietly asked if there were any more questions. A couple of people spoke angrily about being abducted, but most sat in their seats and appeared to Sean to be listening.

Zadrus offered people the chance to return to their homes if they wished, and reiterated that for those who considered staying, they could go forward in time but could not come back. He suggested if that was too frightening, they should leave now. In the end, thirty-four people agreed to stay. Zadrus drew them together and explained if they should change their minds, it would still be possible for them to return home for the next couple of months.

Sean was speechless when he left with Werrimen. He wondered how he'd tell the others that people had agreed to stay, of their own free will.

CHAPTER 3

Jemma sat beside Sean and listened while he recounted the events of the evening. Although happy to see his excitement at their success in attracting people to join them, she wasn't particularly pleased by the prospect of increasing their numbers. The man with the scarred face had managed to evade their security, probably Pritchard too, so how could they be certain the new ones would be safe. Her mind was in such a tangle when they went to bed that her body wouldn't give in to her exhaustion until the early hours of the morning.

She stayed in bed when Sean got up, but sleep wouldn't come so, after staring at the ceiling for another hour, she got up and sat on the edge of the bed, wondering what to do. Zadrus had cancelled their meeting that morning. He expected to be needed by the new people on board. She'd been shown how to access books and movies through her communicator, but she'd done that almost every day since her miscarriage and she was fed up with it. It'd been over a month now since she'd left their apartment by herself. Going to the dining room the day before with Sean, she'd been terrified to let him out of her sight. Her friends had seemed afraid to come anywhere near her, which was her own doing, but all she'd wanted was to crawl inside her own skin. She was acting like an invalid instead of the self-assured professional who'd fled from Earth only six weeks ago, and she didn't want Sean to be ashamed of her, but she suspected he was.

She was tired of everyone telling her that her best chance to be safe was to develop her capacity to protect herself and worse, reminding her how she'd done it before. Prior to this latest assault, she'd been quite confident in her own ability. Now, she had no confidence.

From her own experience, she knew that exercise was the best treatment for depression, but she was still weak, and there wasn't enough room in the apartment to stretch out and start to rebuild her strength. If she was to have any chance of finding herself, she'd need help, and she'd picked up her communicator more than a dozen times but hadn't been able to bring herself to activate it. If she didn't do something to help herself, she'd go crazy, stuck within these four walls, no one to talk to or to interact with most of the day. She'd actually heard someone in the dining room say, 'Poor Jemma. It's so sad.' To hell with that. She grabbed the communicator, let it unfurl in her hand and shouted, 'Liam,' before she could change her mind. Zadrus had included him in the people who were allowed to escort her.

'Hey Jem, good to hear from you,' said Liam. As the PE sergeant at SCARF, he'd helped her meet Hunt's demands, even when she'd thought it beyond her. 'How are you?'

'I'm okay. Where are you? I'm not allowed to go out by

myself.' She gulped in a breath, well aware that that was an excuse and Liam would probably see through it.

'No worries, I'll come to your apartment. We can find somewhere quiet to chat.'

After she closed the communicator, she sat back on the bed. She didn't know whether to laugh or cry. He'd been waiting for her to call. It was less than a minute before her communicator lit up again.

'I'm outside Jem,' said Liam.

She froze and stared at the door. What if Pritchard had got to him? Liam had chosen to join them on the spaceship. He didn't have to. He said he wanted to stay working with Sean and his team. But was that the truth? Pins and needles crawled through her hands and feet, and her heart raced. Struggling for breath, she gripped the side of the bed.

The screen on the wall lit up. 'Sergeant Liam Cleary is standing outside your door,' said the haughty male Sidlown. 'Do you wish to see him?'

'Yes, I do.'

'Then proceed to the door.'

'What if it isn't him? What if he wants to hurt me?'

'I have identified him. There is no error. His vital signs do not suggest deception.'

Liam spoke again, this time sounding concerned. 'Are you alright Jem? Should I get Sean?'

'No. God no. Don't get Sean.' She ran to the bead and waited for the door to open. 'I'm sorry Liam, I'm struggling.'

'I know that mate. Let's go sit somewhere quiet and chat.'

'I don't know if I can. Could we talk here?'

'I don't think that's the best idea. I'll stay with you. Come on. Let's go for a walk.'

He led her to the disc and down to another level on the craft, which was, as yet, unoccupied.

She followed him into a lounge room.

'I'm assuming you want to start working out again,' he said.

Still struggling to breathe, she walked beside him. 'I have to start doing something. You won't tell anyone, will you? You won't tell Sean?'

'Sean'd help you.'

'I know, but right now he has to be ashamed of me. I want to wait until I can make him proud of me again.'

'Oh Jem. Sean would never be ashamed of you. Of course, I'll work with you, but there's one condition. Your head's in a bad place. I know why, and I'll do my best to help you, but if I feel you're not getting better, I'll have to speak to Werrimen.'

She gripped the chair and, staring down at her feet, rocked back and forth to steady herself. 'Okay. I don't want Werrimen involved but I understand why you'd say that,' but it was the last thing she wanted. Time to pick herself up and at least appear to be in control. 'Where do we start?'

Liam smiled at her. He'd obviously realised what she was doing. 'Come on.' He led her to the other side of the room where he'd set up a dozen machines, all of which looked familiar.

'Where did you get these,' she said, running her hands over the treadmill that had been the bane of her life at SCARF.

'Werrimen asked the Council of Earth Leaders to provide

us with suitable equipment. I think they were embarrassed by how they'd behaved, and they told her to take whatever she needed. So, she did. There's more up on your floor. I've kept these for my use only up to now.'

He'd organised the room into a workable gym and, by the look of it, he'd made good use of all the machines. In the corridor outside, he'd marked out a four hundred metre stretch and then divided it into fifty metre sections. He suggested that they start their test there.

She stood on the line at the start and waited for him to tell her to go. She'd just managed a hundred metres, with Liam doing little more than walk beside her, when her shortness of breath forced her to pull up. Frustrated by her diminished speed, and her lack of stamina, she sat on a bench to catch her breath before following him to start the next task. Although she achieved less than a quarter of her previous weight target, Liam seemed confident that if she stuck with it, she'd get there. In her heart though, she doubted she'd ever recover.

She steeled herself to persevere and the first couple of days were painful, but by the end of the third day she'd started to improve, and Liam no longer threatened to involve Werrimen.

'Jem, there's something I want you to do tomorrow,' said Liam, as he walked her back to her apartment.

Her breath hitched as he touched her shoulder with his hand. He looked so serious. 'Okay,' she replied. 'If I can.'

'I think you can. I'm going to wait for you tomorrow morning in my gym.'

'What do you mean?' She looked around frantically. Did

he have someone watching? 'I can't go all that way by myself. I'm not allowed out of the apartment by myself.'

'Yes, you can,' he said calmly. 'When Zadrus first asked me to be one of your escorts, he told me to use my judgement. You've done so well over the last few days that I think you're ready to take the next step.'

'No. No, I can't. Please don't do this to me.'

'We're here,' he said, pointing to her door. 'It took less than a minute. You can do it.'

When the bead responded to her, and the door slid open, Liam smiled and walked away. She jumped inside so the door would be shut before he'd left her corridor. Sick to the core at the thought of having to walk down the corridor by herself, she sat on the edge of the bed. Tired from her exercise, she stretched out and allowed herself to drift off to sleep, not waking until Sean returned and sat beside her.

'Hey,' he said, quietly. 'You okay?'

'I am.' She smiled and reached up to him. It felt so good when he responded by wrapping his arms around her, so safe, and she sighed.

'Okay, what's the matter?' He eased back a bit, and a slight frown creased his face.

'Nothing's the matter,' she replied, snuggling into him. 'I love you so much.'

'I love you too, and because of that I know something's bothering you. Do you want to let me in on it?'

'I will, but I need to think it through first. Can you give me a bit of time?'

'Of course. Just remember I'm here, and if you need a hand all you have to do is ask.'

'I know. I just have to work a few things out for myself first.'

'Okay,' he said, standing and pulling her up with him. 'Let's go to dinner.'

She sighed. The last thing she wanted was to face all those people again. 'Can we order some dinner here?'

'No, best to go out. Just a quick dinner. Say hello to a few people, then straight back. Come on.'

If she objected, she knew he'd give in, but that would be drawing him further into her nightmare and she'd already done enough of that. He hadn't asked much of her since the miscarriage. Surely, she could lift herself enough to do this for him. She slipped her hand through his arm and turned towards the door, surprised by his broad smile as he brushed her forehead with his lips and opened the door.

People seemed a bit different when she got to the dining room, still cautious but there were smiles. Some even murmured, 'Hello.' She sat next to Hunt and made sure she responded to his questions, even laughed at one of his jokes, at which point he squeezed her hand and nodded. Mary and Erin were more at ease, too. They'd stopped fussing. Although she accepted it was due to her more relaxed attitude, she wondered what Sean had said to bring about the change. When he reached for her hand under the table, she realised how lucky she was to have him in her life.

It had been such a big day that, when they got back to

their apartment, she collapsed onto the bed and was asleep before Sean joined her, but she tossed and turned all night. She dreamed about everything that could go wrong when she left the apartment to join Liam in the morning and woke in a cold sweat to find herself enclosed in Sean's arms.

'Shh, it's okay,' he whispered. 'Why don't you tell me about it?'

'I'm so confused. I don't think I can put it into words.'

'Alright, join me in the shower then.'

'That'll be a tight fit,' she said, laughing. Their tiny ensuite was functional but not much more than that.

'Uh huh. Sounds good to me.' He grabbed her hand and helped her squeeze into the tiny recess. 'Mm, cosy.'

She happily folded herself into him, feeling better than she had for weeks.

After he left, her mood dropped. She had to go outside by herself and use the disc on her own, but she knew she couldn't afford to stand there pondering all the possible consequences, she'd never do it. After pulling on her uniform, she strode to the door and forced herself to walk through. She was so focussed on making her way down the corridor to the disc, that she didn't see Liam until she'd almost walked into him.

When he grabbed her shoulder to stop her, she jumped back and raised her fists, stopping just in time to avoid making contact with his jaw. 'You bastard,' she said, slipping her hand back into her pocket, and laughing. 'You didn't trust me.'

'I trust you implicitly, but I wasn't sure how you'd cope. I'm here to help, mate.'

'I know.' To Liam's credit, he hadn't stepped back, nor had he attempted to overpower her to stop her from striking him.

'Let's go over what just happened,' said Liam. 'Come with me back to your doorway. The bead will open the door, but don't worry about it.'

Arms crossed in front of her chest, she stood in front of her opened apartment and stared at him. 'Okay, what now?'

'Don't be defensive. Time for a rethink. What can you see from where you're standing?'

'Long corridor. Both ways.'

'Can you hear anything?'

'No, just us.'

'Can you see the disc?' said Liam.

'No, just the edge of it.'

'Would you have been able to see me, if you'd looked up?

'Don't think so. You were standing on the far side of the disc when I walked into you.'

'And ...?'

'And what?' She stopped and stared at him, but he didn't answer. 'Oh, I get it. Be aware of your surroundings. Look, listen, smell, sense. Yeah, okay, General Liam.'

'How much of that did you do when you left your apartment?' he said, ignoring her sarcasm.

'I was focussed on getting to the disc. It's the first time I've done it by myself since ... you know.'

'Yes, I do know. Can you see how your fear impaired your judgement and increased your risk?'

'Yeah, yeah. I get it. Let's go.'

'Jemma stop, this is really important.' He took hold of her arm and forced her to look at him. 'People like Pritchard, and his ilk, prey on vulnerability.'

'I am vulnerable.'

'You are, and we have to tackle that.'

'That much I know, but you have no idea how hard that is. I don't know where to start.'

'Recognising it is a huge step forward. Now we can go and begin our workout and we'll work on how to tackle it together. Okay?'

She nodded as she followed him to the gym to start her warm-up exercises and had just commenced a run on the track around the corridor, when she sensed someone behind her. She swung around, hoping it would be Liam, but it was Dan, Sean's brother, and his second in command.

Liam stepped between them and whispered so only she could hear. 'Well done. Good awareness.'

Dan skirted around him and fell into step beside her. It was all so damned easy for him. 'Good to see you up and at it, Jemma.'

'Go away.' She ignored him and concentrated on her run.

'Jem, I'm hurt. Don't you want to work with me?'

'No.'

When they returned to Liam, Dan stopped, a more serious expression on his face as he requested a report. Liam hesitated, he wouldn't want to upset her by letting Dan know that her recovery was progressing well, or the step that she'd taken that morning, but she had no doubt he'd provide the information. Even though they were continually told rank no longer had meaning, Liam had been a sergeant, Dan a lieutenant-colonel. Liam looked at her, then turned to Dan and informed him that she could do most things, although he thought she still needed supervision.

Jemma flopped onto a stool and waited for them to finish, cursing the interference but Dan squatted in front of her, looking serious.

'I'm pleased you did this by yourself, Jemma,' said Dan. 'We've all been so worried about you. I considered pushing, but I wasn't sure if you were ready. We're working as a group now, mainly to help the General and Nik recover. Even Anthony, Mary's son, is working with us. I'd like you to join us, too.'

'I'm not ready to work with anyone else. Physically, or mentally. Liam understands.'

'So do I, but our aim has to be to get you back to the way you were. Here's the deal. I come down and work with you and Liam each day, just me. After another week, we reassess, and if Liam and I think you're up to it, you re-join the team. Okay?'

'No, it's not okay. Why can't you just leave me alone to work through this myself? My protective custody doesn't exist anymore. I'm no longer part of your Army. I don't have to do anything you say.'

'Well, that's not quite right. You know Zadrus has appointed us to maintain security on board until we get to where we're going, and he suspects we'll have to continue in that role. He made it clear that as his Prehling, he wants you to be part of our group.'

She let her head drop forward into her hands. Zadrus had inducted her to train as a Trustee, which made her his Prehling, a kind of apprentice. She wanted to walk away from Dan, but there was nowhere to run or hide on a spaceship. Just like before, she'd end up having to go along with them. 'What if I'm not ready after another week?'

'Then we'll go another week, but the decision will be mine and Liam's.'

'God, I hate you sometimes.'

'No, you don't.' He gently turned her around to face him. 'I care about what happens to you, Jem. If I have to force you forward, I'm prepared to do that but, for now, an agreement will do. Otherwise I'll have to talk to Zadrus.'

'Arsehole.'

His smile just made her irritation worse. She stood to leave, but he blocked her path.

'Alright,' she muttered.

'Good. Come on, we'll do a quick combat try-out.'

If she didn't do as he demanded, he'd talk to Zadrus, maybe even Hunt. If she did work with him, she'd end up exhausted. Sean was already worried. If she needed even more rest after her workouts, his worry would increase. Bugger Dan. But he stood there patiently, and she had to answer.

'How about tomorrow?' she muttered.

'How about a little test today? Not too hard, just enough to show me what you can do. You know you want to please me.'

'No, I don't,' she growled. 'But you won't let up.'

Dan was gentle as he went through a series of punches, stances, and blocks. 'We'll do an hour in the gym, and then an hour of combat each day. I'm looking forward to working with you. It'll be great.'

Great was not the word that sprang to her mind. 'I take it I don't get out of here until I agree?'

'Now Jemma, would I be that manipulative?' He stood with his arms folded in front of his chest.

His 192 centimetre, heavily muscled frame, was every bit as big as Sean's. There was no way she could get around him.

'God, you're a bastard, just like your General. Alright, I agree.'

'Excellent, and I'll take that as a compliment. Don't forget he's your General too, Major Anderson. Now, let's find Sean and get a coffee.' Hunt had convinced her to apply for a professional commission while they were still on Earth. He'd believed that it would allow her more freedom, since her protective custody had restricted her to the SCARF site. But Pritchard's final attack had happened not long after, and it hadn't worked as he'd planned.

'Prick,' she muttered, shaking her head at Dan but, so long as he didn't let anything slip to Sean, she'd go along with him. They found Sean in his office on the control floor.

'I called Jem,' said Dan. 'We're going for a cuppa. Want to join us?'

Sean looked at her, a slight frown on his face, but he said nothing as he got up from his desk and, taking hold of her hand, joined them to walk to the nearest dining room.

The banter and competition between the men had always been entertaining, but now, somehow, it made everything seem more normal, taking her focus away from her own woes. It made her realise she really did belong to this group of people whose company, she reluctantly admitted, she enjoyed, and that was bizarre in itself. She'd only become a part of the military group when Sean had rescued her from a strange blue light near her mountain research station. He'd then done his best to protect her from Pritchard. Now they'd all been abandoned by their government and left in the care of aliens because, although human, they were all born on another planet, a planet that none of them could remember.

Dan joined her for every session over the next week. He didn't overtly push or bully her, but she was aware that he picked up his pace beside her each day, and slowly increased her weights. He didn't make her do more in the combat sessions but expected her to respond quicker and from different angles. More than once, his fist connected, and even though she knew it wasn't full strength, it still hurt and left the odd bruise.

Partway through the final session of the week, Dan asked her to sit with him on a bench. 'I think you're ready to join the rest of us for training. Liam will still supervise everything except combat, but we'll go easy there for the moment. Are you happy to do that?'

'No, but you won't let up until I do.'

'You're right, but I'd like you to be happy about it.'

'I'm not devastated. I feel stronger now. Will you wait until tomorrow, so I can talk to Sean tonight?'

'Fair enough. Make sure you're with him when we start tomorrow.'

'Yeah, alright.'

He jumped up. 'Good. Let's do a bit more.'

He increased everything, the number of circuits of the corridor, the weights, the number of push-ups, chin-ups and sit-ups. Then he kept her moving right through her combat session, no simple static exercises. Well, that made it clear, she was into it again. Physically, she knew she was fine, and had been for a while. Mentally, that was a whole other question, although she did feel a bit better. Liam wanted her to act as if she wasn't scared of running into Pritchard. Maybe that would get her through but, really, it was a damned lie, and deep inside she knew it.

She joined Liam and Dan for lunch, then Liam escorted her back to her apartment. Exhausted, she hit the bed for a rest. When Sean came in that night, she asked him to wait before they went to dinner, so they could talk.

He sat beside her, stroking her hair. 'Are you going to let me in on what's had you upset. I know you've been cooking something up with Dan, but he won't tell me, so what is it?'

'You might be annoyed with me, but here goes.' She told

him the whole story including how Dan had interfered and taken over, and that he'd now demanded she join the team.

Sean sat quietly for some time and her worry about how angry he might be with her welled up inside.

'Why didn't you ask me to help you?' he said.

It hadn't occurred to her that he might feel hurt she'd sought help from someone else, yet it was something she'd had to do by herself. She couldn't spend the rest of her life terrified to do anything unless Sean was by her side. 'You were already so worried about me, I thought if I could get fit and sort my head out, you'd be impressed with me.'

'Oh sweetheart, I'm impressed with you every minute of every day. I'm thrilled that you took it on yourself to do the work, and that Liam worked with you. And you probably won't like it, but I'm also happy with Dan that he got in and helped without spilling the beans.'

'You're not annoyed with me?'

'Of course not. The only thing that's ever worried me is that General Hunt, or Zadrus, might try to push you to start before you were well enough, and they had begun to make noises. I'm pleased you took the initiative.' He held his arms out to her and pulled her in close. 'Come here, and let me show you just how impressed I am.'

Jemma continued to improve over the next few weeks and her confidence to move around the spaceship by herself was almost back to normal. One morning, two months after her miscarriage, she found Sean and Dan racing across the big lounge room that had been converted to a gym. Then they argued about who'd won. To her, it'd looked like a dead heat and, although she knew it was a mock fight, she thought they were about as likely to listen to reason as a pair of charging bulls. She turned her back to them, still laughing, until she saw Nik in trouble on one of the machines.

Nik often pushed too hard, which Jemma understood only too well. They both still had a long way to go to recover. Jemma ran to her, yelling to Sean that she needed help, and hoping that he'd actually hear her above his crap with Dan. She needed all her strength to hold Nik up against the high-level balance beams and was so engrossed as she listened to Sean shouting instructions while Dan climbed up to untangle her, that she didn't notice Hunt and Zadrus walk in.

It took several minutes to extract Nik from the machine and settle her on the floor, but she'd become quite short of breath. Not knowing if it was just due to her panic or if Nik had done some more damage to her lungs, Jemma called Werrimen for help. The terrorists shot Nik before they left Earth, and her right lung had collapsed. It had taken all the ingenuity of the aliens to save her life. She'd done so well since then that Jemma feared this could be a serious setback.

Looking up for the first time since finding Nik in trouble to see Werrimen rush in, Jemma's eyes were drawn to Zadrus and Hunt, standing quietly out of the way. She ignored them as she helped move Nik to the alien version of a gurney that would take her to the medical centre.

Hunt stopped Dan from running out alongside her and then waited until everyone else had joined him. 'Is Nik alright?' he said, quietly to Dan.

'Think so. Werrimen's worried that she might have collapsed her lung again. I need to go to her.'

'Right. Give me a few minutes, then you can go.' He turned to look at Sean, his eyes resting on Jemma for an uncomfortable time. 'Listen up. Something has happened on level six. Many of the residents have been infected by a virus.'

Jemma inhaled sharply, aware that both Sean and Dan had moved in behind her. 'Pritchard?'

'We don't know,' said Hunt. 'But it is the same virus.'

Sean gripped her arm and whispered something that she didn't hear. She pushed both him and Dan away and took a step towards Hunt. 'I told you I saw one of Pritchard's thugs. The day I got sick. You wouldn't believe me.'

Hunt glanced at Zadrus before answering. 'I'm assured this virus is well known throughout the universe. We can't assume Pritchard is behind this outbreak.'

'Of course, we can.' She glared at him then wheeled around to Zadrus. 'Where the hell else would it have come from?'

'Zadrus tells me there are multiple possible causes,' said Hunt. 'If someone we brought on board was infected, it would spread quickly.'

'I know that a large number of people have joined us in the last month, but have any of them come from somewhere other than Earth? Did this virus have the influenza A virus embedded within it? Earth's influenza A?'

Zadrus drew himself up and took a breath before answering. 'No, they did not. Yes, it did. We must not be focussed on the source. It is most important now to eradicate the virus and treat the patients first.'

'We do have to focus on the source,' shouted Jemma. 'You can eradicate it all you like, and he'll re-release it.'

'First,' said Zadrus, his voice now stern. 'We must treat the patients.'

'Sticking your head in the sand won't make him go away,' snapped Jemma. 'So, how the hell did he get on board? You told me you checked everyone.'

'No system is perfect. It is possible that he slipped through, although we have no proof he is here.' Zadrus sounded calm, but she didn't miss his fists clenched by his side.

'No, damn it, who else could have done this?' She felt Sean by her side, but she shook him away again, she wasn't backing down. 'Where in hell is he? Why aren't you looking?'

'Is all our group here?' Hunt stepped forward, clearly not prepared to wait for the exchange between Jemma and Zadrus to play out. He had the familiar growl back in his voice. 'Level six is now isolated.'

Jemma stared at Hunt and Zadrus and Sean, all of whom stood there passively watching her. She couldn't work out if they were being deliberately evasive or just didn't get it. 'What use is that? You didn't notice him there in the first place. Or on our level. What makes you think he's still there? He could be right outside our door as we speak.'

Hunt's silence, as he waited for her to finish, cut through the already tense atmosphere. 'Let me continue,' he said, finally. 'All the occupants of that floor have been treated and are now cleared of the virus. Everyone else on the ship must now be cleared. All of you will proceed to the virus treatment room.'

'Fine,' said Jemma. 'But where the hell is Pritchard?'

'I will answer that,' said Zadrus. 'We have increased our surveillance, but I cannot guarantee we will find him. Nor can I be sure that he is the culprit. We will continue looking.'

'Of course, it's him.' She buried her head against Sean's chest. 'It's him,' she sobbed. 'You know it's him.'

'Level six is now off limits to everyone except Bellamy and O'Leary,' said Hunt, raising his voice above hers. 'Are you all clear?'

'Abundantly,' snapped Jemma, but Sean didn't let her say anything more. He steered her towards the virus treatment complex.

*   *   *

After the treatment, Sean led Dan and Jemma back to the medical centre to check on Nik who, now breathing better, was surprisingly cheerful even though Werrimen had confirmed a collapsed lung. Leaving Jemma with Nik to give her a chance to cool down, he grabbed Dan and headed down to the control level. He also wanted to know what Zadrus had done to locate the perpetrators, but he thought he had a better chance of getting that information if they could speak quietly in Zadrus's office without Jemma present.

Hunt sat beside Sean. He spoke quietly. 'Do I have to have a chat with Jemma?'

'No. For God's sake, leave her alone. I'll sort her.' Sean realised he was growling and forced himself to soften his voice. 'These people have come bloody close to killing her three times now, and we know that Pritchard's fixated on getting hold of her. She's angry, but she's also scared.'

'I know.' Hunt sighed. 'I feel for her, but we have to get her focussed, specifically because she is his target. You've got twenty-four hours. Then she fronts me.'

Sean leaned back closing his eyes. Jemma had every right to be angry, but Hunt was also right, her anger put her at risk. It was only a few months since they'd learned of Jemma's position on her planet and that her parents and her grandfather had both been murdered by Fredrick Pritchard. If Pritchard, or his people, really were on board this craft, as Jemma believed, then her life was at stake.

When the meeting concluded, Zadrus asked Sean to remain behind. After the others had left, he turned back to Sean. 'I would like to speak to Jemma about this, just the two of us. Will that present a problem for you?'

Sean sank into the nearest chair. 'Jemma has been through so much. I don't want her hurt more.'

'Have I ever hurt her?'

'No. God, no.'

'Then you must understand I will not harm her now. Would you please find her and send her to me?' He held up his hand as Sean went to speak. 'You may accompany her here, but I wish to speak to her alone.'

Although Sean remained worried, he went in search of

Jemma and found her still with Nik.

'Hey,' said Jemma. She sounded cheerful, but her eyes narrowed slightly as she looked at him.

'Hey yourself. You feeling better, Nik?'

'Yes thanks,' but she too stared at him as though his concerns were written across his face.

'Excellent. I just need to drag Jem away for a bit.' He reached his hand out to Jemma and was pleased, in one way, that she accepted it and stood next to him, but worried about how she'd cope with Zadrus.

'What's happened?' she said, as they walked.

'Nothing specific. Zadrus wants to talk to you. He wouldn't say why.'

'Is he angry with me?'

'No, I don't believe so. I think he's keen to help, but I suspect he wants to chat about your reaction today.'

'Okay, we'll go find out, then.'

'No,' said Sean. 'He wants to talk to you on your own.'

'Oh.'

His heart almost stopped when she stood still and looked up at him, some of the old fear coursing through her eyes again.

'We're here,' she said, trying to make her voice sound light and bright. 'I'll call you when I'm finished. That's if I live through it.'

'You'd better live through it.' He leaned down to kiss her. 'I won't be far away.'

*   *   *

She pressed the button on the communicator outside Zadrus's office and the door opened straight away. Zadrus stood on the other side, a broad smile on his face.

'Come in, my dear. It's good to see you.'

'You saw me an hour ago,' she said, returning his smile.

'I did.' He pointed to a chair and sat beside her. 'Now take my hands.'

She felt the usual jolt, then rested back to allow the warm, calm sensation flow through her body. Werrimen had tried while she was still in the medical centre, but she'd been weak and stressed and somehow her link with Zadrus, even though she thought the world of Werrimen, seemed stronger. She wasn't sure how long it was before he rested back and released his grip.

'You are a strong woman, Jemma. I do not want to focus on the past. I want to talk about moving forward.'

'Find Pritchard and get rid of him. Then I can.'

'No. I agree Fredrick Pritchard, or Drick, as I know him, is a problem, and we will continue to search. But if not him, there will be someone else. I need to know that you can take care of yourself.'

'I kind of did, that day,' she said.

'Yes, you did. But then your fear soared out of control.'

'I'm working on it.'

'I know. We have talked most days. Now I think it is time to get back into your trustee training. Would you work with me on that now?'

'I guess.' What else could she say? It was his spaceship and he was in charge.

'Good. When you come to see me each morning, I will let Mary know that you will stay a little longer.'

Every day for the next three weeks she spent two hours with Zadrus, accepting his energy through his hands, and talking about her fears. He helped her look back over what had happened by touching his hand to her neck and enhancing her memory, and she was relieved that her description of events on the day of the miscarriage seemed to convince him that she really had seen that man. He'd just begun instructing her on how to use the same techniques with people to enhance or alter their memory when, on the final day of the three weeks, he told her that he had a full complement of people prepared to join their mission and they were ready to go.

The Sidlown crew went into overdrive, preparing lounges on each floor for the journey, each of which would cater for fifty humans, and two crew. A variety of rails were placed to help people move during the journey. Seat belts and harnesses weren't necessary as the chairs moulded around the person to hold them in, even if the ride became rough, but they were warned motion sickness was common. Each lounge had a couple of bathrooms and food was replenished with ample supplies for the journey along with water, but hot food and drinks were a risk and wouldn't be available. No one, even the Sidlown crew, really knew what to expect. Despite their history with time portals, no one on the ship had ever been in one. All the advice the Sidlowns offered was based on the experiences of others.

There were now 9,462 humans on board, and 187

Sidlowns. Each of the twenty floors had five Sidlowns on duty. Hunt had resumed his management role, and Jemma did her best to assist Sean, but there were only eleven active people in their team. Nik was doing much better as was Anthony, but neither was ready to be rostered for a full shift. Werrimen was still unhappy with Eric and Mary's failure to inform her of the problems on Earth, given that they were experienced Trustees, and she wouldn't permit them to be fully involved with security as yet.

Despite regular patrols on each floor, Sean relied heavily on the Sidlowns to weed out any trouble. Still, even with the large number of people on board, there were few problems, the occasional scuffle or argument, but nothing serious. So, when they were ready to start on their journey forward to eighty years in the future, all the Anders people were directed to one lounge, leaving the security of the other floors to the Sidlowns.

Jemma accompanied Sean to the prepared lounge early one morning to begin the journey. She hadn't been able to eat breakfast, and even now her stomach lurched at the thought of what they were about to do. They'd been advised that although safety harnesses were available, they shouldn't need them unless the journey became too rough, as the seats would hold them in. Just seconds after Zadrus's voice came through to tell them that they had entered the time zone, the craft began to vibrate. Jemma gripped her seat and saw Sean and most of the others doing the same. A few hours into the journey, she needed the bathroom, which turned out to be more difficult than she'd realised. People sitting between her and the wall with the rail grabbed her hand each time she lost her balance and, by the time she reached her destination, she felt like she'd just completed a ten-kilometre run. The shaking and rattling continued throughout the journey and, a few hours in, she had to fight off an overwhelming nausea. She hoped the people of Earth would be using the intervening years to reach a lasting peace, because otherwise, if the aliens proved to be right, they'd find a decimated planet, and nothing would be normal.

CHAPTER 4: 2064

The War Begins

CANBERRA: FRIDAY 13TH JUNE 2064

19:00 hours: Duty Officer, Major Gerard Hunt, ran up the steps two at a time, his briefcase raised to protect his face from the bitterly cold wind and driving sleet. A sergeant, standing just inside the door, greeted him by name but still directed him to the transparent security cubicle in the middle of the foyer to verify his identity. Most nights, the bureaucratic delay frustrated him, but tonight he was happy to stop for a moment, catch his breath and soak up the ambient warmth. He strode to his office, a glassed-off box in the middle of a large, sterile room filled with desks and computers. The staff in the outer room ignored him as they went about their business with a practiced efficiency, interrupted only by the occasional chatter of an incoming signal. He could have shut himself away like some other officers, *maintaining a distance* they called it, but he liked contact with his people, so he checked for urgent messages then walked out to greet the junior officers and other staff. He asked small, but personal, questions about family or mutual interests, then checked in with the Military Police detachment on the floor before returning to his office. Nothing much ever happened on these shifts. His role was to take charge if a problem arose that was beyond the capacity of the junior officers. But after a couple of hours, he'd completed all the paperwork in the in-tray and, with nothing left to do, he settled in the lounge chair, raised the footrest, leaned back, and closed his eyes.

Raised in a military family, his decision to join the Army had been expected. His father, Brigadier Campbell Hunt, served in the Fundamentalist War of 2025, and his grandfather, Major General Alexander Hunt, distinguished himself in Afghanistan and Iraq, until he was lost in the line of duty, during a bio-terrorist attack in 2020. Gerard had grown up dreaming of action and military honours, yet his father's war, a futile attempt to crush elusive and unpredictable insurgents, hadn't resulted in peace. It had put a stop to further fighting, most nations fearing the nuclear capacity of every other nation and, as a result, Gerard and his generation had never seen active service. He didn't want war, but he longed for the chance to prove himself. It felt like he'd completed school at the top of his class, only to find there were no universities. Of course, that wasn't true and he'd done very well at University, but he dreamed about the kind of officer he could have been and imagined himself performing gloriously in the fields of Flanders, or the jungles of Vietnam. His pleasant dream was interrupted when someone grabbed his arm.

02:30 hours: 'Sir, wake up. Come on, wake up, it's urgent.'

He shook off the fellow's arm and sat up, rubbing his eyes. 'Yeah, yeah, what's up, Sarge?'

'We've lost contact with Washington DC.'

'Is the satellite down?' He yawned, annoyed at being woken for a communication system crash.

'No, I've checked. And I've tried all the systems. Nothing.'

Still half asleep, Gerard walked towards the viewing screen in his office. 'Is anyone else affected?'

'Not that we can find.'

He yawned again as he turned on the screen. 'Right, call the UN office in New York. See if they know what's … holy shit, look at this.' The display covered most of one wall and the resolution made the scene feel like it was happening within the room.

As staff gathered behind him, Gerard stared in disbelief, unable to move. The same clip played over and over. Three missiles zoomed through the air in quick succession, a few seconds between each one. The first appeared to land directly on America's White House and a massive explosion shot debris everywhere, including towards whoever held the camera, followed by a mushroom-shaped cloud that billowed up into the atmosphere. He swore and gripped the back of a chair. What the hell? People lay still on the ground. Others ran, some screamed. Many had bloodied wounds. All were covered in ash and rubble.

He'd barely managed to catch a breath when the camera moved to the second missile. It landed to the North-East.

He'd lived in Washington DC, knew it quite well, although he couldn't identify this site, but the explosion was clear enough, followed again by the fireball and subsequent cloud.

The third missile headed directly towards the camera. Then nothing. Just static.

Everyone in the room was silent, all eyes fixed on the screen, until the muffled sound of a printer caught the Sergeant's attention. 'Sir, there's a flash. It's headed Extreme Security Threat.'

He stared at the Sergeant for a couple of seconds, mute. God, think. He had to do something. 'Right, give it to me. Where are the MPs?'

'Sir, here.' A tall, very fit, and heavily armed woman stood to attention.

'Lock-down this building. Notify headquarters in each state and lock them down. MPs to every parliamentarians' house. They can stand guard, ready to evacuate. Where's comms?'

'Here, sir.'

'Get a link with New York. Keep trying Washington. Try the UN.'

Gerard grabbed the secure office phone and pressed the emergency key.

A few seconds later, he heard the General growl. 'This had better be good.'

'Sir, turn on your screen. I'm on my way to pick you up.'

CHAPTER 5: 2096

The War Must End

Earth Date: Friday 23rd November 2096

10:00 *am.* Lieutenant-Colonel Matthew Hunt flew low over the latest target of the nuclear missiles. Canberra, his home for most of his life, was in ruins. His military college, Duntroon, had been erased — broken bricks and debris scattered across the acres of ground he'd once known so well. The proudest moment of his life had been on those grounds, when at the graduation ceremony, his father, General Gerard Hunt, had taken the salute.

He stared down at the scattered fragments of the once thriving city. A church spire without a church; fireplaces without houses; a lift-well with its elevator intact but no building. Rubble, twisted metal, and ash as far as he could see. Displaced algae and weed framed discrete masses of concrete and metal in the muddied water of Lake Burley Griffin.

Matt dragged his eyes from the window. His mission was about people, not the wreckage of buildings, or the destruction of landscape they could see from the air. But he knew in his heart no one could have survived. As the helicopter set down, the crew continued to stare silently out the windows. The expressions on the faces of his staff, frozen in their seats, spurred him on to get outside.

'Get your radiation suits on. Full checks, suits and oxygen.' No one moved, all eyes glued to something outside the window. Someone called, 'What's that?'

'You're just delaying,' growled Matt as he moved back to the window. 'Jesus … What the …?'

A large grey metal sphere, around fifteen metres in diameter, that looked as though it had been squashed in at the top and the bottom hovered in the sky on the other side of the city. Suddenly, the thing took off at high speed, towards the East.

Someone yelled, 'Where'd it go?'

'No idea,' muttered Matt but, like everyone else, he kept looking. 'There've been multiple reports of those things in other places. First one I've seen, though. They haven't presented any threat, but no one's been able to tell me what they are. Forget it for now. We've got a job to do.'

No one shifted.

'Move,' he yelled. Two people jumped up, and then the rest followed. He looked back through the window, then forced himself away, grabbed his protective suit and dragged it on. Made from a soft, light fabric, it had to work perfectly in the toxic atmosphere. The suits were impermeable to radiation, but not to other atmospheric elements. Odours and heat could seep through, and the unpredictable Canberra weather at this time of the year could be exceedingly hot. They'd have to work quickly.

The patch of road on which they'd set down was relatively unscathed but, even though final checks of equipment and oxygen had been completed, nobody seemed willing to open the door.

'Alright, everyone out. Move, move, move.' Matt continued to yell until all, apart from the pilot, had alighted. He wouldn't have to do more. They'd done this so many times before, the routine of the search was automatic.

Without landmarks, it was a challenge to establish their position, but as Matt turned and looked up the hill, the steps of the original Parliament House stood proudly in front of an abyss which had once been the centre of Australian Government. Behind him, singed scraps of paper fluttered in the soft breeze before settling on the mangled debris of the National Library, where he'd met Dana, his wife. Now, his family home and his memories were all gone. Every town he'd surveyed, after the missiles struck, had shocked him, but this was much more personal.

Somewhere in the distance, a bell tolled. It sliced through the eerie silence like thunder and startled him back to the present. An overpowering smell made him cough. Not just smoke. Burnt flesh perhaps, rotting in the stifling heat of the day. Sweat poured down his face, and condensation inside his mask made it difficult to see. Something crunched underfoot. It was charred, but soft to touch. He squatted down to turn it over. With a strangled scream, he pulled his hand away and reeled back, almost knocking his Sergeant over. The arm of a small child, singed and covered in soot, filled every field of his vision. He grabbed at his mask. He wanted to vomit. The Sergeant tackled him to the ground and held his arms.

'Leave it alone. Do you want to die?'

Maybe. What kind of life was this? Tears welled in his eyes.

The Sergeant reduced his grip allowing Matt to sit up, but he didn't remove the hold altogether. 'You've seen too much, sir. Been there too many times. You're going straight to the helicopter.'

'No, the others have to go first.'

'No, sir. You're doing as I say.' The tough, older, war-hardened Sergeant held Matt's eyes with a fierce stare.

'That's mutiny Sarge.' Matt tried to return the stare but couldn't keep it up. The Sergeant had a clear edge over him in his distressed state and he could appreciate what his NCO was trying to do.

'Don't care,' said the Sergeant. 'You're doing it.'

Matt sighed but turned towards the helicopter. There were times to fight and times to admit defeat. He'd rarely felt defeated in his life, but now he did. The Sergeant helped him up the stairs and shut the airlock behind him. Liquid sprayed almost immediately from many angles. He held out his arms, and turned slowly, as he'd done so often before. The liquid neutralised the worst of the radiation on the suit, then hardened to a gel which trapped any remaining contamination onto the outside, like a cocoon.

Once the spray stopped, he commenced his practiced routine. Remove the helmet, take off the protective suit and boots. Place them in the decontamination cupboard. The airlock wasn't much more than a metre square, just big enough to manage two people in an emergency, with a small bench seat on the right side of the doorway, and the door to the cupboard on the left. It was like being in a vacuum, both physically, and emotionally. He should have been angry, screaming, shouting, demanding revenge. But he felt hopeless. There was nothing anyone could do. Hundreds of thousands of people, and everything they'd worked for and held dear to them, wiped out in an instant. If human life itself held so little value, so little meaning, what was there left to fight for?

The machine interrupted his thoughts, asking if he was ready to start his own decontamination. He raised his hand to key in the appropriate sequence but could only stare at the screen. He raised his hand again. Every individual had their own personal sequence, their military ID, and no one ever forgot their military ID.

Waves of nausea charged through him. He'd forgotten his military ID. He struggled to breathe.

The pilot's voice sounded through the intercom. 'Problem, sir?'

'The numbers. Can't remember the numbers.' He began to shake as he stared at the keypad.

'Use the emergency sequence. Look up, you'll see it.'

Just above the keyboard was a sign. **If no ID, use these numbers — 12341234.** The emergency sequence normally triggered an armed response, and he formed an image of the pilot raising her weapon at him. Using both hands, one to steady the other, he keyed in the emergency numbers, then sat on the bench dressed only in his underwear. Sobs convulsed through his body. When the green light flashed, and the procedure was completed, he stood and walked unsteadily into the next room where he dressed in the military uniform of which he had once been so proud.

The pilot waited just beyond the door. 'Sarge told me what happened.' A seasoned veteran herself, she ordered him to his seat, shoved a glass of water in his hand, and kept him talking. He fixed his gaze on the radiation alarm, which would sound if any of his people were contaminated, but it remained silent as the last crew member completed the boarding process. It struck him as ironic that the biggest advance to come out of thirty years of fighting was the perfection of the radiation suit, and the capacity to neutralise radiation in the air lock.

'Head back to Newcastle,' he whispered.

The usual atmosphere after a mission was jovial, but today it was quiet, sombre. Like him, they'd lost hope. Less than a month ago, Matt had organised the evacuation of thousands of people, including the entire Australian Parliament, from Canberra to the old Newcastle University, in response to intel. Many thousands more had refused to go. He closed his eyes. Someone quietly cried. Soft comforting murmurs drifted back to him. Until today, he'd thought there was still some chance of peace and recovery. But not now. The image of that little arm had burnt indelibly into his memory. Whole families wiped out. Towns obliterated. No one really knew who they were fighting anymore. Or why.

Closing the screen to separate himself and the pilot from the rest of the crew, he set up a secure line to General Gerard Hunt, his father. 'There's nothing left here, sir. Search and Rescue can come in, but they won't find anything.'

When the General eventually spoke, Matt could hear the helplessness in his voice. 'Are you and your crew okay, son?'

'Yeah, just shocked. This is the worst site we've seen. It's horrendous.'

'Right, head back here. We'll talk more when you arrive.' A short pause followed. 'There is something else you need to know, and I don't want you to hear it from anyone else. Two other young women have disappeared.'

'For Christ's sake dad, what's going on?'

'I wish I knew. I've got the MPs out looking. But nothing yet.'

'They haven't found Dana?'

'No son, I'm sorry.'

'We saw one of those weird metal flying things, today. Looked like they were assessing the damage to Canberra. Are they taking the women?'

'No idea.'

The pilot interrupted him as she gave the command to prepare to disembark. The transport bus to take them to the University site pulled in close to the helicopter, extending a walkway to secure a seal onto the unopened door. Matt walked to the back of the bus and sat by himself, closing his eyes.

'Sir, try not to think about it,' said the pilot. 'Today's been hard. Too hard. We have to look to the future now.' She looked away. 'If we can find one.'

But that was all he thought about. His childhood had been in a world that was still at least functional. Born shortly after the initial conflict began, he had no concept of a world at peace. He'd only ever known turmoil. The conflicts had dragged on now for more than thirty years. Terrorist attacks, missiles, poisoned water sources, biological attacks. Cities, even whole countries rebuilt after they'd been bombed, and slowly the people would return to something like normal lives. Then the terrorists would move on somewhere else. He'd led several *peace-keeping forces* in other countries. Now he realised it was all just a kind of damage control. Politicians pretending to do something useful, but all they'd ever done was delay the inevitable. One great political, bloody game. And today, all he could feel was guilt. It was an irrational guilt, he knew that. He couldn't have changed anything. But even so, he'd gone along with it, been part of it. Really believed he was helping. How could he have been so stupid?

CHAPTER 6: 2099

A New Era

Earth Date: Monday, 9th March 2099

10:00 *am:* The vibration in the spaceship ceased as suddenly as it had begun. According to Jemma's watch, it was now two days after they'd entered the time zone, although she wasn't sure if it would be accurate. Was it possible that they could have moved eighty years into the future in that time? All doubt was wiped away when Zadrus appeared, on the big screen, to announce that they were in orbit around Earth in the year 2099. Everyone stared at the screen, but no one moved.

Jemma could hardly breathe and, when Sean wrapped his arms around her, she nestled in. Perhaps she could give him some comfort too. When she finally looked up, she smiled at the number of others doing the same. Hunt held Erin, Nik was with Dan, Eric, Mary and Anthony huddled together. Relieved that everyone had survived the journey, unscathed, her thoughts turned to what would come next. The modern

Earth would be a far different place, good or bad, from the one they'd left behind. She held onto Sean when he suggested they return to their room for a shower and change, afraid to let go as it sank in that everything she'd ever known was gone.

'Right through the journey I wondered if we'd made the right decision,' said Sean, quietly. 'But we're here, and we have to deal with it, no matter what we find.'

'Yes, we do.' Before they'd left Earth, she'd had dreams of finding her sister who'd disappeared after their parents died, of setting up house in the country with Sean and raising a family of happy, healthy, rural kids, of horses, cows, chooks, and working dogs, and of becoming a renowned expert, researching the endangered animals she so loved. None of those things would happen now, or at least not in the way she'd anticipated. She stood under the hot water, hoping it would wash away her anxiety. It didn't, so she waited for Sean and, together, they headed back to the lounge, neither saying anything until Jemma's communicator sounded.

'How are you,' said Zadrus, smiling.

'Good, thank you. We're all fine.'

'I am relieved. Would you please come to my office?'

'Okay. Sean and I can come straight down.'

'No, my dear. Just you for the moment.'

'Oh. Right.' She stared back at Sean as the communicator shut down, hoping he'd have some intelligent suggestion to help her cope, but he looked as nonplussed as she felt.

'You'd better go,' said Sean.

'I don't want to go anywhere by myself.'

'Happy to walk down with you if you're frightened.'

'No,' she replied, squeezing his hand. 'I'm not frightened. I'm pretty well past that now. It's just … oh God, … I don't know. It's just I don't want to let you out of my sight. At least while I can see you, I know you're here, and I'm not alone.'

'Oh dear.' He drew her into him. 'It sounds silly, but I know what you mean. We're in Zadrus's world now, and everything we do is going to depend on him. We know we can trust him, so it'll be okay.'

She took one last look at Sean, then let go of his hand and headed to the disc to take her down to the control room floor, and Zadrus's office.

'Oh good,' he said, when she arrived. 'We can go now. General Hunt and I are going down to have a look at the new settlement. I would like you to join us.'

'Wouldn't you be better to have Sean with you?' she asked.

'You are my Prehling, you will accompany me,' said Zadrus. 'Sean will accompany Werrimen when she needs him. You may both have to take a security role with General Hunt. It will all depend on what we find when we get there.'

She stared at her feet and, to his credit, he waited to let her speak. 'I don't want a security role. I want to learn all I can from your scientists and get involved with researching our new environment.'

'I will facilitate that if possible,' he replied, as he led her to the landing bay. 'But first, we must find out what is there.'

She sat quietly in the transporter, staring out the window at the countryside as they approached and she was marginally puzzled, although not quite sure why, that the bush looked just the same as it always had. As the transporter eased into a spot behind a large red brick building, she leaned forward for a better look. The sculptured gardens took her breath away. Designed and organised splashes of red and yellow framed the red bricks. Softer colours lined the front. When she followed Zadrus out of the craft, she bent down to touch a flower. Familiar perfumes wafted up and she gasped with delight at twittering birds that flittered in and out of the bushes. 'This is beautiful,' she exclaimed.

A sign on the door of the building heralded ADMINISTRATION, and a Sidlown woman walked through the door to greet them.

'We are happy with our gardens,' she said, smiling at Jemma.

'As you should be,' said Zadrus.

'We have worked hard,' said the woman. 'I am Shardene. Welcome to the East Australian Settlement. I presume you are Zadrus.'

'I am Zadrus. At your service madam.'

'No, your reputation precedes you. I am at your service.' She bowed her head towards Zadrus.

'Thank you. May I ask how long you have been here?'

'I have been Earth Commander for four years,' she replied. 'Our people, with the humans, have constructed everything you see. I will show you around later.'

'You have achieved much. Now would you please fill me in on what happened.'

Fascinated by the respect this woman showed Zadrus, a man she'd never met, Jemma had already edged back towards Hunt when he touched her arm to indicate she should follow his lead and position herself a short distance behind Zadrus.

Shardene explained how war had devastated Earth, from the bombing of Washington DC in 2064, to the final, devastating escalation in 2094 which had destroyed all of Earth's major cities. A routine IPL patrol had arrived in 2095, and were so shocked by what they found, that they contacted all of Earth's remaining governments. By 2096 all of Earth's communication systems had been lost and governments who'd held out, finally gave in and accepted the IPL's help.

She was effusive in her praise of those who'd established the settlement and managed its development, their skill and determination, given just twenty Sidlowns and less than a thousand humans, although there was still much to be done. She went on to describe a settlement in South America that was not progressing well and explained that the original Sidlowns from the East Australian settlement had moved there to help. Zadrus looked at his feet and, even to Jemma, it was obvious what was coming.

'I know the plan was for you to return to Sidlow, Zadrus. Would you consider delaying that to take over here. It would only be temporary, and I understand I am asking a lot of you.'

Zadrus stood in silence for a few moments, and Shardene did not interrupt.

Jemma was sure he'd put his own needs aside, to help both the people here and those on the ship who depended on him so heavily. She could only imagine the turmoil in his mind as they all waited quietly for his answer. His decision would impact Werrimen and probably the entire crew of his spaceship. It wouldn't be a decision he'd take lightly.

'I would be honoured to take over here,' he said. His face was blank as he spoke.

'Thank you,' she replied. 'I am deeply grateful. Your presence will help us far more than you can imagine. I presume the message we sent back would have reached Earth command around the year 2000 to explain the war and the damage.'

'Yes, but it was not complete, and arrived much later than 2000,' said Zadrus. 'We ascertained you wanted people brought forward but did not know why.'

'Ah, I see.' She smiled. 'That explains your surprise. Now, I presume you wish to do a tour of the planet to see what has happened.'

'Yes, I do. May we look around the settlement first? It will help me to be able to prepare the people I have brought with me before I allow them to disembark.'

'Of course. There is one other matter I must address before you leave. Many of the humans here suffered terribly, and we needed the help of local leaders like the young man who helped establish this settlement. He worked hard to encourage people to accept us, particularly those who were injured or sick.' She moved around Zadrus and looked directly at Hunt. 'I would specifically like to introduce you to that young man, General Hunt. His name is Matthew Hunt, and he was a lieutenant-colonel in the Australian Army.'

Hunt flinched but steadfastly returned her gaze. 'Hunt is a common name.'

'Yes, but this young man tells a story of his great grandfather, Major General Alexander Hunt, who disappeared from a facility known as SCARF. I believe that to be you.'

'Jesus.' Hunt flinched. He stared, first at Jemma, then at Zadrus. 'Does he know I'm here?'

For the first time since they'd arrived, she relaxed. 'I am not cruel. I have warned him, but of course, when I last spoke to him, I had no idea what to expect either. I must warn you, I have seen images of his father, and you look very much like him, so please understand that he might be quite shocked.'

Jemma put her hand on Hunt's arm. 'Are you okay?'

He stood mute for a moment, before turning to her, 'Yeah, but I've no idea what to do here.'

'I'm amazed,' she said, smiling. 'I didn't think there was anything you didn't know how to handle. Maybe you should do what you're always telling me, one step at a time.'

His face softened into a smile but before he could respond they were interrupted as a man, around Sean's age, rushed into the room.

'Holy shit.' Matthew Hunt stood stock-still and stared at the General.

The older Hunt managed to speak first, although his voice shook. 'Fucking hell.' He looked at Jemma, then Zadrus, then the Commander and finally back at the young man. 'If I didn't know better … I mean, Jesus … you could be my son.'

The younger Hunt walked up to the General and pushed

his face, roughly, to the left. 'No scar. My father had a scar on the right side of his neck. You could be his bloody twin. Is this … is it some kind of joke? It's pretty sick.'

'No joke,' replied Hunt. 'I don't know what to say.'

Jemma couldn't hold back a laugh. Matt raised one eyebrow as he stared at her, just like Hunt. 'I'm sorry, it's not just your looks. Your facial expressions, and mannerisms are identical.'

'Sure,' said Matt. 'This is too crazy for words.'

'It is, but it's real. I guess we'll have to take it one step at a time,' replied Hunt.

Amused to hear him quote her, it occurred to Jemma that others on the ship might also discover they had family. How would any of them cope? She wasn't sure how the Hunts would deal with it, given the look on both their faces.

The Commander interrupted. 'It is time to go back to your ship. You will have plenty of time to get to know each other later. Zadrus, once your passengers are ready to disembark, come back and I will arrange a formal handover. Things here are currently peaceful, but that could change. Our relationship with the people of Earth is still somewhat fragile. You must be prepared for it, and ready to deal with anything.'

'I would like to leave Jemma, my Prehling, here to talk to Matthew,' said Zadrus.

'Of course. It pleases me to hear you are training someone from Earth,' said Shardene.

Zadrus nodded, then turned to the younger Hunt. 'Matthew, please tell Jemma about your experiences, and any security issues that you may have here. We will meet when I return, to discuss how we handle those issues together.'

Jemma stared at him. Surely, he wasn't planning to leave her here by herself. She knew he'd want the inside story and presumably thought she'd have a better chance of getting it, and the look on his face made it clear she shouldn't argue.

*   *   *

Surprised by how alone he felt without Jemma, Sean sat well away from anyone else, and stared at the ceiling, until a large hand on his shoulder made him look up.

'Sean, we will work out what to do when we get there,' said Werrimen, gently. 'Come with me, now. Zadrus and General Hunt, have requested we join them in the viewing room.'

'Where's Jemma?'

'She is waiting in the settlement for us.'

'They left her there by herself! You can't be serious,' he snapped.

'She is not by herself,' replied Werrimen. 'I would have expected you to trust Zadrus by now.'

'I do,' he sighed, as he followed Werrimen to the disc. In the control room, Zadrus and Hunt stood together in front of the viewing window. Both looked grim. Neither spoke as Sean joined them, so he stood beside Hunt and waited, aware that everyone on the ship would be gathered near a viewing screen and waiting on directions from Zadrus.

'Below, you will see planet Earth,' began Zadrus. 'There

has been considerable damage. You must prepare yourselves to be shocked as we move closer.'

Sean heard someone swear, as they looked down on Canada. Vancouver was gone, a vast expanse of ocean in its place. Further down the west coast of North America, Washington state, and much of California, were gone. They were a long way from the East Coast, but Sean imagined the damage there would be even more severe given that was where the bombing began. Further south, the strip of land which connected North and South America, and had contained the Panama Canal, was now ocean. Panama, Jamaica, Haiti and the Dominican Republic were missing. Costa Rica, which had played such a large role in determining his future, was also missing, although South America seemed mostly intact. Across the Pacific, where Indonesia had been, there were now four small islands. To the south, New Guinea hadn't changed, and the north-east of Australia seemed unscathed.

Further south, Queensland's Glasshouse Mountains and Scenic Rim were on the edge of the ocean. Brisbane, the city he'd known so well, was gone. The Gold Coast was gone. It was like some giant had taken a massive bite out of the East Coast of Australia around the border between Queensland and New South Wales. Parts of the land mass between the cities he'd known as Sydney and Melbourne was still there but looked like multiple small islands. At least Tasmania appeared intact. They flew over the Southern Ocean, and across the Antarctic icecap, then turned north to travel up the West Coast of Australia, which was relatively unchanged.

But as they flew across the centre of Australia heading back towards the settlement in the east, they encountered a massive river. The craft changed direction, and turned north towards the Gulf of Carpentaria, to find where it flowed into the ocean, before tracking the river down to the top of South Australia. Once they had seen the length and width of this river, they turned again towards their destination, the East Australian Settlement.

Zadrus spoke again. 'I realise most of you will be shocked, as am I. There is some good news. Enough solid land exists to establish settlements. In fact, many have already begun. Some countries cannot yet be salvaged. An example is North America. It had more bombs per square metre than any other continent, and it will be a long time before we can look to find suitable settlements there. Climates have been chosen which are neither too hot, nor too cold, so that we can conserve energy. There are forty settlements throughout the planet, and in time, there will be more, but for the moment forty is enough.

'Much work has been done by those already in the East Australian Settlement to which we are headed. They have constructed a Transparent Energy Membrane, or TEM, around the settlement to protect us from radiation. You will not be able to see it, and it is not a barrier against movement, but you must remember that outside the TEM, the air is not safe. Fences have been erected to warn you not to cross into the unsafe area but there are no locked gates. You will be free to come and go as you please. Water purification plants have been established and there is sufficient to drink, but it is rationed for everything else. More will be explained after we land.

'You must understand the people here have suffered for many years. They will be suspicious, and some might even be hostile. Please be patient. Prepare to land now. Return to your quarters and collect your belongings. We will advise you further as we approach our landing zone.'

He shut down his microphone and turned to Sean. 'There were almost ten billion people on Earth in 2064 when all this began. Now there are less than one million and they cannot survive without our help.'

Sean waited through a long pause, after which Zadrus told him about Hunt's great grandson, Matthew, which explained the look he'd seen on Hunt's face when he'd entered the viewing room. 'I left Jemma down there to hear Matt's story. She is my Prehling and I plan to increase her training now.'

Sean's body slumped. 'All she wants is to do her research. Why can't you leave her be?'

'You know why,' said Hunt. 'If the terrorists have managed to follow us here, she is at more risk than any of the rest of us. She believes they have, and I suspect she is right.'

Shouts interrupted them as the new settlement came into view. Many people ran to the small windows desperate for their first glimpse. Sean didn't join them. He wasn't at all convinced they'd be able to fit in, returning to Earth eighty years on. It was arrogant to assume that these people who'd been through so much would open their arms and welcome the newcomers into their community. And, through all of it, he had to work out, yet again, how to protect Jemma.

He lingered in his room, as he packed for Jemma as well as himself. Others would be milling around the doorway, eager to get out and see their new home. They could go first. He couldn't stop thinking about that blue light, on the mountain, and how it had resulted in this. He relived that event almost every day, looking for any tiny thing he might have done differently, but they were here now, no point in rehashing the past. He needed to get down there, find Jemma, and start to get on with their new life.

Jemma had walked around the settlement with Matt, and together, they'd viewed more than a dozen buildings, Administration, Hospital, Quarantine, and multiple accommodation blocks when he stopped at a small café at the base of one of the buildings. He explained how the settlement had developed and outlined some of the problems they'd faced, although he quickly brushed over the negatives which, she thought, was very like his great grandfather. Keen to understand what they'd been through, she listened carefully. It wasn't just to be polite; she was genuinely interested.

'Would you like to see an apartment?' said Matt, walking towards the bead of the nearest block. 'They're all much the same, restricted access, residents and security only, although a small number of us are authorised to enter all blocks. We can't walk into apartments, except in an emergency and, even then, I have to request an override.' He flicked a sideways look at her then, grinning, ran for the stairs and proceeded to bound up them.

'Bastard,' she muttered, but, realising he was testing her, she took a deep breath and charged after him. He was almost a full flight ahead when she reached the first step, but she had no intention of allowing him to win, she'd learnt that much from the General. She caught up on the fourth floor, shot him a smile, and tore past.

'One more flight,' he yelled, doing his best to reach her, although he was now well behind.

Using all the energy she could muster, she ignored him and spurted up the remaining flight, beating him by five steps. She sat at the top, heaving for breath and laughing.

'Impressive,' he muttered, but he also had a big smile on his face.

Jemma held out her hand. 'Did I pass?'

He took the proffered hand and helped her up. 'Very well. You're a lot fitter than I am.'

She grimaced. 'Don't let your great grandfather hear that.' Doing her best to imitate Hunt's voice, she went on. 'I expect every member of my team to be at peak fitness. No exceptions. Do I make myself clear?'

'Hmm, might have to work out how to avoid him then.'

'Wouldn't bother. Better to give in and do what he wants.'

His eyes narrowed slightly before he responded. 'Alright, guess I'll work it out as I go. Let's have a look at an empty unit. I programmed this one before we started looking so I could get in. I don't know which one they've allocated to you yet, but it'll be similar.' He walked halfway along the corridor, then stood under a bead. The door slid open to reveal a large, furnished apartment.

After several months in the tiny spaceship cabin, it looked heavenly, not just big, but downright luxurious. A soft, plush carpet covered the floor. It felt remarkably like wool, although she knew it couldn't be; there were no sheep in the new settlement. The bedroom was twice the size of the spaceship bedroom although it was set out much the same, large double bed, bedside tables and walk-in wardrobe and ensuite. In the next room, a large leather-look lounge suite was nestled in front of a wall-mounted entertainment system, similar to the screen in their apartment on the spaceship.

'C'mon mate,' said Matt. 'I'll be happy to show you how to use all this stuff once you've settled in, but we'd better keep moving now so I can show you everything before your husband arrives.'

'Lead on MacDuff,' she replied.

'Who?' He looked puzzled.

'Just an expression from my era. I guess we'll have to get used to each other's way of speaking.' She followed him back down the stairs, then up a long pathway towards a thick patch of bush.

'We're heading to the factories,' he said. 'They're separate from the living quarters. Deliberately, of course. Noise control, odour control.'

'Okay.' As they walked through the bush, she was surprised to find it open out, revealing at least a dozen large buildings. The first two were dedicated to food production, hydroponically grown fruit and vegetables. Another building further along manufactured palatable proteins from beans, lentils and other legumes she didn't recognise. Then there were others that manufactured clothing, furniture and electrical devices. A building at the end stored dehydrated and frozen foods.

'We've been filling this building all year,' said Matt. 'We didn't know what we'd need or how many people we'd have to feed, so we stored as much as we could.'

Behind all the other buildings, was a large kiln. Beside it were stores of bricks and other building materials.

'Matt, I'm really impressed. What you've achieved in the last couple of years is amazing.'

'Thanks, but we'd all be dead if it weren't for the aliens, and all the electronics and food production are their design, although they have shown us how. They want us to be self-sufficient.'

'I understand, but they couldn't have done it alone either. You, and your people made it happen.'

He shrugged. 'I guess. What else would you like to see?'

'I saw a large dam as we flew in. They talk me up as a trustee and part of the military, but the truth is I'm neither. I'm a scientist. My field is ecology and I used to research the habitats of endangered animals. That dam could be a really good place for me to start.'

'Oh wow. Can't wait to hear that story. We'll go back that way, then.'

She hadn't noticed until he pointed out that the bush surrounded two sides of the settlement, hiding the factories to the east, and the dam to the south. As they walked, he showed her the purification plants, the power source for the TEM, and the pumps that took water to the hydroponic sheds. On their way back, she admired the quality of the buildings, all built with red clay bricks, presumably from the kiln. These people had built hope from despair, erecting enough facilities for ten thousand people.

As they neared the Administration building, a shadow crept across the settlement. Matt grabbed Jemma's arm and dragged her into the foyer. Others had done the same. Not one of them had looked up at the sky.

'Matt.' Jemma hesitated as she spoke. 'Look up. It's not a storm. It's the spaceship.'

He stepped back to the doorway and followed her gaze. 'Oh God. You must think I'm a complete fool.'

'No,' she replied, 'I don't, but I would like you to tell me more about what happened here, so that I can understand.'

'That'll take a bit,' he replied, with a sheepish smile. 'The big problem was the damage to the ozone. Even with the TEM in place we've had terrible storms. They start with overpowering darkness, usually followed by chain lightning, hail the size of tennis balls and belting rain that cuts like you wouldn't believe. People have been killed in the winds alone. You can't stay upright if you get caught in them. The Sidlowns set up lightning attractors at the edge of the settlement to pull the lightning away, but those who've been hit didn't stand a chance.'

Linking her arm through his, she encouraged him to walk outside. 'I want to hear all about it, but we'd better head out to the landing zone for now.' She'd only ever seen the mothership through the window of a transporter and, as she watched the ship continue its slow journey above them, she was struck by how much more impressive it was from the ground. People slowly crept out from the buildings and gathered around them to watch. Some seemed fascinated, but others cringed and clung to people near them.

Matt couldn't take his eyes off it, and she stood beside him so they could experience the landing of the massive craft together. Similar in shape to the smaller transporters, it was many times their size, around 300 metres in diameter and, she estimated, seventy metres in height from its base to the top of the dome. Four evenly spaced V-shaped fins projected from the middle of the ship and they spun horizontally around the circumference. There were twenty rows of windows that started just above the fins and extended to the top of the craft. When the spaceship reached the landing zone, it stopped a hundred metres above the ground. No wind, no emissions and utterly silent.

'Do you think they'd let me in to have a look at how this thing works?' said Matt.

'I have no doubt they would agree to that,' said Jemma, pleased by Matt's fascination. 'Zadrus will welcome your interest.'

'Have you seen the controls? Do you know how to fly it? Just imagine being the first human to fly one of these.' He grinned. 'Sorry, it's just … well, it's extraordinary.'

'Don't be sorry. I've had much the same thoughts, and I know they want to teach us everything they can, so we can become self-sufficient. But it'll take time, we have to be patient.'

'Yeah, the aliens here have said the same thing.'

There was a soft whirring sound from the craft as it commenced a slow, vertical descent to the western landing zone. Below the windows and fins, a rim of lights flashed continuously as the spaceship came down. Matt explained that one of his first tasks in the settlement had been the design and development of the landing zones. He'd been told to build three and each had to be large enough to cater for a single mothership, plus half a dozen smaller transporters, so about 500 metres in diameter. He'd thought that was far too small given the crafts were so large, sure that they'd need a runway. So, he'd placed them in areas that allowed room for expansion. He'd located the landing zones on each border of the settlement, leaving out only the southern end because it held the dam. His rationale was that if emergency evacuations were ever necessary, he'd have one close to residences on the western border, one near the factories and industrial sites on the eastern border, and one close to the proposed new Quarantine Centre and Hospital building on the northern border, but still close enough to residences to take their overflow. This one was about to land on the western border.

He strode to the landing zone and continued to look up, awestruck, unaware of anyone around him, until Jemma grabbed his arm. 'You'd better move back a little. We don't want it to land on your head.'

She, too, was impressed by the smooth descent of the ship. It stopped just above the ground then the V-shaped projections were slowly retracted. Nothing more happened until a door opened at the lowest row of windows, revealing a Sidlown in the doorway. A blue light shot down underneath, and two Sidlowns floated down through the light to ground level. They walked around the outer edge, apparently checking the landing zone. The ground crew said something to the Sidlown in the doorway and he disappeared inside. Again, nothing happened for several minutes until six points, evenly spaced around the craft, pulsed with intensely bright red lights. Each light flashed a beam towards the ground which moved around for a few seconds as if looking for something.

'I'm told the lights are to identify the best point to put down the stabilising feet,' said Jemma, almost as awestruck as Matt when the lights steadied, and the feet began to descend. Once they were in place, the blue light underneath the craft went out and the hatch closed. Shortly after, a set of stairs emerged from the doorway on the lowest floor. Finally, people started to collect inside the open doorway.

Jemma watched with Matt as the first of the new inhabitants disembarked. Their gaits were stiff, and they seemed uncoordinated, as they slowly and carefully made their way down the steps from the ship.

'God,' muttered Matt, 'what've we got? We need workers, not cripples.'

'You saw me when we landed, but I'm alright now,' said Jemma.

He groaned. 'If they can all run like you, I'll be obsolete.'

'You'd better work on it then, most of the military people

are better than me.' Before he could answer, Jemma spotted Zadrus float down through the blue light.

He quickly made his way over to her. 'I hope you've had an enjoyable time.'

'We have,' said Matt. 'Jemma's pretty slippery.'

Zadrus frowned. 'Slippery?'

'Sorry, means she can run fast.'

'Yes, she is fast,' said Zadrus. 'Now, I suspect you have some concerns about the people joining us today. It is my role to ensure a smooth transition. I left Jemma here so you would see that she is just like you. Many of the new people will be confused. You must understand they have no idea what has happened here, or why Earth is in such turmoil.'

'I don't think any of us really understands that,' replied Matt. 'We just have to try and do something about it.'

Jemma moved away from Matt and Zadrus to allow them to talk, desperate to see Sean, although she suspected he'd organise others out first. It was a late spring day, the sun warm on her skin, so she didn't mind waiting. The clear blue sky stretched from horizon to horizon, with not a cloud in sight. It felt so good to be here. Most of the valley and distant hills she could see would have been grazing paddocks long ago. Even with the re-growth and scrub, it had the familiar look and smell of the Australian countryside. She was exhilarated at the prospect of living normally again, whatever that would turn out to mean.

When Sean arrived, he showed her on his communicator the location of their new accommodation. They were to be housed, along with all the other security people, in a block close to the Administration building. Matt showed them to their apartment. He pointed out a coffee lounge at the base of the building, before escorting them up, in the disc, to their floor. Once he'd ensured they could get into their room, he left them to it.

'Come on down when you're ready.'

'Well,' said Sean, drawing her into him once the door was shut. 'I guess we're home.'

'Guess we are,' she replied, and heard herself giggle. 'Sorry, this is just so strange.'

'It is. I see they've delivered our stuff.'

'Yeah, what there is,' replied Jemma. They'd left SCARF with one suitcase apiece. The aliens had provided uniforms. And that was the extent of their worldly possessions.

'Not a bad apartment.' Sean walked into each room, looking back at her between each one. 'Big enough.'

'Mm,' murmured Jemma, and she walked out onto the balcony. 'Nice view.'

They stared at each other, but Jemma broke first, and was weak with laughter when Sean's smile turned into a chuckle. She slipped her hand into his and together, they wandered around the apartment, touching things as both seemed to have a need to make sure everything was real.

Still holding hands, they found the stairs down to the café. 'Nice not to have to use that damned disc,' muttered Sean.

'True. Although they are in all the buildings here.' Jemma had intended to fill Sean in on her talks with Matt, but they'd both been too shocked to chat, and Matt was already in the café when they stepped inside. It wasn't much different from coffee shops of their own era, except Matt had explained that everything was free.

'It took all of us a while to get used to it,' said Matt. 'We don't have money. The settlement provides everything we need, and the aim is to treat everyone equally. Everyone has to work, unless they're so physically impaired, they can't.' The aliens have always said they'd deal with anyone who didn't pull their weight … my words … but I've not come across anyone who wasn't doing their best. I think most of the people who've been here since the end of the war are just so grateful to be alive it wouldn't occur to them to slacken off. Might be tougher to police it all now, though.'

'Yeah, I suspect it will,' said Sean.

Jemma wasn't taking much notice of the conversation. She felt uncomfortable with the number of people in the café who stared at them. Even though they were dressed the same, it seemed that they stood out, maybe because they were still a bit unsteady on their feet. She thought she could see something in Matt's eyes too. Probably just caution, but maybe a bit of fear. She didn't think antagonism, but she wasn't sure.

Matt smiled at her. Perhaps he also felt uncomfortable. He extended his hand to Sean. 'Good to meet you properly. Grab a coffee and join me.' He pointed to a table.

Fortunately, both Jemma and Sean knew how to use the servery, so they ordered their drinks, then followed Matt.

'What do you think so far?' said Matt.

Sean grinned. 'We had no idea what to expect, thought we might be coming to tents, and trenches for toilets. What you've achieved is incredible.'

'I'm pleased you approve.'

'We don't just approve,' said Sean. 'We're really impressed at how you've built a whole city from nothing. It must have been enormously difficult.'

Matt smiled again, and this time his face had relaxed. 'Well, we knew we had to be ready for when you outsiders arrived.'

'So, that's what you call us,' said Jemma.

'Oh, I'm sorry. That was a bit rude. We didn't know what to expect. Someone came up with that name, and it seemed to stick.'

'Gosh, I guess we'd better call you insiders then.'

He smiled, 'Sean, you're obviously military. I take it you work with my great grandfather.'

Sean nodded. 'Yeah, about fifteen years. Zadrus told me about you and the General. That's bizarre. It never occurred to me that any of us could come across relatives.'

Jemma wandered away, leaving the men to chat. She didn't want to get involved in a *new* versus *old* military comparison. She just hoped they wouldn't find an *us* and *them* attitude like the *insiders* and *outsiders* terms seemed to suggest. Not confident to head too far away from their building, she headed back up to the apartment and stood under the bead. At least here, the doors were numbered. Theirs was 7002 – floor seven, apartment two. Unable to settle, she wandered again between rooms checking appliances, sitting on the bed, then shifting to the lounge until her eyes alighted on the entertainment system, although 'system' was a strange word for the three-metre square patch on one wall. It was much the same as the one on the spaceship, although this one wasn't rude when it asked what she wanted. Once before at SCARF, Nik had told Artie, the control system there, to take them to the beach and it had been a magical experience, so she thought she'd try a concert from her era. Shocked that it took her straight there, she felt like she was right in the heart of it, sitting in the front row and looking up at real performers. She could hear the music, felt the vibration of the percussion instruments, and was sure she felt a drop of water as the musicians threw themselves around the stage. Transfixed by the sense that it was so real, she sat for a while before telling it to stop so she could return to the lounge room in the apartment.

Thinking about what had happened to them over the last few months, she asked to be taken to the area on Springbrook Mountain where she'd had her research hide. When the scene cleared around her, she stood in grass a metre high, but as she walked east to the old SCARF site, she pulled up sharply at the edge of a sheer cliff face and stared down at the ocean. The rainforest and towns between the mountain and the old Gold Coast beaches were gone. She dropped to her knees, and blinked several times, but her eyes hadn't deceived her. There was nothing but ocean as far as she could see. Sean hadn't had time to tell her much after he'd landed. Perhaps he'd seen this on the way in.

Movement to her left made her look up. A Norellian sphere, the type used by Fredrick Pritchard, hovered above the SCARF boulder. A light shining down from its base moved slowly in her direction. Surely, Pritchard couldn't see her. She wasn't actually there; this was an illusion created by the entertainment system. She screamed, 'Stop,' and waited for the entertainment system to pull her back. As her surroundings cleared, she edged to the window of the apartment and looked for any sign of the sphere, but there was nothing. With no idea if it could find her, she had to tell someone, so she used her communicator to call Zadrus.

'Would you come to my office, please,' he said, 'so that we can discuss it.'

He was waiting when she arrived. His new office was quite impressive, much larger than the one he'd had on the spaceship, although the furnishings were similar, more functional than opulent. He ushered her to a lounge chair and sat beside her.

'Tell me about this Norellian sphere you saw,' said Zadrus.

'It had to be an illusion,' said Jemma. 'Travelling to SCARF was an illusion. It couldn't have been real.'

He shook his head. 'No, I doubt that. You see what is there, even though you are not really there.'

'They shouldn't have been able to see me then if I wasn't really there.'

'That is not necessarily correct. However, when you called to stop, they could not have followed you.' He paused for a moment and took her hands in his. 'You were convinced that Pritchard, or his people, were on the spaceship so we can't dismiss the possibility that it was him. However, it may also be someone from this era who has tracked your tattoo. It doesn't really matter. We are going to have to talk seriously about your security.'

'I'll be careful. Please don't wrap me in cotton wool again.' Since Zadrus's team had interpreted the tattoos which confirmed her link to Anders Major, everyone had been exceedingly protective: Zadrus, Werrimen, Hunt, Sean, even Dan and Nik. Each of the humans in the group had similar tattoos, but they'd accepted that she had an exulted position, which she found ridiculous, but she couldn't convince any of them.

'I had planned to give you time to settle in, and to work on your fitness with General Hunt, but if they are here, I do not think we can wait. We will recommence our Trustee training tomorrow morning. Let me tell you what I will require of you. My Prehling accompanies me when necessary. I will sometimes give you an instruction, and you will obey me. Mostly, when I want you to do something, it will be a request, and you will be free to argue with me. But I will not tolerate argument if it is an instruction.'

She sighed. Zadrus was in charge of the settlement. He had the right to make the rules and issue instructions. Sean would tell her to knuckle down and go along with it until she could determine her own path. 'How do I know if it's a request or an instruction?'

'That will be up to me to make clear.'

She looked up to see Hunt standing in the doorway before

she'd had the chance to answer and feared the worst. Zadrus probably planned to *instruct* her to do something now, given he'd organised Hunt's presence.

Zadrus had a warm smile on his face as he reached out to shake Hunt's hand. 'Good evening General.'

'Good evening,' replied Hunt, flashing a questioning look at Jemma before focussing on Zadrus. 'I'm no longer a General, remember, just an ordinary citizen.'

'We will discuss your status in a moment,' said Zadrus. 'First, we must tell you about an incident.'

Zadrus was up to something, and it wasn't just about her. Given the way Hunt looked at her, he clearly didn't know either. Maybe he'd come out on her side with whatever it was.

Hunt flicked his eyes back to Zadrus. 'What incident?'

'Jemma has seen a Norellian Sphere.'

'Shit. Where? Fill me in, Jemma.'

She sighed as she looked between the two of them and proceeded to retell the story.

'Fucking hell,' said Hunt, when she'd finished. 'I'd hoped we'd left all that behind.'

'Appears not,' said Jemma.

'Alright,' sighed Hunt. 'We'll have to be vigilant. Now, there was something else you wanted to discuss with me, Zadrus.'

'Ah.' Zadrus looked at Hunt for a moment with, Jemma thought, a rather amused look on his face. 'Are you opposed to resuming your old role, maybe not as a General, but to take charge of the security force?'

'Alright, you'd better come clean.' To Jemma's amusement, Hunt raised his eyebrows. 'What do you want me to do?'

'I am pleased you are willing to listen.' Zadrus paused, just long enough to build some tension between them. 'Given all that has happened, we will need more than a simple police force, I feel. Shardene told me of a few incidents that suggest there is still some trouble outside the settlement, and I don't yet know the extent of the problem. I would like you to get started with the security force quickly. Werrimen and I are the most senior IPL members on Earth, and will have a broader role than this settlement, so if the problems I've been told about are widespread, it may be that we will need to extend it to other settlements, preferably with you in charge of the entire force. I am informed that you are now the most senior military figure on the planet.'

'Jesus,' said Hunt, staring back at Zadrus.

'I apologise. I did not mean to shock you, but I feel with the spaceships starting to arrive, we will need to increase security. I am not proposing an Army at this stage but would like to establish this force so that it would not be too difficult to formalise a military structure should it become necessary. We must start immediately, to get the infrastructure in place, and be ready.'

'Bloody hell, you don't want much.'

'It is probably not as bad as it sounds. Young Matt has already begun the process. I will call for him to come and speak to us.'

'He might resent my usurping his authority.'

'No, I don't believe so. He told me that he often feels out of his depth. I think he will be happy to have someone senior here with him, even if it is his great grandfather.'

'Happy to discuss it,' said Hunt. 'Please don't call him yet. From what you say, Matt has suffered a great deal, and I will not distress him further. You must let me determine how to handle this.'

'Of course. Have a seat. I will pour you a scotch. I have a small amount left although it will soon run out. Such a pity,' said Zadrus.

Hunt shifted his head to one side. 'I'm quite sure you didn't keep Jemma and myself here for a quick drink, and a social chit-chat.'

Zadrus poured the scotch, handing a glass to Hunt, then one to Jemma, before he finally spoke. 'We must discuss Jemma's future. I have already told Jemma that I plan to intensify her Trustee training.'

'I understand,' said Hunt. 'Clearly, there is a real threat here, but I would like her to decide for herself what she wants to do.'

There was concern in Hunt's eyes. She'd had this conversation with him before, but suspected he'd back Zadrus now, given the Norellian Sphere. Hunt was, after all, military to the core. Zadrus was the boss and Hunt would see it as his role to follow Zadrus's instructions.

Zadrus stood, walked around the desk, and pointed to the chair he'd just vacated. 'This will be your office now, General. Please take your seat.'

Hunt hesitated at the sudden change in direction before complying, sitting in his new chair, his hands resting on his lap. He waited until Zadrus finished talking about the Norellian sphere.

'Our joint focus must be Jemma's safety,' said Zadrus. 'We know she is Pritchard's main target. Her training must be upgraded. She will become part of your security force.'

'We need to discuss this.' Jemma stood, her arms folded in front of her.

'This is not a request, Jemma,' said Zadrus.

She took a deep breath, calming herself so she could mount a rational argument. 'I understand why you're focussed on my security, and I'm prepared to work with both of you, but I'm a scientist, not a soldier. I want to document the animals, birds, and insects that have survived. I need to do that for my sanity.'

She found Hunt's nod reassuring, but Zadrus stood there like a statue, no expression and no response.

'Right, your work with General Hunt, and myself, is priority,' he said, finally. 'Whatever time is left over you may use for research. If the situation changes though, our requirements for you will change.'

Hunt stood. 'Jemma, call Bellamy. Tell him to come here. I need a minute to organise a meeting with Matt, and I'll be back.'

CHAPTER 8

Sean had stayed talking to Matt for a couple of hours, no idea of Jemma's fright from the Norellian sphere. They'd discussed how the settlement had developed, and now he wanted to know more about Matt, how he'd come to be here, how he'd survived when so many others had perished, what he envisaged for the future, keen to get an idea of what kind of working relationship they'd be able to establish. Hunt had yet to establish his hierarchy and whether Matt would be above or below him. Whatever happened, he wanted to be prepared. He liked what he'd seen of Matt, and Jemma had obviously taken to him.

'When I arrived,' said Matt, 'the settlement wasn't much more than a bare paddock. Linzole, who was a Sidlown like Zadrus, was the Supreme Trustee here. He put me in charge of security from day one. I had to learn how to use the alien technology and all their surveillance techniques in a hurry. He helped me a lot, but only a handful of military people survived, and none of them were officers. After the initial chaos settled, I spent most of my time training others. Linzole announced that I was the boss and pretty much left me to it. Sometimes it was bloody rough.'

'Did you know we were coming?' asked Sean.

'I did. But I knew nothing about you. Linzole kept saying you'd be people just like us.' Matt shrugged his shoulders. 'I couldn't fathom how that could be. Still, you're here, and my concern now is how you'll impact the settlement. With the arrival of the spaceship, we've expanded from less than a thousand people to more than ten thousand. My people are exhausted – the war, the recovery, the building. It's been hard. They can't do much more and they've seen so many things no human being should ever see.'

'Everyone who's arrived here today knows they'll be set to work straight away. There's never been any doubt about that.'

'So I've been told. It'll be appreciated.'

'How about you?' said Sean. 'Do your memories trouble you?'

'Yeah, some. I've mostly come to grips with it all though,' he said, with a sigh. 'There's only one that still gives me nightmares. My wife disappeared without a trace, a few weeks before Newcastle was bombed. We searched everywhere, but we couldn't find any clues, and they won't let me go back to Newcastle to look. It's still too contaminated. One day I will. I dread the thought of finding her body, but at least that way I'd know what happened.'

'Gee mate, that's rough. Maybe I can help in some way.'

Matt shrugged. 'It's too late to find anything, but I'd like to look.'

'Understood,' said Sean. 'I'll talk to the General, and to Zadrus.'

'The General. What's he like, really? Jemma seemed to think he'll make a few demands.'

Sean laughed. 'He will, but he's tougher on her than anyone. He has good reason. I'll explain later. I know your great grandfather very well. He'll expect to lead. Will you be okay with that?'

'Relieved really. A lot of the time I've had no idea what I'm doing. I come from a long line of Generals, and it was assumed I'd get there one day, but they all had the one before to guide them. I'm happy for someone else to shoulder the crap. If I can't work with him, I'll walk away. I don't believe any of the aliens would stop me. Linzole kept telling me he wanted to start training me as a Trustee, but there's never been time. So, I could go that way, maybe learn to fly those weird machines.'

'I've no doubt you'll get on with the General, and that he'll support whatever decision you make. He's tough and he's hard, but he's also fair, although Jemma might disagree with that.'

'Thanks, I appreciate that, and I can't wait to hear what's so special about Jemma.'

'There's a lot that's special about her, but let's focus on you for the moment,' said Sean. 'You've got to be exhausted. You need a break, the time to make decisions about what you want to do, with no pressure from anywhere.'

'Yeah, maybe. We'll see what happens. Jemma said you were a full colonel.'

'I was, but I don't think any of that counts anymore. The General will always be the General, because we can't see him any other way, but the rest of us are just who we are. We'll work out our pecking order as time goes by.'

'I think the Colonel might always be the Colonel too,' said Matt, laughing. 'I've already seen how people respond to you.'

'I'm not important. Tell me about the Trustee thing. You haven't met Werrimen yet. She's someone you'll immediately pick as a leader, and she's started me training with her, didn't give me a choice.'

'Yeah, and now that Linzole is gone, I don't even know if it's still an option.'

Sean laughed. 'I suspect they've got you well and truly pegged. But they worry me a bit. They're so controlled and respectful towards each other. We're both used to Army discipline, and I'd hate to tell you how many times I've suffered in your great grandfather's command. The aliens must use disciplinary measures to get that kind of control.'

Matt nodded, 'Suspect you're right. When Newcastle was bombed, my father was killed, along with just about everyone else I knew. It was only days before they were due to come up here. The grief overwhelmed me, and we were all shocked. Everything stopped. I couldn't function. Linzole, who'd always been kind and encouraging, yelled at me. I was floored, but I clearly remember his words. They still give me a chill.'

'Okay. Go on.'

'He said, "You are the leader. Not only your staff, but the entire community looks to you for guidance. Right now, you are leading them to a very black place, and I will not allow it. Deal with your grief privately, but publicly you must show a positive face, and healthy leadership." I somehow managed to say *yes sir*. But what he said next bothered me more.'

'Sounds like he was trying to shock you into action.'

'Suspect so, but he told me I was such an important person to the community that if I didn't sort myself out, I'd be punished, and that punishment would be swift and severe.'

'Did he specify what the punishment would be?'

'No, never,' replied Matt, shuddering. 'After he left, I grabbed some grog, the stuff we'd made here which was pretty rough, and proceeded to write myself off. When I came around, I looked in the mirror, and realised I was an idiot. Then I did exactly what Linzole told me to do. Once we were back on track, he praised me, and offered to take me on as a Trustee. I never got as far as being sworn in and, same as you, I wasn't keen to push it.'

'No, I haven't been sworn in yet, either,' said Sean. 'But I doubt I'm going to get out of it. Werrimen's tougher than Zadrus and, I suspect, Linzole. Matt, the General won't want to wait too long to get us all together. He'll probably call a meeting tomorrow morning, if not tonight. When you get there, just be very clear about what you want to do, and don't hesitate to tell him. I'll back you up, but honestly, I don't think you'll have a problem with him.'

They talked some more until Sean's communicator sounded. He detached it from his belt and looked at the screen. 'Hey Jem. What's up?'

'I'm in Zadrus's office. Could you swing by here please, after you've finished with Matt.'

'Sure. Leaving now.' Sean frowned as her image faded from the screen. Her face had been taut, and her eyes unusually narrow when she'd spoken. He'd seen her distressed often enough to pick up on the signs, and she was with Zadrus, which was a particularly bad sign given she'd gone back to their apartment to rest. That all added up to trouble. He asked Matt for directions to Zadrus's office. As he said a quick good night, Matt's communicator buzzed, but Sean ignored it and ran for the Administration building. Dashing through the office door as it slid open, he dropped into a chair beside Jemma. 'Are you alright? What happened?'

'I'm fine. General Hunt just left. He thought we should discuss it together. He's on his way back.'

'Shit.' Sean looked up to see Zadrus smiling at him. 'I'm sorry, sir. I was worried when I saw Jemma's face.'

'Do not be sorry. I understand. Let us wait for General Hunt. In the meantime, Jemma, tell Sean what you saw.'

She'd just finished recounting her experience of the Norellian Sphere when Hunt returned but hadn't had the time to tell Sean about Zadrus's demands.

Sean looked cautiously at Hunt. 'Evening.'

Something about Hunt's demeanour had changed and Jemma suspected Sean had sensed the same thing.

Hunt nodded before walking around the desk and taking his seat.

'Okay,' said Sean, his eyes firmly focussed on Hunt. 'What's going on?'

'Jemma's told you the story?'

'Yes.'

Zadrus stepped forward. 'I have asked General Hunt to set up a security force. You, of course, will be part of that, as will Jemma.'

'Oh Jesus.' Sean's grip on Jemma's hand had firmed. 'So that's what this is all about. She doesn't want to be part of any security force. Surely, we've got enough people here. Why can't you leave her be?'

'Her birthright precludes that,' replied Hunt, quietly.

'Birthright!' muttered Jemma. 'More like birth curse.'

'I know,' said Hunt, and his look reassured Sean that he was equally distressed about doing this to her.

'Do I have any choice in this?' asked Jemma.

'No,' replied Zadrus.

'Oh, I think you do.' Hunt was smiling. 'You can come quietly, or you can join us kicking and screaming. I'm not fussed. Either way.'

'I wouldn't give you that pleasure.'

'Pleased to hear it,' returned Hunt. 'Now, logistics.'

Sean interrupted Jemma before she could retort. 'What do you have in mind, sir?'

'Bellamy, you'll be my 2IC of course. I want you above Matt, for the moment, at least. I'll have both Matt and O'Leary report to you, directly.'

'It feels like you're downgrading Matt, sir,' said Sean.

How quickly they fell back into their old ways, thought Jemma. In the last two minutes, Sean had already used the word 'sir' twice. She looked up to find Hunt staring at her. He must have figured she didn't like the direction of the conversation. Wouldn't take a rocket scientist.

'Thoughts, Jemma?'

'Matt has built this security group single-handedly, against tremendous odds. He deserves your respect.'

'He already has it. As soon as I leave here, I'll be talking with him. Problem is, we don't know him or how he operates. Probably best if I'm not the one to judge given our relationship. Hence, he'll report to Bellamy and we'll progress from there. Satisfied?'

'Not really, but it's not up to me,' said Jemma.

'Good, glad you recognise that.' Hunt stood, which seemed to be his new way of telling them they were dismissed. 'Get some sleep, both of you. We'll work out your new role later, Jemma, but you don't need to be at the first meeting in the morning.'

'Fine. Goodnight General. Goodnight Zadrus.' She turned and walked out the door. The way her legs were shaking she hoped Sean would be close behind her.

Next morning, after Sean had told Dan to round up the SCARF group, he took Matt to one side.

'I have no idea what Zadrus is going to demand of us,' said Sean. 'He's upped his requirements of Jemma, so I think we have to be prepared for anything. Can you give me a signal if there's something you're not happy with? I don't know if I'll get through to Zadrus, but I can get through to the General. Of course, I may not win, but together we can give it a damn good try.'

Matt smiled. 'I'll do my best to let you know. Mind you, I'll have my own say. I'm way beyond caring who I antagonise.'

'Pleased to hear it, but I'm trying to let you know I've got your back, and I'm damned sure down the track I'll need you to have mine.'

'I have no doubt you're right,' replied Matt.

'Can you introduce me to your key people before we go in,' said Sean. 'Give us a chance for at least a bit of familiarity.'

'Sure.' Matt beckoned three women and two men to join him. 'These are my team leaders. We called ourselves the Core Intelligence Group, or CIG. I can't remember who came up with it, but somebody did, and it stuck.'

'Good name,' said Sean. 'Okay if we keep it?'

'Of course. Our role was originally policing but, over time, the aliens started to gear us to look for external threats, don't think any of us knew what that really meant. The internal policing's been simple enough. Most people are just grateful to be alive. They haven't been interested in behaving badly. Plenty of problems from drinking too much, but we usually just lock them up for the night. They're almost always contrite, and embarrassed, the next morning.'

'Okay,' said Sean. 'What about the external role?'

'That's more difficult,' replied Matt. 'We've had to get a handle on the alien technology. Then it's about looking for something out there, even though we've never really known what we were looking for. So far, it's all been good.'

'Jemma and Nik are really good with the alien technology, so hopefully they can help too. Are there any other issues?'

Sean wanted as much as he could get, before he went into the meeting.

'There are still people living outside the settlement, but we don't know much about them, and haven't had the staff to go and look. Most who come in are ill. We provide medical help, then take them to the quarantine centre for three months. We keep surveillance on them after, but we haven't had any problems. It's just that we don't know who else is out there, or whether they present any kind of threat.'

Sean nodded. 'Have you ever seen any kind of craft that didn't look like the IPL ones?'

'Yeah, we have. A few weeks ago, one of my people reported something that looked like a perfect sphere. It took off at great speed, before we had a chance to intercept.'

They were called into the meeting before he could question Matt further, but after Jemma's sighting of a Norellian sphere, he had to accept that Pritchard, or others from his organisation, were here. As they walked into the room, he wasn't pleased to see Matt's people congregate on one side of the room, his on the other. Early days, but he'd have to deal with it if the groups were to be successfully integrated.

Hunt announced Zadrus had instructed that they were all to work together as a team, and he be in charge, Sean second in charge. There would be two divisions, Matt to head one, Dan the other. Sean noted a slight flicker of Matt's eyebrows and restlessness from his people as Hunt quickly dismissed the group, telling Sean, Dan and Matt to stay.

After they'd had left, Hunt threw himself back into his

chair. 'Matt, we've already discussed that Zadrus made it clear yesterday I'm to be in charge.'

'I have no problem with you taking charge. In truth, it's a relief. But you made my people felt marginalised.'

'I apologise if I did that, but I thought it best to state the facts and leave no doubt.' Hunt dropped his head. 'None of us really know how to handle this, but from today, *your* people, and *my* people, have to become *our* people. I'm relying on the three of you to make that happen.'

'Simple recognition would have been a good start,' muttered Matt.

'Sir.' Sean jumped in before Hunt had time to growl at Matt. 'We should put aside time for all security people to get together to exchange ideas. Maybe the morning exercise sessions you suggested to Jemma could include everyone.' The way Hunt and Matt both leaned back in their chairs, arms crossed in front of them, it was obvious to Sean that their relationship would have to be built first.

'Exercise, no,' replied Hunt. 'Morning sessions are for you, me, Matt, O'Leary, Denis and Jemma. We are the management team. Matt, let me know if any of your people should be included. Liam can organise a second session for everyone else. If it helps, we can attend the second session, but ours is separate. Daily sessions to exchange ideas is well worth a thought, Jemma to be included. For the moment, I will remain remote.'

'Jesus, I don't want to include Jemma.' Sean muttered.

'You know I'd let her be if I could,' snapped Hunt. 'I wasn't given that option.'

It was Sean's turn to sit back in his chair. 'So, the aliens are running the settlement?'

'No, not entirely, but we can't survive without them. Zadrus has defined how our structure will work and we have to deal with it. When it comes to Jemma, he has plans, and I'm not entirely privy to them. Convince her to go along with him. If he's pushed too far, I have no idea what the consequences will be for her, and I don't want to find out. She and I have reached a truce, but I doubt that will work with him.'

'Christ almighty.' Sean realised he'd be unable to change decisions already made, so after extracting some agreements for the exercise and information sessions, he ran to find Jemma.

She was sitting on the ground, leaning against a tree outside the Administration building. Dropping down beside her, he picked up her hand and looked into her eyes. 'Did you chat with Zadrus?'

'Yes. He'll let me do some of my research, but I'm right back into training with both of them as of tomorrow.'

He sighed. 'I'm sorry, Jemma. I didn't anticipate this so soon. Let's make the most of it while we can. Want to join me, with Matt and Dan, for coffee?'

She nodded. 'Sure, why not?'

'Come on then. Last one there pays.' He took off towards the café.

'Oh, you bastard,' she yelled after him. But she did follow and was laughing as she ran.

*   *   *

Five o'clock in the morning was not Jemma's favourite time of the day, and when Sean nudged her to get up, she groaned and rolled over. Drips of water on the back of her neck at 5:30 a.m. did nothing to enhance her mood. 'Go away,' she yelled. 'I'll start tomorrow.' The smile on Sean's face didn't help at all.

'No, we're starting our fitness training today, and we're not going to be late. Come on.' He grabbed her hands and dragged her up from the bed. 'In the shower. I'll have a cup of coffee waiting.'

'Gee, thanks.' The drink they called coffee in the new settlement was a murky brown liquid that tasted like a cross between the coffee she knew and tea. It was made from a hydroponically grown plant and flavoured with a whitener made from bean paste, which made the whole thing taste green. She'd have much preferred a good latte with chocolate sprinkled on the top, and maybe a shot of caramel.

'Are you still in the shower?' called Sean. He told the shower to turn off as he strolled into the bathroom, a steaming cup of something in his hand, and grabbed her arm, but pulled up sharply to a stern voice from central control.

'Have you suffered violence Dr Anderson? Shall I call for help?'

'No,' they screamed, in unison.

She fell into Sean's arms laughing. When he realised that she'd saturated his clothes, he chased her back to the bedroom and stood over her, his arms folded in front of his chest while she dressed, but this time he was laughing too. After downing the coffee, she ran for the door. 'What's keeping you? Bet you can't beat me today.' She skipped down the stairs and ran for the path towards the gym, stopping only when she crossed into the foyer of the big gym building, and she felt his arm around her chest pulling her back.

'You cheated. I demand a replay,' he said.

'Nope you were just too slow. Must be getting old.'

Neither of them noticed Hunt, standing inside, until he spoke. 'Would the adult responsible for these two children please step forward.'

'I believe that would be you, sir,' replied Sean.

'Fine, then you'd better both hit the track. Give me ten laps to warm up. It's full size, four hundred metres. And Bellamy, this time make sure you beat her.'

'Not a tinker's chance in hell.' She took off towards the track at the other end of the large building, skirting a suspended floor, and multiple exercise and weights machines. One of the long walls of the building was flipped up and formed a kind of awning. Outside, she could see an Olympic-sized swimming pool and a large paddock beyond. Sensing Sean not too far behind, she entered the track and commenced her run.

Her mind wandered as she began the last lap, and Sean had not only caught up but passed her. He was now a good five metres ahead. Not prepared to let that happen, she forced herself to pick up her speed and eased closer to him. With just ten metres to go, she sprinted past. He also tried to put on a new spurt but couldn't catch her.

After setting Dan, Nik and Matt on the track, Hunt

turned his attention back to Jemma and Sean. He pointed to the suspended floor. 'Bellamy, I told you to beat her. Get over there and give me a hundred push-ups. Jemma, if you had enough in the tank to fly past him, you should have been trying harder earlier, so you can give me a hundred, too.'

To her surprise, as she dropped down beside Sean, Hunt moved to her other side and did the same thing. They finished their push-ups, moved on to sit-ups, then weights machines, and before she realised, it was 7:30 and time to hit the showers. When she'd finished, Hunt told her to get some breakfast and make sure she was in Zadrus's office by 8:30. He obviously wasn't worried about her fitness, or Sean's. He had Liam checking the others, and as she walked past, Matt was struggling to keep up. She'd talk to him later. Maybe she could help.

Still not entirely sure how to deal with Zadrus, she took Hunt's advice not to be late seriously, and arrived with minutes to spare. Zadrus welcomed her in and invited her to sit.

'We knew each other quite well at SCARF,' he said. 'Do you still trust me?'

'I do,' she replied. 'I know you're worried, but I need you to trust me, too.'

'You are very intuitive,' he said, smiling. 'Now, we have much to discuss.' He took her hands in his. As usual, she felt the warmth flow through her. It made her feel good about herself. When she looked up at him, he seemed pleased.

'Your reaction confirms my belief I will be able to train

you.' He put her hands back in her lap and moved around to the other side of the desk.

'I will test you to get an idea of our next direction. Please sit back, close your eyes, clear your thoughts and describe the first thing that comes into your mind.'

She shrugged and did as he asked. The first thing she saw was a very large tiger, with enormous eye teeth, maybe a sabre tooth. A man stood beside it and the tiger's head was at about the same level as the man's head. Next, she described an ocean scene with trees, of a type she'd not seen before, behind a large stretch of golden sand. The trees were some kind of palm, but very lush. The next scene was of a space-ship, but unlike anything she'd ever encountered. It was long and cylindrical but, in the middle, a large disc projected out either side. The height of the disc was about the same as the cylinder and it had three rows of windows in it. She thought the whole thing was about 200 metres in length. Finally, she saw people eating something, probably a fruit. It was bright red, with a series of green stripes running down it. As some-one bit into the fruit, juice ran down his shirt. The inside of the fruit was a bright yellow.

'We have finished,' said Zadrus. 'I have never known anyone to pick up those images exactly, as you just did. I am certain you and I are meant to work together. We are finished for today.'

Now almost 11:00, she was due to meet Hunt. He'd scheduled a daily meeting with her, before his second round of senior officer training sessions. She carefully shut Zadrus's door, then walked a short distance down the corridor, before turning towards the stairwell. She stopped to give herself a moment to relax. Hunt had told her to try for a positive spin on whatever it was that Zadrus demanded, and she guessed she'd have to do just that. With only a couple of minutes left, she flew down the stairs and ran headlong into Hunt as he also walked towards the training room. He grabbed her by the shoulders to slow her down, a broad smile on her face.

'I take it you're running so you won't be late for me. Glad to see you're so keen.' When she scowled, he laughed and opened the door, ushering her in ahead of him. The room was much the same as the training room she'd known at SCARF, twenty metres long and fifteen metres wide. Cushioned mats covered the floor and the lower half of the walls. Hunt squatted cross-legged on the floor and indicated to her to do the same.

'I've scheduled these meetings so we can talk about what you're doing, with Zadrus, with me, or anyone else for that matter, and to tackle problems. I don't plan to bully you, Jemma. I had planned to leave you be for a while, but Zadrus hasn't given me a choice after you saw that sphere and, from my perspective, there's more. I'm going to need all the help I can get to develop this security force. You're a thinker, and you have good insight into people. I value your point of view and your ability to come up with creative and practical ideas.'

'I'm happy to talk to you, and to train with you, but I thought you were going to support me to have my own life.'

'That was my plan, and still is, but we're going to have to achieve that differently.'

'Then I'd like to change my uniform from the security one

to an ordinary one.'

He sat back on his haunches, seemed to be contemplating her request. 'No, I don't want you to change your uniform. It offers you some privileges that others might not have.'

'I don't want privileges. I don't want to stand out and, no matter how you spin it, I'm not part of the security group.'

'Yeah, you are, even if you don't recognise it, but we'll leave that for the moment.'

'If you really see me as part of your group, and if you trust me, you'd have made sure the bead to this room would recognise me to let me out.'

'Perhaps you should trust me a little more. Have you tried the bead?'

She stood and walked to the door. The bead opened within two seconds. 'Oops, sorry,' she said, turning back to him just as Sean, Dan and Nik arrived with Matt.

Hunt smiled. 'You can work with O'Leary today. Bellamy, take Matt. Denis, you're with me.'

Nik looked terrified as she stood opposite Hunt. Jemma shook her head. She understood that he wanted to be sure they were all up to par, but suspected he was also about to test how well Nik had recovered. Now that they knew she was Jemma's cousin, they considered her to be almost as much of a target as Jemma herself.

After their session, Jemma told Sean she was heading to the dam, then ran for the door before Hunt had time to hassle her further. The dam was relatively isolated, making it the quietest place in the settlement and after the morning she'd had, she was keen to find somewhere to relax, but didn't realise Nik had followed.

'Mind if I join you,' said Nik.

'No, that's good. We can escape them together for a while.'

They entered through a thick line of trees and Jemma was enthralled by the sparkling stretch of blue water in the dam. She sat on the bank and smiled at a family of ducks as they swam by.

'Wow,' said Nik, dropping down beside her.

'Yeah, I agree. Want to help me document the surviving animals.' She reached in her pocket for a small disc Zadrus had given her that could capture images and, at the same time, record her spoken descriptions of both the animals and the environment. She could do the same on her communicator, but this disc would be dedicated solely to her research. She'd felt it was meant as a peace offering from Zadrus.

A couple of dragonflies, one blue, one red, buzzed around some native bees close to where she sat. She clapped her hands to her face. 'Do you know what this means, Nik?'

'No, but I bet you're going to tell me.'

'Bees mean we've got a chance of being able to grow fruit trees and vegetables naturally. It's our best hope of survival.'

'Okay.'

Jemma wriggled around to investigate a rustling sound beneath a small shrub, delighted to see a skink move quickly away and, a bit further back, a small bearded dragon.

'Just hope I don't step on a snake,' muttered Nik.

'Snakes are good,' said Jemma. 'Mind you, I'd hoped to

find native rodents, or kangaroo and rabbit droppings, but I haven't seen anything like that. And there should be galahs, lorikeets, sulphur-crested cockatoos, crows.' She jumped up and reached out her hand to help Nik up. 'It's only day one. We'll search harder tomorrow.'

Focussed on finding animals, she hadn't realised how far they'd walked until they came upon the small building that housed the filtration system Matt had shown her on the day they'd arrived. A man walked out from the side of the building, and she called out to greet him, but he ran out of sight. 'That's strange,' she said, looking back at Nik. 'I guess I shouldn't have expected them all to be friendly like Matt.'

'No,' replied Nik, pulling out her weapon.

Jemma stared at Nik's hand. Her own instinct had been to respect the man's privacy and leave him be, but four men ran from the building and stood directly in front of the women. They weren't armed, but two of them held buckets.

One of the men, standing just centimetres from Jemma's face, growled. 'What the hell do you want?'

'Nothing,' she said, surprised by his attitude. 'We're just studying the animals. Who are you?'

'None of your damn business.' He shoved her in the chest. Not prepared for a physical attack, she lost balance and fell backwards.

Nik aimed her weapon at him, but he threw his bucket and knocked it from her hand. All four men ran off. Jemma recovered first, grabbed the bucket and pulled out her communicator to contact Sean.

CHAPTER 9

Sean hadn't specifically asked Jemma to attend his first team-building meeting, but that didn't stop him swearing when he realised that she'd taken off. His annoyance was selfish, he knew, but he'd have particularly liked her there, close to him. She had a knack of cutting through irrelevancies to get to the core of a problem, and then suggesting solutions which were often out of left field, but always practical. Still, his top team was himself, Dan and Matt, and building that rapport was paramount.

Dan and Matt were already sitting in his office chatting amicably when he walked in, so he quietly ordered morning tea from the servery at the side of his office, then sat opposite and waited for them to finish. Between them and, hopefully, with the help of Jemma and Nik, they were about to set the direction for the entire settlement. If Zadrus had his way, that would extend across the entire planet, and he'd never known Zadrus not to get his way. They had to get it right. If they didn't, the consequences could be devastating. The responsibility of what they were about to tackle was enormous, yet he'd always approached challenges head on, and that's what he'd do now.

The influx of people from the spaceship and the impact they would have on this previously tiny settlement had to be addressed urgently. Policing and security, and ensuring people behaved themselves, was priority. The combination of Matt's people and the SCARF contingent should be able to handle it in the short term, so long as they worked together. But they had to also think long term, which would mean finding, recruiting and training more people. He was confident Dan could adapt to either role. He suspected Matt could too, so he'd have to figure out who to put where, as he went.

Integrating his people with Matt's people also had to happen quickly. Cliques, when everything still hung in the balance, could easily undermine their success. He waited for a natural lull in the conversation between the two men. 'Alright, I'm thinking two units, each of you to take command of one.' Both men shrugged their shoulders which he interpreted as acceptance. 'We'll shuffle staff, so that each unit will have half of your old crew Matt, and half of the military people who've just arrived.'

'It's too soon,' snapped Matt. 'I accept that'll happen eventually, but you've got to remember what we've been through. We've survived by clinging together.'

'Yeah, I get that. Our group has clung together too, for different reasons, but it's also been traumatic for them. We've all got to expand our thinking now. I know it won't be easy, and you two, more than anyone, will bear the brunt of people's anger. The three of us will also have to work closely as a team and be prepared to let each other know if there are problems.'

It was a risk, but Sean genuinely believed that both Matt and Dan could make it work.

'I don't think we've got much choice,' said Dan. 'Matt, your guys are going to have to tell us everything about the past eighty years as well as what's been happening here. The only way we'll understand is if we work together. And I think our people have something to offer, too.'

'It's not that I disagree, but it needs to be slower.'

'I don't think we've got that option,' said Dan. 'There's already weird shit happening here, Norellian spheres, Jemma sighting Pritchard's people, and other stuff you've talked about.'

'I suppose you're right.' Matt sat back in his chair and rubbed his eyes. 'Alright, we'll try. There'll be snags.'

'Yes, I agree,' said Sean. 'So long as we're on the same wavelength, we'll sort things as we go.'

'Sure.' Matt didn't look convinced, but he'd stopped arguing.

'We'll meet daily. Plus, I'm available 24/7 if you need me.' Sean jumped when his communicator vibrated. He didn't realise how tense he'd been. The gadget opened out to show an image of Jemma, bent over and helping Nik to her feet. She stared at something in the distance.

'Hi Jem, what's up?'

'Nik and I are at the dam. There's something wrong here. A group of men attacked us.'

'Shit.' Sean swivelled around to stare at Matt. 'Are you safe?'

'I'm pretty sure they're gone, although they might be hiding. We're about to go after them.'

'Don't chase them,' said Matt. 'Wait until we get there.'

'But they'll get away.'

'Don't care,' said Sean. 'Matt's right. Stand down until we get there.'

Sean ran for the door. Matt and Dan followed and as they ran past Zadrus's room, heading for the roof and the nearest transporter bay, Sean called to him, 'Would you join us, please. I'll fill you in on the way.'

Zadrus caught up surprisingly quickly, given his size. 'What is the problem?'

'Someone's had a go at Jemma and Nik. They're okay but we need to get to them.'

'Had a go?'

'Sorry. Someone attacked them.'

'Oh, I see.'

Sean led the way into the transporter which took off immediately and, less than two minutes later, landed on a flat stretch near the filtration plant, a large building flanked by four smaller buildings and four treatment ponds. One large pipe carried water from the plant to the main part of the settlement and another from the plant to the factories. Between the buildings and the pipes were multiple hiding places.

'Weapons out,' called Sean. 'Check each building.' They each carried an alien stun weapon, which could immobilise, but not kill. Made from a seamless piece of metal, the weapons looked like sawn-off shot guns. There was no trigger and no sight. On top was a blue-coloured light which helped the user aim in the right direction. It could be set from a light stun through to full immobilisation of the victim. In Sean's mind, they were the best item the aliens had provided. It meant they no longer had to kill perpetrators to stop them. Even better, each weapon was programmed to its user, so if the user was overpowered and the weapon taken, it was immediately rendered useless.

Dan ran to the nearest building and turned the handle. He threw the door open. 'Shouldn't these doors be locked?'

'Yeah,' said Matt. 'They should.'

Both rooms in the small building were empty. Sean and Zadrus cleared another building.

Jemma stood with Nik at the front of the filtration building. She called as the men came near. 'It's only us. There's no one else here. You can put your weapons down.'

'Stop there,' Sean waited for the other buildings to be checked before running to the women. 'Are you both okay?'

'Yeah, we are,' said Jemma. 'They left pretty quickly, although we didn't know how far they'd gone. I thought it was best to call you.'

'I'm glad you did. Come on back to the transporter. We can talk when we're safely inside.' Once the doors were secured, he turned to Jemma. 'Tell me the rest.'

'It was bizarre,' said Jemma. 'We were walking close to the buildings, when four men ran out at us. Two of them had buckets. They appeared to be testing the water, like scientists or students. When they charged at us, I thought we were going to have to fight them. Nik aimed her weapon at them, and they threw the buckets at her. Then they ran. We grabbed the buckets, thought someone could analyse the residue.'

'Good thinking,' said Zadrus. 'Had you seen any of these men before?'

'No, and they weren't really running from us. They were scared of someone, or something. One of them kept saying over and over, *he won't accept this. We've failed.*'

'We need to know what was in those buckets,' said Zadrus. 'It is odd they did not attempt an explanation, just straight to the attack. I do not like it. We are vulnerable at the dam. It is large, and we cannot adequately patrol it in its entirety. We will step up aerial surveillance, and I will see if our current surveillance crafts have seen anything. Have the buckets checked quickly.'

Jemma nodded. 'I'll take them in as soon as we get back.'

Once back in his office, Sean sat at his desk, his chin perched on his hands. He found it difficult to comprehend anyone in this community would behave this way, but if there was a subculture emerging, they had to find it and weed it out before it took hold. He called the lab, hoping they might have identified something useful.

'No toxins,' the scientist told him. 'I'm waiting for a bacterial analysis.'

'Bring it to the meeting room. I'll wait for you there.' Sean called Zadrus, Jemma, Nik, Dan, Hunt and Matt to join him.

Half an hour later, Anthony buzzed in on his PTD.

Jemma ran to greet him. 'I thought you could walk now.'

'I can, but this thing is fun.' He grinned. 'Just trying to make light of it. I can't walk very far yet.'

'Okay,' Sean snapped. 'You can catch up later. What have you found?'

'Yes, sir.' Anthony gave a mock salute but became serious when Sean bared his teeth ever so slightly.

'It's odd,' he said. 'I thought there'd be something else, but this is it. We found cryptosporidium. It didn't seem to make sense. But as I thought about it, it's really quite clever.'

'Yes, it is a very clever rouse.' Zadrus gave an unusually wry smile.

Sean frowned. 'Does somebody want to let me in on it?'

Jemma picked up the analysis. 'Cryptosporidium is a common contaminant of any large body of water. If it's in high enough concentration, it can cause quite a nasty dysentery, so if residents were to become ill from the water, the dam managers would look like fools. Purification plants often can't get rid of it, and it would take time to spread right through the water supply, so by the time people became sick, these idiots wouldn't be linked to it.'

'I get it,' said Sean. 'Victims would get sick, but it wouldn't kill them, although I suppose the elderly or frail would be at risk. But why do that?'

'It is aimed to undermine,' Zadrus answered, with a sigh. 'People are still nervous after what they have been through. All they need to do is create doubt about the competence of the IPL, some unrest, and we lose the trust of the general population. Our society is fragile, and still quite unsafe from the outside environment. It would not take much to destroy it.'

'Okay,' said Sean. 'So, we have to get to the bottom of this, fast.'

'Yes,' said Zadrus, with a sigh. 'I have an uneasy feeling about who might be behind it.'

'Who?' Concerned that Zadrus was withholding something, Sean pushed. If there was a threat, he needed to understand it, so he could be ready.

'There are numerous possibilities,' said Zadrus. 'I hope I am wrong, and it was just a childish prank. But I am worried we might have a serious problem. Has anyone checked the security cameras?'

'I have,' replied Matt. 'We found clear photographs of four of the assailants. I've checked our files. We can identify two of them, a teacher and a factory worker. No obvious links. No history of any wrongdoing. We brought them in but got nothing. Neither of them could explain what they were doing, or why they were doing it. They seemed perfectly normal people until we asked about the buckets, and their presence at the dam. Then they became vague, but they didn't seem to be deliberately evasive. We've moved them to the Quarantine Centre for observation, but we can't keep them too long without arousing suspicion. I think we'll have to let them go and try to keep them monitored.'

'What about the other two? Do you have any leads on them?'

'No, and the two we questioned hadn't met them before this morning either. Said they just showed up.'

'Stranger by the minute,' muttered Sean.

'Yes,' said Zadrus, 'Focus on the two you have not identified. Keep us informed.'

Convinced now that Zadrus knew more, Sean tried again but Zadrus was impervious to his pleas.

Hunt held the group back after Zadrus had left. 'New rules.'

Sean groaned. He was tired of all the demands on Jemma and he had no doubt that Hunt's *new rules* would be mainly aimed at her.

'Don't look at me like that. Jemma, you can keep moving freely within the compound, but if you want to go outside the tree-line, or the fence-line, you will require an escort. Denis, the same applies to you.'

'Okay,' said Jemma, surprised he hadn't demanded a permanent escort.

'I want you and Denis to take on a new role. You will be on call to the Quarantine Centre, to meet anyone who comes in from outside the city.'

'I'd like to discuss that, sir,' replied Sean.

'Go ahead.'

'I'd prefer to rotate it among several people.'

'You don't have several people.' Hunt sighed. 'Look, under normal circumstances, I'd agree with you. For the moment, you, O'Leary and Matt have your work cut out to address that deficit. Denis and Jemma are the only remaining members of the management team. They have the skills and knowledge to conduct investigations.'

'Sean, I don't mind,' said Jemma. 'It would kind of give me a purpose. I don't like being the princess that everybody has to look after.'

'But it takes you away from your research.'

'We'll trial it for a month,' said Hunt. 'I don't think the role will be onerous.'

His argument effectively shut down, Sean had to accept that Jemma and Nik now had a new role.

Over the next few weeks, Jemma and Nik encountered several people coming in from outside the settlement, ordinary people who'd found a way to survive, mostly just outside the boundary, but well within the TEM. Various methods had been used to obtain clean food and water, from old shops to farm animals, sealed water tanks and deep bores. After a routine three-month stay in the Quarantine Centre, each person was offered a standard residence in the settlement. Zadrus still talked about the possibility of outside influences, but nothing could ever be proven. And try as he might, Sean could never get him to define what he meant by outside influences.

* * *

Three months after they'd first arrived in the new settlement, Jemma had settled into a regular morning routine, an hour in the gym, sometimes longer, then meeting with Zadrus, mostly to talk about everyday events. One Sunday morning, she had just finished showering after a particularly gruelling gym session, but hadn't yet dragged on her maroon uniform, when Sean called to hurry up.

'Sunday's supposed to be a day of rest,' she retorted. 'I'll be ready when I'm ready.'

'Okay grumble-bum, you can explain your tardiness to Zadrus.'

'Bugger off,' she muttered.

'I heard that,' said Sean, grinning. 'Come here.' He pulled her into a hug.

She nestled in with a big sigh. 'I'd just like a bit of a break sometimes.'

'I know. Go along with them and do your best. They'll ease back soon enough. Problem is, Zadrus and the General are really worried.'

'I know.'

'Go on.' He swivelled her towards the door. 'I'll follow as soon as I've had a shower. Now that I can get in there, that is.'

She made a face as she left and headed down in the disc, but before she left the building, the communicator on her belt sounded.

'Hey Jem.' Nik, dressed in the standard blue uniform that most of the population wore, smiled up at her through the screen.

'Hi Nik. Why are you dressed like that?'

'Undercover,' she said grinning.

'Undercover?'

'Yeah. Matt asked me to change to this uniform.'

'I know you work with Matt now,' said Jemma. 'But you're still security.'

'It's just temporary. Matt's had regular meetings with those men who attacked us at the dam. He's worked hard trying to get them to trust us. A few days ago, they started carrying on about some group they claim is being set up to *save us.*'

'What from?'

'The IPL, I think.'

'Shit. Does Sean know?'

'I imagine so. Matt's not a lone ranger.'

'Alright. How can I help?'

'Not sure,' said Nik. 'The group's a bunch of weirdos. They reckon the IPL are going to destroy us all. I made the mistake of saying if that's the case why haven't they already done so? No one answered, but a couple of them looked like they were going to attack me.'

'I don't think you should have anything more to do with them,' said Jemma. 'They sound whacko.'

'Matt knows what I'm doing. Anyway, I went to one of their meetings, and there was talk, lots of talk about someone living outside the city.'

'Yeah, you hear that all the time.' Jemma started onto the pathway towards the Administration building. 'Mostly, it's rubbish, but every now and then they find someone. So, what?'

'I thought it was just rubbish at first too, until they said that he's related to you.'

'That's ridiculous. Have you told Zadrus, or General Hunt?'

'No,' said Nik. 'Thought I'd nose around a bit more first. Then I'll have better information to present.'

'For God's sake, you'd better talk to Sean.' She turned away when another call came in. 'Hang on, Nik.'

'Morning Jemma,' said a nurse. 'We've just had a man present. He's very frail. I need to get him to the hospital quickly, but if you want to come over, you might be able to talk to him before the transporter arrives.'

'Thanks. On my way.' Jemma flicked her screen back to Nik and told her about the man.

'I told you,' said Nik. 'There's something strange going on here. Do you want me to come with you?'

'No, I'll be alright. Just keep your communicator handy in case I need help. It's probably nothing. Go talk to Matt. He's your boss.'

'Yeah.' Nik laughed. 'I was told I was too close to Dan.'

Jemma hoped Nik would do as she'd asked, but she didn't have time to worry about it as she made her way to the Quarantine Centre. She'd get the story, then contact Sean to fill him in, tell him about Nik at the same time. Uncomfortable though it was, she reported directly to Hunt. Apparently, she was too close to everyone.

The nurse looked up as she walked in. 'This is Mr Patrick Reilly. We're ready to go to the hospital, but you can speak to him while we wait. No stress, please.'

Jemma nodded and turned to the man. 'Hello, Mr Reilly. I'm Jemma, from security. Do you feel up to talking to me?'

His mouth dropped open, and he stared. 'Jemma?'

'That's right. You made the right decision to come in. You look very unwell.'

'Sure,' he replied. 'You did say Jemma. What's your surname?'

'Anderson.' She perched on the side of his bed. 'Jemma Anderson. Where have you come from, Mr Reilly?'

'Not far.' He paused for a few deep breaths. 'I needed help, so I decided to try here.'

Jemma wanted to reassure the man, he looked so ill, but Hunt had tasked her with finding out everything she could from anyone who approached the Quarantine Centre. 'Do you live alone?'

Mr Reilly nodded, but continued staring. 'You look familiar. What was your name again?'

'Jemma Anderson.'

'You can't be.' His deep green eyes pierced through hers, in much the same way Sean's stare had affected her when they first met.

'Can't be what?' His stare made her uncomfortable, so she smiled, and stood back, out of the way of the nurses. 'We can talk more later. You need the hospital now.' As she watched him go, she had the sense that he also looked familiar, but she shook it off. Thinking it unlikely that he'd told the truth about living alone, she notified Sean so he could track the man and his treatment.

When she arrived at the hospital the doctors, waiting at the entrance to the Emergency Ward, were already looking at results from blood and imaging that had been taken en route.

She waited in the background until she recognised the doctor Sean had rescued from Costa Rica along with Anthony, Therese Morgan.

'Hello Jemma,' she said. 'Good to see you again.'

'Lovely to see you up and around,' replied Jemma. Last time she'd seen Therese, the woman had been even less mobile than Anthony. 'Does anyone know what's wrong with Mr Reilly?'

'I think I do, but it's strange. There are lesions in his pleura and his lungs are filled with fluid. It was supposed to have been eradicated forty or fifty years ago.'

'Okay,' said Jemma. 'I'll bite. What is it? Can you help him?'

'In our day, I'd have said it was terminal, but I suspect the aliens will have some ideas. I'll ask Werrimen.' She turned back to the patient. 'Have you ever worked with asbestos?'

'I don't think so,' he replied.

'Your problem looks like mesothelioma, the cancer that arises from asbestos exposure,' explained Therese. 'It can only be definitively diagnosed on biopsy, but I'm almost certain of the diagnosis. The image showed calcified plaques in your pleura which are a classic sign. The disease has infiltrated your lungs, causing fluid to build up in there. We need to drain that fluid to help you breathe before we do anything else. I'll talk to my advisers then and see what else we can do.'

'Thank you,' said Mr Reilly. 'I appreciate all your help.'

'No problem,' replied Therese.

'I've read about mesothelioma,' said Jemma, walking away with Therese. 'Why do you think that's odd?'

'All buildings which contained asbestos were demolished decades ago.'

'Could he have been infected before then?'

'Doubt it,' she replied. 'I'll have to check, but I think the demolitions would have happened before he was born.'

It took several hours for Therese to be satisfied that he was stable. Jemma was about to leave when she was interrupted by Sean on her communicator.

'Do you want to tell me what's going on?'

'Yeah, I'll join you in a few minutes.' But on her way to his office, she was interrupted by another call from Nik.

'Jem, can you spare a few minutes?'

'Yeah, sure,' she replied. 'I'm walking back to Admin from the hospital.'

Nik ran up the path to join her. 'Well, what do you think? Is he the man they were talking about? You know the Rescue Earth Group.'

'Don't know, but either way, it doesn't make sense.'

'No. I just spoke to one of the nurses who escorted him to the hospital. She said he's adamant he has to talk to you.'

'Let's go see Sean. He can decide what to do.' It often annoyed Jemma that she had to defer to Sean, but this situation was so bizarre, she needed his view. 'Did you report to Matt?'

'No, haven't got there yet. I was digging around here.'

'God Nik, he's going to slaughter you and, if Sean doesn't know, he'll slaughter the pair of you. You'd better come with me.'

Jemma knocked on Sean's door and he waved her in.

'Morning ladies. Would you like coffee?'

'Good Lord,' said Jemma, laughing. 'That was so last century. But yes, I'd like a coffee.'

'Was it now? Would you prefer if I'd said "Enter", and while you stood stiffly in front of my desk, I then growled, "Report?" Is that it?'

'No dear. Oops, I mean colonel dear.'

'Well then, since you're going to be a smart arse, get your own coffee, then sit down and fill me in.'

'Yes sah.' Jemma blew him a kiss, then retreated to the servery for her coffee.

'Bit of respect wouldn't go astray,' muttered Sean.

'I respect you more than you can ever imagine honey-bun, but this is serious.'

'God help us.' He walked back to his desk shaking his head. 'Grab your coffee, sit down, cut the crap and tell me what's going on.'

Jemma opened her mouth to answer.

'Don't,' he said, glaring at her. 'Denis, ignore her and fill me in.'

Nik started the story and Jemma added details here and there.

'How long have you known about this group, Denis?' said Sean, when they'd finished.

'About a week. My commander asked me to take a look.'

'Matt asked you?'

'Yes, sir.'

He went on, but Jemma didn't miss the flicker of irritation that crossed his face before he managed to cover it.

'Right. We need some tangible information. Jemma, how do you feel about going back to talk to Mr Reilly?'

'Yeah, I plan to, but I wanted your thoughts on how to tackle it. There's something about him, a sense of familiarity, but I can't put my finger on it.'

'Understood,' replied Sean. 'And there's something else.'

'What else?' said Jemma.

'Something's prickling at the back of my neck.'

'What? You tell me not to talk in riddles.'

'Yeah right. You never met my sister, did you?'

'No.'

'She married a man by the name of Patrick Reilly. Just feels like a hell of a coincidence, or a set-up. But I can't see why anyone would do that.'

'Okay, but he's supposed to be related to me, not you.'

'I get that, but the coincidence with his name is strange, given my brother-in-law. We might sleep on it. I'll get Matt onto seeing if he can find anything on this Patrick Reilly or where he comes from. I guess his name is not that uncommon.'

'No,' replied Jemma. 'But still ...'

'Alright, I'll look into it. Stay away from the hospital for now. I believe you're both up for training on the alien tech this afternoon, so you'd better get into that.'

As they left, Jemma heard him calling Matt, and had no doubt Matt was about to cop a blast for not informing him of a potential threat.

*   *   *

Sean suspected Matt was so used to working alone, that it hadn't occurred to him to report in. That would have to change. He considered discussing it with Hunt but, given the complex relationship between Hunt and Matt, thought it better to manage the situation himself.

'Matt,' he said, into the communicator.

'Morning boss,' replied Matt, looking cheerful.

They'd been getting along so well that Sean didn't really want to pull rank, but he knew the time had come. 'My office, please.'

'Sure. Something wrong?'

'We'll discuss it when you get here.' Sean shut down his communicator and waited. They'd do this standing.

Matt ran in, puffing. 'What's up?'

Pleased, in a sense, that Matt had been concerned by his call, Sean changed his mind and told Matt to sit while he walked around to the other side of his desk. He fiddled with a pen. Although nobody used ball-point pens in the new era, he liked the feel of it, and it helped him collect his thoughts. 'Do you have any active operations?' he said, finally.

'No,' replied Matt. He frowned and sat forward. 'If I've done something wrong, tell me.'

'Denis was in here, in a blue uniform.'

'Yeah, she's doing a bit of digging around. I thought it best if she dressed the same as the people she's talking to. There's been gossip about some bunch stirring up a bit of trouble. She's not doing anything dangerous.'

Sean leaned back in his chair. 'Have you spoken to her this morning?'

'No, not yet. We're meeting shortly.'

'Did you know about this Rescue Earth Group?'

'Yes. I don't think they're a problem, but I wanted to be sure. I think they're just whingers. She's under strict orders to only meet in public places. She was headed to a meeting yesterday afternoon and she's due in soon to debrief.'

'So, you haven't spoken to her since that meeting?'

'No. Oh God, don't tell me something's happened to her.'

'She's fine, but I'm not happy. You left a relatively inexperienced officer in the field without adequate back-up. That's resulted in a significant development this morning that you don't know about.'

'Mate, I'm sorry, but God-damn-it, I told her to contact me straight away if there was a problem. Is she in trouble?'

'She's safe, but I'll come back to what happened,' said Sean, standing and walking to Matt's side of the desk. He perched on the edge and stared down at Matt. 'I'm concerned that you identified a group of dissidents, and you didn't inform me.'

Matt stared back up at him. 'Shit man. I really didn't think they were a problem. I'd have informed you if I did.'

'I'll accept that for the minute,' sighed Sean. 'Matt, we're a team and we're going to have to agree to a few rules.'

'Sean, I have no problem with that. Now, for God's sake, what's happened?'

Sean stood. 'Get a coffee.' He recounted everything Nik

and Jemma had told him, pleased that Matt interrupted with questions several times.

'Damn it, I thought she understood me,' said Matt. 'She should have reported in straight away.'

'Agreed, and you should have supervised more closely. I'll call Denis later and have a word with her.'

'My performance was inadequate,' said Matt. 'I apologise. It won't happen again. Would you leave Denis to me? Like you, I need to assert my authority.'

Sean thought about it as he walked back to his desk. 'Alright, that's fair enough. We need to fill in the General before you do that though.' At the look on Matt's face, he laughed. 'I won't dump you in it. How we operate is between you and me. The General has to be informed about Jemma. Come on, let's go.'

If it turned out that there was a link to Pritchard, either through Reilly or this Rescue Earth Group, Sean would be right behind Hunt reeling Jemma in, although it would hurt him to do so.

Hunt looked up as the men entered. 'You look like a pair of happy Vegemites.'

'Vegemites?' said Matt.

'Oh dear, before your time I'm afraid,' said Hunt. 'What's up?'

'Something's happened,' said Sean. 'It involves Jemma and Denis.'

'Right. Is that why they weren't at training this morning?'

'Yeah, partly.'

'Should O'Leary be here?'

'Probably,' replied Sean.

Matt interrupted. 'Sir, I stuffed up. I didn't let Sean know there was a problem before it blew up.'

Hunt sighed. 'Have you discussed it with Bellamy.'

'Yes, sir.'

'Bellamy, are you satisfied?'

'Yes, sir.'

'Work it out between you then. Matt, find O'Leary and bring him in.'

After he left, Hunt looked at Sean. 'Do you want me to talk to him?'

'No. Best if I can sort it.'

'Right, wait until O'Leary arrives then fill me in.'

Although aware of Hunt's stare, Sean paced across the office while he waited. As soon as Dan walked in, Sean began.

'Damn,' said Hunt, finally.

'Damn alright,' muttered Sean. 'It just doesn't make sense. Jemma's at the centre of this, yet again, and my gut says there's substance to this story, but neither of us can work it out.'

'Wait and see what he has to say for himself,' said Hunt, his voice calm, but Sean could hear the underlying concern. 'You're satisfied she'll be safe with him?'

'Nik will be with her, and we'll station a couple of people outside the door. The thing that worries me is how that Rescue Earth bunch knew about him.'

'That's probably more concerning than the fellow himself.'

'Suspect you've got to run with it until we find out,' said

Dan. 'A lot of weird things have happened to Jemma since we've known her. Pritchard and his cronies probably were on the ship that brought us here, even though we couldn't find them. It wouldn't have been hard to hide, and Zadrus couldn't rule out the possibility that they could have the technology to get past the IPL's screening.'

'Agreed,' said Matt. 'Truth is we don't know much about the people still living outside the settlement, either. So far, those we've found have been ordinary people who've found a way to survive, but we haven't had the resources to go out and look. It's possible people from Anders have infiltrated. For now, we have to make sure Jemma's safe, and find out what we can from Reilly.'

'Is Jemma cooperating?' said Hunt.

'Yes, she is,' said Sean. 'But she's frightened again.'

'Of course. I'll get more involved with her then. We can't let the fear get out of hand.' Hunt leaned back and sighed. 'I seriously don't want to have to be hard on her.'

'No, definitely not,' replied Sean. 'I want her to have some freedom, to work out what it is that she wants to do. But I want her safe, too, so if it comes down to it, you'll have my support.'

'Good.' Hunt nodded. 'We'll try to avoid it. I'll fill Zadrus in.'

*   *   *

Jemma didn't take much in from her training session on the alien technology and overnight, she tossed and turned. She'd started to get up when Sean came out of the shower and told her to stay in bed, and that he'd square it with Hunt. He reset the alarm before he left, for another hour. When it sounded for the second time, she forced herself to get up, and headed into the shower recess. She did her best not to think about Patrick Reilly as she stood under the warm, soothing water, until she realised that she had to get moving. She murmured for the shower to cease and reached for the large towel she still preferred, although they'd been advised, for the sake of hygiene, to use the air dryers.

Pulling on her uniform, she wondered if one day she'd be able to wear other sorts of clothes. Today would have been a jeans and T-shirt sort of day. She didn't mind the uniform, which looked like a one-piece jumpsuit but was actually shirt and trousers. The material was light and soft, not unlike parachute silk, but when the shirt was tucked in, it seemed to stick to the waist of the trousers, making it appear to be a single piece. In summer, it stayed loose, and allowed the breeze through, so despite the long sleeves and full-length trousers, it was cool, but in winter, it firmed to the body, and insulated against the cold.

Breakfast would have to come later, her meeting with Zadrus was at 9:00. She pulled on her shoes, brushed her hair, grabbed her bag and ran for the door. After securing the apartment, her communicator vibrated, and she swore at the delay.

'I've just checked with the doctors on Mr Reilly's progress,' said Nik. 'He's still very ill, but determined he has to see you.'

'Okay, I'll meet you at the doctor's office.' She raised her communicator to let Zadrus know she was going to be late again. When she arrived, Nik was trying to help Therese retrieve her notes from the previous day. Late twenty-first century computers were fully interactive. The thing asked, in a haughty tone of voice, if she wanted them alphabetically, in order of presentation, or current location. Nik swore at it and requested order of presentation.

'Well,' it responded, 'do you want views on your desk, or printed?'

'Oh, for Christ's sake, printed,' she yelled at it.

'Hmph. Done,' it replied, and shut itself down.

Jemma laughed as Nik grabbed the notes and slammed them on the desk, right next to the moody computer. Therese flicked through the notes, then led them to the Emergency Department to find out where Mr Reilly had been moved to. She expected to find him in a medical ward and was surprised he was still in one of the Emergency Department's short-stay rooms. He looked even more frail this morning. His feet dangled over the end of the bed. She guessed he was quite tall, but he was so stooped when he stood, it didn't show. Probably, under better circumstances, he'd have been quite a handsome man, but now he was gaunt, unshaven and struggling for every breath.

As he spoke to Therese, he continued to stare at Jemma, then he stood, with a great deal of effort. 'I must speak to you, Jemma.' His voice held a sense of urgency, almost desperation.

'Certainly, but I'm late for a meeting now. Would it be

alright if I come back in about an hour?' She was more than late to meet with Zadrus, and she had to fill Sean in.

'Of course,' replied Mr Reilly. 'But please come back. It is important.'

She waited until she was outside to call Sean and was surprised that he answered as soon as she spoke. He must have been waiting.

'Are you okay?' he said.

'I'm fine. I'll give you the basics then I have to head to Zadrus.'

'Change of plans. Meet me at Jamie's café. General Hunt and Zadrus are going to join us there.'

'Oh, sure. I'll head there now.'

*   *   *

Sean left the building quickly so he could appreciate a few minutes in the sun. He needed a bit of time by himself, to think. It was good not to have to dash across busy roads or wait for streetlights. With no road vehicles in the new settlement, most people walked, but if they needed a vehicle, they used the small aerial transporters that zipped noiselessly overhead.

Jemma called out as he was about to walk in the door. Relieved to hear her voice, he whirled around and picked her up, then held her tight.

'Put me down, you'll embarrass Nik,' she said, laughing.

'Nik will cope. Let's go inside.'

They each ordered from the menu. Along the wall, display

cases showed cakes and meals neatly arranged on a couple of shelves. But they were all images and continually changed. The food they ordered slid onto the counter within minutes, looking like it had just been cooked. Sean shook his head, one day he'd get used to this technology. He found a table in a corner out of the way to wait for Hunt and Zadrus to arrive.

Zadrus began as soon as he walked in, even before he sat down. 'Jemma, Nikola, what have you found out about this man?'

'Not much,' said Jemma. 'He was so ill when he arrived that I couldn't get much out of him. But this morning, he asked to see me again.'

'Did he say what he wanted?' asked Hunt.

'No, but I'll go back as soon as we're done and chat to him.'

'I don't like it,' said Sean. 'But we need to find out what's going on.'

'Agreed.' Hunt drummed his fingers on the table. 'Is it possible he's telling the truth that he's been living close by?'

'Yes, it is,' said Matt. 'We've rescued many people from nearby in the last couple of years.'

'My understanding is that they were very thorough when they cleaned the asbestos out of the buildings,' said Sean.

Matt nodded. 'And if they couldn't clear the asbestos, they demolished the buildings and buried the materials in the desert.'

'So, asbestos contamination shouldn't have been possible,' said Sean.

'I have been told the same,' said Zadrus. 'But there might

have been a hidden building. If asbestos inspectors did not know it was there, they couldn't have cleared it. We need more information.'

'Jemma, I'm going with you when you go back.' Sean took hold of her hand. 'We don't know anything about the fellow, or what kind of threat he might pose.'

'No, but he's frightened. I'll go in alone. He's too weak to do me any harm.'

'I'll organise an earpiece,' said Zadrus. 'We can listen and be close by. Are you comfortable with that?'

'I'll stick with her,' said Nik. 'Mr Reilly didn't seem to be bothered by me being there before.'

Sean didn't realise how hard he'd squeezed Jemma's hand until she gasped and pulled it back. 'Sorry. I'm worried.'

'I know,' she replied. 'I won't take any risks.'

Sean walked back with her but stopped at the room next to Mr Reilly's, where Zadrus fitted the earpiece. He hugged her as she left. There wasn't much more he could do.

CHAPTER 10

Jemma stood outside Mr Reilly's room, holding the door handle, but she couldn't bring herself to turn it. After everything she'd been through, it surprised her that she was so unnerved by one sick elderly man. She didn't for a minute believe that he'd been living out there by himself and, if Nik's Rescue Earth people were right and he was related, there'd probably be other family. She had to find out and, if he was a fraud, she had to know that too … and, more importantly, why.

'You don't have to do this,' said Nik, startling her back to reality.

'Yeah, I do. There's something about him, although I can't quite put my finger on it.' She grabbed Nik's hand. 'You won't leave me, will you?' She didn't feel physically threatened, the man was far too ill, struggling for every breath, but she didn't want to do this alone.

'I'll stick to you like the proverbial glue,' said Nik. 'Come on. Best to get it over and done with.'

Mr Reilly's face lit up as soon as she stepped inside. 'I'm so pleased you came back.' He pushed himself off the bed and tried to stand. His body shook.

'Please don't stand for me.' Jemma ran forward and eased

him back onto the bed. Once he was settled, she did her best to smile and appear to be at ease. 'Okay Mr Reilly, what can I do for you?'

'You've already done an enormous amount for me. Please call me Pat.' He stopped to heave in some air and, when he spoke, he could only say a few words without stopping. 'I believe we might have a family connection. That sounds peculiar I know. Please hear me out.'

She wanted to say it wasn't just peculiar, it was impossible, but she whispered, 'Go ahead.'

'Thank you,' he said, taking one of her hands in his. 'I'm not sure where to begin. I recognised you. From my mother's photos. I heard your name. I knew I had to speak to you.'

'Your mother's photos?'

'My mother's name is Jemma. She was born in 2016. Named after her aunt. Her mother's name was Thera Anderson. Does that make sense to you?'

Jemma ripped her hand away. He was claiming to be her sister's grandson. That would make him her great nephew. But he was fifty-six, and she was twenty-seven. He couldn't be. She forced herself to calm down and respond. 'My sister went missing after our parents died. I never saw her again, although I missed her terribly.'

He tentatively reached out to touch her hand again before going on. 'I grew up with stories of my great aunt. She disappeared without a trace. My grandmother had a terrible accident. Lost her memory. The FBI located her when you went missing. Your only surviving relative. My grandfather sent her back to Australia. Her daughter was my mother. She was three years old at the time. They stayed in your flat while the police investigated. My grandfather couldn't leave his business in the States. He disappeared just after she came to Australia. He left her okay, financially. Had a sizeable estate. She was alone with a baby, though. Spent the rest of her life searching. Refused to believe you were dead.'

He rested back on the bed, looking drained, and Jemma wondered if she should leave him to rest, but she had to hear the rest of the story. She took a deep breath and told him to go on.

'We knew you were married to a military man. He went missing at the same time. His sister came back from America. With her husband, Patrick Reilly senior. Police introduced them to gran. They became firm friends. Great aunt Cheryl helped gran recover. Their son was Charles Reilly. My mother and Charles grew up together. Both told me it was a foregone conclusion that they'd end up married.'

Jemma's chest felt tight. 'Do you know the name of the military man?'

'I've been trying to remember. His sister was Cheryl Bellamy. Cheryl Reilly after she was married.'

'Sean?'

'Yes, yes. That was it.' He gripped her hand as he lay back on the bed, his face glowing with sweat.

She leant forward, until her head rested on her knees. Someone might have told this man about her relationship with Sean, but it was feasible that Thera and Sean's sister could have become close. They shared the same tragedy. And she had recognised Sean's eyes in Pat the day she met him. She was still trying to process his story when the door flew open behind her, and Sean raced into the room.

Pat lifted his head to look at Sean and gasped. His breathing suddenly deteriorated until he was gasping for air. He clutched his chest. Nik hit the emergency button while Jemma and Sean did their best to calm him as they waited. They held onto each other, unable to speak as the doctors worked on Pat.

When his breathing finally slowed, Pat held out his hand to Jemma. 'I'm sorry. It was such a shock to see your friend come in. He's Sean Bellamy, isn't he?'

'He is, and he's my husband. Sean this is Pat Reilly.'

Sean nodded. 'Pat, I knew Patrick Reilly, your grandfather. I was at their wedding, and I knew Charles, your father, as a little boy.'

Pat smiled. 'I recognised Jemma the minute I saw her, but I can't believe you're both here.'

Sean sat beside Jemma on the bed, his arm around her. 'I can see why your mother and my nephew would have been thrown together, but it's your grandfather, the man Thera married, that I'm interested in. Can you tell us anything about him?'

'Of course,' he replied. 'I knew my gran very well. She lived to the age of ninety. A beautiful, caring lady. I never met my grandfather. She didn't remarry. Kept his name. For my mother's sake, I think. It was Pritchard.'

Jemma took in a short, sharp breath. 'What was his first name?'

'Fred. He owned some big pharmaceutical company. Started by his father last century.'

Thera had been stuck in America when her parents had died. Pritchard had informed Jemma that he'd *found* her following an accident, and later married her. If Pat was to be believed, Pritchard had, at least partially, told the truth. 'Pat, did they ever find Fred Pritchard or his body?'

Sean raised his eyebrows, then nodded and turned back to Pat. 'Yeah mate, that might be important. We'll explain later.'

'No. Police said there was an explosion. One of his factories. So intense that anybody near its centre would have been vaporised. He'd been there that morning. Several people missing after it. None of their bodies were found.'

'So, no proof that he died,' murmured Jemma.

'No, not as I understand it. I need to ask some questions, too.'

'Of course,' said Jemma. 'We'll answer whatever we can.'

'Both my grandmothers had photos of you. Neither of you have aged. Am I talking to Jemma and Sean? Or their great grandchildren. Out of respect for my mother, I have to know. Do you understand?'

'I do,' Jemma said quietly. 'We also need proof.'

'I can get the photos. And all the documents mum has. At home.'

Jemma felt Sean's grip tighten on her hand. 'Your mother is still alive?'

'Yes,' he replied. 'She's eighty-three, but still quite strong.'

'I'm having trouble taking in what you're saying,' Jemma

said, her voice little more than a whisper. 'The aliens res-cued us and moved us forward in time. To us, everything that you've described happened a matter of months ago.'

'For us it was eighty years ago.'

'We're going to have to think about what you've just told us,' said Sean. 'You'll need time to think too, but for now, we should leave you with the nurses to rest. We'll come back later and talk more.'

Pat leaned forward towards Sean. 'You will come back, won't you?'

'We will,' said Jemma. 'We're not going anywhere, and it's going to take you some time to recover.'

To Jemma, it all seemed to be a family thing, that she and Sean would have to work through, just like the General and Matt. She'd know for sure once she saw the photos but, in her heart, she felt that Pat was telling the truth.

*   *   *

Sean escorted Jemma back to Hunt and Zadrus to debrief, then returned to the hospital so he could talk to Pat on his own. He'd been expecting Pat's claim that he was related to Jemma, and he'd been geared up to help her deal with it, but it hadn't occurred to him that he could also be related. He hoped Pat was telling the truth, and that their sisters had found each other, but was astonished to be told that their offspring had married. Yet, it wasn't really so far-fetched that the two women might have clung to each other to get through, after he and Jemma had disappeared. The odds against finding their daughter and grandson here, though, had to be astronomical and, never one to believe in coincidence, that bothered him. When he walked into the hospital room Pat was asleep, so he sat on a chair beside the bed, and waited until Pat opened his eyes and noticed him.

'I'm sorry,' Pat said, with a start. 'I didn't know you were there.'

'No, no. I wasn't going to wake you, not after your collapse this morning.' Sean raised the back of the bed and helped Pat to get comfortable. 'Mate, I've got to ask you more about your story. You seem to be an honest person, but I need to be sure, in my own mind, before we go further. My wife suffered greatly at the hands of Fredrick Pritchard, and I'll do anything I can to avoid her suffering further.'

'I don't know anything about that. You might have to fill me in as we go. Ask anything you like. I'll do my best to answer.'

'My understanding is that there's heavy radiation outside our city boundary,' said Sean. 'But you've survived there for years. You're ill now, but it's to do with asbestos, not radiation.'

'I don't know,' said Pat, after a deep breath. 'I can't explain it.'

'Understood. Would we be able to speak to the people you've been living with out there?'

Pat shook his head. 'Oh dear. I don't know.'

'I realise this is hard for you, but if I'm to help, I need to know who's there.'

'Yes, I guess you do. Alright.'

'It struck me, this morning, that the odds of you being here, in the place where we landed, are astronomical. Can you tell me how you came to be here?'

'Probably not as strange as you think. As the East Coast started to collapse, people moved inland. A lot of them came south of the Queensland border. I moved here first with my family. Dad was killed early in the war. Mum came with us. We intended to bring my brother, Pete, and his wife and family. They had to sell their cattle. No one wanted to buy. Everyone was walking away from farms. Then all the lines and satellites were down.' Tears rolled down his cheeks as he recalled everything that he and his wife had done to contact Pete, but they never heard from him again. The only realistic conclusion was that Pete was dead.

'If it's too hard, we can take a break,' said Sean, aware of Pat's clipped sentences as he worked to take in air. 'I need answers, but I don't want to cause you any more pain.'

Pat shook his head, 'No, you need to know you can trust me. About a year after we bought the farm, I found a huge underground bunker on the property. No idea who built it. Or why. It was professionally finished. Given the fixtures and fittings, probably mid-twentieth century.'

'Hence the asbestos,' said Sean.

'I guess so. I did all the work to get it into a usable state. I had the most exposure.'

'Our mentors believe they can cure you, so keep your hopes up.'

'Thanks. The world was getting into trouble. I stored

enough water for about ten years. Grabbed as much canned, dried, and frozen food as I could get my hands on. I built a filtered compressor for oxygen. Electricity was through a wind engine, solar panels and battery cells. I built them all.'

'That would've been one hell of an achievement,' said Sean.

'Hard work, but it paid off. We did well for a long time. A few months ago, I had to get outside. Probably the first signs of my illness. The farm was remarkably good. Hydroponics shed had seed and chemicals. All sealed in bottles. The seeds germinated. I couldn't believe my luck. Then I found animals — cattle, goats and chickens. They were healthy. Gave us fresh eggs, milk, and vegetables. It felt like heaven.'

'Who else did you have living with you?' said Sean.

'My wife. Our son and daughter-in-law. That's it.'

'Okay. Are any of them ill?'

'No. Mum's slowed up a bit, but everyone's healthy.'

'What if we took a transporter out there to check on them? Would they talk to us?'

'I doubt it,' replied Pat, staring at his feet. 'They'd be too frightened.'

'Why?'

'Because of the things we saw.'

'What sort of things?'

'When we left the farm. Let me go back. I found my old hydro-electric car. Amazing. It was still in good order. Had to fiddle with the motor. It finally started. I stuck to local roads first. We came on an enormous waterway. We'd expected to find grazing land. Used to be a town there too. Didn't know what to make of it.'

'We saw similar sights when we arrived,' said Sean. 'There's a massive split right through the centre of Australia, starting in the Gulf of Carpentaria, and extending almost down to Adelaide.'

Pat paused to steady his breathing. 'My son yelled to get down. He saw a flying craft. Like nothing we'd seen before. Just above the treetops. Heading towards us. I dragged everyone behind some bushes. It landed fifty metres away. Several people jumped out. Ordinary people, but all armed. Seemed to be looking for someone.' He shuddered. 'One of them touched something pinned to his chest. It worked like a loudspeaker.'

'I've seen something similar,' said Sean. 'It's a translator but it can also be used to enhance the voice. Go on.'

'He demanded everyone come out. Reckoned they wouldn't harm us. They'd take us someplace safe. We didn't move. It felt wrong. A man emerged from the lower end of the valley. Someone in the craft fired. Killed him. Jesus, it makes me sick to think about it. We stayed where we were until it took off. Then we fled back to the car. I drove as fast as it'd go back to our bunker.'

'God,' said Sean. 'It couldn't have been the IPL. The weapons they carry don't kill, only stun.'

'This man was killed. They shot him through the heart, and I saw the blood gushing.' Tears rolled down his cheeks.

'Can you describe the craft?'

'Big metal ball. No wings. Just a sphere.'

'Shit. Sort of confirms something Jemma saw just after we arrived here.'

'Okay. Couple of weeks later we ventured out again. Tried other directions and saw the signs here. All said come on in. When I got worse, family made me do that. The rest you know.'

'Pat, someone told Jemma about you the day before you arrived.' Sean frowned. 'Did you speak to anyone before you got here?'

'No, we only made the decision an hour before I came in. I had no idea Jemma was here until I saw her.'

Sean leaned back and stared at him. Someone, unknown to Pat and his family, had known they were there. The Reillys had bought the farm well after Pritchard's disappearance, so even if he were back, he couldn't have known about it, unless … 'Pat does your mother have a tattoo on her right hip?'

'She does. She doesn't know much about it, though. Said it had been there all her life. Her mother also had one and it was a mystery to her, too.'

'Jesus.' Sean was torn about how much to say but, if Pritchard could track Pat's mother, she was in grave danger and he'd need Pat's support to be able to act quickly enough to protect her.

'Pat, I have a lot to tell you, and most of it revolves around Fredrick Pritchard.'

'Okay.'

'Pritchard didn't die in a factory fire. We believe that he's managed to follow us here, although we don't know how. For reasons I'll go into later, he's after Jemma. The problem is, I believe he'd be prepared to use your mother to get to Jemma. We have to get to your mother first so we can protect her.'

'I don't know what to say,' said Pat. 'I believe my grandfather genuinely loved my grandmother. I always wondered why he didn't take her with him.'

'Good question,' replied Sean. 'We have to bring your mother in here if we're to protect her. Will you agree to that?'

'Of course. Pretty much confirms we're family though.'

'Pretty much. You don't have a tattoo, do you?'

'No, but my father had one as well as my mother. My grandfather was long gone when I was born. I never met him and now I'm glad that I didn't. Neither of my parents knew what the tattoos signified.'

'Okay. I'll organise a DNA test, only way we can really be sure, but your mother is priority.'

'I'm happy to do the DNA. I need to know the truth as much as you do. For my family's sake. My problem is from asbestos. I know there's no hope. You'll be convinced of our relationship when you meet mother.'

'Pat don't give up,' said Sean. 'The aliens are far more advanced than human scientists, and they believe they can cure your illness. Your family will have to go into quarantine, but you'll be able to be with them as soon as you're well enough. I need to speak to the doctors and find out what we have to do to take you there safely, and I'll organise a transporter.' He handed Pat a communicator, explained how to use it, then called Matt to organise a guard and headed to the next room where Hunt waited with Jemma, Dan and Nik.

'Hospital's working on oxygen,' said Hunt. 'A doctor will have to go with him. Matt's organising a PTD, like the one Anthony uses, and he'll join us as soon as that's done.'

'Okay,' said Sean. 'I believe he's telling the truth. I just have to get my head around it.'

Jemma nodded. 'That's how I felt too. The DNA test should tell us more. The thing that's always bothered me, even when Pritchard told me about it, is that my sister was seriously injured in America, and nobody notified me. I've been wondering lately whether there was really an accident or if Pritchard faked her injury. They called her daughter Jemma so at least one of them knew who she was and that she was related to me. Either she didn't lose her memory, or he knew all along who she was.'

'Yeah,' said Sean. 'I suspect you're right and I'm damned sure that Pritchard intended to use your relationship, to reel you in as soon as he had the opportunity.'

'Yeah, but hang on,' said Hunt. 'Pritchard is a vicious terrorist. Is it really possible that his family didn't know?'

'I'm sure Pat was telling us the truth,' said Jemma.

'I agree.' Sean turned to Hunt. 'We have to approach his family with some trust. We can keep a close eye on them in quarantine.'

'I guess something like this was bound to happen eventually,' murmured Matt.

'You mean because we're outsiders,' snapped Jemma. 'Maybe the same will happen to you some day. I doubt you're immune just because you're an insider.'

'Hello-o-o-o-o. Already has.' Matt grinned and tossed his head towards Hunt.

Jemma blushed, but she had to laugh. 'Sorry, I'm just too shocked to compute it all.'

'Right,' said Hunt, smiling. 'We don't know what this is all about and, until we do, everyone with a tattoo is restricted to the precinct around the Administration building.'

'You mean Nik and me,' said Dan. 'They've never come after me.'

'Doesn't mean Pritchard, or whoever's doing this, won't come after you now if he can't get hold of Jemma or his daughter. Don't forget, he did kidnap Nik once. And as you know, I also have a tattoo, as do several of the others who came with us.'

'I can look after myself,' growled Dan.

'So can I,' said Jemma. 'And Nik too. But he got us.'

'Don't grumble any of you. If you have to go outside the restricted area, you need my permission.' He glared at Dan. 'All of you.'

'Deja vu,' Jemma muttered.

CHAPTER 11

Sean headed to Werrimen's office to fill her in and found Zadrus already there, pacing and frowning. Werrimen stood, as always, with her hands clasped in front of her, patiently waiting for him to settle down.

'Good morning Sean,' said Werrimen. 'Zadrus has told me about Mr Reilly. What is your impression?'

'He's genuine.'

'I suspect you're right,' said Zadrus. 'I am most disturbed by his statement that he saw someone murdered. If it happened after we arrived, it could be Pritchard, but we must not close our minds to other possibilities.'

'No,' said Werrimen. 'Do you think this man's memory is sound, Sean?'

'I do. He's very ill, but his mind is clear.'

Werrimen exchanged a look with Zadrus that Sean couldn't quite interpret.

'What did you mean by *other possibilities?*' said Sean.

Zadrus threw himself onto the chair behind his desk and stared up at the ceiling. 'Long before we arrived, the IPL took the decision to concentrate on developing the new settlements and assured the residents that they were safe. Unfortunately, there is always a risk although it was not anticipated so soon, and they thought they could manage without troubling the already devastated human population.'

'So, do you know what is going on?'

'I have my suspicions, although I am not certain.' Zadrus covered his face with his hands. 'There are other beings in the universe, some even in this galaxy, who are not friendly. Given current events, we must be alert to the possibility of their presence.'

'We must also be sure before we make accusations like that public,' said Werrimen, although her frown suggested she agreed. 'Has IPL command reported any unfriendly craft, either here or outside the Earth's atmosphere?'

'I contacted them this morning. They have seen some activity, but not in this hemisphere.'

'For God's sake,' said Sean. 'I need to know who or what we're dealing with, and how to fight them.'

Zadrus nodded. 'You are right, but I need more information before I can properly advise you.'

'Then that is settled,' said Werrimen. 'While we work on that Sean, you and Jemma should go out and see if this man's claim of being family holds any credibility. The spherical craft he saw and the attack on Jemma at the dam are concerning, but there is nothing we can do until we identify the unfriend-lies or see their craft.' She looked up as Jemma joined them. 'Ah, good timing. I have just suggested to Sean that you go out to meet Mr Reilly's family.'

Jemma nodded. 'Agreed, but before we go, I need to fill

you in on an attack that we've just been informed about at the school. Poisonous gas was released into the air-conditioning. Two of the teachers were overcome, but they both managed to stagger outside and stopped anyone else from entering the building. They're now in hospital. Matt's gone to inform the General. He asked me to find you, Sean. Nik and Dan have gone to investigate.'

Zadrus thumped his fist on the desk. 'We must get to the bottom of this.'

'It'll be that bloody Rescue Earth Group,' said Sean.

'What do you know of this group?' snapped Zadrus.

'Nothing,' replied Sean. 'They're apparently antagonistic to the IPL. Nik had started to infiltrate them, before Mr Reilly came in. I've stopped that investigation for the moment.'

'Yes, I think that is wise,' said Zadrus. 'I will follow up with the school. You should retrieve Mr Reilly's family quickly, before Pritchard, or whoever is behind this, can get to them. We have a sample of Mr Reilly's DNA. The scientists are comparing it to each of yours now. Check on that, then head out there.'

'The other thing that's bothering me,' said Sean, 'is that the area Reilly describes is well outside our boundary fence, so it wouldn't be protected by the TEM, yet he and his family were able to cope in the open atmosphere. Even if he is related, we need an explanation for that.'

'Oh, of course,' replied Zadrus. 'There is a valid explanation. I thought you knew. Initially the limit of the TEM was just outside the fence. At that time, the Reillys would have been safely shut in their bunker. As the settlement grew, the capacity of the TEM was increased, so that the area covered now is almost eighty kilometres outside our boundary. By the time they emerged from the bunker, their area would have been covered. My apologies, I thought you were aware of that.'

'Oh. I had no idea. There's so much for us to learn that I'm not across everything, yet.'

'Yes, I understand. Go to the lab now, and see if you are related to this man,' said Zadrus. 'Whatever the result, take Mr Reilly to his farm, and see if you can convince his family to come back with you.'

Sean walked with Jemma to the lab. Neither spoke, although they exchanged an occasional glance as they waited at the lab for Anthony, who was now the chief scientist.

'I hope you're ready for this,' said Anthony.

'You've found a link, haven't you?' Sean remained standing, his arm still around Jemma.

Anthony nodded. 'I've not come across anything quite like this since we've been here. There's a strong crossover between your DNA, Jemma, and Pat Reilly's. And there's a strong crossover between his DNA and yours Sean. He's close, not first degree, but not too far away from either of you.'

'What does that mean,' said Sean, 'not first degree?'

'It means that he's not our father, brother or son,' said Jemma. 'But he's closely related to us, so cousin, nephew, great nephew is logical.'

Sean stared straight ahead, then drew Jemma into him. It was true. A woman in her eighties was Jemma's niece, and a man in his fifties was not just her great nephew, but his also. So, how should they act when they meet Jemma's niece? He eased her back. 'Are you alright? We don't have to rush out there.'

'Yeah, I think we do. We have to accept what he says now and see what else is coming. Let's go to the hospital and pick him up.'

'Right then,' said Sean. 'I don't want to give the hospital any warning we're coming. We both need to appear calm and casual for his sake.'

Pat sat on the side of his bed. He had an expectant look on his face. 'The DNA test verified you are related to both of us,' said Sean.

He looked delighted, but Sean wasn't prepared to waste time discussing it.

'I've organised a transporter to take us out to meet your family.' Sean stopped, and looked at Jemma. 'Our family.'

Tears ran down Pat's face. 'Thank you. I so wanted to be right on this. I'm delighted to meet you Great aunt Jemma. Great uncle Sean. Would it be okay if I were to hug you?'

Jemma smiled and moved closer to him. Tears formed in both their eyes. Sean joined them, but was the first to break it off, his tone quiet, but firm. 'The transporter is waiting on the roof to take us there.'

Pat was organised into a PTD which was a small craft in itself. When the nurse waved her hand over a screen at the top, it lit up, and she told it to move forward. It lifted a few centimetres above the ground and slowly moved. She told them that the chairs could rise up to twenty feet, although they had built-in sensors that stopped them from hitting the ceiling of a room or crashing into a tree.

Pat's breathing became shallow as they approached the transporter. His hands gripped the side of the chair and he told it to stop.

'I guess you haven't been in one of these before,' said Jemma. 'They're very comfortable. We just need to get you up through the blue light and you can lie down again inside.'

He vigorously shook his head. 'The only time I've seen anything like this, someone was killed. Are you sure these aliens are what they say they are?'

'Oh, of course. I understand.' Sean walked inside. 'I trust the IPL, and my people are waiting in here. The pilot, and co-pilot are both Sidlown, and I know them. We wouldn't do anything to harm you, and we've both been in these numerous times. They're safe.'

'The craft you saw. Did it look like this?' said Matt, returning to them from inside the transporter.

'Similar, but a bit different too. The metal was much the same, but it was a sphere, and a bit bigger.'

The craft they were about to enter looked like a flattened sphere, fifteen metres in diameter. The central rim where they were headed, projected out from the surface of the sphere by about a metre. Jemma had slowly edged Pat forward during the exchange and, by the time they'd finished speaking, he was at the entrance. With some gentle encouragement, he agreed to go inside. A reclining chair had been set up for him next to the pilot so he could rest in comfort but, at the same time, give instructions on how to get to his home. They lifted into the air with barely any sensation of movement. Pat directed the pilot along a road, the only route he knew.

Neither Sean nor Jemma had been outside the settlement's boundary before, and Sean wasn't sure what he'd expected out here, but it wasn't this. All around were lush green fields. There was some regrowth, but not much. There had to be animals out here keeping the grass down, but how could that be? Even though the atmosphere was better now, these areas had been so badly devastated no animals should have survived. He was nearly knocked off his seat as Jemma rushed forward.

'My God, it's a kangaroo,' she cried.

Sean grabbed her, 'Jemma, back here and sit down.'

'No. Sean look. It's a kangaroo.'

'Bloody hell, it is.'

Pat nodded, 'Yeah, we saw quite a few roos.'

Jemma sat back in her seat. 'Sean, do you realise how exciting this is. Kangaroos have survived the devastation. Pat found some animals on his place. Maybe other animals have survived too. I can't wait to get the chance to see what else is out there.'

Matt looked at Sean, started to say something, then shook his head and sat back.

'Whatever it is Matt, spit it out,' said Sean.

'Alright. I don't know how much you've been told about that period just after the war, but, when we went out trying to find survivors, we sometimes found perfectly healthy people. Every health check known was done and we didn't find anything wrong with them. It seemed like there were safe pockets, although we never worked out what the difference was. This area might be one of those safe pockets. I just don't know.'

'So, if there are enough safe pockets, there might be enough cattle, sheep, even poultry to redevelop farms, and eventually live real lives.' Jemma couldn't sit still as she spoke.

'True, but it's going to be some time before we're able to find out. For now, let's concentrate on the task at hand.' Sean turned to the pilot. 'How close are we to the farm?'

'Almost there,' replied Pat. He directed the pilot to an area he thought should be safe to land as it would be relatively concealed if there were any other craft around. Still in his PTD, Pat followed Sean down through the blue light, to the ground, where he pointed to a clump of bushes. He stood, not wanting his family to see him in the chair. Sean supported him until they reached a wooden panel tucked inconspicuously beneath a rocky outcrop. Jemma and Matt shifted the panel to reveal a door through which three people, a woman about Pat's age, and a younger man and woman, emerged. All had tears in their eyes as they ran out to greet him.

Sean, with Jemma beside him, stood very still. These people were probably relatives, and he could see them sneaking looks his way.

The younger man stepped away from Pat. 'Dad, who the hell are these people?' Pat's wife, and the younger woman, stared from Jemma to Sean, then back to Pat.

'This is Jemma Anderson, and her husband Sean Bellamy,' replied Pat, with a smile.

'Fair go, they're the spitting image of the photos, but that Jemma Anderson and Sean Bellamy would have to be over a hundred years old. What the hell's going on?'

'We need to go inside. I'll explain it and introduce you properly then.'

Although the young man still looked suspicious, he was polite as he showed them, and the others, into the entry foyer. Pat took his family to another room, leaving Sean, Jemma and Matt to stare around the massive space.

Photographs and paintings covered the walls. Directly opposite the entry was a poster size photograph of Sean in his military uniform, accepting something from Hunt.

'Holy shit,' said Matt, pointing at the photo. 'You almost look impressive.'

'Very funny. I remember that photo. We'd just returned from Afghanistan.' He gently turned Jemma to her right. 'There's two photos of you too.'

She followed his gaze to the two posters. 'Oh, my goodness ... I remember them both. That's Thera next to me, on the farm. I was about fifteen. The other one's a couple of years later, the night of my formal. And that's Henry, our kelpie, with us. There's a big chunk out of his right ear where he took on a seven-foot kangaroo and lost. We left him on my uncle's farm, intending to go back quite soon. I never knew what happened to him after the floods. I thought he'd been another victim.'

Sean whistled, 'Nice dog, but I think I could fall for the girl.' He walked behind her and wrapped his arms around her shoulders until a scuffle behind interrupted them. A chocolate-coloured kelpie ran to Jemma.

'Henry,' snapped Pat, as his wife ran forward to control the dog.

The dog would have knocked her off her feet if she hadn't already collapsed to the floor. 'That can't be … it can't be Henry.'

'No,' said Pat. 'Not your Henry. He's about eight generations further on, but still has your Henry's blood in him.'

'But he was lost in the floods.' As Sean helped Jemma to her feet, she reached down to pat Henry and absent-mindedly checked his ear.

'No, he survived,' said a soft voice behind her. 'Neighbours found him. When father heard, he flew him to America, hoping it would help mother's memory, but it didn't return until she got back here. Jemma, is it really you? And Sean too?'

'Yes Mum, it is them,' said Pat.

Jemma stared at an elderly woman, no idea what to say.

The woman walked towards them and pointed to another photo on the wall opposite Jemma's photo. They were both in it, cutting the cake at their wedding.

'How on Earth did you get that?' Jemma walked over and raised her hand to touch the image. 'Only SCARF people attended our wedding.'

Sean looked between Pat and his mother. 'We need to know,' he said gently. 'How did you get it?'

'Father said one of his people was there. He was overseas himself at the time.'

'Must have been that fake scientist,' murmured Jemma. 'The one who tried to get me outside and lure me away from SCARF.'

The family stared at each, no one seemed to know what to do, until the elderly Jemma walked forward and put her arms around the younger Jemma. 'It is so wonderful to see that you survived. My mother never gave up.'

'I wish I could have found her before we left, but everything was in such turmoil, we didn't have a chance. The IPL told us that they had both Thera and Sean's sister, Cheryl, under surveillance and both were safe.'

'I'm sorry everyone,' said Sean. 'We can't be sure we weren't followed, so we can't risk being out here too long.' He turned to the older Jemma. 'We need to work out how best to help you. Pat has to come straight back with us, he's too ill to be out of hospital for long. Would you consider joining him? I think your safety could now be compromised. We can come back for your things later. There's ample room for the four of you on our craft. How many dogs do you have?'

'Henry, his lady and three puppies,' said Pat.

'What do you think we should do, Pat?' said Jemma senior.

Jemma jumped in. 'It'd be wise to come back with us. We can offer you some protection, but our medical people can check you out to see if anyone else is in the early stages of Pat's illness.'

Pat smiled. 'Mum, I agree with Jemma. We have to, at

some stage, trust someone.' They looked at each other, but there was no time for further discussion as Matt ran into the room, yelling.

'Aircraft approaching. Everyone inside.'

A deafening noise was followed by a tremor that ricocheted through the bunker, then multiple loud explosions. The last of Matt's staff dashed into the room, slamming the front door shut, one of them yelling, 'We're under attack.'

Sean ordered everyone into the back room, while Matt bellowed orders to the base controller.

'They're on their way,' said Matt. 'We just have to hold out until they get here.'

Sean turned his attention to the security screen Pat had used to look outside before he'd decided it was safe to leave the bunker. 'Jesus, that's a Norellian sphere.'

'It's the same as the one we saw. The one that killed the man,' said Pat. 'We only saw humans come out of it though.'

'I'd say Pritchard's here,' Sean muttered to Jemma. 'His people are all human.'

'Mrs Reilly, we need to be ready to go when help arrives,' said Matt. 'Pack necessities only. We can supply clothes and most things you need, and we can come back for your things when we know it's safe. Pat, is there any other way out of here?' Pat and his wife drew a quick map showing alternative exits.

Matt's instructions jarred Sean back to the present. The bunker was a large structure. He counted at least ten bedrooms, four separate living areas, two kitchens and dining areas, an enormous storeroom, even bigger than the entry foyer, and various engine rooms for air-conditioning, oxygen supply, water purification, sewerage. It also had three safety exits other than the front door.

'Right, we'll use this exit as soon as our transporter arrives,' said Sean, pointing to one that was close to a small clearing. 'They'll give us cover so we can run out. Mrs Reilly, grab what you need. Jemma pack up the dogs, then help Pat. Matt, have the pilot go back to our transporter once we get cleared, see if it can still fly.' The noise at the entry door grew louder until, suddenly, there was total silence.

'That'll be our people,' called Matt.

'Prepare to go,' ordered Sean. 'Jemma, you're with Pat. Matt assist Mrs Reilly. Someone grab the dogs. Get into the craft as fast as you can. Run underneath. Use the light.'

For a time, once they were safely in the lounge, Jemma stared at Sean without speaking. She'd just found family, and she was sitting in an alien transporter, cuddling a dog on her lap. It started as a smile between them, but gradually built into hysterical laughter. Jemma senior seemed to understand, and she reached out one of her hands to each of them, as only she could.

*   *   *

'I'm so confused,' said Jemma, resting her head on Sean's shoulder. 'This has really driven home how much we've lost.'

'I know what you mean. A day at a time.'

She smiled up at him. 'Yes, General.'

'And don't you forget it.' He threw both arms around her, stroking her hair as he whispered, 'Remember our mantra. So long as we've got each other, we'll get through.'

She buried her head against his chest and lost herself in his strength for a moment but when she looked up, Matt had squatted in front of them.

'Sean, I know you're struggling to cope here, so I've organised a few things with the General to give you time to work things out.'

Sean nodded. 'Thanks.'

'The General has ordered security for both of you, and your family, around the clock.'

Jemma sat up straight, ready to react, but fell silent when Sean firmed his grip, stopping her from pulling away.

'I'll take the Reillys, excluding Pat of course, to the quarantine centre,' said Matt. 'They've arranged a large ground floor unit, suitable for Mrs Reilly, the family and the dogs. You're to take Pat back to the hospital, and settle him in. We'll all meet at the administration centre once we're finished.'

Even though Jemma knew her family was safe, she had to fight an irrational fear that she might lose them again when they left the transporter. As they lifted off again, she concentrated on Pat and, back in the hospital, she remained so focussed on settling him in that she didn't notice Sean leave.

Pat dropped off to sleep quite quickly, but it took her some time before she relaxed enough to give in. She tiptoed to the door and carefully opened and shut it to avoid waking him. A touch on her shoulder made her swing around, hands raised to fend off an attack. She hissed out a breath when she realised it was Hunt. 'For Christ's sake. What do you think you're doing?'

'Sorry, didn't mean to frighten you.' He steered her away from Pat's room. 'Do you remember there was an attack on the school this morning?'

'I might be a bit overwhelmed, but I'm not demented.'

Although he smiled, he clearly didn't plan to be distracted by her sarcasm. 'I'm pleased to hear that. O'Leary and Denis are waiting to report. I'd like you to join us. Bellamy's already there.'

'Where?'

'My office. Let's go. I've got a transporter on the roof.'

'We could walk,' she snapped.

'We could, but we're not going to.'

Realising how tense she'd become, she followed him through the blue light without responding further, then sat quietly using the time to focus and unwind.

'We're here,' said Hunt, and walked with her through the blue light and down on the disc to his office where Zadrus waited, looking serious.

'Good afternoon,' said Zadrus. 'I would like to start as soon as you are ready.'

'We're ready,' said Hunt, pointing to a chair next to Sean for Jemma, while he walked around his desk to his own chair.

'Thank you.' Zadrus turned to Nik. 'Would you please tell us what you know about this Rescue Earth Group, Nikola.'

'Sure.' She took a nervous look at Hunt, then Matt who

nodded to her to go on. 'Matt continued questioning those people who attacked us at the dam. They talked about some aliens who don't belong to the IPL, said these aliens believe the IPL is only interested in collecting and removing Earth's resources and will, in the end, kill off Earth's inhabitants. He asked me to go undercover, find out what I could. They had lots of stories about how the IPL murdered people towards the end of the war and caused irreparable harm.'

Zadrus nodded. 'How did you feel about that?'

'I questioned myself as to whether I could have been deluded into trusting the IPL, but I dismissed that. They had no evidence for their claims, and when I questioned them, they'd become irrational. It was really hard to understand because, on any other topic, they were logical, analytical, and intelligent.'

Zadrus dropped his head back and stared at the ceiling. 'Have they told you the name of the planet?'

'One of them said that it sounded like elephant but that wasn't quite right.'

'Could it have been Ailazant?'

'Possibly, but elephant was the best I could get from them.'

Zadrus's face suggested to Jemma that he wasn't happy with that piece of information, but his next question surprised her. 'Did you join them?'

'Hang on.' Dan jumped up and stood directly in front of Zadrus. 'Nik's not the guilty party here.'

'I am not accusing her of anything,' replied Zadrus, his face softening a little at Dan's protectiveness. 'I am checking how far she's infiltrated.'

'It's okay,' said Nik, urging Dan to sit down. 'I've already told Matt that I joined them when they started telling me about Jemma's family. I thought it was the best way to get information.'

Zadrus nodded. 'Did you know about the school beforehand?'

'I heard about it this morning and reported to Matt straight away. While he was looking for Sean and the General to let them know, Dan and I headed down but, by the time we got there, it'd already happened.'

Zadrus stood for a while, deep in thought. 'Have any of you seen a Zant?'

He was met by quizzical looks.

'My apologies. People from Ailazant are known as Ailazantians, but usually referred to as Zants.'

'No,' said Dan. 'The only aliens I've ever seen are your people.'

'No, I haven't either,' added Nik. 'I only saw humans at their meetings but, there was one occasion when I went on a patrol in one of their crafts that I got a brief glimpse of a figure running past a partly open door. The being was very short, probably no more than a 120 centimetres.'

Dan pulled his chair close to Nik. His face was almost as dark as Zadrus's uniform. 'You didn't tell me you went skylarking on their aircraft.'

'No, I didn't think you'd be happy about it.'

'You're right there.' Dan leaned in close to Nik and ignored everyone else in the room. 'They could have taken you anywhere. Pat saw them murder someone. Were you going to pull the trigger too?'

'Steady.' Hunt stood beside Dan. 'Let Denis tell her story.'

She hesitated before pulling her eyes away from Dan. 'The people I went with weren't murderers. I felt safe. That's the thing. They're only rabid when they talk about the IPL. I don't believe any of them would have been involved with murder. Besides, Pat Reilly described a Norellian sphere. The one I went on was different, more oblong.'

Zadrus nodded. 'That would be a Zant craft.'

Hunt walked back behind his desk. 'Right. Zadrus, who or what are the Zants? Could the craft that attacked the team today have belonged to the Zants?'

'Yes, I am afraid so. From the reports, there were two different types. Sean and Pat saw a Norellian sphere. Matt has also described another, more elongated craft such as the Zants use. It would appear they are helping the Anders rebels.' Zadrus sighed. 'Zants are anti-social beings. They have plagued the IPL for millennia. Whatever we have, they try to steal. Wherever we go, they interfere, often without reason. They are antagonistic to everyone and do not worry about who they harm. They will tell you the IPL attacked their planet in the beginning. There is an element of truth to that, but it only happened because they had attacked several other planets. The IPL launched an offensive to wipe out their weapons facilities. They were heavily involved with the war on Anders Major, so I am not surprised to hear they have teamed up again. They have never needed a reason for their aggression. It is simply their nature. If they are here, they must be stopped.'

He looked at Dan before continuing with Nik, 'Do you feel you could go back to the Zant supporters Nikola, to get more information?'

'No way,' growled Dan. 'It's far too dangerous. She doesn't have the experience or the training for that kind of operation.'

'I beg to differ,' replied Hunt. 'I have been working with her for some time, as you know.'

'That's not the same as experience.' Dan flung his chair aside as he stood. 'We may not have marriage ceremonies here, but as far as I'm concerned, Nik is my wife. I won't have her put in that kind of danger.'

'Steady mate,' said Sean. 'You know how I feel about everything that's happened to Jemma, but if Nik could keep going, she's our best shot at getting information.'

Matt stood to face Dan. 'We don't have anyone else in there, Dan. Hell, we didn't even know they existed until this happened.'

'No, damn it,' yelled Dan. 'The risk is too high.'

'Would anyone care for my opinion?' Nik sat with arms and legs crossed, glaring at Dan.

'Doubt it. Don't forget you're a weak and feeble female,' Jemma murmured. She wasn't unsympathetic to Dan's fears. She knew how much Nik mattered to him, but the attitude that both she and Nik had to be constantly protected some-times went too far.

'That'll do.' Hunt was the only male in the room who

had always seen both herself and Nik as capable of defending themselves, but she groaned as he continued. 'You can both show us that you're not feeble when we get to our next combat training session.'

Sean leaned over Jemma's shoulder and whispered. 'You brought that on yourself.'

She glared back but didn't respond.

'Denis, are you prepared to continue? Shut up O'Leary,' said Hunt, as Dan leaned over his desk.

'Yes sir, I am,' said Nik. 'And yes Dan, I am.'

Dan sat back on his chair, still muttering, 'We're going to do a lot more training then.'

'There is something else,' said Zadrus, but he faltered.

'You need to tell us,' said Hunt. 'We can't fight back if we don't understand what's happening.'

'Yes, you are right.' Zadrus looked at each of them. 'All of you, as well as Pritchard, were born on Anders Major, and you know that he was a prominent figure in the rebel faction. But I suspect you don't know the reason your people had to escape when they did. The Zants had invaded Anders. The rebels subsequently allied themselves with the Zants which is why I believe that Pritchard, probably with the help of modern-day rebels from Anders, has again linked himself with them. If so, they are a very dangerous combination.'

Hunt stared at him with his mouth open. 'We'll meet tomorrow morning. All of us. We'll have to decide now what we do to protect both ourselves and the rest of the community.'

Too tired to take in much more, Jemma took her leave,

while Sean stayed behind for a private discussion with Hunt. Accepting that she had to have her security guards with her now, she called to them. 'Come on Heckle and Jeckle, you can tuck me in.'

Her smile faded when they reached the apartment. The front door was ajar, and papers were strewn across the floor. The sofa had been pushed over, and the bedroom was in a shambles. One of the guards ordered her to stand aside and, with his weapon drawn, went in. The other guard notified his command and remained with her until reinforcements, including Sean, arrived. Jemma stood watching. She couldn't speak, couldn't move, while they combed the apartment for clues to the intruders. Sean whisked her away, to the high security apartments, which were largely occupied by CIG people, leaving others to pack their things.

As they entered the new apartment, she forced herself to focus enough to speak, 'Sean, what's going on?'

He shook his head. 'I wish I knew. I guess we have to accept it's Pritchard.' Standing in front of her, his hands on her shoulders as she started to sob, he drew her into him. A guard was to be stationed outside, and there were regular patrols around the building all night, much more security than for normal residential buildings.

CHAPTER 12

Overnight, Sean remained troubled by Nik's summation of the Rescue Earth Group, even more so now that he knew Pritchard or at least Anders rebels, were involved. But no matter what the Rescue Earth Group claimed, he didn't believe that the IPL had an ulterior motive. They could have left Jemma to die in Costa Rica, and they didn't. They could leave everyone in the new settlement to die, but he was confident they wouldn't. The problem was he had no concrete evidence to justify his trust. Unable to rid his mind of the niggling doubts, he approached his boss before the morning workout.

'I know,' said Hunt. 'I've had the same thoughts myself, but I've seen no sign of ill intent. None of us would be alive without them. We're going to have to put our faith in Denis to find out.'

'Yeah, I agree,' said Sean. 'I'm not happy about putting her at that kind of risk, although I won't say that to Dan, but I can't see any other way.'

'No, and I understand his fear, but we've got to stand back from it,' said Hunt. 'Denis is very capable. She knows the risks and she's determined to go ahead. Mind you, I suspect some of that determination is in direct response to O'Leary's attempts to stop her.'

'Probably.' Sean smiled. 'A bit like Jemma. My problem is that we don't really have any idea of the risks. She's our best hope, so I'll get her to organise a meeting with her contacts as soon as we've finished training.'

No one seemed able to settle that morning, so Sean gave up and headed the group to his office. Matt had already organised the equipment to listen in, which he quickly activated. When Sean was satisfied that they were all ready, he gave Nik the signal to contact Caroline, the woman who'd introduced her to the Rescue Earth Group.

'The school was meant to be a statement,' said Caroline. 'We wanted publicity so we could reveal ourselves to the world and warn the IPL to leave peacefully. No one was supposed to be hurt, but when the IPL thugs arrived, and the press was silenced, it wasn't safe to reveal ourselves.'

'Okay,' said Nik, shrugging her shoulders at Sean.

'Will you be free to join us at our next meeting? It's in two weeks.'

'Yeah sure. Let me know where,' said Nik, when Sean signalled to her to end the call. 'Talk to you soon.'

'*Silence the press?*' said Sean, staring at Nik. 'No one would stop the press from doing anything. They were all reporters before the war ended. They know their job. None of them would be *silenced*.'

'No, it's crazy.'

'Alright,' said Sean, not at all sure what to make of the conversation. 'Let's go to our combat session.'

Hunt listened as Sean filled him in, then he nodded and

turned to address the group. 'Denis, you're with me. It's time for you to move to the next level. Bellamy, take Matt. You can step up now too, Matt.'

Sean smiled at Matt's grimace. Dan had already started working with Jemma. He appeared to be taking his temper out on her, but she was more than keeping up with him. Sean bent down, ostensibly to adjust his boots, but mainly to hide his grin, as the others groaned. Matt struggled more than anyone else, and Sean quietly arranged to meet with him later to come up with a plan to bring him up to speed. For the moment though, Nik had to be the focus.

Hunt spent the next two weeks raising his demands and pushing everyone to their limits, although he focussed mostly on Nik.

Sean found himself damping down the grumbles, but he also had to work hard physically, and was relieved when the day of the meeting finally came around. He called Nik, on her own, to his office to ensure she was prepared. Impressed by how calm she appeared, he led her to the conference room to meet with Hunt and the rest of the team, and for Zadrus to explain the equipment they'd have available to them.

'I have attached a tracking electrode to Nikola's belt,' said Zadrus. 'It is too small to be detected. Some of you have permanent tracking devices and we should, I feel, fit all of you with them later. I will organise hearing pieces before you leave.'

'Thank you,' said Hunt. 'Denis, there is no room here for any maverick behaviour. You will obey any orders you are given through your hearing piece. Bellamy and I can both speak to you. If anyone else sees anything that you need to know, one of us will pass it on. Do not take risks. If you feel unsafe, get out of there.'

'Yes, sir. I've no intention of being a hero, but I'll do my best to get information.'

Dan stood behind her and buried his face in her hair. 'Take care.'

'I will. Stop worrying. I'm looking forward to the party you're going to throw for me tonight.'

'I love you,' he whispered. 'And I'm going to be close by.'

Sean was concerned that all the fuss might overwhelm Nik, but she seemed to be holding it together very well, and at the allotted time of 3 p.m., he told her to head out. Matt followed a couple of minutes later, then Dan and finally himself. Zadrus, Jemma and Hunt watched from a small room where Jemma had taken charge of the monitoring system. Security nodes, too small to be noticed unless you knew they were there, had been installed into every building by the aliens. Jemma worked on activating them so that they had both vision and sound.

The meeting room was well within walking distance, but Sean insisted that Nik call a transporter and stay in the vicinity of other people at all times. When she jumped off at the building where the meeting was to be held, Matt, who had been in the same transporter, followed. Sean and Dan weren't far behind, alighting together then separating so both had a good view of her. Sean saw Caroline first. He whispered into his speaker while Dan, who had a camera attached to his shirt, transmitted a close-up view of the woman to Jemma. Sean stayed a few metres behind Nik, but Dan continued on so that he was a similar distance in front of Nik. Matt took up a position outside the building and gazed around, as though waiting for someone.

'There are two very small beings at the front of the meeting room,' said Sean. 'I haven't seen anything like them before. Both are about 120 centimetres in height, large heads compared to the rest of their bodies. They've got long, spindly arms. The hands extend well below their knees. Their legs are long, too, but their trunks are very small. Most striking feature is the eyes, large, black and penetrating. Big ears, flattened backwards, noses and mouths are very small. One of them seems to be speaking, but his mouth is barely moving.' They were quite different from the Sidlowns who, despite being large, seemed a lot more human than these beings.

'Caroline,' Nik whispered, so low that Sean could just hear. 'Who are they?'

'A group of aliens who want to help us fight off the invaders.' Caroline spoke with a religious type of fervour which worried Sean.

'Sir,' said Sean. 'Don't think we can leave Nik there much longer. Too dangerous.'

'Not yet,' replied Hunt. 'Stay close. I've already sent more CIG staff in to back you up if you need to extract.'

Nik spoke again. 'Caroline, they look very different from the aliens we've seen before.'

'They're a different race. From a planet called Ailazant. Don't worry, they're trying very hard to help.'

Sean heard Hunt order Nik, through her earpiece, to stop asking questions, just before a hush came over the room. The alien who appeared to be in charge held up a hand, and the crowd responded with total silence.

The being introduced himself as Landi and began. 'I must thank everyone for attending today. It gives me great hope for the future fight we must have to regain your freedom.'

'Jesus,' muttered Sean. Landi's voice was whiney, smarmy, but the humans in the room seemed entranced. 'Is this being recorded? Everyone needs to see this.'

'I've got it,' replied Jemma.

Landi continued. 'We must agree on our next target. The best way to cause havoc would be to contaminate the water supply. We propose to use a poison that will make the water taste bad, but not harm anyone. The IPL efforts will be directed to cleaning the water supply, while we proceed to take over the Administration building.'

Most people in the room clapped as if he'd just announced the second coming.

'I will leave you now for your leaders to organise the details,' said Landi.

'Denis,' said Hunt, 'agree with anything they ask of you, then get out as soon as you can.'

'Jemma, quickly,' exclaimed Sean. 'Zoom in on the humans standing behind the speakers. The one in the middle, around a hundred and eighty centimetres, dark hair, supercilious smile.'

Jemma did as Sean asked, then cried out, 'Oh God. It isn't. Is it?'

'Yeah,' replied Sean. 'It bloody well is. Pritchard. And his goons. There's no doubt now. He's here, and the bastard's working with the Zants. Alright, I'm getting Nik out.'

Nik was already responding to Hunt's orders. She told Caroline that she was prepared to assist with anything she could, and was allocated a security role, to stop anyone coming near the dam when the poison was being delivered. She said her goodbyes and turned towards the transporter bay.

'I'll be in touch with the date and times,' said Caroline.

'Alright Nik, keep going, quickly,' said Sean, through his speaker.

'Don't look back, Denis,' said Hunt. 'I've ordered the rest of the CIG team to go after Pritchard. The rest of you follow Denis.'

Nik turned and ran to the transporter, jumped on board, and almost fell into a seat at the front. Sean jumped in after her and sat behind. He let out a breath, ready to relax, until he heard someone shout.

'Are you going to the admin building?'

'Yes,' said the pilot.

A man jumped on the craft and sat opposite Nik. 'I need a coffee. How about you?'

'No, I really need to hit the sack,' said Nik. 'I'm up early tomorrow.'

But the fellow was insistent. 'You need a few minutes to relax.' He extended his hand. 'I'm Manuel Perero.'

Sean heard Matt curse. 'Sean, use your speaker to tell Nik to be careful. He's one of ours. Tell her to stay where there are plenty of people. We've got to get to her quickly.'

Nik put her head down as though she was really tired so she could listen to Sean, then turned back to Manuel. 'Alright, but it has to be a quick coffee.'

When they landed, she walked in the direction of the main staff dining room. Manuel suggested a quieter coffee shop, but Nik shook her head and kept walking. Sean walked in, not far behind, and sat on the other side of the room. Dan joined him within seconds.

Still through their earpieces, they heard Manuel say, 'I won't beat around the bush. You look like someone who can take care of yourself, so I'm going to ask you to take a bigger role. We need someone to take the poison to the dam. You'll have escorts, but we still need someone competent holding the poison. Would you be prepared to do that?'

'Well, I can't see any reason not to,' she said. 'Are you worried about ambush, or people within the organisation?'

'Both,' was the response. 'I'll contact you next week to go through the details.'

'Okay.' Nik stood and walked out of the dining room. 'Shit, Perero's following,' she muttered.

'We're right behind,' said Sean. 'Get ready for an intercept.'

'Hey Nik,' said Jemma, walking past from the other direction. 'There's a big meeting in the conference room. Coming?'

Hunt was speaking to someone on his communicator when they arrived, and his voice was tense.

Jemma walked up to him, hands on hips, and glaring. 'Damn it,' she said, as soon as he'd finished. 'Pritchard. Again. Have they got him?'

'No,' he snapped, as he closed his communicator.

'This time we've got to fight back,' said Jemma. 'I'm not going to sit back and wait for him to attack again.'

'Agreed,' replied Hunt. 'These Zants are a problem too. We need Zadrus's input. We're no longer on a level playing field.'

'And we have another problem,' said Sean, joining them. 'Manuel's one of Matt's staff, a CIG officer, so we also have to work out to what extent these bastards have infiltrated CIG.'

Jemma gaped at him. 'You've got to be joking.'

'I wish I were,' said Sean, questions running through his mind now about Matt, although it was Matt who'd alerted him to Manuel's CIG status. Surely, he wouldn't have done that if he was part of this damned group.

'Did Pritchard see any of you?' said Hunt.

'I don't believe so,' said Sean. 'But if some of his cronies were in that meeting, any of us might have been seen. Maybe the reason we haven't been able to identify some of the attendees, or the fellows that attacked Nik and Jemma at the dam, is because they're Pritchard's people.'

'Or people from the modern Anders,' said Dan.

'Yeah, or that.' Sean turned back to Hunt. 'We've got to find a way to work it out.'

Nodding, Hunt turned on a large screen at the front of the room and told it to take notes, then turned back to the group.

'This is bigger than we'd thought. We need to put together what we know. Matt, you have a history with Manuel. Have you seen any evidence of treachery or insanity?'

'I know him well,' replied Matt. 'He's not insane, and until I heard that conversation, I'd have trusted him with my life.'

'Track his most recent jobs, interview the people he's worked with,' said Hunt. 'See if you can get any clues. O'Leary can help you. We need to proceed at speed. Denis, keep talking to Caroline. Bellamy put Pritchard's image out there and try to find him.'

Everyone looked up when an urgent alert on Jemma's communicator interrupted them. 'Mr Reilly's in trouble,' said a nurse. 'I went in to check on him. His oxygen had been turned off, and his medication list altered.'

Matt then had an urgent alert from the security officers stationed in quarantine. Someone had invaded the Reilly's flats. They, fortunately, hadn't been there at the time. They'd been visiting the centre's nurse for their routine checks and had stopped at the cafeteria for a meal.

Hunt flew into action. 'Bellamy, issue a general alert. I want all available staff called in. Matt, O'Leary, go to the Quarantine Centre. Bellamy, Jemma, Denis, with me to the hospital.'

*　　*　　*

Jemma clung to Sean when she found Pat, pale and struggling to breathe, sitting on the edge of his hospital bed. She could smell his fear, yet there was little more she could do than pray that he'd pull through. Nik showed her Pat's electronic chart which was about the size of a small tablet computer from her era. She cursed when she saw his vitals, oxygen saturation way too low, carbon dioxide far too high.

'I've turned up his oxygen,' said the doctor. 'I can't leave it there for too long though, it'll increase his carbon dioxide and that could be fatal. Hopefully, the drugs will kick in, so we don't have to ventilate.'

Jemma's breath caught. She remembered how hard it had been for her when she was ventilated after the bushfire, and she wasn't convinced that Pat would have the strength to cope with it.

Pat made a strangled sound and lifted his hand to attract her attention.

Jemma flew to his side. 'Do you need something?'

'Feeling a bit better,' he whispered, although the wheeze made it hard to understand. 'Don't worry.'

'Pat, can you tell us what happened?' said Sean, gently easing in between them.

'A nurse told me I had to try breathing for myself,' he said, his words constantly interrupted by his need to take a breath. 'He turned the oxygen off.'

'Any idea who the nurse was,' Sean demanded, looking up at the staff.

'No,' said the doctor. 'In fact, all the nurses on roster tonight are female which is unusual in itself. This nurse was male, so I know he wasn't one of ours. But he did have some medical knowledge. The medication he placed in Mr Reilly's cupboard was a sleeping pill, which might seem innocuous, but given Mr Reilly's condition, it could have been lethal.'

Matt muttered, 'Manuel was a nurse in the Army before he joined us after the war. Can you remember what he looked like, Pat?'

'Where the hell's the security guard?' snapped Hunt, as he raced into the room.

'On it,' called Matt.

Pat looked surprised, 'I last saw him around ten minutes before the nurse arrived.'

'Sir, over here.' Matt was in an empty room across the hall. He'd removed a gag from the guard and was pulling bindings from his hands and feet. 'This is Sergeant Richard Li. He felt something sharp against his arm, and that's the last he remembers until he woke in this room.'

'Okay, listen up,' said Hunt. 'Have two security guards around the clock with Mr Reilly and another two with his family. Jemma, Denis, stay with Sergeant Li until he's fully roused and can give a description of his attacker. This facility is now in lock down. No one in or out without clearance. Is that understood? Everyone else with me.'

When the doctor muttered something about a police state, Hunt apologised but he remained firm. 'The situation is now so grave we have no other option.'

'It's just not enough,' snapped Jemma, glaring at Hunt. 'We need to know what's going on. First, it's our apartment. Now, it's the Reillys' rooms. Pat is Pritchard's grandson for

God's sake. Why would he put his grandson's life at risk? None of this is making any sense.'

'No, it isn't,' replied Hunt. 'He's obviously targeted Pat, and just as importantly Pat's mother, to get to you. We just have to keep trying to find him and shut him down.'

Swearing, she turned her back on Hunt and squatted beside Li, doing her best to reassure him. If Pritchard was prepared to put his grandson and his daughter at risk just to get to her, how could they predict what he'd do next. 'Can I get you anything?' she said to Li.

He shook his head. 'Give me a minute. I've just got to clear my head. I heard what the General said.'

She let him rest for a few minutes, then quietly began to question him. When he was finally able to give a description of his attacker, it jelled with Manuel.

'Matt,' she said, into her communicator.

'Yeah mate.'

'He's described Manuel.'

'Okay, I thought he would. We've found Manuel. He's been taken to the Administration building. You'd better join us here.'

She left Li with the medical staff, grabbed Nik, and headed out. Manuel, shackled to a chair, cheerily greeted her as she walked into the room, and spoke to Nik as if they were old friends on any normal day in the office, yet, as soon as Sean mentioned the Rescue Earth Group to him, he stopped talking, his eyes glazed over, and his face became expression-less. He seemed utterly confident that he was on the righteous path. He couldn't explain why he thought that, or even why he had joined them in the first place.

Jemma fell asleep on a couch as Sean, Matt and Dan, with Zadrus, continued through the night questioning Manuel. She jumped when Hunt called everyone to order.

'Everyone here?' said Sean, looking more tired than Jemma could remember ever seeing him.

'Go ahead,' said Hunt.

'Manuel claims that the Zants set up a higher-level operation to ensure the success of their operations. They recruited several CIG operatives. Manuel doesn't know how many, and he doesn't have names. There were never face to face discussions between them, and he couldn't identify anyone. I believe him to be telling the truth. Zadrus has tested him, and he agrees with me.'

'So, how are they getting people to join them?' said Jemma. 'And what do we do now?'

Zadrus shook his head. 'I don't know yet. I will work with Manuel and try to deprogram him. First, I must work out how he was initially programmed. The Zants have numerous techniques, so it may be slow. For the moment, I will keep him isolated. I do not believe he can be of any further use to this investigation.'

'We're all fatigued,' said Jemma. 'I'd appreciate a rest break, and I think others are worse than me. Could we please adjourn and meet back early afternoon?'

'I agree,' said Sean, with a sigh. 'You go. I'll round up with the General, and then follow you. Take a transporter. I know it's not far, but it'll be safer.'

She was past arguing about the security guards who followed her when she headed for the transporter with Nik, and she wasn't aware that Dan had followed, until he put his hand on her shoulder, to tell her to stand back while he checked inside the craft. Two CIG guards stood by the pilot. Dan nodded to them and ushered her in. The guards stared at her without uttering a word. She'd started to move into a seat when she saw Dan and her security contingent moving towards the front of the craft, their weapons drawn. Instantly alert, despite her tiredness, she heard a scuffle and then watched helplessly as Dan and the guards walked back, their arms outstretched.

'Sit down and shut up,' said a man, his weapon aimed at Dan's head.

When Dan reached her, he pointed out the window.

'Oh my God, Dan. We're heading away from the settlement. We'll be out of Earth's atmosphere soon.' She grabbed his arm. 'We've got to stop them.' She pulled her communicator off her belt, but it didn't light up.

Dan was shaking his communicator, then shook his head. 'They've blocked them somehow,' he muttered.

She jumped up. 'We've got to do something.'

The men shifted their weapons to aim them directly at Jemma.

Dan, gripping both her arms, pulled her back down. 'Stay calm. Those are rifles, not alien weapons. He looked up at the man with the rifle. 'Jeremy, please explain what's going on? You belong to CIG. What are you doing here?'

'It's time to expose the IPL and we can only do that through the Rescue Earth Group,' responded Jeremy, tersely.

'What's wrong with the IPL?' said Jemma.

'Don't be so naïve,' he snarled. 'Enough chatter. We're nearly there.'

'How the hell are the Zants manipulating these people?' she whispered to Dan. 'He clearly has no idea why he's doing this.'

'You're right. Hopefully, we'll get some answers soon.'

She looked back through the window and gasped. A massive spaceship loomed above, similar in size to the IPL ship which had brought them here in the first place, but more oblong in construction, and not quite as tall. The external walls of IPL ships were very smooth with evenly spaced windows and exits and were always a consistent colour, a deep greenish-grey. This ship, on the other hand, had a rough appearance to the external shell, the windows randomly placed, differing between floors, and the colour, while mostly a dark grey, varied from the top to the bottom.

"Christ almighty, Dan. It has to be a Zant ship. We can't allow ourselves to be taken onto that.'

'Don't think we've got much choice. See what happens when the transporter docks.'

'What the hell,' exclaimed Jemma, when she saw Caroline waiting for them in the landing bay, but she fell silent when Dan shook his head at her.

'Well, it looks like you win Nik,' said Dan. 'Now that you're back with your friends, you won't have any more use for us.'

Nik gave a barely perceptible nod in Dan's direction.

Caroline ran to Nik. 'Are you alright?'

'Yes, I'm fine.'

She motioned to Jeremy. 'Take the rest of them to the holding bay.' Her voice softened. 'Nik, you come with me.'

'Are you sure they won't be hurt,' said Nik. 'They're all innocent victims, just like we were.'

'No, no, we're trying to rescue people, not harm them.'

When Jemma was pushed roughly towards a nearby room, one of her security people attempted to protect her, but he was quickly overpowered. The walls were seamless, once the door had shut, not even a clear division between them and the ceiling. There was something that appeared to be a window, but given they were in space it probably wasn't and, even if it were, it wouldn't be a useful escape route. Worse, their captors were trained CIG operatives. Overpowering them was unlikely.

Roger, one of Jemma's guards, a strong, muscled man of African heritage, tapped each of them on the shoulder, and indicated to cease talking. He pointed to a small, square object on the wall, which she suspected was a listening device. Dan, Roger and Kurt, her other guard, used a kind of sign language with each other to plan their attack when they had their chance. Jemma tried to glean some idea of their plans so she could find a way to assist.

*   *   *

When Sean was alerted that the transporter carrying Jemma

had gone off course, he dashed to the control room on the top level of the Administration building. The measures in place to prevent unauthorised entry to this room were tight and, although he understood the need, the delay to gain access in the emergency was more than frustrating. First, a security-pass to enter, then his ID tag, which contained a magnetic key to open the door to a small secure chamber, then the bead, and finally, a spoken password which had to recognise his voice, before he could get through to the inner control room. Failure at any stage set off a security alert.

'What's the problem?' he yelled, when he finally broke through into the room.

'Sir, look at the screen. Dr Anderson's craft is heading upwards. It's already beyond our atmosphere.' Despite the distance, he could see every detail of the transporter, from its navigation lights to its windows and doors.

'Jesus,' gasped Sean. He'd only ordered the transporter to ensure the women's safety. Now they were gone, and he had no clue what to do about it. Although he was grateful that Dan was with them, he knew that there was no way any of them would have agreed to a detour like this. His brain refused to function. He called Hunt.

'Shit,' said Hunt. 'Have you tried contacting them?'

'Of course. No response. Their personal communicators should still be in range. But nothing.'

'Alright, on my way. Contact Zadrus.'

Hunt and Matt ran in together. They stood beside Sean and they too, stared at the craft, which was still travelling vertically, and had just picked up speed. All three men stared helplessly at the screen.

'What is the problem?' said Zadrus, as he also entered the room.

'The transporter carrying Jemma, Denis and O'Leary has left our atmosphere,' said Hunt. 'We've been unable to make contact.'

Sean asked the operator to zoom out from the image on the screen so he could see if there were any large crafts in the vicinity to which they might be heading, but still nothing. 'Do you think a Zant ship could be so close by?'

'Perhaps,' replied Zadrus. 'European command has been tracking a Zant craft in the Northern Hemisphere. It would not take much for it to have moved closer to us.'

'Right,' said Hunt, striding to the large conference table in the centre of the room. Despite the look of horror on his face, his voice was loud and firm. 'Everyone over here, now. Zadrus, can we project that image onto the wall and make it larger, so we can see whatever is out there?'

'Certainly,' replied Zadrus, ordering central control to shift the image. He then joined them at the conference table.

'Listen up,' said Hunt. 'We must assume our guards and pilots have been overpowered. Zadrus, should we send a crew out after them? I need your advice.'

'I doubt there is much point, yet,' said Zadrus. 'The hijacked transporter has too much start.'

'Sir,' said Matt. 'Look at this.' There's a larger craft. The transporter's about to dock on it.'

'By all the stars,' muttered Zadrus. 'Zants. That answers our question. Even if we could get a craft there quickly, there is little we could do. We would not be able to dock on their ship, and we could not fire on it, as our own people are on board.'

'I agree.' Werrimen's voice made Sean jump. She moved so damn quietly he hadn't realised she'd joined them. 'Has anyone in the IPL had recent contact with the Zants? We will need a communication channel to make it clear to them that we know what they're up to.'

'I spoke to European command a couple of minutes ago and they are working on it now,' said Zadrus.

'Good,' said Werrimen. 'I have been informed there is an IPL ship not far off. I will have them change direction and investigate. That will be quicker than sending out a transporter, but of course, you are right, Zadrus, it will be purely for surveillance. Still, making ourselves seen will be useful.'

Sean was fascinated at how Werrimen had quietly taken charge, and Zadrus had moved aside to let her, but he didn't have time to dwell on it.

'Right,' said Hunt. 'We've got seven people up there, Jemma, Nik, Dan, two guards, two pilots, and potentially others. Am I correct?'

'Yes sir, I've checked,' said Sean. 'The guards are Kurt and Roger, both of whom are well known to Matt.'

'They are, sir,' said Matt. 'And, like Manuel, I'd have trusted them with my life.'

'Understood. We can't afford to trust anyone at the moment. What about the pilots?'

'I've asked for those names. I spoke to the guards just before they left. If they've been turned, they're bloody good actors. Matt can you ask around to see if the pilots or the guards have been behaving differently?'

'On it.'

'You will stay close to me, Sean,' said Werrimen softly, so only he could hear. 'We do not know what is about to happen. We must work together.'

'I know.' Sean wanted to argue. In fact, he wanted to find the perpetrator and punch his lights out. But he would maintain control and didn't believe he needed a babysitter.

'At the moment, my judgement is better than yours,' said Werrimen. 'If we receive bad news, I will handle it, not you.'

'Fine,' he replied. He couldn't, no wouldn't, contemplate something happening to Jemma, but he had to stay occupied. Immersing himself in the search would be his best approach. And, if something did happen, he'd decide at the time who would handle it.

'I should have anticipated this kind of action,' said Zadrus, with a sigh. 'The Zants will see our people as rich prizes. I do not think they will do them any serious physical harm because they know our reaction, and that of the rest of the IPL, would be aggressive and swift. I think they will be like Manuel when they return. But, if Pritchard is with them, they may not come back.'

'Forget about who's to blame,' snapped Hunt. 'Forget about worst case scenarios, I need to know what we can do to get my people back.'

Zadrus shook his head. 'I cannot be sure. The Zants are masters of manipulation.'

'I might have a clue,' said Matt, as he returned. 'I've just been told that one of my people was found outside the city about an hour ago. He was dazed but coherent. He said he was forced into a Zant craft along with several other people.'

'Can he name the others?' said Sean.

'I believe so,' replied Matt. 'Apparently they all lost consciousness and, when they came around, the people he was with were carrying on about the evil IPL, and how they needed the Zants to help them. His memory from then until he was dropped back in the field is hazy. He was disoriented, so he called for help.'

Zadrus frowned. 'That gives me a few ideas about what they might be doing. Get a list of names of those who were with him, then bring this man, and Manuel, to the Medical Centre. Round up everyone he names and bring them in to me also. Werrimen will work with you here.'

Sean passed on the directions through his communicator, then looked at Matt. 'Anything else?'

'Yeah, there is. They were instructed to assemble at the uniform factory, at 2 p.m. tomorrow. He didn't have any more information, but they were specifically told to ignore evacuation orders from the IPL once they were inside. Their ultimate plan is apparently to take over the Administration building.'

Sean checked on the map and looked to Werrimen. 'I think it's the only factory with direct line of sight to the Administration building. Am I right?'

'You are,' replied Hunt. 'I'm not sure what advantage that gives them, unless they plan to bring the factory people to the Administration building, once they have control.'

'Maybe,' said Werrimen. 'When it comes to the Zants, don't assume anything. We will have to be ready for whatever they plan.'

'Right, then we need to organise quickly,' said Hunt. 'Bellamy, stay here and help me coordinate the search for Jemma.'

Christ, another babysitter. Before he could retort, Hunt ordered Matt to bring all CIG operatives in, and secure them within the Administration building, until they could be checked and cleared.

Accepting that he was stuck in the control room with Hunt and Werrimen, Sean assisted Matt to contact the CIG staff. Excluding those with Jemma and Nik, they found all but three officers. When Matt contacted the wife of one of them, she said she thought he was at work. He was the first to be written onto Sean's suspicious list. Since no one had seen the other two, they were also written onto the list.

Matt had every remaining CIG officer brought into the control room, one-by-one. Sean helped him question them and, as the night progressed, they identified three more for the suspicious list. They'd now listed two pilots and eleven operatives, including Manuel, then the man who they'd found wandering and those who were with him. Sean reluctantly told him to add Dan, Nik, Jemma and her two guards to the list.

Hunt gave him a sharp look, then nodded. Eighteen people under the control of the Zants was far too significant and, despite their questioning, Sean realised he couldn't be certain that the ones they'd cleared were genuinely safe. They might just be smarter than the others.

CHAPTER 13

As the hours ticked by in the Zant spaceship, Jemma began to fear the worst. Dan and her two guards did their best to reassure her that the fact they'd been left alone and unharmed was a good sign, but she didn't feel particularly comforted. Finally, a door opened, and Nik and Caroline were pushed into the room. She wanted to run to Nik who looked distressed, but Dan held her back. Now that she realised his attitude to Nik was all an act, she didn't argue.

'What?' snapped Dan. 'Have you come back to gloat?'

'They've asked us to speak to you, to explain their plans to rescue Earth from the IPL. Would you please listen?' Nik had her fingers crossed in front of her chest as she spoke, and again, Jemma saw an almost imperceptible nod pass between her and Dan. Caroline stood beside her and looked smaller to Jemma than she had earlier.

Dan put his hand up to stop an angry outburst from Kurt. 'Yes, we're prepared to listen, but you'd better be convincing.'

Caroline stepped forward. When she began, her voice was almost a whisper. 'When we arrived in the East Australian settlement it was rough, no buildings, and fences everywhere to stop us escaping. Thousands of us were crammed into tiny quarters. We had the clothes we stood up in. Water and food were strictly rationed, and we were starving, dirty and frightened. Many of our people died, some of my closest friends.' A sob escaped and she had to pause. 'We had no contact with the outside world. We didn't even know if there was an outside world.

'Our only shelter was tarpaulins strung over poles. Toilets were pits, no showers. We were given a ration of water each morning and had to make it last the whole day. Most of the time, we just sat under the shelters and had nothing to do until building started for the first living quarters which were essentially Army huts. Some people worked on furniture, others to make clothes, and a few on the plumbing. It was hard work, but when the huts were finished, and we were able to move inside, we felt a bit better. The Sidlowns cleansed and purified the water, so we finally had some running water.

'Once we started building the permanent structures,' we walked between the camp and the building sites each morning and night. That's when the Zants approached us. They took us on board their craft and explained the IPL's history of aggression, just like they'd caused on Earth. I was so exhausted, I passed out as they were talking to me. A Zant caught me as I fell. The others who were with me, all had the same experience. The Zants were so caring. They invited us to join the Rescue Earth Group, and we were so impressed with them that we did and, even though living standards have improved, I can't just conveniently forget the atrocities I saw. So, I'm here to ask you to listen to us, and to the Zants, and to approach what we have to say with an open mind.'

Kurt stepped forward. 'Dan, Jemma, Nik, you weren't here at that time, but I was, and I'm shocked by Caroline's interpretation of what happened. I'd have died without the IPL's help. Many people did, from injuries or the lack of food and water. The IPL begged Earth's governments to change. They repeatedly warned they'd have to mount an offensive to shut down the terrorists. When they did act, it was swift and devastating. They did their best to minimise harm to innocent people and to locate the injured and help them.

'Fences were there to define the safe area, not to keep us in, and the IPL worked incredibly hard to get enough food and clean water. They were scrupulous in their rationing so everyone, including themselves, had an even share of the available water. They took the same approach with the food.'

'I know they worked hard to get things running,' said Caroline. 'But the truth is they caused the devastation in the first place.'

'But,' said Roger, 'did you not read of the extent to which they tried to avoid aggression? It was in the newspapers for a long time before they acted.'

'They should have found another way,' she replied with a defiant tilt of her head.

'Caroline, may I ask you a question?' Jemma interjected quietly.

'Of course.'

'When you passed out, had they given you anything to eat or drink?'

'They may have. I don't remember. We were so exhausted.'

'I don't understand your question Jemma,' said Dan.

'You can faint from extreme dehydration as your blood pressure drops. But it's extremely unlikely they would all have been equally dehydrated at exactly the same moment. Something was done to manipulate these people, chemicals in water or food, or something else to induce the faint. That would explain how the Zants were there ready to catch the people as they fainted.'

'Good point,' said Dan.

'They helped,' said Caroline angrily. 'They would never hurt us.'

Before Jemma could continue, a door opened. She hadn't seen a Zant in person before and was surprised by their small size and frailty, but they were all armed with a long stick-like weapon. There was no aggression as they asked the group to follow them, but she had no doubt the aliens would use their weapons if provoked. They walked along a corridor to a large conference room. Landi waited there to greet them.

He pointed to some seats arranged around a large table. 'I would like to help you understand why we are trying to resist the IPL.' He smiled, in a way that made Jemma shiver. 'Around five centuries ago, Earth time, the IPL attacked my planet. They did not leave enough of the planet's surface viable to enable anyone to re-inhabit. Since then, we have followed them around the galaxy, trying to show people how to resist them. I would like to show you some footage of the devasta-tion on Earth for those of you who weren't here to see what happened, to show you what Caroline saw, and help you understand the IPL's motives.'

They watched the film for almost an hour and Landi con-tinued to smile throughout. Jemma sensed that Dan and the others shared her discomfort but, as they focussed on each other, they failed to notice Zants had walked up behind each of them. It was too late to resist when she felt alien hands on their shoulders, and she passed out. When she recovered, she was in a reclining lounge chair and was offered a hot sweet drink, which she gratefully accepted. Landi, and the other Zants, checked each of them, offering blankets and ensuring they were comfortable. He asked if the film had made them realise the need for the Rescue Earth Group. They all, except Nik, agreed, expressing shock that they hadn't seen through the IPL before. Jemma was puzzled as to why Nik stood at the side of the room with a fixed smile on her face.

'I'm so pleased you understand why we are concerned,' said Landi. 'We will keep in touch over the next few weeks. My staff will now show you to a private transit lounge while I organise your transport home.'

Once they were settled in the lounge, Caroline was the first to speak. 'Now do you see why we feel we have to resist the IPL? They've caused so much death and destruction.'

All nodded, and even Kurt wondered aloud why he hadn't realised it before. He'd seen all the hard conditions and the suffering but had never questioned it. Nik murmured quiet agreement, but a puzzled look on her face made Jemma ask what was wrong.

'Oh, nothing, I was just thinking about all we'd been through, then I thought about all the reports I have to catch up on. It just all seems a bit daunting.'

They accepted her response, but Jemma wasn't convinced. She'd sit quietly and wait until they'd landed back on Earth, then ask again.

*   *   *

Sean and Matt had just finished questioning the CIG people when Zadrus returned with a small silver bar in a container. 'My apologies this has taken so long. I had to be sure. You will find one of these located in the neck of any person who has been manipulated by the Zants. This one, from the man you found wandering this morning, is faulty. Although I have never known the Zants to make this kind of mistake, it is most fortuitous for us.'

'Jesus,' said Sean and Matt in unison.

Zadrus smiled. 'Indeed. This tool will enable you to locate the devices. Come with me and I will show you how to use it.' It was a small box around five centimetres square and one centimetre deep. Held over one of the silver objects, it emitted a loud, high-pitched, screeching noise.

Sean checked Hunt and Matt under Zadrus's guidance, then Matt checked him. Once they were sure of how to work it, Matt had each of the CIG operatives brought back to the control room. Sean ran the device over individuals they had considered suspicious first and all were affected. Of the others, one who they'd previously cleared also had a bar. Zadrus recommended at least an eight-hour rest following the removal of the devices as he expected the victims to be fatigued.

After they'd finished, Werrimen called Sean to join her at the tracking screen. Hunt stood with them as she explained the IPL patrol had reported that a small craft had separated from the Zant ship and was on a trajectory back to Earth. She worked on the screen until a Zant transporter came into view, then began to track its descent. Half a kilometre above the ground, it suddenly disappeared from the screen. 'By the stars,' she muttered. 'They've cloaked.'

'What do you mean?' said Sean, grabbing her arm. 'Where the hell are they?'

'Stay calm,' she replied. 'They've established a shield to stop us from seeing them. I will extrapolate from their trajectory prior to the cloaking and map out a potential landing zone.'

Her map covered an area that was far too big to check from the ground, so Sean began to organise transporters until he was interrupted by a voice on his communicator.

Nik, tears streaming down her face, cried, 'Sean, help me.'

'I have your location Nik. We know what's happened. We're on our way.'

'They're all acting weird. I don't know how the Zants affected them, but it didn't work with me. Please hurry.'

'I know mate. We'll be there in a few minutes. Keep your communicator channel open. It gives me your coordinates.'

He rushed, with Matt and Zadrus, to the closest transporter, along with several security staff. He wasn't sure how many and didn't care. He wanted to be up and moving.

'The Zants did something to them,' continued Nik. 'Afterwards, they acted like they were looking after us, comfortable chairs, hot drinks, blankets to keep us warm. I pretended to go along. Landi smiled at me as we headed back into our transporter, like he knew it hadn't worked with me. He gave me the shivers, but I didn't care. All I could think about was getting home. Sean, they went crazy. Carrying on about how the IPL attacked Earth, trying to destroy it. I pretended to fall as I got out of their transporter, acted like I'd sprained my ankle. I didn't expect them to buy it, but they did. They just walked off, even Jemma and Dan. There's something really wrong with them.'

'Okay Nik,' said Sean. 'We're nearly there. Stay calm. We'll sort them out. Do you …'

Suddenly, Dan's voice interrupted them, resounding through the communicator. 'I came back because I was worried about you, Nik. You've called them. Don't you understand they're our enemy? I thought you loved me, thought you trusted me.'

'I do love you,' said Nik. 'I was talking to your brother.'

'No brother of mine. He's in bed with the enemy.'

'Oh shit. We need to hurry,' said Sean. Less than a minute later, they landed, and Sean jumped out through the blue light. He ran to Nik, ordering Dan, who was standing over her, his face taut with anger, to get on the ground. Although the others hadn't returned yet, Sean was sure they would, particularly when they saw the IPL craft. Dan flicked his eyes towards Sean, allowing Nik the split second she needed to break away. She ran to Sean, waving her arms. Jemma charged between the two men and Sean realised he'd have to be firm with her, although he had no idea how she'd react. He pushed Nik towards Zadrus and took hold of Jemma's arm. 'Come with me. You're safe now.'

'No, Sean,' she said. 'They're dangerous. The IPL want to kill us. You've got to talk to Landi. He knows what's going on. He'll help us.'

'I know sweetheart. Just bear with me for a few minutes. I want to check that you're okay. Then we can talk.' It took all his strength to stay calm and in control.

Jemma shrank back when Zadrus came close and held the device against her neck.

'I know what he's doing honey,' said Sean. 'This is safe. You must trust me.' Although she didn't fight, the fear in her eyes gutted him.

Zadrus worked quickly to remove the device, and once it was out, she slumped into Sean's arms. He picked her up and took her into the transporter to rest on a lounge chair beside Nik who was already there, leaving Matt to sort Dan and the guards.

'They implanted a device in your neck, but I think it is not working properly,' said Zadrus, shifting his focus to Nik. He held the tool over her neck. 'Even so, I will remove it for your safety. Do you have a headache?'

'Yes, but it's okay.'

'It was brave of you to contact us under the circumstances,' said Sean.

'I didn't feel brave,' replied Nik. 'I was dead scared. I had no idea what they'd do if they heard me. They were so antagonistic.'

A short time later, Matt reported that the others had tried to resist, but with weapons drawn on them, all the silver bars had been removed.

Jemma groaned, holding out her hand to Sean.

'It's alright sweetheart,' he said, supporting her to sit although she was trembling and struggled to respond.

'Nik, I'm so sorry,' said Jemma, once she was able to speak coherently. 'I don't understand how I could have thought that way.'

'You must not feel guilty,' said Zadrus. 'You had no control over your thoughts, or behaviour, once the bar was in place. You were externally manipulated.'

'Nik,' said Sean, 'were there any other humans on board?'

'Not that we saw.'

Sean felt so far out of his depth that he had no idea what to do next. The Zants had to be stopped and, although he respected and trusted both Zadrus and Werrimen, it bothered him the extent to which he had to rely on them to solve his problems. Helplessness was not a feeling which sat well with him. He had to find a way to get up to speed.

The trip home was much slower than the trip out had been, which gave Sean time to organise rooms in the hospital for each of the victims, including Jemma and Nik.

He left the hospital, once he'd settled them in, and headed back to the Administration building.

Werrimen waited at the landing bay. 'We are about to speak with European command, and I want you involved,' she said to Sean. 'We will see if they have managed to contact the Zants. General Hunt is already there. We should join him.'

'Yes, ma'am.' He followed her to the conference room.

A small group of Zants was visible on one screen. They sat very quietly, with fixed smiles on their faces. Another screen showed a group of five humans, who Sean assumed were the European leaders.

'Can we get on with this,' snapped Hunt. He was pacing like an angry bull, although he looked relieved to see Sean.

'Of course,' said Zadrus. 'We will let the Zants think that our people are still missing.'

'Speakers about to go on now,' said the operator. 'They will be able to see us. Quiet please.'

Victor Klein, from the European command, began. 'Landi, I would like to introduce you to the people present with us.' He named Hunt, Sean, Zadrus and Werrimen. 'We have heard some disturbing news from our friends in the East Australian Settlement. They tell me a number of their people are missing. I'm just wondering if you could shed some light on this.'

'I'm so sorry to hear that you have lost your people, Victor. But I'm sure you realise we do not have a presence in that area, so we have not been able to observe any unusual activity. We have adhered to our agreement we would not interfere with the way Earth's cities are re-established. Of course, we will notify you immediately, if we should come across them.' He bowed his head, as if in deference.

Viktor spoke again. 'We have also been reliably informed you plan an aggressive mission in that region. Can you explain that?'

'No, no, this is not true. We are like the rest of the IPL and are merely interested in keeping the peace. Once we are invited to help, we will be only too happy to do so.'

'Thank you. Please keep us informed of anything you hear.' Viktor terminated the link, advising the East Australian command to stand by until he secured their interface.

'What a slimy bastard,' said Sean. 'Are they all like that?'

'Mostly,' said Viktor. 'You can't ever trust them. But back to the matter at hand. They're not admitting to anything yet, so I don't think continuing the conversation is of value. My main purpose was to let them know we are aware of their plans. Are your people alright?'

'Yes,' said Sean. 'But Zadrus found some small silver bars implanted in their necks which he says they've used in the past. We've removed as many as we can find, and the people who had them don't seem to have any lingering after-effects, just a temporary headache and fatigue.'

'Can you send us some samples of them?'

Zadrus shook his head. 'No. Unfortunately, they disintegrate after a while in the atmosphere and there is no preserving medium that works with them once they've been activated. Prior to implantation, they are quite inert. Unfortunately, even the faulty ones in this group have crumbled. I will send information and the tools to detect and remove them.'

'Hopefully, they will back off now that they realise we know what is afoot,' said Viktor. 'What kind of help will you need if they do attack as planned?'

'I doubt they'll back off,' said Sean. 'They seem too sure of themselves. Their supporters have been told to assemble in the factory and I think we should allow that to happen, then we can confine a large number of their victims into a small area, which will give us a chance to remove the devices.'

Hunt nodded. 'Agreed. We should concentrate as many crafts as possible in that area too, just before the allotted time, so any assistance there would help. It might just stop them in their tracks.'

'That sounds like a good idea. I will request assistance from the IPL here,' said Viktor. 'Zadrus, I understand that you will also involve other members of the IPL. Let me know if you need any other resources. We'll do what we can to assist.'

When the link was terminated, Hunt turned to Sean. 'Bring all our staff in. They can bunk in this building overnight. Make sure all weapons are operational. In the morning, we'll divide into three. One group will defend the Administration building. The second will secure the factory and remove the bars from any Rescue Earth members who turn up. The third group will set up an alternative command. We have to contemplate the possibility that the first two groups could fail.'

Aware that each city had a bunker with its own oxygen,

water and food supplies, Sean assumed that Zadrus and Hunt would lead that group.

'Matt,' said Sean. 'You're best placed to take the Administration building. Pick out your strongest people and get them organised.'

'I will join you, Matt,' said Werrimen.

Sean nodded. 'When Dan recovers, he can lead the team in the factory. Jemma can take charge of removing the bars. Nik can join Zadrus in the command centre to help with surveillance. We'll discuss it more, but I suspect it will be best for me to also go to the factory, and we'll need the bulk of trained security people there. The Rescue Earth members will be fairly hard to handle when they arrive, maybe even worse when the bars are removed, and they find out what was done to them.'

Leaving Matt to liaise with Hunt and the aliens, Sean made his way to the hospital. It was only about three hours since the Zants had released his people, but he needed them back on deck, particularly Dan, as soon as possible even if they hadn't fully recovered.

Jemma, Dan and Nik were sitting together in easy chairs when he arrived, a nurse fussing around them.

Jemma saw him first and jumped up. 'Are you alright? What's happening?'

'I'm fine,' he said, brushing a quick kiss on her forehead. 'It's you I'm worried about.'

'Don't be. Muscles are a bit stiff, and I'm a bit fatigued. We're all in the same boat. We'll get over it.'

'Okay, sit down, and I'll fill you in.' He told them about the meeting with European command and their allocated roles for the next day.

'Are you serious?' said Jemma. 'You want me to babysit.'

'We'll head over and get started,' said Dan, quickly. 'Come on, everyone.'

When Nik hesitated, Dan looked back at her. 'I'm so sorry.'

'Jem, we should go, too,' said Nik, once she tore her eyes away from Dan.

'Sure,' muttered Jemma, but she stood in front of Sean, staring at him, her hands on her hips.

'What?' he said.

'You want me to remove the bars? I'm capable of helping you get everything organised. It's time to stop mollycoddling me. I've recovered from all my traumas, and I can do most things. I need to be in there helping you.'

'You will be helping me. The people with bars are going to fight us and I consider you to be the best person to handle that. You're physically capable of subduing most who'd try to attack, and you have exceptional communication skills to handle anyone who wants to argue.'

'Don't try to con me. You're still wrapping me in cotton wool.'

'Okay, let me put it this way,' he said, taking hold of her shoulders and pulling her around to face him. 'I'm the boss, and until you learn to follow my orders, I won't be giving you any tougher assignments.' He turned on his heel and strode off. 'Come on, Dan.'

'Oops,' said Nik, easing in behind her. 'You need to come with me and calm down before you say something you'll regret. I'm not defending Sean, but he has to manage this whole operation and, as much as he loves you, you're just a small cog in the wheel he has to get turning. Put yourself in his position and imagine trying to manage you.'

'What?' Jemma shifted her stare to Nik, her temper rising at the smile on Nik's face, but she stopped herself from snarling when she thought about what Nik had said. 'Recovering from that bushfire was hell. Bringing myself back after the miscarriage was bloody hard, even touch-and-go there for a while. I'm physically fit, and I'm emotionally stronger than I've ever been. Sean, more than anyone, knows how much work I've put in, and now he's treating me like I'm his personal assistant, not capable of anything unless he's looking over my shoulder.'

'For crying out loud, Jem. If you sit in a corner and meditate for five minutes, you'll realise you're talking rubbish. He's got every right to be worried about you. He cares about you more than life itself. He does not see you as a simpering little thing who can't function without him but, I'd say, he does want to keep you close. I saw a look on Dan's face when he heard that we were going to different places. Neither of us are happy about it either, but we have a job to do, and we'll both follow orders. Flouting his orders in a situation like this is not the way to win him around and prove that you're up to doing more.'

'Why have you got to be so damned rational?' retorted Jemma. 'I don't come from a world where people give each other orders. I'm used to thinking for myself.'

'Then you'd better wake up to yourself, because that's the world you're in now.'

'He's my husband.'

'He is, and Dan's my husband. If Dan gave me an order in an emergency, I'd do as he said and adjust, if necessary, as I went along.'

'I don't know how to handle this.'

'No,' said Nik. 'That much I understand. But you do have to face reality. This is the world we have, at least for the foreseeable future. If you love him, sort it out with him, and work out how to manage the situation you're in.'

'You sound like the bloody General.'

Nik laughed. 'I'll take that as a compliment. Now, go on, make up with Sean.'

'Alright, I'll go talk to him.' She didn't get the chance to talk to him as he flitted between Dan and Matt, ensuring they had everything they'd need. Then he sought advice from Werrimen on how to handle anything the Zants might do. Jemma gave up and went in search of Zadrus to ask his advice on how to remove the bars. He showed her the device and how to use it, then sat her down to discuss how she should cope with the aggression he expected from the Rescue Earth Group. Once he'd finished, she settled back in a lounge chair and fell asleep, unaware of anything, until Sean shook her shoulders, just before dawn.

'Rise and shine,' he said, brushing her hair away from her face.

She sat up, shaking her head and struggling to work out

where she was. When she looked up to see concern in his eyes, she felt ashamed of the way she'd responded to him a few hours earlier. 'I'm sorry,' she said. 'I won't let you down. Zadrus gave me instructions on how to remove the bars and how to handle the people afterwards.'

'I never thought for a minute you'd let me down, but I didn't have time to explain my decision. Come on, we've got to move.'

She walked with him, hand in hand, to the roof where the command group had begun to assemble. Nik and Dan were already there, in an embrace that suggested they were afraid they might not see each other again, but they separated when they saw Sean. Dan walked with Nik to the transporter which would, under the cover of darkness, take the command group to the bunker. When she'd left, Dan assisted Sean to check the group who were to stay in the Administration building. Then, shortly after sunrise, the factory group headed out. Sean was surprised to see that others had already started to arrive, but he shrugged it off and ordered his group to blend in to get a sense of the overall mood.

The day passed with no sign of any Zant presence, and tensions began to rise. Early in the afternoon, people began to move into the factory. Most of them sat around chatting, but still there was no sign of the Zants. Sean was about to contact Hunt to suggest they'd been duped when all the communicators in the room vibrated.

A message flashed across the screens, 'DO NOT DRINK THE WATER.' Almost immediately, Sean's handpiece also vibrated, showing Hunt's image. He held up his hand to silence Jemma, and those around him, so he could listen to Hunt, well aware that what he did next could determine the outcome of the whole operation.

'Alright sir, I'll pass it on,' said Sean, as he shut down the screen.

'What's happening?' Jemma took hold of his arm before he could turn away.

'Bad news.' He kept his voice low. 'We have to avoid freaking the crowd. Let Dan know we need to spread out and be ready for anything.'

Once Dan and his people had placed themselves strategically around the room, Sean hoisted himself up onto a chair, mainly to ensure that he could observe any action that could hint at trouble. 'Everyone — listen up. I've been advised there is a problem with the water supply in the Administration building. When taps were turned on, people became very short of breath, collapsing within minutes. There are at least five dead, and many others seriously affected. We do not know if the water in this building is safe. Please use the bottled water in the fridges. Do not, under any circumstance, drink the tap water. Thank you.'

'Christ almighty, Matt's in that building,' said Jemma. 'And Werrimen.'

'I know,' replied Sean. 'But there's nothing we can do from here.'

Someone at the back of the room bellowed, 'Our Zant leaders said nobody would be hurt. These people are lying to us.'

'That's right,' yelled someone else. 'Landi said they'd lie to us. Try to make us evacuate. Well, we're not going.'

Another man shouted, 'Damn right. Stay put.'

Sean motioned to his operatives to move in. 'That's the safest course of action,' he said, in a loud voice, forcing himself to stay calm. He didn't have enough people to control a riot. Priority had to be to remove the bars from those affected as quickly as possible.

'Given the situation in the Administration building, everyone in this room is to be checked medically. You will not be permitted out of here until you have been checked. Please be aware that we are armed and will use our weapons if there is no other option.'

Insults were hurled at Sean from several points in the room.

He stepped down from his chair and signalled to Dan to take charge. 'Time to start on the bars. Probably should have started earlier, but we'll get into it now. Jemma, go after the loud ones first.'

'Yes boss.' She ducked out of his reach as he swung his arm into a pretend punch.

He turned away to answer his communicator again, then took a deep breath before turning back. 'Bloody Zants have stormed the Administration building. They've taken control. General Hunt has no idea how many people are dead.'

'What about Matt,' said Jemma, 'and Werrimen?'

'He doesn't know. Be aware that it's possible some of the people here have more information than I do, so take care.

They may have some other plan up their sleeves.'

'Dear God. Can this get any worse?' said Jemma. 'Let's get on with it then. The sooner we get those bars out, the better. Zadrus said to expect a fair bit of anger, so we all need to be on alert.'

'Yes, General Anderson, we do.' Sean grinned at her retreating back as she set up to do her job, but he wasn't taking her concerns lightly, and he maintained a careful watch across the room. He wasn't surprised that all those who identified themselves as members of the Rescue Earth Group had a bar, and one by one the bars were removed by Jemma with Dan standing nearby. He was surprised though, that a small number of people didn't have bars. All were there alongside someone who did, but he made a mental note to keep an eye on them. To enable Jemma to work at speed, he left Dan to maintain control and took it on himself to explain to each individual how they'd been manipulated. Most were furious with the Zants, and many offered to help. To avoid giving them time to think about what had been done to them, he decided it best to keep everyone busy and assigned each person to a rotating shift to keep watch until they received permission to move outside.

Although the factory was now under control, Sean ordered his staff to stay alert and report anything suspicious. It wouldn't take much for the mood to splinter. The factory was a basic structure used to manufacture the uniforms they all wore. There were four large rooms on each floor, with a few smaller rooms scattered, including bathrooms. Most people curled up to sleep after the bars were removed, which Sean considered appropriate given they hadn't had the mandatory eight-hours rest. Fortunately, modern bathrooms didn't require water for flushing, otherwise tempers could really have boiled over.

Now, it was a waiting game, too soon to relax since they were surrounded by potentially volatile people.

'Shit, I heard shots,' someone cried.

Sean yelled, 'Get down. Get away from windows and doors.' He edged towards a window and opened a slit in the shutters. Another shot.

'Get down. Get down. And stay there,' he yelled, as he picked up his communicator.

Jemma crawled over to him. 'What's going on?'

'Zant crafts are patrolling up and down between buildings. I just saw them shoot two people who tried to run from one building to another. They killed them.'

'God help us. Are you sure?'

'No doubt,' replied Sean. 'There's blood all over them. And there's something else.'

'Hopefully, it can't get worse,' she replied.

'Not sure,' said Sean. 'The Zant crafts are more oblong that the IPL transporters, so they're quite easy to identify.'

'And?' said Jemma, shuddering when she saw the look on his face.

'And, I saw a Norellian sphere.'

'Pritchard,' she spat back.

'Yeah, I'd say. Zadrus has been focussed on the Zants, but

Pritchard's out there. He might just be watching but, knowing him, I doubt it.'

Communicators around the factory lit up, along with large screens at several points in each room, all with an image of Zadrus. 'Everyone must remain inside,' said Zadrus. 'Help is on its way from our European and Asian settlements. Do not risk your life, or the lives of others who may try to save you. You cannot hope to overpower the Zants.'

As the night dragged on, anger turned, as Sean had feared it might, towards the IPL for not letting people know about the Zant threat. The mood continued to deteriorate, so he set up small groups, each under the direction of a CIG official, some to check and ration the water supply, others to guard exits, others to monitor communications.

None of the CIG people slept that night and Sean, despite his own exhaustion, pushed himself to keep going. He'd need another plan if there was no resolution by the morning, but for now, it was critical to keep the peace at all costs. As morning dawned, he peered through the base of the nearest window. The area outside the building was quiet and deserted and a couple of people took it on themselves to open the door. He called them to get back, but they remained standing in the doorway until, suddenly, a Zant craft flew low between the buildings.

'Get back,' yelled Sean, again. 'Shut the door and get away from it.'

Doors and windows were again locked down and Dan herded everyone back into the centre of the factory floor.

There were no arguments and people huddled together, particularly when more shots were heard.

'That sounded like return fire,' whispered Jemma, but jumped to a loud sound, like something hitting the outside wall.

'Think you're right.' Sean crawled back to the window and peered out. A two-person Zant fighter craft lay on the pathway just below. There was no sign of life, but he wasn't prepared to risk anyone going out to check. 'Tell Dan to settle everyone down. I'll chat to the General. I think we're in for a bit of a wait.'

The firing ceased for a short time, but there were repeated episodes throughout the day, and there was nothing anyone in the building could do. With most of the people subdued, Sean ordered half his staff to rest. Although he knew from Hunt that the IPL had worn down most of the Zant resistance, he prepared everyone for another night in the building. No one objected. He figured they must have accepted now he really was there to protect them.

CHAPTER 14

Just after midnight, Jemma gratefully accepted Sean's direction to take a six-hour break. She curled up on some blankets in a corner, away from everyone else, and was asleep within seconds. When she woke, the warm early morning sun was caressing her skin and, for a moment, she imagined herself stretched out on the couch in her Gold Coast unit but, as she opened her eyes, she remembered the awful truth. Most people were still asleep, and it was eerily quiet. All the aircraft and weapon noise had gone. Not sure what to make of it, she crawled to the door, opened it a crack and peered out.

Sean seemed to materialise beside her. 'I'm told the Zants have withdrawn from the city,' he whispered, but he didn't look confident. 'The IPL haven't yet declared they have control, but the General says they're close. I'm waiting for the signal to move out.'

'I'd like to have a look,' said Jemma.

'Okay, but just look. Don't go out. The IPL are still checking. It shouldn't be long until we're cleared.'

She opened the door, and cautiously stepped into the doorway. The scene that confronted her took her breath away, and she had to grip the doorhandle to steady herself as she ran her gaze over the debris, scattered as far as she could see. Wrecks were strewn across all the open spaces that surrounded the factory in which she stood. She could see remnants of at least three downed Zant crafts closer to the Administration building, although pieces were spread over such a wide area it was hard to be sure it was only three. Bodies littered the landscape, Zants around their crafts, and Sidlowns and humans who must have tried to run between buildings. Their peaceful settlement had become a warzone.

Unable to speak, she turned back to Sean and sank into his waiting arms. His communicator vibrated and he spoke to Hunt without letting her go.

'We can go now,' he whispered. 'Transport's about to land to shift us.'

While Sean organised people from inside the factory to waiting transporters, Jemma walked outside to Dan and tried to help him direct people from there. Still numb with shock, she jumped when Sean took hold of her arm, but followed him quietly to a smaller transporter.

'We're going to the bunker to meet with Zadrus,' said Sean. 'Dan will join us as soon as he's got everyone here sorted.'

She broke down when Matt, already on board, stood to greet them. 'I thought you were dead.'

'No,' said Matt, smiling as he patted himself down. 'Not dead, but I don't mind admitting I was scared.'

'What happened? We heard that people died.'

He nodded. 'Several did, the ones closest to the source of the poison were most vulnerable. They were overcome before we realised what was happening.'

'Dear God, this is madness,' said Jemma.

Matt faltered as he began to explain. 'When we realised the smell coming from the taps was poisonous, we all grabbed the nearest heavy object and started to smash windows and ventilation outlets to get fresh air in. The Zants overpowered us within minutes. We were too weak to resist. They went to amazing lengths to ensure we were comfortable, gave everyone who showed signs of poisoning, an antidote, including me. I felt better as soon as I got it.' He shook his head. 'When the IPL stormed the building, the Zants surrendered. No fuss, no attempt to fight back, like it was all part of their plan. I got the impression the whole thing was pointless.'

Jemma comforted him, but something dawned on her as she looked around. 'Where's Werrimen? She was with you, wasn't she?'

Tears welled in Matt's eyes.

'Matt, where is she?'

'She was one of the first to be hit. Last time I saw her, she was unconscious. Two Sidlowns had her on a gurney. She was breathing, but she looked awful.'

'Oh God. Does Zadrus know?'

'He does. They rushed a medical team to her. It'll be the end of him if she doesn't make it.'

'She'll make it. I'm sure she will. She's tough.' Jemma wiped the tears from her face. 'God, this can't be happening.'

'About to land,' said the pilot.

Looking down, all she could see was a sports oval with a variety of flat playing fields and a small, old-fashioned clubhouse, but nothing large enough to house everything they'd have needed during the crisis. As they landed, a door opened at the end of the clubhouse that was closest to their landing pad and the General walked out.

His face lit up as he saw Jemma, Sean, and Matt. 'With me. Hurry. It's unsafe out here. Where's O'Leary?'

'Coming,' replied Sean. 'Pilot's going back for him and a couple of others.'

'Okay. Follow me.' Hunt pressed the palm of his hand against a flat metallic looking plate just outside the door through which he'd emerged. Inside was an empty room but, at the back, was a set of stairs and he walked towards them.

The stairs widened out at the bottom and Jemma shook her head. She should have expected the cavernous, ornate foyer and the multiple hallways. The SCARF facility had been equally elaborate and, just like SCARF, there were multiple doors and corridors opening from the foyer. Hunt led them down a long hallway which appeared to finish in a dead end, but he pushed a tiny black disc into a slot that appeared in the wall as he approached.

Jemma stared at the slot. 'What the ...?'

'Camouflage,' said Hunt. 'Very restricted access. We've got three more security measures to get through. Everyone, stay close.'

He held his security pass, a small square plastic-looking

card that was attached to his shirt, against a box on the door. Another door opened. Then he spoke a series of seemingly unconnected words into a small communicator. The final door slid open revealing a large room with multiple screens. Area names were printed underneath, including one that said Earth command, and another, IPL Command.

'We're here,' said Hunt.

Jemma peered at the screen. 'Who's that?' A being, similar in height to Zadrus, filled the screen, but he looked frail, and his skin had a reptilian texture. He sounded anxious.

Zadrus stood in front of the screen, leaning forward and gesticulating towards the being as he spoke.

'We first noticed it this morning. Go out and investigate. Determine if you can contain it. Go quickly. You have more than ten thousand inhabitants in your city now. If we must evacuate, we will need many crafts. Get back to me as soon as you know. Keep me informed.' The screen shut down.

Zadrus turned to the newcomers. 'Are you all well?'

'Yes, we're good,' said Jemma. 'Matt's told us about what happened in the Administration building. Have you heard how Werrimen is?'

'She is now conscious.' Zadrus paused and focussed on the ceiling. 'It will take a while for her to recover but she is strong, and I am confident she will do well. She is in safe hands and we must not bother her with our current problem.'

'God, I hope you're right,' said Jemma.

Zadrus smiled. 'I believe I am.'

'But why did they do it? said Jemma. 'Matt thinks that the

way they surrendered, it was all pointless.'

'He is probably correct. The whole episode you have just endured might have been a distraction.' Zadrus shook his head. 'Matt, you go for your medical check. You were exposed to the toxic fumes, and we do not actually know what the antidote was that they gave you. Report to the medical centre, here, in the bunker. I have a team waiting for you.'

When he'd gone, Zadrus continued. 'When some of the implanted silver bars proved to be faulty, I became suspicious. The Zants do not make that kind of mistake. They are far too clever. I focussed on the factories because I thought their underlying plan was to take over the Administration building. But, unfortunately, that was another ploy. They wanted me to think they were after the Administration building, so we would concentrate all the settlement's resources there. Which is exactly what we did and left everywhere else in the settlement vulnerable.'

'So, we effectively did what the Zants wanted?' said Hunt.

'Yes, and Dragile believes he has found their real goal.'

'Who's Dragile?' said Jemma.

'The person I was speaking to when you arrived,' replied Zadrus. 'He is the Fleet Commander.'

'What did he find?' said Sean.

'IPL crafts conduct regular patrols just outside the Earth's atmosphere. This morning, one of the ships called in a major disturbance to our dam system. On closer inspection, they concluded someone had contaminated, and almost drained, the dam. It is now a distinct red colour.'

Hunt interrupted, 'I've ordered some crews to go out and investigate.'

'No,' responded Zadrus, 'I would prefer that you ask them to report to the IPL Commander who is proceeding there now. We don't know what has happened or what the Zants have done. Our people are more experienced in dealing with them. They must take charge.'

'Of course,' said Hunt, although Jemma noticed a slight narrowing of his eyes. 'I'll redirect them.'

Even though she was shocked that Zadrus and his people could have been so easily duped by the Zants, Jemma could see no point in allocating blame. They'd have to deal with whatever happened now.

'Zadrus,' said Jemma. 'If they've drained the dam, they must be looking for something on the dam bed. What could be there that they'd be after?'

'I do not know. The Zants are a greedy race,' he said, with a sigh. 'They will do almost anything to get hold of things they define as valuable or that might be useful to trade in other parts of the Universe. Perhaps they wanted the water, or minerals that people on Earth would not consider valuable. I have called Pat Reilly to join us. Hopefully he will be able to cast light on what is there.'

'Oh no, he's too ill. You mustn't stress him.' Pat had been in charge of a geological survey before the war, and she was sure he'd know all there was to know about the structure and resources of the dam, but his health was far more important than their need for information. She turned in response to a noise behind her and could hardly believe her eyes.

Pat walked through the door. He didn't have an oxygen mask, and he stood straight and tall, at least as tall as Hunt, maybe closer to Sean's height. He'd been so stooped when he was ill, she hadn't realised. Now she could see a familiar twinkle in his eye, one that she'd known so well in her family. In fact, the similarity to her father was striking, the dark brown hair with a smattering of grey-green eyes and rugged good looks. A broad smile came over his face when he saw her, and he reached out to her.

'It's such a relief to see you. I was told that you were safe and well but it's not the same as seeing you. And Sean, too,' he said, when Sean, who'd walked up behind, squeezed his shoulder.

Jemma sat with Pat as Zadrus explained the minerals the Zants valued and asked if he had any idea what the dam might hold.

'There were a lot of different mineral types in the area, but nothing of any real interest that I could imagine,' said Pat. 'I've been thinking about that man who was shot after the craft landed near our farm. I had the feeling they were looking for someone in particular and we've concluded that they were after mum, but is it possible they wanted my maps?'

'If Pritchard's involved, he probably was tracking your mother's tattoo, but whether it was to find her, and subsequently Jemma, or get to you, who knows,' said Hunt. 'We know that he's in cahoots with the Zants. There might have been a dual purpose.'

'One of the people in that craft looked familiar, although I couldn't see him clearly,' said Pat. 'A male, late-forties, dark hair, average height and quite slim. My deputy, Ross Simpson, was like that but he was very religious, and wouldn't have been swayed by greed. In any case, he had his own geological knowledge. But there was another person, my Chief Executive Officer, an administrator with no geological training. We often joked that he and Ross could have been twins. He'd need maps or Ross or me to find the deposits. I never really trusted him but, dear God, could he have turned so bad?' Pat slumped back in his chair.

'We have to consider the possibility,' said Sean.

'And,' said Jemma, 'there's another possibility. Your description fits Pritchard. He probably would look familiar to you given he resembles others in the family.'

'That's a good thought,' said Sean. 'Let's start by working out what the Zants want. Could you help us identify the deposit areas and types of minerals?'

An IPL scientist stepped forward. 'Excuse me, I might be able to help here. I know the kind of minerals they go after, so if you know what's in the area, we might be able to narrow it down together.'

While the Zants were after the minerals, Jemma had no doubt that Pritchard would be conjuring some other plan, probably helping the Zants, so that they'd help him in return. It was beyond her how any human could be persuaded to voluntarily associate with either the Zants or Pritchard. Those with bars had had no choice, but what could possibly convince others to do so?

Criminals and terrorists in her era were driven by monetary gain or a strong religious or political belief, but the society the aliens had helped develop here didn't have those motivators. There were no restrictions on religious beliefs, and people were encouraged to express their political views so everything could be openly discussed. People in the new settlement came from all sorts of cultural and ethnic backgrounds, and she hadn't come across any prejudice. Most people were just relieved they'd survived and happy to live together in peace. Since there was no economy, desire for possessions didn't really seem relevant. If someone indicated they wanted a different type of dwelling, a particular possession, or a trip or holiday, it was made available to them, if at all possible. If they didn't like what they were doing, then as soon as they let someone know, they'd be offered something else or a study program to improve their work situation.

When she told Zadrus what she was thinking, he explained, with a sigh, that he'd seen it before. 'They offer people power, which can be almost hypnotic to some. The Zants, on your home planet, Anders Major, offered people the chance to rule when they took over, promised to make them kings, or queens, or to give them enduring power over others. The concept of becoming absolute rulers drew many people in. On other planets, I have seen them offer a life of luxury or immense wealth. Of course, they never deliver on their promises.'

Before she could discuss her fears regarding Pritchard, Pat returned with the IPL scientist.

'We think we know what they're after,' said Pat. 'This region has large deposits of several minerals. No one has ever sought to mine them because, in the main, they're so plentiful elsewhere it hasn't been worth it. The main one is zircon, but there's also ilmenite. Both are plentiful in the sand that lines the dam above its clay base. Before we excavated the dam, we had long discussions about the minerals that'd be lost under the water, but strategically, it was the ideal place, both in terms of its proximity to the old city, and because it was an area with very heavy rainfall. It takes runoff from several directions, so we thought it would always be full, and it has been.'

Jemma stared at him and laughed. 'I used to often buy cubic zirconia jewellery because it was really cheap,' she said.

'No, no, cubic zirconia was a manufactured jewel, not a mineral at all,' said Pat. 'Zircon is a mineral which comes in a wide array of colours. It's plentiful on Earth. It was sold as the *poor man's emerald or ruby,* but these gentlemen tell me that on some planets, it is more valuable than a diamond would be to us.'

'So,' interrupted Zadrus, 'for them to get hold of the zircon, they would have to drain the water. Is that correct Pat?'

'Yes, and probably dry some areas completely, in order to place the type of mining equipment they'd need, unless they have something more sophisticated than I know. I'm not sure what the red colour is though. Maybe the water that's left has taken on some of the mineral colour, or I guess it could have exposed a red algal bloom. We'll have to test it. Scientists need to get out there now, and I'd like to go along. It's alright

Jemma.' He smiled, as he saw her start. 'I'm still a bit weak but I'm improving every day. I'm up to it.'

'I'm sure you are, but please let someone medical go with you,' she replied. 'You don't know what you might find there.'

The large screen lit up. 'Investigation Team to Command.'

'Yes, report,' responded Zadrus.

A Sidlown man stood forward, his image filling the screen. 'The dam levels are dangerously low, and the water is highly concentrated with something. A large channel has been cut through the dam wall on the southern side of the dam and the area to the south of it is flooded. So, they weren't after the water. There is a large area around the dam that has been fenced off. We cannot get close to the machinery to check what they are doing but there is a lot of activity. Armed guards at the entrance threatened us, so for the moment we have retreated. Most of the guards are human and from what we can see, at a distance, the machinery operators are human. There are some Zants around, but not many. Someone has disconnected the town water supply from the dam. The pipes that lead to the reservoir tanks have been removed completely and the reservoirs sealed off. The tanks are full, and the water is completely safe in those tanks, so the settlement is not in immediate danger. We need your instructions on how to proceed.'

'See if you can find any water with the red colouring outside the fence, then stand down,' Zadrus replied. 'We are sending out a crew of scientists who can test it. They may also be able to identify the equipment. We think we know what they are after but need confirmation. Once they have finished,

I want you to return to base. Leave a small surveillance team behind who can report any changes to the situation. Do not confront them.'

'Okay then,' said Pat. 'We'd better get moving.'

'Certainly, but you will be accompanied by security Pat. You may still be a target,' said Zadrus.

'I'll be surrounded by other scientists,' replied Pat. 'They should be security enough.'

Jemma shook her head. 'Please do as Zadrus asks. We don't understand the Zants and, if Pritchard is there, God knows what he's up to.'

'Alright. For your sake, I'll accept. I'm deeply grateful to this community. You saved my life and the lives of those in my family. I want to give something back and I'm up to it now. Jemma, please understand, I have to do this.'

Sean jumped up. 'Okay then, I'm going too. I'll keep a close eye on him, Jemma.'

'Can't you send some of your people?' She hadn't anticipated Sean's reaction. She wasn't happy about Pat going out there, but with Sean going too, the two men in the new settlement who meant everything to her, were both about to place themselves in danger. Sean was the most competent person she knew, and he wouldn't shy away from the challenge. Refusing to do something himself that would put his staff in danger, just wasn't in his psyche.

'Hang on,' said Jemma. 'Why don't I go too. I'm more qualified to assess the extent of an algal bloom than anyone else here.'

'No,' replied Hunt.

'It's not up to you.' Jemma slammed the papers in her hand onto the table.

'I'm afraid that I agree,' said Zadrus. 'If Pritchard is there, you and Pat together are too much of a target.'

Dan stood. 'I'll go, mate. Pritchard won't get past Sean and me together.'

Jemma turned away from Hunt and Zadrus and walked with Sean to the transporter that would take them to the dam. 'Please be careful. I can't envisage my life without you.'

'Don't think that way sweetheart. I'll be back before you know it.'

'You'd better be.'

Sean drew her into his arms and held her tight. 'I love you,' he murmured.

'I love you too.'

He eased her back. 'I have to go.'

'I know. Promise me, you'll hurry back.'

'I'll do my level best.' He kissed her forehead, then leapt into the transporter.

She watched the transporter until it was out of sight, then, as she felt Zadrus's hand on her shoulder, she turned and followed him back into the bunker. She remained on tenter-hooks, pacing at the back of the room until Hunt called her to help Nik with surveillance. She doubted Nik needed her help, but it would give her something to do, so she followed Nik to the bunker's control room and familiarised herself with the equipment.

It was two hours before Sean's group called in.

'What have you found?' snapped Jemma. 'Is Pritchard there. Or one of his spheres?'

'Nothing like that,' said Pat, standing beside Sean so she could see him. 'But it is a bit odd. The colour in the water is due to a soluble dye. It's not toxic at all.'

'That is odd,' said Zadrus, as he and Hunt moved closer to Jemma. 'Probably intended to confuse. We must remain alert. We still have no idea what the Zants will do next.'

'Understood,' said Sean. 'We're concentrating on trying to get some direct evidence that it's the zircon and ilmenite they're after. We've been scouting round the perimeter for a possible entry point where we won't be seen. I plan to go in and try to get some of the product they're mining. We have a small mineral analyser that should give us a broad idea.'

'No,' said Jemma. 'Sean, for God's sake. That's far too dangerous.'

Zadrus looked from Jemma to Sean. 'Provided you can find a safe entry and exit, it may be better than waiting. They will be expecting us to use force, so their resources will be geared towards fighting off an attack unit. They shouldn't be suspicious of a single individual. Do not linger. It must be in and out. If something goes wrong, I am not sure what the consequences will be. If the Zants capture you, I cannot predict what they will do. I doubt they would harm you, but you must be very careful.'

'I've got a listening device,' said Sean. 'I can change clothes so that I look like I'm part of one of the work crews. My implanted tracker should still be working. I'll be okay.'

'You must understand the volatile nature of the situation you are entering,' said Zadrus, as Sean stepped away from the communicator.

The person with the reptilian skin, to whom Zadrus had been speaking earlier, had quietly re-appeared on the screen. 'No, Zadrus, do not send in a single person. The Zants have far too many tricks. He cannot possibly hope to outwit them.'

'Unfortunately,' responded Zadrus, 'I think we are too late to stop him, so we must make the best of it. Sean is very capable.'

'Alright, get back to me as soon as you know anything.' The screen shut down although he continued to mutter.

Zadrus smiled, 'He is swearing at us. While I find that amusing, we must take this situation very seriously. I will not hesitate to call for external support if there is a problem. Is everyone clear on that?'

Although Nik had organised equipment to track Sean, and Jemma knew he was sensible, he had no knowledge of these beings. Zadrus's concern had Jemma fuming. He should have stopped Sean. She'd had a bad feeling from the beginning, but there was nothing she could do other than sit with Nik and listen like everyone else.

CHAPTER 15

Leaves crunched a few metres away from where Sean had walked, looking for a good entry point. He bolted behind a stand of trees and stood absolutely still.

A man called to someone else, although Sean couldn't see either of them. 'Keep going. I'll catch up.'

'Gotcha,' replied a female voice.

Sean shrank further behind the biggest of the trees when he heard a man undoing his trousers. He didn't dare move and remained still for several minutes even after he heard retreating footsteps. With a few deep breaths to steady himself, he edged out for a better look. Whoever the people were, they'd gone.

Staying close to the scrub, and watching carefully for any sign of movement, he crept towards the boundary fence. Satisfied that the area was deserted, he straightened up and strode to the edge of the Zant-controlled territory. Although the edge of the dam was a couple of hundred metres away, the red hue extended as far as he could see. Long-dead trees rose like ghosts through the exposed dam bed, along with old sheds and houses that'd been swamped when the dam was first established. The stench of rotting fish and weeds was overpowering.

Feeling a lot less assured now than when he'd made the decision to go in, he retreated behind the trees to wait for the sun to go down. He knew Hunt wouldn't attempt to contact him in case he was in a vulnerable situation, and thought about calling in, but decided against it. He didn't want to be told to cancel his mission, so he waited quietly until it was dark, and he was confident that there was no one else around. The section of fence he planned to use had thick scrub close to it, which he thought could be useful if it became necessary to retreat in a hurry. Burning an opening in the metal fence using his IPL multi-tool, he said a silent prayer of gratitude for the alien devices. It not only cut metal, but it could repair it and, as soon as he was through, he turned back and closed his entry point, then edged out from the shadows.

The core of the mining operation, where he needed to be, was at least two kilometres away. Getting there without drawing attention to himself could be tricky, particularly given the dam bed was boggy, and he'd have to skirt the edge. He'd walked around a kilometre and had relaxed enough to settle into a comfortable rhythm, when a bright light flashed into his face.

'What the hell are you doing here?'

It took a minute to make out the man behind the light, not the fellow he'd encountered outside the enclosure. This one was larger, bulkier and armed with a menacing-looking old-fashioned rifle.

'Just, … just, er … checking the site for the next operation,' he stammered.

'I didn't know they were looking at more sites,' growled the man.

Sean paused for a few seconds to compose his voice. 'They want an alternative site found, so if the current one becomes too wet, they can move the equipment somewhere else. It's just a precaution as I understand it.'

'Okay, but you're not supposed to be anywhere by yourself. Make sure you've got someone with you if you're wandering around again.'

'Sure. I'll be more careful.' He'd have to do better if he was to get out of here in one piece. He turned and walked briskly away from the man, maintaining a fixed smile in case the fellow followed, or he ran into anyone else with a lethal weapon. He gasped when, a bit further on, he recognised his neighbour from the new apartment block, Kiri Payoosh.

'Hey Sean,' called Kiri. 'I didn't know you'd joined the dark side.'

'Oh, hello Kiri.' Jesus, he had to pull himself together but, despite all his undercover experience, he was so far out of his comfort zone here that every new glitch was taking all his energy to manage. 'Good to see you. I've been involved for a couple of months, what about you?'

'Gee, I only came in three weeks ago, but what a buzz. I can't wait to see the other planets. What will you choose, the summer lifestyle or the winter one? He grinned as he planted a loud kiss on a large, red zircon. 'You little beauty, what a future you're about to give me.'

'Oh, I don't know,' replied Sean, struggling to make his

voice sound light. 'I like the sunshine. Are you getting plenty of good stones? How's the machinery holding up?'

Kiri grinned as he replied. 'The zircons are fabulous. And we're getting bucketloads of sand and ilmenite, so we're doubling the rewards.'

'Fantastic.' Sean forced a smile. 'Have you come across many people we know? I haven't.'

'No, not many,' Kiri replied, 'a few people who worked on the water supply, and building developments. So, you might see faces you recognise without really knowing them.'

'Okay,' said Sean. 'Hey, can I check your samples? I'm trying to determine which areas are best, so I can get you the best possible grounds.'

'Sure, no worries. The drillings are over here, and the washed stones are in the corner. I bag the best site you come up with.'

Sean smiled, 'That's a given.' He picked up some of the drillings, ran them through his fingers and into the portable mineral analysis machine in his pocket which, fortunately, didn't require much to do its job. Then the same with the washed stone.

Thanking Kiri, he moved away from the light and started his report, hoping that the command centre could still hear him. 'You should have received an analysis from two samples by now. The stones look like zircon to me, but they've also stored the tailings and I think that must contain ilmenite. They've got sand in mounds, and I'm sending that through now. I'm just going to cast my eyes around the rest of the operation and then head out through the main gate. I don't want to run into a patrol again in the darker areas.'

*   *   *

'You need to get him out,' cried Jemma, well aware that the beings he had to get past had been responsible for the death of so many over the last few days. Although he seemed confident that he'd be out within minutes, Jemma could feel the tension from both Zadrus and Hunt and that made her even sicker as she worked to manage her own fear.

'I'm sorry, my dear,' said Zadrus. 'Sean is on his own, which he knew when he went in. We have no means of extracting him. We do have our best IPL and CIG operatives, waiting to help him when he reaches the front gate. For the moment, we have to rely on Sean's ingenuity, and you know that he has plenty of that.'

She knew there was nothing they could do. It was all up to Sean, but sitting here waiting was a nightmare.

'We're getting the readouts,' called Nik.

Jemma rushed to her side, relieved to have something on which she could focus, although she didn't really understand all the lines and squiggles on the charts that emerged.

'Main mineral is zircon as we thought it would be,' said Pat, easing her aside so that he could look. 'There's ilmenite in the sand, and the sand's silicon rich too as I expected.'

'You look puzzled, Jemma.' Zadrus stood behind Pat to look over his shoulder at the printouts.

'Yeah, I am. Australia's rich in all those minerals. Why didn't the Zants just set up somewhere else, away from the city, where they wouldn't be noticed? If they'd sought permission from Earth Command, they'd have most likely got it. Why here? Why now?'

'You're forgetting they equally cannot operate outside the TEM,' replied Zadrus. 'They need the same concentrations in the air as we do, and cannot tolerate radiation, so that would hamper such an operation. They also don't like to do too much manual work for themselves and they will see the humans as expendable. While they have plenty of humans around them, they know that the IPL will not mount any offensive campaign.'

'Or are they here because this is where Pritchard wants to be?'

Before anyone could answer, they were interrupted by Sean chatting to people on his way back to the fence.

'He's let his guard down too early,' said Zadrus.

'Fifty metres to go,' muttered Hunt. 'He needs to be more alert now.'

Jemma waited in silence, afraid to breathe. If he kept his head, he could be out in a few more seconds. Suddenly, a different voice rang out, and she froze.

'Ah, Mr Bellamy, it is so kind of you to join us. Could we invite you inside to discuss our operations?'

'Oh, my God.' Jemma gripped Nik's arm. 'That's Landi's voice. They've got Sean. What are we going to do?'

'Stay calm,' said Zadrus, his voice loud and resounding.

No one uttered a sound.

'For the moment we will listen, get enough information to formulate a strategy,' said Zadrus. 'They may be so sure of themselves they will just let him go and send him back with a message. Or they may keep him captive. I am confident they will not hurt him; they would know by now that we are watching and will retaliate.'

'They won't harm him, he's too good a catch.' Hunt moved behind Jemma, resting his hands on her shoulders. 'We're not sitting back, Jemma. We have a tactical group standing by to go in after him.'

*   *   *

Sean considered making a run for it, but too many guards with old-fashioned rifles stood between him and his escape route. His best chance of escape would be to stay out in the open and keep Landi talking until the IPL could get into place to intervene.

'Landi, you've cut the city's water supply. Could you explain that?'

'Certainly, Mr Bellamy. We need this area drained of water to carry out our operations. I'm afraid you will need to find an alternative water source. You have a lot of resources available to do that, so it shouldn't present too much of a problem. I do hope you can forgive us.'

'Could I invite you to join me in a meeting with the East

Australian Settlement Management? Perhaps we could help you organise things in a way that would satisfy everybody.'

'I'm afraid your IPL partners are very antagonistic to us, and so a meeting would be futile, I think. No, you will have to accept our hospitality until we have finished our operations here. We will endeavour to make you as comfortable as possible, but I cannot let you contact your colleagues for the moment. I do apologise for any inconvenience, but necessity forces my hand. Please accompany me inside to your new quarters.'

Sean looked around frantically for his rescuers. He spotted Dan behind the fence, but he was blocked by dozens of armed humans inside the fence. If Dan's people fired, there'd be a blood bath which meant an immediate rescue wasn't going to happen. For now, there was nothing he could do other than follow as Landi demanded.

One of Landi's people held open the door to a small silver structure that looked like a garden shed. Landi followed him in, then led him to a flight of stairs at the back and down to a large open space. It was very similar to the underground IPL facilities he knew so well. Numerous doors were dotted along the surrounding walls. All of them were shut.

Landi leaned forward until his eye was close to a round object beside one of the doors. He inserted a small black rod, presumably an electronic key, into a slot beside the door. Once Sean was inside, Landi shut the door. 'These are your new quarters Mr Bellamy. You have a room to yourself and a shared sitting room. Your meals, and a change of clothing, will be brought to you and, if you require anything to make your stay more comfortable, please let your minders know and they will provide anything they can.' Landi gave him a sickly smile and then left.

Sean sat on the bed, working hard to suppress the sense of dread coursing through him. Refusing to let himself be overwhelmed, he realised he had to find a way to let the IPL know what lay beneath the shed. He stood and walked out of his room. The door opened onto the sitting area and, on the other side, was another room, presumably for the person with whom he was sharing. Multiple potted plants were scattered through the open space and the ceiling appeared to show the sky. It had to have been created by a combination of visual images and holograms, but he grudgingly admitted, it was well done. Still, he wasn't about to be lulled by the comfort-able appearance of the place. Despite the advanced features, it was still a building and every built structure had weak points. He'd just have to find them. No idea if the team back in the bunker could still hear him, he decided his best course of action was to talk and hope they were listening.

'Okay, hopefully this is coming through. I was intercepted inside the main gate. We walked about one hundred metres to the west of the gate, to a small metal shed, around three metres square, beside an exceptionally large gum tree. Don't be misled by its appearance, it's like the bunker. There's a major structure underneath. We came down a set of stairs at the back, then took the fifth door on the right. Landi used a key, possibly magnetic, to gain access. It also needed his eye print. Inside, there are two lockable rooms and a large shared sitting room. I can't recall a shed when Jemma and Nik encountered those men at the dam so, presuming the underground building was here, there must be another access. I'm apparently sharing with one other person. I haven't met him or her yet, but I'm looking.'

'I don't trust company, that's why you haven't seen me. Who are you? And who were you talking too?' A tall, slim man, late forties or early fifties, stood in the doorway of the second room. He had grey hair and looked gaunt which may have made him appear older than he was.

'My name is Sean Bellamy, and I'm part of the city's security force. Who are you?'

'Ross Johnson. I've been here for over a year. I was a geologist before the war, and I think I'm useful to them. They're looking for minerals.'

'Yes, they are,' replied Sean. 'I've heard your name. Pat Reilly is working with us.'

'You know Pat?' Ross demanded, rushing forward. 'He's alive? How did he survive the attacks?'

Sean stepped back, no idea if this fellow was to be trusted. 'Yes, he's alive. He and his family hid in a shelter on their farm, until he sought our help because he'd become ill. The aliens we work with, the IPL, treated him, and he's now doing very well. He's helped us work out what the Zants are up to. Pat thought you'd died.'

'I suspect everyone thought that. I know about the IPL. My wife and I were rescued by them, but the Zants grabbed me when we were walking back to the camp one night. They knew who I was, and what I did before the war, which has always puzzled me. I haven't given them much information, but they wear you down, and sometimes they got more than I intended.' He sat back onto his chair, shaking his head and muttering to himself.

It was obvious that Ross's isolation had impacted his mental health. He'd clearly stopped fighting but offering sympathetic noises wouldn't get the man motivated. 'We need to find a way out,' said Sean.

'It's hopeless,' said Ross. 'If you try to stand up to them, they hit you with a weapon they call an equaliser. It's like a high-tech cattle prod, gives an electric shock, and it's got a needle on the end that injects a toxin.'

'Alright, we'll have to find a way around them. Will you work with me, watch them when they come in? I need to know every move they make if I'm to come up with a plan.'

'Why not? Might reduce some of the boredom.'

'Good man.' Sean hoped that Hunt and Zadrus had heard this conversation. While he might be able to work out how to get out of this room, he didn't think they'd get far without some help from outside.

*   *   *

Even though it was clear Sean was trapped in an underground prison, hearing his voice helped Jemma calm down. At least she knew now he was alive.

'Bellamy's just given us clear directions on how to get to him,' said Hunt, sounding equally relieved.

'It is not enough,' said Zadrus, shaking his head as he leant over the map of the dam. 'There are several hurdles before the shed, and we don't know how many they are holding there. It is unlikely that Ross is the only prisoner.'

Matt had stood back, listening to Sean, then Hunt and Zadrus, but now he slumped on a chair next to the conference table. His skin was grey, and he was hyperventilating.

Hunt rushed to him. 'What's wrong, Matt? Slow your breathing. Deep breaths now.'

'Ross's story.' Matt rolled his head back and stared at the ceiling. 'None or you were here when this city was set up. Hundreds of people disappeared. My wife was one of them. She was pregnant.' He heaved a breath and clutched Hunt's arm.

'Take your time,' said Zadrus, looking equally concerned.

'There was never any sign of a struggle. We had no idea what became of them ... presumed they were dead. When the IPL made themselves known, most of us thought they were behind the disappearances which is why we struggled to accept help in the beginning.' He looked up at Zadrus. 'I'm sorry but you have to understand. We were always told that aliens were a myth.'

'I do understand,' replied Zadrus, sighing. 'It is possible that the Zants were here long before we arrived.'

'Is it also possible that my wife, and all the others, are still in some other part of that facility?'

'It is worth considering, but it would be unusual for the

Zants to keep their prisoners in one place,' said Zadrus. 'Most likely, those taken years ago have been moved on.'

There was a protracted silence before Hunt spoke. 'Matt, if it's too hard for you to be involved in the rescue attempt, we'll understand.'

'No, I can put my own problems aside. You need me here. I'll be okay.'

'I will report what you have just told me to IPL command and get an investigation underway,' said Zadrus. 'I was unaware there were many missing.'

Jemma did her best to comfort Matt. This was going to be as much about his wife now, as it was about Sean. Her admiration for Matt, given everything he'd suffered, soared. Despite the horror of losing his wife and then his father, he'd thrown himself into rescuing others and developing the settlement. She had no doubt that, like her, he'd need to be active and involved, in order to get through. She'd have to learn from him and do the same, lift herself above her grief and make herself useful.

'Right then,' said Zadrus. 'Everyone, join me, please. We must plan what we are to do.'

'O'Leary will take the lead in the field,' said Hunt. 'We can't go in with weapons blazing. I've called him back in to talk strategy.'

Matt glared at him, but Jemma knew Hunt would want Matt close until he'd evaluated his emotional state.

'I'm so sorry to hear about your wife,' said Jemma. 'I didn't know.'

'I don't talk about it.'

'Don't be angry with the General. He's as concerned about you as he is about Sean.'

Matt nodded but looked away. 'Yeah, I know.'

Zadrus ordered his technical team to get Dragile back on the large screens. 'We need outside help with our current problem,' he said as they waited. 'We must rescue all the prisoners from the Zants, detain the humans who are helping them, and then move the Zants off the surface of the planet. We cannot do that on our own. Come with me to talk to Dragile. We will leave Nikola with the listening equipment in case Sean speaks again.'

Dan walked in as the screens sprang to life. He looked at Jemma but took his place next to Hunt without speaking.

'I hope you have good news for me.' said Dragile.

'No, I am afraid not,' responded Zadrus. 'In fact, I have very bad news.' He recounted what had happened and requested the help he thought they'd need.

After a lengthy silence during which Zadrus motioned to those around him to say nothing, Dragile spoke. 'I did not think it was a good idea to send a lone human in, but having done so, we've obviously learnt some things. I agree with you, we cannot assume there are only two prisoners there. The set-up is too elaborate for just two. Keep listening to Sean. I will have our ships detect lifeforms within that building, see if we can get a count. We must set evacuation plans in place for the settlement, in case we fail. Other settlements are already on alert to assist if needed. Let me know if any other information comes to hand. I will pass on anything I find, as soon as I receive it.'

When the screen shut down, Zadrus ordered everyone back to the conference table. Before he could start, Sean's voice sounded again.

'Ross, I was just wondering, have you been out of this area at all since you've been here?'

'Yes. They often took me to a large room to interrogate me. I can't tell you exactly how we got there, but we went outside the door and then across the open area, onto a moving platform which took us down some levels. I don't know how many. When the platform stopped, we'd be in the bigger room.'

'Excellent! That tells me the building has several stories, so it's larger than I realised. Did you come across any other humans during those trips?'

'Well, not to speak to, but often someone else would be coming in when I went out or moving out as I was brought in. There was one person who I saw on several occasions. They called him Pete. On one occasion, there was a lady with him. Her name was Sharon. Mostly, I only saw people once. I just remember Pete, because there was something familiar about him, but I couldn't place what. They didn't seem to care if I heard people's names. I guess there was nothing I could do with the information, so it didn't really matter.'

'Can you recall any other names?'

'Yes, would you like me to write a list? It'd give me something to do,' replied Ross.

'Please do write the list. You know I'm thinking there's

something familiar about the names Pete and Sharon,' said Sean. 'Oh hell, I know. Pat's brother Pete disappeared, and his wife's name was Sharon. He probably looked familiar because he looked like Pat. They may have thought he could lead them to Pat.'

*　*　*

Pat arrived back in the conference room at the tail end of Sean's conversation as Ross described his encounter with Pete and Sharon. There was no mention of the children. Pat stood, staring into space, his face blank.

Hunt ordered a break. There wasn't much they could do until Sean spoke again, so Jemma urged Pat to take a walk with her. They left Dan huddled in a corner with Hunt, Matt and Zadrus to stare at some maps. She had to hope that they'd come up with a workable strategy, and quickly.

When they returned, they found Zadrus speaking earnestly into his communicator.

'No, no it is fine. Just some minor issues we have to clear up. Everything is under control. You rest. Your health is all that matters now.' He closed the communicator and, with a loud sigh, dropped his head onto one of his large hands.

'May I go and see Werrimen?' said Jemma.

'Yes, of course. But do not tell her about Sean or the dam. I do not want her to worry. Don't forget he is her Prehling.'

It seemed to Jemma that Werrimen had all the care available to her that she needed, but Zadrus looked so tired, and she knew he wouldn't rest until Sean was rescued. In that instant, she realised how much Sean's loss had affected everyone. She made up her mind there and then, to stop thinking about herself, and to offer her support to those who were taking active roles in Sean's rescue. She could manage her own terror privately.

She followed Hunt when they were called back to the screens, surprised to see Landi on one, Dragile on another.

'No, no, I have no knowledge of Colonel Bellamy's whereabouts,' said Landi.

'You have been seen and heard talking to him,' said Dragile.

'No, you are mistaken. However, I must warn you that if any attempt is made by your people to enter our grounds, they will not survive.'

Zadrus and Dragile both sat back and stared at each other. 'Landi, you must realise that the entire IPL is watching you. Should you cause our people any harm, you will pay dearly.'

Landi continued to smile. 'Stay away from my site and no one will be hurt.'

Dragile slammed his hand onto something which terminated the link, swearing as he did so. 'That would have to be the most irritating creature I have ever encountered. I have more IPL security on their way to you. This threat must be stamped out quickly to make it clear no further intrusions will be tolerated. Anything less will be taken as weakness. Discuss the situation with your people. I will pursue my leads. We'll speak shortly.'

Jemma suspected there was much more to come when Zadrus turned to address them. Most of Matt's old team, including those who now reported to Dan, had arrived in the conference room, along with several of Sean's old team. When Zadrus told them of Sean's abduction and the take-over of the dam site, their initial shock turned to anger, as it dawned on everyone that the mission to save Sean was now, most likely, a mass rescue. From the looks on several of their faces, it occurred to Jemma that some of them may also have lost family during the last months of the war.

Nik's voice interrupted the protracted silence, 'Sean's planning to break out, so you may find some help coming from the inside.'

Zadrus stood. 'Did he say how?'

'I think he intends to overpower the guard who brings in the meals. Sounds dodgy to me.'

'Dodgy?' said Zadrus.

'You know. Hairbrained. Can't work.'

'Oh, I see.'

'I don't think we can rely on Sean succeeding,' said Dan. 'Anything could go wrong for him. We have to devise a plan from the outside. If we're met by him once we get in, fantastic. But we can't rely on that.'

Jemma suspected Dan already had something in mind, and she was nervous to interject, but she felt she had to say something. 'It seems to me the biggest barrier we have is whatever Landi's using to protect the perimeter. If that threat can be eliminated, we might be able to use our greater numbers to overpower those in the compound.'

'Yes,' responded Zadrus. 'Some of our IPL members are very familiar with the weapons the Zants use. They are already out there.'

'We have another problem,' said Matt. 'We don't have a prison. We use the quarantine station to watch people, but we haven't had to deal with criminals at this stage. So, where will we house them, to interrogate them? And after?'

'You are right,' said Zadrus. 'We have a couple of options. We can convert one of the secure buildings to a temporary containment area, deal with the longer-term problem once the crisis is over. We could also land a large spaceship if necessary and process them from there.'

'Right then, we should get started,' said Hunt.

Zadrus received a report that Landi's protection was simple incendiary devices, but the triggers were hidden. They could be set off by body heat, so walking anywhere within the vicinity could cause an explosion, which meant that casualties were inevitable, no matter how much care was taken by the investigators.

CHAPTER 16

When the evening meal was delivered, Sean mentally documented every move the guard made. It bothered him that he couldn't pick if the guard was male or female. There were no distinguishing features. He knew it shouldn't make any difference, but he'd prefer not to attack a female. Putting that thought out of his mind, he told Ross to stop speaking and to write down his observations, in case the Zants were monitoring their conversations, as he suspected. He also stopped his attempts to transmit information to the IPL, no idea if they could hear him, anyway.

'It must be nice to finally have someone to share a meal with,' he said, when Ross joined him at the table.

Ross smiled, 'There've actually been quite a few folks through here. They'd stay a few weeks, and then be told they were going to their permanent facility, never anything more than that, but it was clear the facility wasn't here on Earth. I was once told I'd be shifted to the permanent facility, but it hasn't ever happened, and I'm thankful for that. The whole thing felt suspicious, and I doubt they were told the truth about where they were going. I actually wondered if they were to be …you know …um … murdered.'

'Okay, let's not go there. We're better off to put our energy into working out how to deal with our own situation.' He placed a piece of paper in front of Ross which had printed on it, *are you prepared to try when the guard comes back?*

Ross nodded, but they were still eating when the door again opened. It was too soon for the guard to have returned. Sean rose, ready for whatever was about to happen. He gasped when a human male entered the room.

'Good evening Sean. I'm pleased to finally meet you face to face.'

'Jesus,' exclaimed Sean, gripping the back of his chair. 'Pritchard. What the hell do you want?'

'You know what I want.'

'If you think I'm going to lead you to Jemma, you're out of your mind! Particularly now that I know you're in bed with the Zants.'

'You will lead me to Jemma. It's in both of your interests. As far as the Zants are concerned, one does what one has to do.'

'Why?' asked Sean. 'Why are you doing any of this?'

'Oh, I think you're brighter than that.' Pritchard smiled, which made Sean want to pummel him into the ground, but he knew he had to restrain himself if he were to have any chance of getting out and back to a position to be able to protect Jemma. 'I can't leave her free. I had her sister nicely contained until you interfered. I won't allow you to interfere again.'

'All Jemma wants is to live her life,' growled Sean. 'She doesn't want anything to do with you or Anders Major.'

'I'm sure that's how she thinks but, given her position,

what she wants is rather irrelevant, don't you think?' replied Pritchard, still smiling. 'Like it or not, she remains, by birthright, Supreme Ruler of Anders Major. I cannot allow her to take that up.'

Sean gaped at him. 'You're prepared to kill her to prevent her from returning to her planet?'

'No, no, I quite like her. I'll have her placed on another planet that doesn't have access to space travel. If you'll help me get her, you can join her.'

'As if I'd tell you where she is,' Sean snapped.

'Oh, I know where she is. I've been tracking her since I first met her.'

Sean took a breath to steady himself. 'How can I help you if I'm incarcerated here?'

'I can fix that, and I can offer you something that will convince you to help.'

'What would that be?'

'Her uncle Kevson,' replied Pritchard as he turned to leave. 'I'll return in twenty-four hours for your answer.'

'She doesn't have any relatives. There was an uncle with a farm in the far west, but he was killed in the same floods that took her parents. There's no one else.'

'No, he wasn't killed. Her uncle Kevson is very much alive and well, and I know where he is.'

'So, he's in cahoots with you too?'

'No,' replied Pritchard. 'He is not working with me, but I can access him quite easily if you bring Jemma to me.'

'As if I'd do that.'

'If you want your freedom, and you value Jemma, you will do as I say. You obviously need some time to think about it. I will return tomorrow. If you agree, I will secure your release. Seems like a fair deal to me.' Pritchard smiled again, then reached for the door handle and backed out of the room.

*　*　*

Hunt had directed Jemma to organise the large number of security officers who were on their way in from other settlements to help. Although she knew it was to keep her busy, she'd thrown herself into the task to avoid thinking about Sean. Zadrus had made it clear that the Zants would be watching as all the transporters arrived so, when Sean's voice came through again, she was in the process of organising security guards to collect the new arrivals and escort them to the bunker. She forgot all about the arrivals and dashed back to the speaker, desperate for anything that might indicate he was on his way out, but she felt like someone had punched her in the face when she heard Pritchard's voice. 'No,' she cried. 'It can't be. Dear God, it can't be.'

Dan moved closer, wrapping his arms around her to hold her up. 'Shush. Just listen. We might learn something we can use to help Sean.'

She stared at him, unable to form words, and didn't resist when he guided her to a seat. He beckoned to Pat to sit with her, then he joined the others at the communicator, and appeared to be analysing every word.

Pat stroked her hand, although he looked equally shocked. 'Is that my grandfather?'

'It is,' she murmured.

'Sean said he was a criminal, but I think I still had a romantic notion that he'd been misjudged. He is my grandfather after all, but he's downright evil.'

'No, there's nothing romantic about him,' said Jemma. 'Evil's a good word. Someone suggested, when we discovered that he had my sister, that he'd kept her drugged so she wouldn't remember who she was. I suspect that was right. I just hope she had a good life after he left.'

'That much I can assure you. We loved her dearly. Now I'm glad I never met the bastard,' said Pat.

'I wish I hadn't, but if he's got Uncle Kev I need to meet with him.'

Hunt sat opposite her and reached out for her hand. 'I have no idea what to say. We have to focus on rescuing Bellamy first. At least we know where he is. When he's safe, we start work on finding your uncle.'

'I have already requested an investigation,' said Zadrus. 'If your uncle is alive we should be able to track him, unless …'

'Unless what?' said Jemma.

'Unless he has him somewhere that is out of our range.'

'Dear God.' She stared at Zadrus, then at Dan, who'd moved back beside her.

'Stay with Pat until you get your breath back,' said Dan. 'We need to get on with the search.' With a grin, he bent forward into a fake bow. 'Your majesty.'

She slapped his arm but had to laugh. Dan always did that for her. It didn't matter what the problem was, or how badly she was hurting, he seemed to be able to take the sting out of it, yet, once he re-joined Hunt, he was all business. He was so much like Sean.

Still clinging to Pat, she listened to Hunt and Dan as they developed their strategy. They'd have to move at speed, and without showing their hand, so the Zants wouldn't have time to close off access to their building. Dan suggested two teams, one to tackle the building, the other for a surface offensive. He thought both teams should arrive at the same time. The surface team would create a distraction and get the attention of the Zants and their human security. The building team could use the ruckus to get inside.

'It might sound a bit obvious, but Sean managed to get in by cutting through a fence,' said Dan. 'We could do the same, use the cover of darkness, and the bushes in the perimeter, then make our way around to the building. So long as we're quiet and stay in the shadows, we should get away with it.'

Hunt straightened up and stared at Dan for a minute. 'Yes. Good thinking O'Leary. You can lead Team 1 to take the building. Find a way to get in without being seen and find some cover nearby until Team 2 approaches the front gate. Matt, you take Team 2. Make sure you're seen. Do whatever it takes to get their attention onto you, without putting any of your team at risk. That'll buy some time for O'Leary to get inside. Denis and I will coordinate operations at the site. Jemma, you remain here and assist Zadrus with surveillance.'

She desperately wanted to object, but she understood why Hunt had issued that command. She was Pritchard's main target. Her presence at the site could create an unnecessary complication. Yet he was allowing Nik to go, and she was almost as much of a target. Jemma turned her back. If she said anything now, it would most likely inflame the situation.

While Dan and Matt briefed their teams, she waited with Pat for Zadrus to give the go ahead. The munitions team had already cleared many of the incendiary devices, but they were worried because the triggers had been placed in what they termed a 'sloppy' fashion, so they couldn't be sure they had them all. They advised that when a device was triggered, they'd heard a very light 'clicking' noise which they considered a warning, although at best it was a couple of seconds. The actual devices weren't very strong. If hit directly, they thought it possible that the impact could be lethal, and jumping back, even a couple of metres, should be enough to save the person's life.

Zadrus spoke to Dragile and, just before sunrise, gave the order to commence the offensive. Both teams ran to the transporters that would take them to the dam site.

*   *   *

Sean explained to Ross why Pritchard's presence meant he had to escape. Using pen and paper, he outlined his plan. 'We'll overpower the guard and force him to cooperate. As soon as we're out, we'll release anyone we find. Increasing our numbers will give us an advantage.'

When the guard entered, Sean greeted him with a cheerful, 'Hello.'

Ross took the plates, then Sean swiftly overpowered the Zant taking care not to harm him. He had to remain capable of cooperating.

'You are wasting your time,' said the guard. 'You don't have the key to get out.'

'But you do,' said Sean. 'I will require you to use it.'

'No. I will not help you.'

Sean, maintaining a tight grip on the Zant, smiled. 'I'm not asking you to help. I'm telling you that you're going to help. If necessary, we will use force. Now tell me, how many prisoners are there in this facility?'

The Zant cried out in pain when Sean pulled his arm further behind his back. 'I cannot tell you what I do not know.'

'Describe this floor.'

'Sixteen apartments, two or three prisoners in each.'

'Other floors.'

'I am only permitted on this floor.'

'Where are people taken when they leave here?' snapped Sean.

'An orbiting large ship. That's all I know.'

'How often are people shipped out?'

'Every three or four days.'

The full horror of what must have been happening took Sean's breath away. Every three or four days for six or seven years, maybe longer. With no idea how much the IPL had heard, he had to focus even harder on getting the hell out of here.

'Alright, move,' commanded Sean.

The guard stared at him but didn't resist. He turned to the door and used his key.

'Where's the nearest room with prisoners?'

The Zant pointed to the first room.

'Open it,' growled Sean.

Ross took charge of the prisoners, mostly male, but a few females, all between twenty and thirty years of age. They appeared to be healthy. As Sean cleared each room, Ross instructed the prisoners to assemble in the entry foyer. They found twenty-six people on the top floor, but Ross had been sure there were multiple floors, so Sean pushed the Zant down the first flight of stairs to a second floor. Thirty-two people were released there and eighteen from a third floor. He directed everyone up to the top floor, to wait with Ross while he continued down to a fourth, and it seemed final, floor. It had a large open foyer and a locked area at the back. Even with the Zant's key and eye-scan, he was unable to open it, so he turned to go back up. Sensing movement behind, he picked up his speed and, pushing the Zant in front of him, ran to the top floor. 'Okay, how do we get outside?'

'I have never been outside,' the guard replied.

'Try the key you used on the other doors,' commanded Sean, anxious to get moving. The door opened, and he directed everyone out but, before he could follow, a searing pain shot through the middle of his back, so severe he lost consciousness.

*   *   *

Dan ordered his people forward at almost the same moment as the door to the shed opened, but he couldn't get through the surge of prisoners who spilled out through the narrow entrance. He pushed people along until the last one had emerged. 'Sean isn't with them,' he shouted. 'I'm going in.'

Ross had stopped just inside the doorway to wait for Sean, but when he heard Dan he told him, as briefly as he could, what had taken place.

'Any idea how many floors?' asked Dan.

'Sean said four.'

Dan tore down the stairs, directing two of his people to search each floor until he reached the fourth level. It was clearly different from the other three. Uneasy about this level's purpose when he saw the locked door, he waited for the rest of his team, then ordered them to spread out and continue to search. He whirled around when he heard someone, or something, scampering towards the southern end.

'There's something mechanical gearing up,' yelled Matt, as he flew down the stairs.

'Yeah, I can hear it.' Dan ran towards the noise. 'Sounds like a transporter.'

The locked door blocked them from getting any closer. It didn't respond to the magnetic key Dan had taken from the Zant. With Matt's help, he tried to shoulder it open but without success. Others came up behind him and added their weight, but it didn't budge. The mechanical noise continuing to increase, he searched for any other entrance, but there was nothing. His only clue was a set of symbols above the lock.

'Zadrus,' he shouted. 'We need advice.'

'What is the problem?' replied Zadrus.

'Sending a picture,' yelled Dan. 'We can't get through.'

'Look for the key,' replied Zadrus. 'It will have the same symbols on it. I would expect it to be in a recess beside the door.'

'Found it,' yelled Dan.

'Insert it into the lock.'

'A tiny screen slid out. With a touch pad below it.'

'Key in the symbols in the same order as those on the door.'

'Got it.' The door slowly creaked open but as he tried to step through, he was thrown back into the hallway by a massive gust of wind.

'Zadrus,' he screamed. 'They've taken off. You've got to get someone out there to intercept.'

'Already doing it,' said Zadrus. 'Dragile has also sent some fighter crafts.'

'No,' yelled Dan. 'Back him off. Sean's on board and God knows who else.'

*   *   *

Sometime after he was attacked, although he had no idea how long, Sean tried to shift his arms. He cried out with pain. He was shackled to something. It felt like the kind of examination table doctors of his era used, but his vision was so blurred he couldn't see. He froze when Landi's voice cut through his nightmare.

'Do not fight it Mr Bellamy, you cannot escape. I did tell you that before you abandoned my facility. You have cost me a lot of time and money I'm afraid, which is regrettable, although I may be able to recover some through you. I will not harm you unless you force me to do so. It is best if you cooperate, so we can resolve this situation to our mutual benefit.'

'Where am I?'

'That's of no concern to you now, Mr Bellamy,' said Landi.

After Landi left, another Zant, who'd be standing quietly at the side of room, approached. 'I can give you something to relieve your pain and, if you convince me I can trust you, I will move the table into a sitting position and release some of the bindings.'

Sean nodded, and forced himself to smile at his captor.

'Please move onto your right side as much as you can.'

He screamed as another sharp pain seared into his back, but this time it resolved quickly, and as it went, the agony he'd felt when he awoke, went with it. He stared at the Zant.

'My apologies, but I find it is usually best just to use the antidote rather than waste time explaining it. You are less tense that way.'

This fellow seemed genuine, so Sean thanked him and, as his vision cleared, he cast his eyes around the room. It reminded him of an operating theatre with a table in the middle that was covered in instruments. As the back of the bed was tilted upwards, enabling him to sit, he had to stop himself from wondering what went on in this room. He had no doubt that Zadrus would be doing everything he could to find him, so he lay back to allow himself to recover. Fatigue overwhelming him, he closed his eyes.

A Zant, speaking in a hushed tone, woke him.

'There are a lot of crafts following us. Landi's gone too far this time. I doubt we'll get out of this without damage.'

A different voice agreed.

Raising his hand, Sean touched the nearest Zant's arm. 'Could you tell me where we are please?'

The Zant almost choked as he stuttered. 'What do you mean?'

'Are we still on Earth or have we moved out into space? Are we close to Earth?'

'Yes, yes I believe we are orbiting Earth. I do apologise, but I must go, I have things I have to do.'

The Zant ran for the door, and seemed to have difficulty finding it, but it finally opened, and he stumbled through. Sean's gaze turned to the Zant who had earlier administered the antidote.

'Don't ask me. I spend most of my time in this room, and really don't know what's happening. Everyone is under strict orders not to tell you anything, but I can't anyway, so there we have it.' He also scurried from the room, but with greater composure.

Sean frowned, but the tiredness still overwhelmed him, and he drifted back into a sound sleep.

*   *   *

Desperate for something to occupy her mind, Jemma joined the medical team to check the prisoners who'd been released from the dam. Her misery turned to fascination as the Sidlown crew set up a temporary structure for the purpose. They started with a box about two metres square and twenty centimetres deep. With the release of a catch, it expanded to a bigger square around fifty metres by fifty metres. Then it stopped, but, as she moved towards it, a Sidlown held her back.

'It is not finished. It must consolidate before the next phase.'

A few minutes later, the structure started to expand upwards, a metre at a time until, she estimated, it had reached eight metres in height. Another Sidlown walked to the front wall. He attached a small device to the centre, and a door slowly formed. He remained still in front of the door after it had opened, until a swirling mist inside cleared. Then he beckoned everyone forward.

Jemma gazed around the structure as she followed him in. The walls, when in the box, had appeared gossamer thin, but now they were solid. She had to tear herself away from admiring the alien ingenuity so she could help set up tables and unpack instruments and dressings. Once the released prisoners began to arrive, she did her best to be useful, assisting a triage nurse and arranging transport to the hospital where the captives were to be questioned further.

The excellent condition of most of them surprised Jemma as she scanned for implanted devices like the silver bars that they'd found in the Rescue Earth Group. She didn't find any but was surprised to see an unusual tattoo on the shoulder of the first person she checked. He said it had appeared in the last week, but he had no idea how it got there. His roommate also had one. The first either of them knew about it was an itchy spot on the shoulder. By the time she'd finished her checks, she'd found fifty tattoos. Those who had been on the top floor, including Ross, didn't have them. Eighteen people said that theirs had appeared three weeks earlier, about a week before they were shifted to the third floor. The rest, who had been on the second floor, had only noticed theirs in the last week.

Jemma took an image of each tattoo before releasing its wearer to join the others in the transporters. Each tattoo had two lines of symbols with something that looked like an inverted boomerang above. She'd noticed a similar V-shaped symbol when she was inside the Zant spaceship. Puzzled by what she was seeing, she began to compile a report, and once she was satisfied there were no further injuries, she showed Dan what she'd found. He had no idea what to make of the tattoos either, so he escorted her back to the bunker to present her findings to Zadrus.

When they arrived, Zadrus and Hunt were staring at a big screen that showed a large craft, although there didn't appear to be any activity around it.

'Is that where Sean is?' asked Jemma.

'Yes,' replied Zadrus. 'We are watching closely. Now, were there any problems?'

'Not problems,' replied Jemma, handing him her communicator with her report. 'But we found these.'

'Would you connect your communicator to the screen system so we can show Dragile,' he said, frowning at the first of the images. While he sounded calm, his face was white, and his clenched fists suggested a fury that she'd never seen in Zadrus before. With Dragile, he watched in silence, although they exchanged looks at some of the images.

Finally, Dragile gave a loud sigh. 'It was foolish of us to think we could re-establish life on Earth without interference. Government ignorance here has prevented law enforcement agencies from looking into alien abductions, so the Zants, and presumably others, have had a wonderful opportunity to pursue their evil with impunity. It is our responsibility now. We should have seen this coming, and we should have prevented it.'

'So, I take it you know what these tattoos represent?' snapped Hunt.

'Oh yes, indeed,' responded Dragile. 'We know them very well. Zadrus do you have an electrometer?'

'I do,' replied Zadrus.

'May I ask something?' said Jemma, aware of Hunt's arm around her shoulders.

'Of course,' replied Zadrus.

'Are they the same as our tattoos?' Zadrus had long ago identified the origin of the tattoos that she, Sean, Dan, Nik and Hunt all had on their right hip.

'No,' said Dragile, rubbing his hands across his face. 'Yours are an identification that was used by your home planet, Anders Major, to show your family and your position in that society. These are different. Zadrus, call all members of the IEMO to your city. Include your senior people. Request each member to bring a list of people who are known to be missing from their city. I will contact Earth's IPL commander, Shardene, and request her assistance. Then I will make my way down to join you.'

'What's the IEMO?' asked Jemma.

'The International Earth Management Organisation which is made up of the administrators of all the settlements,' said Zadrus. 'General, I need you, Jemma, Dan, Matt and Nik in the conference room. I will answer any other questions there. What I have to tell you must remain confidential.'

Jemma walked beside Hunt. The others followed, all silent.

Zadrus secured the room and enabled an electronic security blanket. 'We know about Pritchard's agenda, and I doubt he cared what the Zants were up to, probably accepted that they were just after the minerals.' Zadrus looked up at the ceiling for a few seconds. 'Having seen the images that Jemma so carefully recorded; we now know otherwise. I have no idea how to tell you this, so I will just say it directly. Throughout history, every planet has, at some point, profited from a slave trade, including Earth. You would not know that, on many planets, human beings are in high demand for that trade.'

Jemma gasped, 'You can't mean that Sean has been taken for slavery? Can you?'

Matt stood. 'And Dana? My wife?'

'Possibly. But they do look after them as you saw today.

Hopefully, realising Sean's value to us, they will give us the first option to *buy* him. That's the best we can hope for at this juncture. We will of course do the same when we find Dana, and any other humans. Please be aware that on most planets, slaves are treated well, although, on some, men might be put to work, often very hard work.'

'How the hell did this happen?' growled Matt. 'Why didn't you notice and why didn't you warn us about the Zants?'

Zadrus nodded. 'I understand your anger, but please let me finish. Many planets have become degraded over time. Lack of food and water on some planets has made their people weak. The human species is physically particularly strong. Many, throughout the Universe, believe that if they hybridise with the human species, they will produce offspring with increased strength and ensure the survival of their own race.'

'Fucking hell.' Matt stared at him in disbelief. 'You mean my wife might have been taken as a sex slave.'

'It is my painful duty to tell you that that is most likely the case. There have been instances of people on my planet buying human slaves for that very reason. It is illegal on Sidlow, and every effort is made to stamp it out, but I would be lying to you if I said it didn't happen. To help you understand, I would like you to look at the image of Dragile. He is, in fact, what most beings on my planet look like. I am the result of an experiment. My parents looked *normal* for Sidlow, but the scientists of the time implanted human sperm, along with my father's genetic material, in my mother, and I am the result. I, and many like me on Sidlow, are half human. While beings like Dragile are still larger than most humans, they are much weaker than those like me. Mostly, my race has achieved our ends by collecting sperm and eggs from humans who volunteer to help us, and sometimes by producing embryos and developing them in vitro. Some planets buy slaves, usually males, and keep them there as a permanent source of sperm. Occasionally, women are taken for this purpose also, but usually their eggs are collected, and the embryos developed elsewhere. Slaves usually live comfortably, but in isolation from any other human being. The tattoos you saw are not just branding marks. They have a lot more meaning. The central image is a symbol for the planet which has purchased the person. The symbols below identify the purchaser. If anything goes wrong with the captors, the purchaser can still identify their own slave through the tattoos.'

The room was silent until Matt exploded. 'My wife, and child, could be anywhere in the universe, in who knows what kind of conditions.'

Dan stood, walked across the room, and put his hand on Matt's shoulder. 'You've got every right to be angry. I can't even begin to imagine how you feel. At least we still know where Sean is, not that it helps us much. We have to focus now on getting them back. All of them, including Dana. Can you do that mate?'

Matt glared at him, then seemed to lose some of his tension. 'Yes, I can. If what Zadrus describes has happened to Dana, I have to find her. And my daughter.'

'We're all with you,' said Dan softly. He turned to Zadrus. 'How do we find them and get them back?'

'That is our major concern,' responded Zadrus. 'Dragile is, at this moment, briefing our leaders and requesting assistance. If there are no more questions, we will start preparing for the IEMO meeting. I will be here for any individual questions you may have.'

'Just one thing,' said Dan, 'should Jemma remain involved with the investigation? I'm sorry mate, but I'm worried the stress might be too much for you.'

'I'm involved,' said Jemma, standing to face Dan. 'Accept it. I need to be here and to know what's happening, and I believe my input can be useful. I'm staying.'

Hunt turned away but she didn't miss the smile on his face.

Zadrus was also smiling as he responded, 'I think it best for Jemma to continue. She is my Prehling and will work with me in headquarters for now.'

CHAPTER 17

While Dan and Matt worked with their staff to meet and brief the IEMO delegates, Jemma waited with Hunt. He did his best to console her, but she couldn't control the cartwheels in her mind. They knew the craft that had taken Sean had docked on a larger spaceship which had been identified as Zant, but that was where it ended. For all she knew, he could already be dead. Hunt, whom she suspected had guessed the way she was thinking, led her to the meeting room so they could at least see what was happening.

The crowd was bigger than she'd expected from the forty settlements, but Hunt explained that each city had sent two delegates, and most had brought their own security staff. In addition, there were two or three IPL Trustees from each settlement, and many more Trustees from the patrolling Earth fleet. She estimated four to five hundred attendees, which meant that getting people in and settled would be a slow process. Every person who entered the bunker had to be screened, scanned for Zant bars, and greeted by one of Dan's or Matt's staff. She suspected that some of their greetings might be closer to an interrogation since neither Matt nor Dan were inclined to trust anyone at this stage. Many of the Trustees, in their distinctive black uniforms, stood at the side of the room, carrying sophisticated-looking weaponry, far from the simple stun weapons to which Jemma had become accustomed.

She looked up at Hunt. 'Why are they so heavily armed?'

'Not sure. The IPL has a lot of experience with the Zants, and we know from everything Zadrus has told us, that they're tricky. Maybe the Trustees are worried about infiltration.'

'I think we'd notice if a few Zants walked in.'

'We would, but we've seen for ourselves how they use humans.'

'Yeah, true.'

'Come on. Let's join the team. Looks like we're about to start.'

There was a hush as Dragile mounted the podium to address the meeting. He was slightly stooped as he walked, and he held onto the railing beside the stairs as he climbed them. His reptilian skin seemed even more pronounced now that she could see him in person, and he didn't look strong, at least not like Zadrus. She smiled to herself when she realised that she'd expected to see a tail, but of course there was none. His body shape was essentially humanoid. It was hard to tell because he didn't stand as erect as Zadrus, but she thought he'd be a similar height, around 230 centimetres. Despite his frailty in comparison to Zadrus, he was an impressive figure and he commanded the attention of everyone in the room as he prepared to speak.

He looked up and began to speak. His voice resounded

throughout the large room as he outlined everything that had happened, including his belief that the humans had been kidnapped for the intergalactic slave trade. He didn't allow time for questions, calling Nik to the stage to provide a summary of all the information that the delegates had provided her regarding missing people. She walked forward as soon as he beckoned, but she looked extremely nervous. When she started to speak, Jemma noticed an anger in her eyes which was out of character, but it became obvious why as she talked about the 2,647 people who were known to be missing. The actual numbers had to be much larger as so much information had been lost in the war. Almost all those on the list were young and fit, and around three-quarters were male, which fitted well with Dragile's belief of why they'd been taken.

A man at the back stood and, staring around the room for support, addressed Dragile. 'We're all too stunned to fully process what you're saying, but one question springs to mind. What are you doing to find all these people? They could be thousands of light years away by now and scattered anywhere on millions of planets. We don't have any capacity to deal with that. How do we protect the rest of our population now that we know what's been going on?'

'We have already started to address each of your points and set emergency procedures in place. I called this meeting to seek your input and to provide you with information. We have begun to develop files on every person we know to be missing. Our next step will be to notify all sympathetic planets of our problem. Most will take this information very seriously and, if there are any slaves, will do their utmost to find them. Some will not be as helpful. On those planets, our Trustees will intervene. Once we have identified all the target planets from the tattoos, we will concentrate Trustee forces there. We know of sixteen planets already. Unknown tattoos have been sent to our Trustee command on Sidlow who, we hope, will be able to identify them. You must understand we are not alone. There are many inhabited planets in the universe and, all but a handful will be angered by what has happened here. Most will mobilise their resources to help in our search.'

Jemma didn't feel particularly reassured, and she suspected most others in the room would agree with her. There was little more Dragile could add and, no matter how hard he tried to reassure the crowd, uncertainty remained so, around 3 a.m., he closed the meeting.

The Australian team gathered around Hunt, Dan and Matt. They'd all been given rooms in the bunker, but no one seemed ready to leave.

'I want everyone to try for some rest.' Hunt raised his hand when people objected. 'There's nothing more we can do tonight. Those of you on guard duty, attend to your stations. Everyone else, get some sleep. We will reconvene at 11a.m.'

Nothing happened overnight, but Jemma jumped at the smallest noise. In the end, she gave up and sat on the side of the bed hoping that, when she went outside, she'd discover the events of the day before had just been a nightmare. Hunt called her to come in two hours earlier than expected and she jumped up. She didn't really care what he wanted her to do.

Anything would be better than worrying about what might be happening to Sean.

He'd already started to brief Dan and Matt when she arrived. It seemed that a crowd had gathered in Administration Square, mainly people who'd been caught up in the Zant assault at the factory. Once news started to spread of the latest Zant interference, their fury had increased. While Hunt and Zadrus feared a riot, it occurred to Jemma that she hadn't reached anger yet; she was still numb with shock.

'I would like your opinion,' said Zadrus, when Hunt finished explaining what was happening. 'When I address the crowd, I think I should describe events directly and outline what we are trying to do. I've always found that it is best to be open and honest.'

Jemma deferred to Hunt in the same way as Dan and Matt, and he smiled which was more irritating than anything he could have said. She'd never wanted to be part of his security force but, every day, she found herself being drawn closer and closer to his core group. Now that Sean was gone, and recognising that Pritchard was prepared to do anything to get hold of her, he'd up the ante. She'd have no choice but to acquiesce. And he knew it.

Hunt had clearly taken the reigns again when he answered Zadrus. 'I agree. Straight to the point is best. These people have every right to be furious. I would suggest that the time has come to upgrade our security force and form an Army, give people a legitimate way to fight back, stop individuals going off half-cocked for revenge.'

Zadrus paused for a moment. 'Although it distresses me, I believe you are right. The Army cannot be limited to this settlement, however, or any other individual settlement. We must not enable internal conflicts. Would you be prepared to take responsibility for setting it up? I am asking a great deal of you.'

'We've discussed this before, so I've already started thinking about how to go about it. Yes, I am prepared to take responsibility. May I also suggest a public forum so that people who aren't involved with the Army will still have a voice and can vent their frustrations. The whole population needs to have the right to be involved. I suggest we develop a model here, then roll it out to the other settlements.'

'Yes, I agree,' said Zadrus. 'I will address the crowd first, then hand it over to you to talk about those things.'

Jemma wasn't happy at the turn this conversation had taken. The fact that Hunt had demanded she join him here meant he'd intended to raise the idea of the Army and it wasn't a big leap to assume he had a role planned for her. That was the last thing she wanted, but that discussion would have to wait. She walked with Nik, making sure they stayed well back from Hunt, to the transporters which would take them to Administration Square. The Administration building was still toxic, so they were to land on the other side and walk around, into the square. All eyes turned toward them and the crowed hurled questions and demands as they made their way to the central stage. It was a permanent fixture and its purpose had been, ironically, for entertainment like concerts or stage plays.

She sensed the mood of the crowd worsening and put her irritation aside to stand beside Zadrus, as she knew he'd want. He began with a succinct description of the events of the last few days. When he reiterated Dragile's message to the IEMO that many of the missing people had been taken for the intergalactic slave trade, the crowd became utterly silent.

'We have no way of knowing how many people are missing,' said Zadrus. 'We will gather all the information we can and have already commenced our search.'

Many people in the crowd slumped down on their chairs or on the ground. They stared at each other, or at Zadrus, until, in the end, someone stood and shouted at Zadrus.

Hunt quickly stepped forward, his hand on Jemma's shoulder indicating he wanted her to stay up there with him. He stood in front of the lectern and faced the crowd. To her surprise, everyone there looked up at him and waited, probably due to Matt's presence on his other side. So many of these people had been through both the war and the recovery with Matt. They knew him well, and of his relationship to Hunt. The rest of the crowd were from her era and would have seen Hunt or Dan or even herself in an official role on the spaceship. Hunt proposed the forum and suggested regular meetings, then went on to pursue the idea of developing a military capacity within each city.

Jemma couldn't decide if the audience was reassured or too shocked to respond, but when Hunt explained the logistics of setting up an Army, she saw many people sit forward to listen. It was her turn to smile. She shouldn't have doubted him. Much as she hated to admit it, he was particularly good at organising and motivating people. Those interested were to bring identity papers the next day, which showed their age, and a summary of everything they'd done in the past. He set a follow-up meeting for three days hence and promised a progress report then. As an afterthought, he said he'd also set up an office for people to report if they knew of anyone who was missing or would like information on people on the missing list, then he thanked them for listening and closed the meeting. She looked at him, shaking her head.

'What?' He had a broad grin on his face.

'You enjoyed that.'

'Yes, and no. I enjoyed having something to do, to take charge of a bad situation and work out how to sort it out. But I didn't enjoy seeing the pain on the faces of those people.' He put his arm around her. 'So, are you with me on this?'

'God, you're predictable. I support what you're trying to do, but I don't want to be any part of your Army.'

'I thought you'd be right behind me.' He lifted his arm from her shoulder and tousled her hair.

'I am,' she muttered. 'A long way behind.'

A spring in his step which she hadn't seen for some time, had him several metres ahead of her as they made their way back to the transporter until someone rushed past, and knocked her off her feet.

Matt yelled, 'Grab that man.' With Dan, he tore after the fellow. Hunt ran back to help her up, taking a piece of paper the man had shoved into her hand. He read it out. 'IF YOU

WANT TO SEE SEAN BELLAMY AGAIN, WAIT OUTSIDE YOUR APARTMENT BLOCK BY YOURSELF AT 10PM.'

'Ignore that now,' said Hunt. 'We'll go back to the bunker and decide what to do.' She ran beside him to the transporter, aware that Dan and Matt had cuffed the man and were heading him towards the hospital, the only place other than the Administration building with discrete interview rooms.

Jemma was on tenterhooks, as she waited with Hunt in the bunker for the men to return, springing to her feet as the door opened.

'Says he belongs to a group of people who worked for the Zants but realised they were doing the wrong thing and left,' said Dan. 'Claims they feared retaliation because they knew too much and were forced into hiding for their own safety, and they're now looking for a way to return to the city.'

'We both think the story's bogus,' said Matt. 'He's got too much knowledge of the Zants to dismiss him entirely, though. We checked him for a silver bar, but he was clean.

Dan shook his head. 'Sir, the Zants are gone. If these characters were afraid of them, they could just have presented to the quarantine centre, and been accepted there.'

Matt agreed. 'I doubt they know anything about Sean.'

'But hang on, what if they do? We can't just ignore them,' said Jemma.

'No, we can't, and they won't come out if they don't see Jemma,' said Hunt.

Dan wheeled around to him. 'You can't put Jemma at that kind of risk.'

Jemma, hands on hips, interrupted. 'I'm prepared to give it a try if there's any hope of getting Sean back. I understand if they're Pritchard's people, that they might simply be after me, but I've got an implanted tracker. You could use it to help locate us both.'

'We have a tracking device on Sean,' said Zadrus. 'It was implanted before we left to come here, so we actually know where he is. The problem is not in finding him, it is in getting him away from the Zant craft. We must wait for them to land and hope that they don't get to a transport zone before we can intervene. Let us stay focussed on the problem here. It is possible you could use Jemma to flush this group out, but I agree with Dan, the risk is too high.'

'Well if you've all finished trashing my idea, perhaps you could let me finish,' growled Hunt.

Dan and Matt, both said, 'Sir,' but Zadrus laughed and Jemma said, as sweetly as she could manage, 'Certainly, General.'

Hunt laughed too. They both knew he'd won. It was only a matter of time before she'd be expected to acquiesce, maybe even call him sir, but she didn't plan to make it easy for him.

'I'm wondering if we can find a trained person who looks like Jemma,' he said. 'If these people do show up, they probably won't scrutinise too hard initially. Eventually, they'll realise she's an agent, but we should have overpowered them by then.'

'I actually think I know someone who fits the bill,' responded Matt. 'Give me a few minutes and I'll see if she's nearby.'

Jemma wasn't happy that they were putting another person in danger in her place, but she knew there was no point in arguing. 'Do you think they know anything about Sean?'

'I doubt it, but we can't dismiss it altogether,' said Hunt. 'My feeling is that they're probably Pritchard's people, as you say, and they want you, but I'm not going to allow that to happen. IPL command is tracking the craft that we believe has Sean. Until they can work out how to board it, or force it to land, there's nothing much anyone can do for him. So, let's see what we can find out through these people. Meanwhile, why don't we go find somewhere quiet, and have a chat.'

A tight sensation crawled into the pit of her stomach as she followed him to a small lounge in the secure accommodation section where they'd all spent the previous night. When he flicked the lever that would prevent anyone else from opening the door, she groaned.

'You know what I'm going to say,' he said, grinning. 'What about it?'

'No.'

'Jemma, I've discussed this with Zadrus.'

'I'll bet you have,' she muttered.

'Come on, sit down.' He sat on the sofa and pointed to the seat beside him.

She threw herself down. Refusing to sit with him would have been churlish and whatever he planned to say, he'd go ahead anyway. 'I don't want to join your Army.'

'I know, but you're already part of the security force on

Zadrus's orders. I want you to step up, and I want you to do it willingly.'

For a moment, all she could do was stare at him. 'Why? Why are you doing this to me?'

'The truth?'

'Please.'

'I have a number of reasons which I'm happy to share with you. But there's one major reason that's making me push you now.' He paused. 'After my conversation with Zadrus, I believe he is going to instruct you to join me. And if you argue with him, I believe he'll force you. Truthfully, I don't know how he would do that, and I don't want you to suffer any further. I think it's best if you don't find out what he might do.'

'Okay, I get that. So, what are your reasons?'

'Fair enough. I have three. Firstly, I enjoy working with you. You're a hard worker, you're physically strong and capable, and you work things out for yourself. Secondly, given the number of attempts that have been made to abduct you, I want you close, which will be easier if you are part of my Army. And thirdly, Sean is like a son to me, and I feel a responsibility for you in his absence. So, are you with me?'

'It doesn't sound like I have a choice.'

He sighed, 'No, I don't think you do. I am happy for you to discuss it with Zadrus first if you would like.'

She leaned back on the sofa and closed her eyes. 'All I want is for Sean to come home, safe and sound.'

'I understand, and I also recognise that this is a terrible time to be asking you to make a decision.' He sat quietly beside her for some time, then leaned over and took her hand in his. 'Jemma, I want you with me, willingly. When this is all over, I will try again to have Zadrus agree to release you. Does that help?'

She sighed. 'I guess. I'll do what you say.'

'Good girl. I'm meeting with Matt, O'Leary, and Denis to nut out our plans. I'd like you to join us.'

With a shake of her head, she sat forward. 'Alright, but you need to remember a serious conversation we had when we were at SCARF.'

'Uh huh. What's that?'

'I'm not a girl, I'm a woman. If you want me to do something, I need you to discuss it, not just bark orders. I won't live in fear of you again.'

'I remember well. There may be times I'll bark orders at you, in an emergency, but the last thing I want is to have you scared of me.'

'Fine, I'll go along with you.'

'Good woman. Is that better?'

'No, it isn't.' She slapped his arm. 'Now, you're patronising.'

When he threw back his head and laughed, she jumped up and walked to the door. 'Unlock the door and let me out.' She stood with her arms folded and glared at him.

'Now who's barking orders?' He grabbed her and put his arms around her. 'Give your dear old dad a hug.'

She had no doubt he cared, but she wouldn't tolerate the way he'd treated her when they first met.

Dan raised his eyebrows when she walked in beside Hunt. 'Don't ask,' she muttered.

Hunt grinned. 'Yes, ask. Jemma's agreed to be one of us. So, I now have four senior officers, five when we get Bellamy back.'

Her jaw dropped. 'You can't make me a senior officer. I have no knowledge of military processes, or rules, or strategies.'

'Works for me,' said Dan. 'I've already taught you heaps, but happy to teach you anything else you need to know.'

'Excellent,' replied Hunt. 'Now that's settled, we can move along.'

'It's not settled. Are you all stark raving mad?'

Hunt grinned again. 'Nope. Now let's get down to business. O'Leary, you'll be my 2IC in Bellamy's absence. I'm going to place you in the new Army as a full colonel.'

Matt raised his eyebrows, and Jemma suspected he was irritated that he'd just been overlooked.

Hunt must have noticed it too, and he turned to Matt. 'Don't look at me like that. I want you to take the running on setting up this Army, including what training we'll have to put in place. You know the people, and the systems available. You're the best one to work it out. You'll also be placed as a full colonel.'

Matt looked a bit appeased.

'Denis, you will continue your work with the alien technology. For the moment, I plan to appoint you as major, but I am not sure where your work will lead you. We can re-assess as we go.'

'Thank you, sir.'

'Now, Dr Anderson, where shall we place you?'

'Private sounds about right,' she growled.

'Hmm, don't think so. Your rank was major, so why don't we start at lieutenant-colonel. You're an intelligent woman, you'll work out what you need to learn. Remember everything is new. Nobody is adequately trained to do what we're going to have to do now.'

'That's just ridiculous, but I don't really care at this point. Why are we wasting time on this? We need to get back to working out how to rescue Sean.' She looked at Matt. 'And Dana.'

'Alright, we'll all take a break,' said Hunt. 'Dragile is monitoring Bellamy, and there's nothing much more that we can do. Be back here and ready to move at 21:00.'

When they regrouped, Jemma joined Matt and Dan as Nik fitted each of them with listening devices.

'Listen up,' said Hunt. 'Our decoy will be in place at 22:00. O'Leary and Matt, use transporter one. Proceed to the top of the Administration building. It's safe so long as you don't go inside. You'll be able to get line of sight to the decoy from there. If they show, follow them. As soon as you notify us, Jemma and I will also follow. Stay in contact with Denis at all times. Zadrus will be here with her. Everyone clear?'

All, except Jemma, said, 'Sir.'

Hunt raised his eyebrows as he looked at her.

She screwed up her nose. 'I'm clear.'

Matt grabbed her arm and pushed her to the other side

of the room. 'Are you crazy? He'll eat you for breakfast if you keep that up.'

'No, I'm not crazy and no, he won't eat me. We have an understanding.' She sighed, why did every male in her life believe they had to rescue her? She knew exactly how far she could push Hunt. But right now, it was time to focus on whether these people really did know anything about Sean's whereabouts. She shook him off and walked back to stand beside Nik until the transporters were ready to go.

At 22:30, Dan called in. 'I don't think they're coming. There's no traffic of any kind out here. Matt's still checking, but nothing so far.'

Hunt sat back in the transporter that was to follow Dan and Matt once they'd spotted their target. 'Okay, return here when you're ready.'

'Hang on,' yelled Matt. 'There's something directly above us. Not one of ours. Quite small. Stand by. We're going closer.'

Nothing more was said for several minutes. 'O'Leary, sir. It's a tiny craft, haven't seen anything like it before. They grabbed the decoy before we could get to them. We're following.'

'Stay on them,' said Hunt, signalling to his pilot to take off. 'We've got you in our sights. We're on our way.'

He focussed on the communicator, ignoring Jemma, and she pulled her knees up to her chin. If anyone was hurt in her place, she'd struggle to live with it.

'It's gone down,' said Dan. 'We're sixty kilometres north of the city, just inside the TEM. It's a valley. A cluster of large buildings, smaller ones at the edge. They appear intact. Looks like an old school, or maybe a university.'

When the small craft landed, Matt followed it down. Jemma looked at Hunt, but he remained oblivious to her as Matt started to speak. 'Please come out, we will not harm you. We are here to help.'

Would they believe him? He sounded so much like the people Pat had described, but she couldn't think of anything better he could have said. Dan reported a door opening, and a gasp as he said that Jemma's decoy had been pushed out and a man had a weapon to her back. Matt immediately repeated his message of no harm, but they heard someone insist he drop his weapon. Jemma jumped when she heard a sharp cry, then several more cries before the communicator shut down.

'O'Leary. Matt.' Hunt bellowed into the communicator, and she was sure if he could have jumped through it to reach the men, he would have.

It was only a couple of minutes before they heard a groan, and then a woman's voice. 'Who are you? What happened.' It sounded like the decoy, a senior CIG operative by the name of Ciara.

'I don't know,' another female voice replied. 'Those people sought refuge from us a few weeks ago and we provided them with everything they needed, but we had no idea what they were doing. They told us there'd be an attack, and to stay hidden in the back building, so we did. When we saw their craft take off and yours still here, we thought there was something wrong. We've been trying to revive all of you since.'

Hunt demanded a report. Ciara complained of a stabbing pain in her back as she got up and turned the visual back on the communicator, and she didn't answer him as she started to move, whirling around every few seconds, and peering between buildings.

'I can't find Dan or Matt,' she cried.

'Stand down,' yelled Hunt. 'We're nearly there. What's your injury status?'

'Don't know. The pain's excruciating, but I've got to find them. Over and out.'

'I repeat. Stand down. You're injured.'

It was obvious from the lack of response that she had no intention of obeying the order. As soon as they landed, Jemma ran to her. 'Are you okay?'

'It's painful but I can get around, and I need to keep going. I let them take Dan and Matt.'

'Rubbish, they overpowered you,' snapped Hunt, catching up with them.

'I should have seen them coming.'

'No, but I'm not arguing with you. Round up the people who live here and find out something about them. I'll organise the search.'

'Sir.'

'I'll help her.' Jemma didn't think Hunt expected to get much from the residents, but helping Ciara was something she could do.

The woman Ciara had been speaking to explained that thirty people had been living in the complex since the war ended. They had good supplies because it had been a university with live-in residences on campus, and they were very close to quite a large town which had only been partially destroyed. A couple of the university buildings had stand-alone generators and once they had found a supply of diesel, they had their own source of electricity. Not knowing if the spacecrafts they'd seen going overhead at various times were safe, they'd maintained strict blackout conditions.

'Probably why we didn't know you were here,' murmured Jemma.

The woman nodded and continued. 'The university had a strong agricultural focus in its day, so we had the resources to set up a small farm to grow vegetables, and we found plenty of canned and frozen meat in the old supermarket, although those supplies are starting to dwindle now.'

'Why don't you come and have a look at our city,' said Jemma, but she didn't have time to pursue it when she saw Hunt running towards her.

'Have you found them?' The look on Hunt's face was like nothing she'd ever seen before. The usual inscrutable mask of control had gone.

'Too late,' he said. 'They're heading out beyond the atmosphere, probably to one of the Zant crafts. Zadrus has informed the IPL Commander we have another abduction.'

'Oh God, will this ever end?' Jemma couldn't think of anything to say to help either of them.

'Hopefully. Grab Ciara. We'll head back.'

CHAPTER 18

There was nothing to do in the bunker and Jemma thought she might to go mad. Nik didn't need help with surveillance but was happy to sit with her to chat when she could. Still, with no new information, all they could do was wait, and she wasn't prepared to sink any further into her anguish at the loss of Sean. She had to get out of the bunker, and she'd wanted to see Werrimen since before Sean went missing, so she called for a transporter. She knew she should have sought Hunt's permission but decided against it. He'd most likely say no, so she'd do what she wanted and deal with the consequences later. All the transporter pilots had been cleared after the attack on the factory, and she knew most of them anyway, including the one who arrived now. He greeted her and, as soon as she sat, lifted off, chatting all the way to the hospital where he touched down on the roof. When she jumped out, he followed, his hand on his weapon. Apparently, there was no one in this settlement who didn't believe they had to protect her. At least when they reached Werrimen's room, he veered off and left her to enter alone.

Inside, a young Sidlown man stared at his boots, while Werrimen badgered him for information. Somehow, she'd found out that Sean was missing. It seemed that when Zadrus had visited the day before, he hadn't mentioned Sean, nor had he been in today, no visit, no call. Werrimen demanded to know what had happened overnight and shouted at the unfortunate young man that she knew something was very wrong. She stopped when she saw Jemma.

'By all the stars,' said Werrimen. 'Something else has happened. What is it?'

Jemma forced herself to smile. 'Do I look that bad?'

'Yes, you do. Tell me.'

Jemma looked at the hapless young man, before turning back to Werrimen, relieved that she obviously hadn't heard about Dan and Matt. 'I've been told not to worry you.'

'Worry me? Do you not understand the lack of information, and the lack of contact from Zadrus, has me exceedingly worried?'

'Yes, I do,' replied Jemma, working hard to keep her voice calm. 'Shall I get Zadrus on the communicator?'

'No. You will tell me what I need to know.'

A nurse entered the room in response to the loud voice. Werrimen waved her away and continued to glare at Jemma. 'Tell me,' she roared.

Jemma glared back. 'Fine, but it's on your head. We had another event overnight.'

'Do not talk around it. Tell me what has happened.'

The young man cringed, although Werrimen was far too wound up to concern herself with him, and it was obvious to Jemma that if she didn't tell her something soon, Werrimen would get up, order a transporter and head to the bunker herself.

As quietly as she could, Jemma responded. 'Dan and Matt were abducted last night.'

Werrimen looked as if someone had fired a cannon into her chest. 'By the stars,' she whispered. 'Where are they now?'

'They were bundled into a small craft and taken out to the Zant ship where they're holding Sean. Pritchard is here in the settlement. We heard him talking to Sean before he was abducted.'

'And this Zant ship, does it look like a normal Zant spaceship?'

'No. Dragile said it's a transport-zone capable ship.'

The look of misery on Jemma's face stopped Werrimen's demands. She reached out, drew Jemma in, stroked her hair, and murmured soothing words. 'We'll get them back,' she said, although her voice was grim. With gentle hands, she raised Jemma's face and wiped away the tears. 'I had better go and take charge of those men. Do you want to come with me?'

Jemma nodded.

'And you, young man, I was told when you were assigned to me yesterday, that you wish to become a Trustee, and I should talk to you.'

'Yes, madam I do, if they will have me.'

She looked more closely at his name tag. 'Well young Osten, you had better join me now. We will see what we can do to advance your career. Looks like I'm going to need a new apprentice.' She smiled at him. 'I am sorry I growled at you, but you handled it well. You will cope with the testing process.'

He bowed his head.

The transporter in which Jemma had arrived was waiting on the roof, and the pilot bundled them into it although he looked surprised to see Werrimen.

'I've been out of action for three days, and what a fine mess they've made,' said Werrimen. 'Withholding information from me. What, in the name of the Universe, do they think they're doing?'

Jemma presumed the question was rhetorical, so she remained quiet even as they landed, and she jumped out of the craft. Werrimen strode away from her and into the bunker, taking the stairs two at a time, before she burst into the conference room where Zadrus and Dragile were engaged in intense conversation through a screen.

'Talking and looking serious,' she muttered to Jemma. 'Do they think that makes them important?' With something that sounded suspiciously like a growl, she walked brusquely to them, ignoring both Jemma and Osten. 'There are over a hundred screens in this room, all of them, except the one you're talking on, are blank. Where are the IPL Commanders? What about the leaders in other settlements? And why isn't this facility in lock-down?'

She looked like she was about to tear both men apart. 'You've lost three humans,' she yelled at them. 'By all the stars in the Universe, how did you manage to do that?'

Zadrus glared at Jemma, which only served to enhance

Werrimen's fury. 'Don't bother looking at her, I had several sources.'

'Calm down Werrimen, we are working on getting them back,' said Dragile, but the look on his face belied the confidence of his words.

Jemma had no doubt that Werrimen was capable of intimidating any Trustee, and that was precisely what she intended to do here. Zadrus had placed a chair near her, and indicated she should sit, by touching her arm. She shook him off.

'You will both stand down.' Her voice was quieter now but had lost none of its intensity. 'I am taking command.'

'You cannot do that,' spluttered Dragile.

'I just did it,' she responded. 'Lodge a complaint if you do not like it, but if you wish to remain a Trustee, I suggest you accept my direction.'

Zadrus stared at her, the start of a smile on his face. He turned to Dragile. 'She can do it. They wanted her to take over Command of Sector 7, which of course includes Earth, when we arrived, but she declined. That was, of course, before all this trouble. Werrimen is the most experienced person here. Look at the number of stars in her crest, eighteen. That's more than yours and mine added together. It is in all our interests that she steps in.'

Dragile muttered something about knowing her history, which Werrimen ignored.

'Right, do the three missing humans have implanted tracking devices?'

'Yes, madam.' Dragile looked sour.

'Earth people say ma'am. While in their territory, I suggest you do the same.' She turned back to Zadrus, who was now struggling to suppress his smile. All the people, IPL and human, involved in the search should have implanted trackers. Do they?'

Zadrus's face reddened. 'All IPL members and senior Earth people do. Not everyone though.'

She yelled at him that it should have been obvious. Every person on the planet should have trackers implanted eventually, but for now, she would at least have ensured that any active staff were covered. She ordered Zadrus to get onto it straightaway, then to meet back in the conference room to give her a full briefing, just herself, Zadrus and Dragile. She wanted to know every detail, in particular what they had and had not done, in order to develop a plan. And she made it clear she was far from ready to let the two men off the hook.

'Come,' she said to Osten, 'I will speak to IPL command while we wait. At least we can do something positive about your career.'

Zadrus chuckled as he nodded for Osten to follow her. 'Your future is bright indeed young man.'

*   *   *

Sean was overjoyed to see Dan and Matt when they were brought into his room, although both were on floating gurneys and unconscious. His happiness waned when it hit him that their presence meant they'd also been abducted. Matt cried out in pain, then groaned, but didn't show any sign of consciousness. Sean tried to run to him, but the Zants waved him back, threatening him with their stick weapon. It took four Zants to pick Matt up and shift him to a couch. He screamed as they lifted him, then fell limp. Sean paced as close to the men as he could get, given the continual threatening gestures from the Zants. Dan groaned. Sean edged towards his gurney and leaned across to gently rub his arm. The Zants didn't interfere this time, they were focussed on Matt. Sean continued trying to rouse Dan, but he pulled away and whimpered.

'Open your eyes and look at me, mate,' said Sean.

Dan struggled to follow the instruction and, when he did, he stared upwards but didn't seem able to focus. 'Sean, is that you?'

'Yeah, it's me. God, I'm glad to see you. Well, in a way. Don't fight the restraints. They'll release you once you've recovered. Trust me, they genuinely don't want to hurt us. We're prime specimens. They expect a good price.'

'Where the hell are we?'

'Zant ship,' replied Sean.

'They hit me in the back with something. I can hardly breathe.' Dan cried out as he tried to turn towards Sean.

'Stay still. Looks like you both got a heavy dose.'

'Both?'

'Matt's here too. He's breathing but he's still unconscious.'

'Shit. I've got to move,' said Dan, crying out again as he tried.

'No, don't move,' said Sean, leaning over Dan again to hold him still. 'They'll give you the antidote soon. They used a kind of cattle prod. It's got an electric current and a hypodermic in the end that injects a toxin. Knocks you out, but no long-term harm. Doesn't damage the merchandise. They call it an equaliser, brings us down to their level of strength, or some damn thing.'

Two Zants waved Sean away. They gently rolled Dan onto his side, then one of them applied the antidote. Sean could only watch as Dan screamed in agony, before passing out again. Two other Zants continued to work on Matt. They had a mask covering his face, which Sean assumed was delivering oxygen. They proceeded to give him the antidote, but he didn't respond. One of the Zants asked for something which he then applied to Matt's skin. Matt groaned, and slowly opened his eyes.

Relieved, Sean left Dan, who was now softly snoring, and walked across to Matt. 'Don't move, mate,' said Sean.

Matt grunted a response, but his eyes remained shut and Sean thought he had gone back to sleep, so he headed back to Dan who was now watching him.

'What did you mean, they don't want to damage the merchandise?' said Dan.

'The price they can get for us is, so they tell me, astronomical. No pun intended.'

'Oh right,' replied Dan grimacing. 'Good news is your tracker's still working, but they can't hear you anymore. Probably got a jamming system in operation. But Sean, the bad news is this ship can go through a transport zone and take us anywhere in the Universe. The IPL doesn't have a ship capable of following them.'

'I knew I'd have to help myself,' said Sean. 'Heaps of the Zants think Landi's gone too far. They're worried their own leaders are pissed off with him. That might be to our advantage.'

Sean stood back when a Zant came in to remove their shackles. The Zant helped Matt, who was still groggy, to stand. When he was satisfied, he moved across, but Dan had sat himself up and rejected the assistance offered. The Zant shrugged and left, although he did check Matt again as he walked past.

'Jesus,' said Dan. 'I feel like a truck hit me.'

'More like a tank,' muttered Matt.

'It'll pass,' said Sean. 'Took me a few hours. They'll return soon and I need to talk to you first. Are you capable of listening?'

Both men nodded.

'I've been watching the discontented Zants. He was one of them.'

'You think he'll help?' Dan stretched his arms above his head as he spoke.

'They won't help voluntarily, but we might be able to trick them,' said Sean. 'Both of you need to rest so that you'll be alert enough when I need to call on you.'

Sean settled himself into a chair and waited, confident now that both Dan and Matt would be able to rouse themselves when he needed them. Several Zants came and went before Sean recognised the one who'd been most critical of Landi. He took the chance to start a conversation and did his best to sound chatty. 'Hello, have you been on this spaceship long?'

'This is my first tour.'

'Oh, are you enjoying it?'

'I do as I'm asked.'

'We're still in orbit around Earth, aren't we?'

'I believe so.' The fellow had started to relax, which Sean saw as his opportunity.

'I wonder if Landi's bosses know that he's taken us.'

The guard grimaced. 'We're all waiting to find that out.' He stopped and slapped his hand to his mouth, tripping, as he turned and charged towards the door.

Sean followed him. 'I feel couped up in here. Do you think we could go for a walk around the ship? We obviously can't go anywhere, so what about it?'

'I will check with my commander, and if he agrees, I will return.' The Zant almost fell through the doorway, catching his foot.

Matt and Dan slowly recovered and, a couple of hours later, were able to sit with Sean and talk. When Landi came in, they were quite relaxed, but it was the human with him that made Sean reel backwards. 'Pritchard!'

'Mr Bellamy, Mr O'Leary, Mr Hunt. It's good to see you,' said Pritchard. 'Mr Bellamy, I have an offer for you.'

'As if I'd trust you,' snarled Sean.

'Now, now Mr Bellamy, don't dismiss my offer before

you've heard it.' Pritchard smiled. 'Your friends interfered with my operation to bring Jemma out of hiding which is why they are here. I have another operation about to start, and I need your help to complete the job.'

'Why would I help you?' Sean stared at him. Surely even Pritchard would realise that he wouldn't put Jemma in danger.

'It's not why you would, it's what will happen if you don't. Mr Landi has kindly given me the option to buy your freedom, and I'm sure he'll include Mr Hunt and Mr O'Leary if I ask.' He looked at Landi who nodded. 'If you don't accept my benevolence you will be taken to a sector on the other side of the universe, with no chance of ever returning home.' He paused. 'Or, of ever seeing Jemma again.' He smiled, but this time it was too much for Sean, who let fly.

'You fucking bastard. You'll pay for this.'

Matt grabbed his arm to hold him back. 'Control it,' he muttered.

'I'm sure you believe you will stop me,' replied Pritchard. 'But you won't, and you must recognise the consequences of refusing to help me. If I cannot get Jemma peacefully, we will use whatever forceful means we find necessary. I will have no problem destroying your settlement, or its inhabitants. The deal is this. Agree to help me, and you will all live. Refuse and, most likely, Jemma will die. That is not my preferred option, but she cannot be left free to return home to Anders Major.'

Sean had no idea if he was telling the truth, or if he had the means to do what he planned. He shook Matt's hand away from his arm. 'Anders Major is not her home. She's never even been there.'

'I am aware of that. Unfortunately, it doesn't make any difference. If she were to decide to travel there and check it for herself, then it could become home. Now, I must have your agreement. Last time, I gave you twenty-four hours, and your actions before I returned were most foolish.'

Dan whispered, 'Agree with him. We can work out what to do later.'

Sean understood Dan's suggestion but, if he agreed, he had no guarantee that Pritchard would be true to his word, and they might be placing Jemma in significant danger. If he didn't agree, Jemma might be in even more danger, and so might all the inhabitants of the settlement, all because of Pritchard's insane obsession with his wife.

'Alright, provided Matt and Dan are included, I agree,' replied Sean.

'A very sound decision, Mr Bellamy. Now it may take a few days, or even a couple of weeks. If Mr Hunt had not interfered with my first approach, I would be able to take you now, and re-unite you with your wife, but I have a second plan in process, so we will have to wait. Landi will not leave until we are ready.' Pritchard walked out of the room, leaving Landi behind.

'I understand you requested a walk outside this room,' said Landi.

Sean fought against his disgust. He'd have to pretend he was prepared to cooperate with Landi because, whether or not Pritchard returned, Landi still had the upper hand. 'Yes,' he said. 'We'd like to stretch our legs and have a look around. I didn't think there'd be any harm in that.'

'Certainly.' Landi smirked as he spoke, clearly enjoying their misery. 'Perhaps you would like to meet some of our other humans on board. Please remember we will not hesitate to use our weapons on you, should you misbehave. On that understanding, I am happy to personally give you a tour of our ship.'

Surprised at how easily Landi had agreed, the men followed him from the room. The Zant ship, although structurally similar to the IPL craft with which they were familiar, was very different internally. There were no muted colours to cover the stark metal walls, and none of the soft texture underfoot. The floors were a hard surface rather like the feel of a ceramic tile, although the floor to ceiling finishes were still seamless. Communicators were regularly spaced in the corridors, but there was no sense of homeliness or camaraderie. Zants scurried between rooms and, as they sped past Landi, they'd lower their gaze and look away. It saddened, rather than surprised Sean, but he thought it best not to comment.

'We will start with the control room. I thought that you might like to see the craft they have following us,' he said, in a sarcastic tone. 'They think they are going to rescue you.'

Sean felt a chill go right through him at the sinister look on Landi's face as he laughed.

'We have ways to get you past the IPL. They won't even know it's happened. It's your own fault. None of you would be here if you hadn't got in the way, but now that you have, you'll go with Mr Pritchard. If that fails, you'll join our Adopt a Human program. I'm sure each of you would realise a very high price.'

Sean glared at him.

'Now, now, Mr Bellamy, I don't want to have to cause you to suffer pain again. I'd suggest you control that temper of yours. Mind you, a feisty human will fetch a much higher price.'

Sean felt Matt's hand on his arm and forced himself to take some deep breaths. Their best hope was to escape before Pritchard returned, and before Landi entered a transport zone.

'A wise move Mr Hunt. I see you have much better self-control than your friend,' said Landi. 'Now follow me to the common room.'

On the way through the next set of corridors, Sean noticed the guard to whom they had spoken earlier. He limped past them with his head down and looked as though he'd taken quite a beating. The men exchanged horrified looks. It was clear Landi had no regard for any other being, including his own kind. Sean had thought Landi dangerous, but this creature showed no remorse and would obviously stop at nothing to get what he wanted, particularly if it involved financial gain. Sean had no doubt that if anything happened to make him or the others less saleable, Landi would kill them without a second thought. He'd have to make sure they all remained healthy and unscathed, if they were to survive.

Landi led them to a large room with a few scattered lounge chairs, and a couple of tables. It was sparse, but at least it did have some paint on the walls. It was about the same size as the room they'd just left, without the medical equipment. Towards the back, a group of humans sat with their backs to the door. They turned around and appeared surprised as the men entered. Sean's spirit lifted, not only for the company, but because now he had several others who might be willing to help, maybe plan an escape, and he was clear in his mind now, they had to escape. Pritchard was evil, Landi far too unpredictable. If something went wrong, who'd know what either of them would do.

Landi left them to stay in the lounge for a while but made it clear that the guards would be with them. Sean couldn't wait to wipe the grin off his face and, in that instant, determined that one day he would. For now, he'd have to rely on his years of training and experience to get through. Step one was to watch, observe every movement and find weaknesses, all while making himself appear impassive. He knew Matt and Dan would be doing the same. As he walked in and sat down where the guards directed, he was pumped, ready for action. There'd be some slip, some flaw in what the guards did, to enable him to overpower them, although not yet. It would take time to thoroughly assess his target, and he needed to know more about the other humans, and whether they'd be with him or against him. Just because they were human didn't mean they couldn't be working with the Zants. Pritchard was human.

Then he saw it, the first point of weakness. As the guards moved to stand behind him, they turned their bodies and, for a split second, exposed their backs to him. Not much, but it might be enough. He smiled and offered a slight nod of his head to the other humans in the room, but when Dan stood, looking like he intended to join them, Sean stopped him. He didn't want to make any move that might upset the guards and, as they didn't know the other humans, he wasn't prepared to risk being vulnerable. It'd be best if the others came to them. They kept the upper hand that way. The other humans were probably also prisoners, but could equally be accomplices, set up to make him let down his guard. Time would tell, but for now, he wanted some distance.

After a few minutes, a woman walked over and sat down. 'Hello, I'm Catarina. I didn't know there were any other people on board.'

Sean introduced himself, Dan and Matt and explained they'd only just arrived. 'How long have you been here?'

She waited for the guard to move away. 'A few months for me, and others have arrived at various times. Where are you from?'

'Australia.'

'I'm from Northern Europe,' said Catarina. 'But others here are from various places including a couple from Australia. I'm glad to see you're all wearing translators. None of us had them with us when we were taken, and we have some people who've had quite a difficult time with communication. She pointed to two Asians sitting by themselves in the far corner, a male and a female. Perhaps you can help us with them?'

'Of course,' said Sean. 'Only too happy to help however we can.' They continued with a relatively inane conversation for a short while until a commotion drew their attention to the other side of the room. Both guards ran over to see what was wrong, and Sean started to get up.

'No, no,' said Catarina, 'it's only a distraction. Make sure you ask Landi to bring you in here every day for some company. Don't argue with him, he is very cruel. The more heads we can get together, the better. It will take a while for him to trust you, but eventually he will leave you alone like us. Just do it,' she finished quickly as the guards returned.

One of Catarina's group was writhing on the floor, on the other side of the room. Sean noticed a guard return his equaliser to its sheaths. The guard returned to Sean and indicated that he, Dan and Matt should follow, and he escorted them to Landi's office.

'I understand there was some commotion while you were in the lounge,' said Landi. 'What was it about?'

'We were on the other side of the room,' responded Sean. 'I noticed someone was in pain, but I don't know whether that was the problem, or whether the guard inflicted it.' He worked hard at maintaining an innocent expression.

After several seconds, in which Landi seemed to be trying to judge whether he was telling the truth, Sean spoke again. 'I wonder if we could spend some time with the other humans each day. I presume they're in the same situation as us, and you're also waiting to move them on. Would that be okay?' Being polite to Landi made him want to vomit, but he'd do whatever it took. He was going to beat this arsehole.

Again, there was silence, but Landi did agree that daily visits to the common room would be fine, although he reminded Sean that Pritchard might return before it could be arranged. He warned them that any attempts to escape, or cause problems, would result in harsh punishment, and they should understand there was no escape, they must simply accept their fate. He motioned to the guards to return the men to the room in which they'd started.

'Thanks for stopping me, Matt, when I wanted to deck Pritchard,' said Sean, once the guards had left. 'I would have loved to do it, but I knew you were right. And for Christ's sake, don't ever tell your great grandfather. He'd flatten me for losing control.'

Matt grinned. 'No worries. I'm getting the impression the old man's a bit of a bastard.'

'He's alright. There's no one I'd rather have in my corner when I'm in trouble.'

'Such as now?'

'Yeah, such as now,' replied Sean. 'If Pritchard returns, we'll have to plan as we go, but if he doesn't, we need to keep going to that common room. We've got to be cautious, we don't know those people, or how much we can trust them. They could just be bloody good actors. It looked like that fellow was zapped and in pain, but I didn't see the stick used. Did either of you?'

Neither had, but Dan thought that if the fellow was acting, he was incredibly good.

'Does the IPL know there are others on board?' said Sean.

'No, I don't think so,' said Dan. 'At least they didn't before we were taken. We were trying to put together a list of missing people because we realised that the Zants have probably been up to this for a long time, but I don't think Zadrus realised there'd be more than just us on this ship.'

Landi escorted them to the common room the next morning and seemed to take great pleasure in advising them that it would be a few more days before Pritchard returned. As soon as he was sure that Landi had left, and the guards were otherwise occupied, Sean, keen to communicate with the two Asians, sought them out and explained who he was. He figured if there was something wrong with the main group, they might have noticed it as they weren't able to join in any activities, unless that was another ploy. He pointed to his translator as he spoke, and both their faces lit up. Watching their lips, he was sure they were speaking some language other than English, but he heard their words in English, and they indicated they understood him. Both had been taken from China and while they could understand Landi and the guards, they could only get short snatches of conversations from the other humans when they were standing close to a guard with a translator. He told them to call on him anytime they needed help, then returned to the table to speak to Catarina. After a few days of the same ritual, the guards seemed to relax, and they were able to chat more freely.

Catarina had been in charge of security in her city and had been taken in a very similar situation to the one in which Sean had found himself.

'Have you ever considered escape?' said Sean, feeling more confident with her now.

'Not yet, but we've been watching. I think our only hope would be to hijack one of their transporters, although that would involve considerable risk.'

'There are a large number of IPL crafts following us,' said Sean. 'I like your idea, but I've been toying with something else. If we took a transporter, there'd be plenty of help from the IPL once we were out. But first, we'd have to get free of this room, then find our way through an unfamiliar ship, past hostile guards, and get to the transporter bay.'

'Yes, I've considered all of that, but we can't come up with a better idea, and I think there are ways around those problems.'

'I'd like to put another idea to you,' said Sean. 'I know how to get to the control room because Landi's taken us there twice now. We might have a better chance hijacking the mothership, rather than a transporter. That way, we'd stop Landi in his tracks and rescue all their prisoners.' The idea was ambitious, but Sean felt confident that it would be possible.

'Wow, you boys think big,' Catarina responded. 'What you're suggesting is a mighty task. There are only fourteen of us, including the three of you, and we've counted at least forty-seven Zants on board.'

'They're quite weak when you stand up to them,' said Matt. 'Our problem is, they have weapons and we don't, but

I'm sure we can confiscate some. I agree we should take the whole ship. Finding our way to the docking bays, and evading the Zants along the way, is probably more hazardous.'

'All right,' said Catarina, 'I'll check with the others and if everyone agrees, we'll start planning. It'll be crucial to get hold of some of their weapons, but to be honest I've never seen one used on a Zant, so I don't know if they have the same effect on them, but we obviously have to try.'

She suddenly sat upright in her chair. 'Stop talking. Your guards are coming, and they look a bit suspicious. Just agree with anything I say now, okay?' said Catarina.

'Oh, my goodness, it's your birthday Sean. Everyone sing happy birthday,' she called, then made a fuss of singing the song and slapping Sean on the back. The guards nodded to each other and moved away again.

It took a few days to get everyone to agree to the plan and work out the details, but they didn't have anyone who could fly the ships.

'I've had lessons on transporters and started a bit of work on large ships,' Matt said. 'But I don't see myself as accomplished.'

'I might just make sure that the Asian people have understood our plans,' said Sean. 'See what they can offer.'

The female of the duo became quite agitated as he explained. 'Yes, yes,' she said. 'I was trained to fly the big ships, before I was taken. I can help.'

Sean slapped her on the back. 'Thank God for translators. That's fantastic mate. You'll be our pilot. We'll back you up, but the flying job is yours. I'd expect the IPL to send a crew across as soon as we notify them. All we should need to do is keep the ship stable. The Zants won't want to crash either, so there might even be some help from them.'

They divided themselves into two groups. Sean, with Matt to back him up, would lead one, Catarina, with Dan, the other. Sean's team included all those who had knowledge of flying and communications. Catarina's team would go first and clear the way to the control room. They agreed to act in two days' time.

Those days passed inordinately slowly for Sean. On the day, a couple of Catarina's people walked over to the guards, ostensibly to say hello but they quickly overpowered the Zants. One of her men was touched by an equaliser and went down, but others were there to back him up, grabbing weapons and keys wherever they could. Her team moved out with the guards in front of them. Sean's team went behind, watching for all possible movement and threats.

'Take us to the control room,' shouted Catarina. A few more Zants were overpowered on the way and in the control room, but otherwise all went smoothly. There were now thirty-four Zants captured, well short of the known numbers, and Landi was not among them.

Sean forced his way to the communications console, while the Asian woman took over the controls. 'Show me how to open a channel,' he growled at the Zant, who sullenly cooperated. 'IPL craft, this is Sean Bellamy of the East Australian Settlement. Please connect me with Dragile.'

Dragile appeared on the screen within seconds. 'Sean are all of you safe?'

'We are, but there's a lot of other humans on board here. We need transport off. For the moment, we've locked ourselves in the control room, but I'd like urgent back-up.'

'It's leaving as we speak. How many humans?'

'Fourteen.'

'Do you have weapons?'

'Yes, we've taken some from the Zants.'

'Please take care. They will stop at nothing to win, and you have now seriously embarrassed Landi. Send an armed group down to the docking station. Have them look at these images of the IPL officers who are about to board your craft.' A series of images of Sidlowns appeared on the screen.

'I'll take a crew.' Catarina jumped in, with a big grin, before Sean could say anything. 'Don't look at me like that. You've got the pilots. I haven't. I can do the security work.' Dan shrugged but stuck close to her side as she grabbed one of the more cooperative Zants and said, 'Show me the docking bay.'

'Oh hello, what is this?' Dragile was heard again. 'A transporter is leaving the ship. Now there's another one. Do not worry about them, we will follow. Do not allow the Zants to trick you into anything. We will see you very shortly.'

Matt guarded the door, while Catarina and her crew moved out.

It was a relieved Sean who welcomed the flight crew when they arrived, and he allowed himself to be bundled onto a transporter, along with all the other humans. A separate transporter took the Zants. A skeleton IPL crew remained on board to pilot the spaceship back to Earth, and search for any remaining Zants.

Dragile had a broad smile as he greeted them. 'Come with me to the meeting room so I can let you know what will happen from here.' Once they were settled, he went on, 'You will each be interviewed individually. Our hope is that you might have information you do not realise is valuable. We are interested in anything you might know about where other captives have been sent after leaving the ship you were on. We are determined to capture these Zants this time, particularly Landi. Once that is over, you will be transported back to your cities and your families. Does anyone need anything immediately? Is anyone hurt?'

There were several requests for showers and changes of clothes.

'Of course. I'll organise rooms for everyone. For the moment, you will each have an escort and your communicators have been disabled. As soon as you have been interviewed these measures will disappear. I am so relieved you are all here and safe. Please let me know, at any stage, if there is anything that I can do for you. Sean, Dan and Matt, would you remain for the moment please?'

Sean nodded, 'Let me introduce Catarina who also had a security role in her city.'

'I am very happy to meet you. Would you join us too please so I can show you what happened to the transporters that escaped?'

Sean filled Dragile in on the visit from Pritchard and his demands while they waited for him to focus his screen.

'I am not surprised,' said Dragile. 'I will let Werrimen know about Pritchard, but for the moment, we will focus on finding Landi. Our transporters followed him, at a distance. He landed south of the main Australian continent, on Fitzroy Island, which surprised us at first as most of the land mass has gone, but the refuelling station that was there, appears to be intact. We have not checked these stations recently because we no longer need them, but he may have additional crafts hidden away. If we can stop him from taking off, then maybe this time we can get him and retain him.'

Sean murmured, 'I'd like to participate when you question Landi and maybe add a few of my own.'

Dragile smiled, 'There are intergalactic conventions which require the utmost propriety in these matters. I understand how you feel, but we will leave it to the experts. Now perhaps more importantly, would you like to connect with your colleagues back on Earth? I believe your wife is waiting to speak to you.'

CHAPTER 19

Sean remained behind when the others left to shower and change, knowing Dragile was about to contact Werrimen. He stood back as Werrimen congratulated Dragile on the rescue and was surprised to hear him admit that he hadn't had much to do with it.

'Dragile, bring the humans you've rescued to the East Australian Settlement,' said Werrimen. 'Have your people fly the Zant ship here also.'

'My pilots have secured the controls of that craft and are heading down as we speak,' said Dragile. 'Please be aware we have not been able to do a complete search of the ship and cannot guarantee there are no Zants hidden on board.'

'Understood. I will organise an armed pursuit team here. I look forward to seeing you.' Werrimen shut down the link.

For the first time since Sean was taken by the Zants, he allowed himself to relax. The Zants were safely tucked away in holding cells, and the humans who'd been rescued were all settled in cabins. In a couple of hours, the nightmare should be over. As preparations to return to Earth got underway, Sean leaned back in his chair to await instructions from Dragile. He allowed his eyes to close until he heard that two of the Zants were asking for a meeting to discuss their release.

Dragile laughed at the request. 'There will be no release. They will be transferred to an IPL holding station to be tried by an intergalactic court.'

Sean had learned not to underestimate the Zants. On so many occasions, he'd believed all was fine, only to have them pull a stunt. He had the uneasy feeling they were up to something now, although he couldn't imagine what it could be, and the Zants continued to insist on a meeting. Dragile finally agreed to meet with them which made Sean even more concerned.

The IPL were, as always, thorough. Dragile had armed guards escort the Zants through the corridors, and he continuously monitored then on the screens in the control room, but they looked too damn sure of themselves for Sean's liking. Suddenly, one of the Zants pulled out a small black box, about the size of a cigarette pack, from somewhere at his side.

Sean yelled, 'Dragile, check his hand. The Zant on the left.' But it was too late. Even as Dragile shouted into his communicator to warn the guards, the Zant raised his arm and slammed the object against a wall. Sean heard a loud bang. The screens went blank. The craft lurched. All power, including lights, shut down.

'Stay calm,' roared Dragile. 'Do not move until power is restored.' He screamed into his communicator, 'Report, report.'

Sean felt like all the air had been sucked from his lungs. It seemed an eternity before a single light flickered on above the central panel and a faint cry was heard. 'It's a bomb.'

He remained still while Dragile checked his controls, unable to comprehend how the Zant could have secreted an incendiary device on board. They had to have been checked before they were put in the holding cells, surely.

Little by little, more lights came on and a screen lit up as a resounding, mechanical voice commanded, 'All sectors secured and locked down, major mechanical damage, evacuate.'

He stood beside the controls, unable to move, as Dragile frantically manipulated the screen to survey the damage. The area where the Zants had been standing was now replaced by a gaping hole. If anyone in that sector had survived, they'd have been sucked out into space. Dead within minutes, but fully aware of what was happening to them. He'd never experienced the mind-numbing fear that now occupied his entire being, even when bombs had exploded near him during the war in Afghanistan. Here, in space, in a fatally damaged ship, he had to stop himself from sinking into the depths of panic.

'Now, listen to me,' said Dragile, taking hold of Sean's shoulders. 'There are ten sectors in this spacecraft. Each sector is like a slice of a pie, and each has all twenty floors of the craft in it. If any one floor is damaged, it is possible to isolate that floor from the rest. The entire sector in which we are currently located is safe and secured from the rest of the craft. All your people are in this sector. They are safe. Do you understand what I am saying to you?'

Sean stood mute.

'We cannot move between sectors until the craft lands,' said Dragile. 'Each sector has access to its own docking bay and transporters. We have an escape route, and we need to use it. Stay calm, and you will be safe. Can you work with me?'

Sean forced himself to focus only on Dragile. He nodded and looked around as Dan and Matt ran in.

'We cannot assist in the landing from this sector,' continued Dragile. 'It is in everyone's interest, including the pilot's, to get ourselves out of the vehicle. Then the pilot can concentrate on landing without having to worry about us.'

Sean continued to fix his eyes only on Dragile. 'Understood. Everyone, with me. Dan, take the rear. Let's go.'

Dragile led them to an escape chute. 'All your people are to be brought here. It is the most central point of this sector. The chute will take you to this sector's landing bay. It is on the lowest level. You will jump into it one by one. Sean, you go first so you can help everyone at the other end.'

Sean froze as he stood at the opening and stared into the cavity of the tunnel. He couldn't see the end and had no way of knowing where it led, or if the section of the ship below him remained intact. He'd been told in the past that, at times like this, your entire life would flash through your mind, and that was exactly what happened. He thought about his parents. And Jemma. He didn't know if he'd ever see her again. He contemplated whether this was the end, or if he'd someday rest in front of a fireplace on a cold winter's night, recounting his adventures to his grandchildren. Somehow, finding a way to cling onto life so he could meet his grandchildren, became paramount.

He stared again at the chute. If it'd been damaged in the blast, he'd be jumping out into space.

'This sector is intact,' said Dragile firmly. 'Others are waiting for you to show your leadership.'

Sean knew he couldn't just stand there, he had to act, to look confident, to reassure. Closing his eyes, he worked to clear his mind. Then he jumped.

A Sidlown Trustee caught him as he rolled through the end of the chute. His mind was clouded by a fog he couldn't shift, but he was aware of someone telling him to stand on the far side of the chute, and to help others as they came down. He automatically complied. Once everyone was down, Sean, Dan, Matt, Catarina, several IPL guards and Dragile, were directed to the farthest transporter. When the doors had closed, and Sean could see a pilot crew in charge of the controls, his mind began to clear. Dan, the only person present who was aware of his fear of flying, sat beside him and chatted, not the least bit concerned that he didn't respond.

As they flew out of the mothership and started to head down towards Earth, Sean turned his head towards Dan. 'Thanks mate.'

'No problem.'

'The mothership will land on Earth once everyone who is not needed to fly it, has been evacuated,' said Dragile, sitting opposite the men. 'There are several areas near the East Australian Settlement, far enough from the residences, that they can use to land safely. If it were to crash, no one on the ground would be at risk.'

Sean watched Dragile pick up his communicator to give his final instructions to the pilots. 'They sound incredibly calm. Aren't they concerned it might crash?'

'Yes, they are,' replied Dragile. 'But they also know that the control area where they are working is strong enough to survive a crash. Except in the direst of circumstances, the crew will walk away. We also have other crafts standing by to follow them down. They will pick up the crew and survey the damage.'

Gripping the edge of his seat, Sean forced himself to look back at the ship. He was astonished that anyone had survived. He had to work to steady his breathing but was unable to tear his eyes away from the mangled mess. At least ten percent of the ship, on one side, had been obliterated, which explained the lean on the ship before they'd escaped.

'How many deaths,' said Sean.

'Thirty-six of my people,' said Dragile, staring at the ceiling before he went on. 'Nineteen Zants. As far as we can tell there were no humans among the dead.'

'God. I'm very sorry to hear about your people.'

Dragile gave a brief nod, then stared straight ahead.

Sean looked outside to see what the other transporters were doing but could only see six fighter crafts travelling in formation alongside them. 'Where are the other transporters?'

'Heading to the East Australian Settlement,' said Dragile. 'Landi has been a problem for the IPL for a long time. He has interfered on many planets and caused terrible destruction wherever he has gone. My people have tracked his transporter and know where he landed. I have instructed my pilots to go there.' He pointed to a spot on the map. 'We must capture him and put him away once and for all.'

'We're with you. Let's get the bastard,' said Sean, amidst cheers from the others.

'My thoughts exactly,' replied Dragile and, for the first time since the explosion, he smiled.

'I know the island where Landi's set down,' said Sean. 'Fitzroy Island. It's near Tasmania. It won't be protected by a TEM, so we won't be able to move out of the transporter without protection.' The gear they'd need would seriously hinder their movement. Even from the time he remembered it, Fitzroy was covered in thick forest and heavy undergrowth, making it a popular spot for competitive bush walks and cross-country runs. It had sorted out the serious competitors from the hangers-on. Given the deterioration in the terrain, the search would be slow, and it would be difficult for Dragile to keep up given he'd also have to wear a protective suit. Dragile's anger was driving him now, and that anger went far beyond what had happened today, but would it be enough to keep him going through the difficult countryside? The look on Dragile's face bothered Sean. Something deeply personal had happened to make him so hell-bent on getting Landi. His anger would affect his judgement, and he might become a serious liability, particularly in an emergency.

Sean kitted up and attached his breathing device, a major advance on those he'd used in his previous life. A small mask that covered his mouth and nose was joined to a light box which attached to his chest like a shield. It was around thirty centimetres square and three centimetres deep and converted nitrogen and oxygen in the atmosphere to breathable air. He stepped out of the craft and looked around. The going was rough, worse than he remembered, with steep, rugged hills and thick overgrown bush. There was nothing to indicate anyone else had been in this area in recent times, but Landi had come down here for a reason. He did nothing without purpose. He'd be nearby, probably watching them as they struggled through the undergrowth.

Dragile managed to keep going, although Sean could see signs of fatigue creeping in, shortness of breath, more frequent rest stops, thirst. They'd walked for a good hour when someone at the front called to get down. Matt crawled past Sean, stopping at the edge of a clearing then beckoned Sean up.

'Check this,' said Matt.

On the far side of the clearing was a small shed, similar to the one through which Sean had been taken from the East Australia settlement. It looked deserted, no sign of movement, no footprints in the surrounding sandy soil, and no sign of a transporter.

'There was one just like that in a clearing in Northern Europe.' Catarina crawled forward until she was next to Sean. 'We found it when we went to investigate a spate of disappearances.'

'I think they're probably everywhere,' said Sean. 'They belong to the Zants.'

'We need to check it out,' said Matt.

'Yeah, we do, but first we need a plan. We've got to assume they're hiding somewhere inside. Someone can scout the shed, see if they can find a way in. But no heroics.'

'Of course not,' said Matt, moving out before Sean had finished speaking.

Sean swore. There was no point in yelling at Matt's retreating back. If, by some miracle, Landi didn't know they were there, raising his voice would draw attention to them, and that's the last thing they needed.

Matt stayed down, hidden by thick bush as he circled around one side, then turned and did the same on the other side, before returning. 'Everything's open. It looks abandoned.'

Sean wasn't convinced. 'Could be they want us to think that. I'm going in. Catarina, cover me. Everyone else, be ready to follow on Matt's lead. Matt, this time wait for my order.'

'Sure boss,' replied Matt, grinning.

Sean ignored him and went on, 'Dragile, I'd like you stay out of the line of fire, so that you can take charge if anything else goes wrong.' If things turned nasty, Dragile would be able to get reinforcements should they need them, quicker than anyone else, and it would keep him out of harm's way.

All remained quiet, but Sean had no doubt Landi would be somewhere around this shed. Stopping on one side of the door, he covered Catarina so she could check inside. Just as Matt had reported, all seemed to be clear, but a set of stairs at the back led downwards, like the shed he'd encountered at the dam. He told Catarina to stay where she was and moved back to the entry to bring the others in but, when he turned back to let her know they were coming, she was nowhere to be seen. His heart sank. He'd only walked three metres from her, looked away for less than five seconds, and she'd vanished. How could he have been so stupid?

Two Sidlown guards had remained with Dragile, but everyone else ran to Sean. He tore down the stairs and along the first floor, reefing open doors and calling Catarina's name. Finding nothing, he continued down.

Matt reached the bottom floor first, and yelled back, 'She's here.'

Several Zants, including Landi, were huddled over a large central table inside a glassed-in room. Catarina was strapped to a chair. Matt, and one of the Sidlowns, fiddled with a small box at the entry, but the door remained secured. A series of clicking noises made Sean spin around. Doors slammed shut at each end of the floor, and by the time he realised what was happening, Landi had shifted to stand beside Catarina.

'I am so sorry gentleman,' sneered Landi. 'I had not planned to involve you in our escape, but I am afraid there is no option. I cannot allow you to go as you will notify others of our whereabouts. There are seats in the room to my left.' He swept his hand in that direction. 'You are not prisoners and will have full access to any part of this craft except this room. Please make yourselves comfortable and enjoy your journey. We will be taking you to places that I am sure you have never been before.'

Landi released Catarina's shackles, and pushed her roughly

towards the door, then shoved her out, quickly closing the door before any of the men could rush him. Sean grabbed Catarina to make sure she was clear. Suddenly, the building shuddered, and there was an ear shattering noise.

Someone yelled, 'It's an earthquake.'

'No. No, this isn't a building,' said one of the IPL guards. "We are in a Zant spaceship and it is about to take off. Take a seat. Hurry. Wait until we are in the air to work out what to do.'

'Shit,' muttered Sean. "Hopefully Dragile's notified Werrimen. We don't want them firing on us. Everyone, move. Get to a seat. Now.' He ran to a comfortable-looking lounge with cushioned chairs and a well-stocked food and drink station, but Sean knew, more than anyone, how deceptive the Zant facilities could be. Once everyone else was seated, he found a chair and strapped himself in, battling against an overwhelming sense of helplessness, to stay alert. He clutched his seat as the craft shot out horizontally over a large body of water, and then vertically upwards. The take-off wasn't as smooth as those he'd experienced in IPL craft, and there was a constant vibration until they were out past the Earth's atmosphere when the ride softened, and he tentatively stood.

'After all we went through to escape, and now we're back to square one,' said Dan.

Catarina glared at Sean, and her voice shook. 'I can't go through this again. We have to find a way out.' She swung around to the senior IPL guard, 'You've got to find a way to get us out of here.'

There was soft muttering, and it wasn't just the humans.

The IPL Trustees seemed equally nonplussed. Sean's mind spun trying to fathom how to calm everyone down and come up with a course of action, but Matt was first to act.

'You've got a choice,' said Matt, positioning himself at the front of the group. 'Everyone, listen. You can sit there feeling sorry for yourselves, or you can apply your brains to finding a solution. We can do what we've done before. If there is an escape route, let's find it. It isn't going to fall into our laps. There might be a transporter somewhere we can get to. Or maybe a long-range communicator. We've all got implanted trackers, so they'll know where we are. Dragile will have called for help. At least this time we're not incarcerated, so get off your arses and help me look for anything we can use to escape.'

*   *   *

'Werrimen, answer me.' Sods of dirt flew around Dragile at all angles as, behind him, the Zant craft headed out across the Bass Strait.

'I am here Dragile,' said Werrimen. 'What is the problem?'

'They are gone. Zants tricked them into a ship. It has taken off.'

Jemma screamed. Werrimen reached out with one arm and drew her in close. 'I know my dear, but you must be quiet now. I need all the information I can get.' She turned to Dragile. 'Do you have another craft following them?'

'Yes, yes. But you do not understand. It is a transport zone ship. They are gone Werrimen. They are gone.'

'Return to your transporter and come here Dragile.'

'We had him,' said Dragile. 'I did not expect him to pull the same trick all over again. We were so close.'

'Leave it to the others.'

'Do not let them fire on him. We need Landi alive. He has the humans on board. He knows where my brother is.'

Werrimen gaped at the screen. 'Emilrad? You believe Emilrad was taken by Landi?'

'I do not believe it, I know it.' His face was a collage of anger, fear and despair.

'Go back to your transporter and come here. We will talk more then.' She shut down the communicator and turned to Zadrus. 'You and I need to talk.'

'Include me in that discussion,' said Jemma, tears streaming down her face. 'He's lost them all. Sean, Dan and Matt were all on that craft. How the hell could this have happened?'

Werrimen nodded as she led them to a quieter room. 'Dragile's wild decisions make sense now. That is not an excuse. He should have advised me, and I could have sent someone else out to help him, but at least now I understand.'

Jemma glared at her. 'No, it's not an excuse. Sean got it all under control, then he lost them. I need to know how to stop Landi. You don't have a spaceship that can go through the transport zones. You can't follow. Sean really has gone now.' She sank into a chair. Her world had just been shattered.

'You are right,' said Zadrus. 'The last functional IPL transport zone compatible ship, from Condona, landed on another planet in the Milky Way galaxy a matter of months ago. Before it could leave to return home, the Zants planted explosives, and destroyed the ship. Condona lacks the resources to rebuild its fleet, so we have nothing.'

'No, no,' said Werrimen. 'We have a ship. Dragile's people took control of the Zant's transport zone ship.'

'What use is it without pilots?' snapped Jemma.

'None,' replied Werrimen.

'What happened to the pilots from the last Condonan ship? The one you said was destroyed after they arrived in this galaxy?' asked Hunt, as he joined them.

'By all the stars in the universe,' cried Werrimen, slapping her hand against her forehead. 'Why didn't I think of that?'

Zadrus stroked her arm. 'Think of what?'

'The Condonan pilots. They can't have left the galaxy without a ship.'

'Of course,' replied Zadrus. 'I will get onto finding them immediately.'

'Good, that leaves me to work out what to do with Dragile. He cannot continue as commander of the team to follow Landi. His judgement is impaired.'

Hunt left with Zadrus, which gave Jemma the chance to ask more questions. 'If Dragile can't command, who will go as commander?'

'Either Zadrus or myself. My problem is that I can't deny Dragile the opportunity to go if there is a chance that he could find his brother. And I can't allow Zadrus and Dragile to go together. Dragile can be a bully and Zadrus doesn't stand up to him well. Zadrus will have to stay here. I must go. Please do not mention any of this until I've had a chance to assess Dragile's state of mind and make a final decision.'

CHAPTER 20

As Earth shrank below them, Sean became increasingly aware that he couldn't allow his people to sit there licking their wounds. Even if they failed, it was better to do something, rather than nothing.

'Alright, on your feet,' said Sean. He waited until they'd all stood, conscious that a few had lagged well behind. 'Let's go looking for a way out of here. Who has a communicator?'

About half indicated they did.

'Right, those with communicators, form up on my left. Everyone else, pair up with someone who has a communicator. Stay in those pairs. No lone wolves. Is there any pair without a weapon?'

Heads shook as Sean walked towards the corridor through which they'd entered. 'Okay, move out.'

Sean, waiting until all the other pairs had gone, had only just reached the doorway when Catarina called, 'We've found their docking bay. Four transporters. I'm going to see if I can get …' A loud bang interrupted her, followed by silence.

Sean demanded a report, but she didn't respond. 'Does anyone know which direction Catarina took?'

'I do,' said Matt. 'I saw her go past the control room and

then straight ahead.'

'Alright, everyone in that direction,' yelled Sean. At the end of the corridor, he charged through an open door and into a large docking bay. Catarina, and one of the Sidlown guards, lay unconscious on the floor, close to a transporter. Dan bent down to rouse her, while Sean headed toward the craft.

Catarina lifted her head. 'Don't touch it,' she screamed before collapsing back down and heaving in some air. 'It felt like a massive electric shock,' she whispered, as Dan helped her to sit up again. 'That's all I remember.'

The senior IPL guard, Rodeg, walked around the craft following the outline of a small red beam that ran along its length. 'It's a security device. We won't be able to remove it.'

Sean was deflated. It didn't seem to matter how hard he fought these beings, they always seemed to get the upper hand.

Landi's voice came through their communicators again, 'Ladies and gentlemen, I suggest you return to your lounge and take your seats. We are about to enter a transport zone. You will be safe if you are seated.'

Sean swore. He wanted to ignore the warning but Rodeg overrode him.

'No,' said Rodeg. 'We must comply. A transport zone allows movement through millions of light years in a very short time, but it is rough. If you are not securely seated, you will almost certainly be injured. We must return immediately to the lounge area.'

Before they'd all locked into their security apparatus,

which was rather like a racing harness, the craft lurched and shuddered violently.

'Hang on,' yelled Rodeg. 'This is it.'

As the minutes dragged into hours, some of the humans became ill, but there was little they could do. They'd just have to endure. Finally, the ride smoothed out and Sean, along with most of the others, began to relax.

'Remain seated,' said Rodeg. 'We are not yet through the transport zone and it will soon become rough again. I can't predict how long we have.'

'Can we get up and move around for a few minutes?' said Matt. 'Just to stretch out.'

'Possibly,' replied Rodeg. 'The Zant ships are rough. Stay close to your seats. As soon as you feel turbulence, no matter how slight, you must be seated.'

Sean made the most of the break, stretching his muscles but, within minutes, the craft again shuddered, and the turbulence resumed. 'Back to your seats,' he yelled. A couple didn't make it. They fell and had to drag themselves up. He had no idea how long it was before they came out of the transport zone. His watch had stopped early into the journey, as had everyone else's, and most of his team, including the Sidlowns, looked exhausted. Some were quite ill but, to his relief, no one had been seriously injured.

'We must rest,' said Rodeg. 'We cannot do much until Landi lets us know where we are and reveals his intentions.'

Sean woke to find Catarina standing in front of him, a grim look on her face. She flicked her eyes towards the side of the room where several armed Zant guards stood in a line across the entrance to their lounge. He reached for his weapon, but it was gone, and he noticed the others doing the same. They had to have been drugged, probably a gas piped through the air in their chamber.

'We are about to land,' said Landi. 'Please remain seated. The planet we are entering does not contain adequate amounts of oxygen or nitrogen in its atmosphere for you to breathe. We will dock directly into a building and you will be free to move into it. Please do not attempt to leave the building. You cannot survive outside.'

When the doors opened, Sean, with Rodeg beside him, led the group out. He continued to look around for any opportunity to overpower the Zants and did his best to resist as he was pushed down a set of stairs, and into what looked like an ordinary docking bay. There were no windows through which he could see if Landi had been telling the truth about the outside environment. The docking bay door shut firmly behind them, leaving Sean in no doubt that they were trapped. They were herded along a hallway to a large, windowless room where they were greeted by several humans and IPL members, most of whom were Sidlown, and a number of other beings who were not familiar, although they seemed friendly enough.

A woman emerged from the centre of the group and extended her hand, first to Sean then to Rodeg. 'Hello, I'm Lena. Please follow me.' She sat at a large table and called for more chairs.

Sean kept his eyes on her as she moved. 'Can you tell us where we are? We were abducted from Earth.'

Rodeg seemed to be equally puzzled by these people. He shrugged his shoulders as Sean looked at him.

Lena sighed, 'We were all abducted. This facility belongs to the planet Ailazant. I can't tell you exactly where we are, but we are not on Ailazant. Most of us have been here for a long time.'

'But,' said Catarina. 'You're human. Your accent sounds South American.'

She smiled. 'Yes, I am human, but I am not from Earth. We all originate from a single planet although no one is clear where. Most of us speak similar languages to your own and we are all essentially the same.'

Sean interrupted. 'So, how do we get a message out?'

'You don't,' she replied. 'We are incarcerated here.'

'There has to be a way to escape.'

'Let me be blunt,' said Lena. 'Inside, we exist. Outside, we die. We live in hope that someone will discover us, and organise a rescue, but realistically that is unlikely. The Zants have used this planet as a safe zone to avoid capture and to dump unwanted prisoners for centuries. We rely on them to maintain it. The facilities are good, and we have plenty of food and clean water. They've set it up so there are areas that resemble the outdoors, and for most of us that does make things a bit more bearable. Would you like me to show you to some quarters? There are plenty of rooms available, so you can take your pick.'

Sean thanked her and motioned to his group to follow. He sensed hopelessness pervading, struggled to fight it himself, but somehow, he'd have find a way to get everyone motivated again to actively seek a way out. Otherwise, they could be here for the rest of their lives. He requested that they be located together, and it took some time to find enough rooms in the same locality to house them all, but finally they did.

Lena explained how to return to the great hall, and where to obtain food and water, then left.

Taking a deep breath and exchanging a glance with Dan to give him strength, Sean called for order. 'Half an hour to check out your room and freshen up, then back here and ready to discuss our options.' Standing in the doorway to his room, he hoped half an hour would be enough to control his own despair. He strode in, washed his face, and made himself perform a few push-ups at speed to get the adrenaline pumping, then returned to wait for everyone else. Lena's attitude bothered him. She'd clearly given up all hope, and if everyone else here was the same, that could be a problem. He'd have to isolate his people so they wouldn't become contaminated by the same sense of despair.

'Well,' he said, as soon as the others arrived, in the most cheerful voice he could muster, 'does anyone have any ideas? We must stay focussed on how to escape. Is everyone with me?'

Rodeg responded first, 'There was a way in, so there must be a way out. The IPL has known for a long time that the Zants have a facility such as this, but we had no idea where it was located.'

'So,' said Dan, 'the IPL has no idea where we are?'

'No,' replied Rodeg. 'We all have trackers embedded, but they don't extend through the transport zones. They will know which direction we went, but that will be the limit of their capacity to follow. If there is someone friendly nearby, they might pick up on the trackers, but we can't rely on that. We have to work with what we've got.'

Sean refused to allow himself to focus on their isolation. 'What do you think of the building we're in?'

'I've wondered if we're in a big spaceship,' said Rodeg. 'As you know the Zants are pretty good at camouflage.'

'Good thought,' said Sean.

'If it isn't,' said Matt, 'then how did they build it? Where did they get their materials? How did they extract them? How did they transport them? Are there other buildings, or other crafts?'

'You're right,' said Dan, slapping the wall behind him. 'The Zants need the same atmosphere as us to breathe, so they must have other crafts here, something to enable them to get between buildings.'

Rodeg nodded, 'And, if we could find something, we could take off, not to Earth, but maybe to somewhere friendly.'

'Good thinking,' said Catarina. 'On Earth, there's an international distress signal. Is there such a thing as an inter-planetary or intergalactic distress signal?'

'Yes, but there is no telling who'll respond,' said Rodeg. 'They may not be friendly.'

'In that case, why don't we spread out and have a good

look around,' said Matt. 'See if we can find a control room. We should stay in our pairs. Has anyone checked if our communicators work here?'

'Rodeg and I tried them before,' replied Sean. 'That's a good idea Matt. Look for any windows or viewing screens that give a view of the outside. Then we can judge if there's anything we can use, like a long-range communicator, or a transporter.' Happy that individuals were now thinking and using their initiative, he allocated pairs, teaming anyone who'd been quiet during the discussion with someone who'd been actively involved.

After a couple of hours of fruitless searching, Sean and Rodeg found a heavily guarded room. It appeared to contain controls for the atmosphere, but no sign of engines or aircraft controls. Even the docking bay through which they had entered was empty. Landi's craft had clearly left.

When he called for everyone to return to the common room, he again sensed despair, but spirits picked up at the food and beverages they found loaded on the dining table in the middle of the big room.

'Careful,' said Sean. 'We don't know where that came from.' A couple of people picked at it. When nothing happened, a few tucked in, and eventually everyone filled their plates.

Once they'd finished, Sean stood at the head of the table and called for order. 'Listen up. Time to start pooling ideas for our next move.'

'What about overpowering a Zant craft when it docks?' said Catarina.

'They're heavily armed,' said Rodeg. 'Not sure if we can overcome that.'

'Store the thought,' said Sean. 'It's something we've done before, but we were already inside when we did that. It's worth considering, particularly if we can't come up with something else.'

'How about pinning down Lena and her crew?' said Matt. 'There must've been attempts to escape before. Just because others have failed doesn't mean we can't succeed. If we can find out what went wrong, perhaps we can improve on it.'

'Good idea,' said Sean.

When no other ideas were forthcoming, Rodeg suggested they consider resting. 'It has been a long day. We can start fresh in the morning.'

Well beyond exhaustion, Sean didn't argue, but he remained alert overnight and was first up in the morning. A meal was again waiting when he walked into the dining room, although there was still no indication of who'd delivered it until a group of Sidlowns arrived. Most were similar in appearance to Zadrus, but one of them looked remarkably like Dragile, could have been Dragile if Sean hadn't known they'd left Dragile behind on Fitzroy Island.

'We thought you might need nourishment, so we brought you some food,' said the Dragile lookalike.

'We thank you most sincerely,' said Rodeg. 'This is Sean. He is the leader of the human group from Earth.'

Sean stepped forward. 'We were on a mission led by Earth's IPL Fleet Commander, Dragile, when we were tricked into a Zant ship and detained.'

The Sidlown's eyes lit up. 'You know Dragile?' he cried. 'Is he safe? I was taken a long time ago and have heard nothing of him, or the rest of my family since then.'

'The rest of your family?'

'Dragile is my brother.'

Rodeg looked shocked as he responded. 'Surely you are not Emilrad?'

The man nodded. 'That is my name.'

Rodeg offered a small bow of his head which Sean now recognised as a sign of deference to a senior person in the Sidlown culture. The anger he'd observed from Dragile, on Fitzroy Island, suddenly made sense. His own brother had been abducted by Landi.

'Sir, we were discussing how to get away from this place,' said Sean.

'Aah. As do all newcomers.' Emilrad sat at the table opposite Sean. 'We have searched every corner of this building and have not identified any means of escape, but we continue to look.'

'Perhaps we can work with you,' said Sean.

'Of course.'

'Do you know where we are?' said Rodeg.

'I know exactly where we are,' said Emilrad, laughing. 'I overheard a pilot talking to a training crew one day. They didn't know I was there, and they were speaking quite openly. The pilot instructed them on their coordinates here and the coordinates of Condona, and how to plot a course between them. I, of course, wrote down everything he said.'

Sean leaned forward, 'Could I have a copy just in case we can find a way to use them?'

'Of course. The thing that pleased me was that Condona is not far from here, a couple of light years in your terms, but in an IPL or Zant craft, that's just a few days. The control room here only has local communicators, but there has to be a long range one somewhere, so they can call for help if they need to. If we could get a signal out, and the Condonans were to pick it up, there might be some hope but, as yet, I have not worked out how to do it.'

'Right,' said Dan, chuckling, more to himself than to anyone else. 'We find a suitable spacecraft, hijack it, traverse a planet without oxygen, find their long-range communicator and send off a signal. Can't see a problem.'

'Sounds good to me,' said Sean. He laughed too, but he wasn't sure the idea was as farfetched as it sounded. 'Getting a signal out has merit.'

Emilrad nodded. 'The Condonans would alert everyone else nearby, but I just haven't been able to find a way.'

'Alright, let's keep that in the back of our minds. Is there anyone in this building we shouldn't trust?' said Sean.

'No, not really. There are around six hundred people here, and you do get some petty disputes and dislikes and arguments, so I take care what I say and who I speak to. Lena is trustworthy and generally looked up to as the leader of the community. She has a lot of information and I often talk to her. If we did find a means of escape, she would be useful, and her assistance would be on the basis that we send a rescue party back for the rest of them, which of course, we would do anyway.'

'I have a question,' said Dan. 'The Zants are so involved in the slave trade, how is it that they leave people alone here?'

'Well, they do not entirely. I presume you noticed the floor that was full of freezers. I do not know how to put this delicately, so I will just say it. That is a human sperm bank. Many human males just volunteer when asked to contribute. They see it as payment for their food and keep. Those who do not will be forced. It is, I am afraid, only an issue for humans as it is the human genetic material that is valued. I am sorry to say this, but I recommend you just accept it as part of being here and go along with it for your own safety. Fortunately, there are not any Sidlown women here, as they would be used as incubators for the embryos. I believe that does happen elsewhere.'

'So why don't they just sell the humans they've got here?' said Sean. 'You'd think that'd be easier.'

'There is one very good reason. For thousands of years, they have managed to keep this place a secret. If they sold you, and you could provide information to lead the IPL here, they have then lost a place which is very important to them.'

Although Sean could feel himself sinking into a deep depression, he couldn't lift himself out of it. The Zants and their ways were unconscionable, and he had no control. There was nothing he could do other than try to stay focussed on escape. There had to be a way, damn it, and if anyone could find it, it was going to be him.

CHAPTER 21

Jemma accompanied Werrimen to the landing site to wait for Dragile's transporter to come in. A line of IPL Trustees stood between them and the craft as it touched down. They carried more sophisticated weaponry than she'd seen before, even compared to the ones she'd noticed at the IEMO meeting, and their uniforms were made from an unusually thick material, a bright orange in colour. Frowning, she looked up at Werrimen.

'Do not worry,' said Werrimen. 'The weapons provide a shield against the Zants' equalisers, and the uniforms are made of a fabric which the toxin cannot penetrate.'

'Wow. They look so serious.'

'Oh, they are, believe me. We have too much history with the Zants to not take them seriously.'

Jemma stood close to Werrimen, not quite sure what to expect as the Trustees entered Dragile's transporter. She suspected that all the Zants who'd been captured by the IPL had perished when the bomb had been detonated, but she didn't want to have anything to do with them if they hadn't. 'Do we have to wait until it's cleared for Dragile to come out.'

'No, I should not think so,' said Werrimen. 'Now I want

you to be aware that I have no idea what condition he will be in when he joins us. He might be angry and ready for a fight, or he might be utterly crushed,' said Werrimen. 'Whichever it is, I will handle him. Do not let him intimidate you.'

Well aware that she had no idea how to deal with someone like Dragile, Jemma agreed but, after he floated down in the blue light, he stood under the craft and stared into the distance. His face was blank.

'Oh, by all the stars, this is far worse than I expected,' murmured Werrimen. 'I will take him to the hospital in case he needs sedation. Stay with me. Let me start, but if you think of anything, feel free to ask.'

As Werrimen approached Dragile, he stumbled across to her. She led him away before anyone else had a chance to speak to him. Jemma followed, a short distance behind, not convinced he would be able to join the mission at all, let alone lead it. In a small interview room, normally reserved for medical examinations, Werrimen eased him into a seat.

'I am very, very sorry ma'am,' he began.

Jemma knew better than anyone how he must be feeling, torturing himself that he'd lost Sean, Dan and Matt, and devastated that he was no closer to finding his brother. She sat beside him and rested her arm on his shoulder. This wasn't a time for recrimination, they needed information that only he had, so anything she could do to help bring him around, she would.

'Now that I know about Emilrad, I can understand what motivated you to do some of the things you did,' said

Werrimen, as she found a chair and sat opposite him. 'I would have preferred if you had involved me earlier, but we must not dwell on that now. I have an idea that might enable us to follow Landi.'

He slumped in his chair. 'We were so close. You know as well as I do, that he will find a transport zone, and all will be lost. Emilrad, and now all these other people are gone forever. I have been so stupid.'

'No Dragile. You are wrong. I have a plan, but you will have to work with me. I need to know if you can lift yourself to do that.'

For a while he stared at Werrimen, but then as if someone had flicked a switch, looked her directly in the eyes. 'What is your plan?'

As Werrimen explained, Dragile began to add ideas.

'Dragile, I cannot allow you to lead the mission.'

'I must,' he replied. 'It is my only hope to find Emilrad.'

'No. I will lead,' said Werrimen. 'You may come, but you must accept I am in charge.'

Anger flashed through his eyes as he glared at her but, after a short pause, he seemed to relax and bowed his head. 'I understand. You are in charge and I will adhere to your authority.'

'Good, then we can proceed. We must return to the bunker now.' Werrimen led the way to a transporter and, as usual, Jemma had to run to keep up.

When they landed, Zadrus charged out of the bunker to greet them, and Jemma stood back as Werrimen moved between the two men but, although Zadrus looked irritated, there was no aggression.

'Fill me in on what has happened here while I have been gone,' Werrimen said to Zadrus.

'There have been a number of events. Reports have come in, from across the planet, of small buildings disintegrating. Hidden spaceships, mostly transport zone capable, have taken off. At least fifty. The Zant ship that Sean and his team captured will land within the next few minutes. The crew who checked Dragile's transporter have remained there to undertake a thorough search of the ship as soon as it lands. I will head there now to check if we can use it.'

'No,' said Werrimen, 'I will go. Dragile can join me, and I think it is best if Jemma remains with me also, to stop her dwelling on her loss. You must find those Condonan pilots.'

'I have located them and have sent a message. I am waiting for a reply, so am free now to go with you.'

'No, it is too important. I do not want to risk missing that communication. I would also like you to reconvene the IEMO, so that everyone can be kept informed. And contact the person who is acting as IPL Fleet Commander, now that Dragile is here. We need to know where Landi's craft is at all times.'

His nod, although a bit stiff, was compliant, and Jemma was amused to hear him mutter as he walked away, but she suspected that Werrimen was asserting her authority to also make it clear to Zadrus that she was in charge.

Jemma had never seen a transport zone craft. Given that the Trustees were so adamant that ordinary craft couldn't travel the transport zones, there had to be major differences. Everything depended on the condition of the Zant ship, and whether it would be satisfactory to undertake the journey through the transport zone. It was her only hope of ever seeing Sean again. It had to be okay. Werrimen seemed confident that they'd find the Condonan pilots in time and Jemma prayed that she was right because, without them, all was lost.

Waiting with Werrimen and Dragile at the landing site, she had a good view of the new ship as it came down to land. It was smaller in diameter than the craft she knew, but considerably longer, and an entirely different shape. The front was cylindrical, about ten metres in diameter, and fifty metres long, not unlike an aeroplane of the early twenty-first century but without the wings. Behind the cylinder was a disc-like projection. It was about twenty metres in height and extended horizontally about fifty metres on either side of the cylinder, so around 110 metres at its widest point. There were four rows of windows around the outside, which she suspected meant four floors. Behind the disc was a further ten metres of the cylindrical shape and the end fanned out into a triangular section with its edges slightly raised. She had no idea what to expect from a transport zone but presumed the shape was to cope with extreme pressure during the flight. She smiled to herself. It was only a matter of months since a flight to her had meant hopping on an aeroplane, and taking several hours to traverse a few hundred kilometres, not millions of light years.

When they were given the go ahead, she followed Werrimen into the blue light which lifted them into the middle section. She was immediately struck by the similarities to the only other Zant craft she'd seen, when Landi had implanted the silver bar in her neck. It was not well-maintained, and there were no creature comforts. Werrimen and Dragile went directly to the controls, but she was curious about the whole ship and, knowing that it had been thoroughly checked, wandered down the corridor.

Werrimen was smiling when she caught up. 'It is ugly, but serviceable. We can fly it.'

Jemma had been wondering how to make some demands of her own, but couldn't come up with a good way, so she blurted it out. 'When you do send the ship out from here, I wish to be on it. I've been pushed into the background. Everyone's been so concerned about my emotional state that I've only just avoided becoming the tea lady. I won't get in your way but leaving me out is far worse than keeping me busy and involved. Work it out however you like, but involve me from here on in.'

Werrimen smiled. 'By the stars Jemma, I would never leave you out, but I am not sure that coming with us is the best idea. How will you cope if we fail to find Sean?'

'How will I cope if I'm here and you fail to find him?' She held her breath as Werrimen stared at her.

'Yes, you are right. You will come with us then.' Werrimen turned and beckoned her to follow.

'I'm glad we've settled that,' said Jemma, surprised by her own temerity, and even more so that Werrimen had accepted.

'Zadrus does not yet know that I will be on the ship with

you,' said Werrimen. 'I am heading back to tell him now. I have already told Dragile I will be in command. Please do not mention it until I have filled him in.'

Nothing more was said in the transporter on the way back. As they walked into the bunker, Zadrus looked up.

'The Condonan pilots are on their way. Thirty-six to forty-eight hours. IPL command has the coordinates through which Landi's craft disappeared, so now we must wait.'

In Jemma's mind, it was a long time to wait, but she had to accept there was no way around it. She saw a look in Hunt's eye which told her something else had happened and he was obviously waiting for Werrimen to finish.

'May I have a moment?' said Hunt. 'I've spoken again to the fellow who slipped Jemma that note. He has now admitted to working with Pritchard.'

'God, will we ever escape him?' she murmured.

'We have to make it end,' said Hunt. 'He told me that Pritchard plans to use Sean to get to you, Jemma. Apparently, he intends to rescue Sean from the Zants and drop you both on a planet from which you can't escape.'

Jemma didn't believe for a minute that Pritchard would trust the Zants to do his bidding or that Sean would reach any sort of agreement with him.

Dragile, who'd been sitting quietly at a table, rose. 'I believe I also have some information on this matter which confirms this fellow's claims. Sean told me that this Pritchard person accompanied Landi to his room just after Matt and Dan arrived. He said he would take Jemma and the three men to a primitive planet. He said you must not be allowed to take up your position on your home planet.'

'Jemma.' Hunt had his arm around her. 'Are you okay?'

'Yeah, I think so. None of this is particularly new, although I suppose the primitive planet gives it a new slant.'

'There was something else,' said Dragile. 'I understand that you had an uncle Kevson, and that you believe he died many years ago?'

'That's right. His body wasn't found, but the police said he couldn't have survived the fall from the cliff where he was last seen, trying to help someone else, during the floods in 2011.'

'Pritchard also claimed that your uncle Kevson is alive and well. He said he would reunite you with him.'

'Yeah, he's said that before but it's not possible. The police were certain Kev couldn't have survived.' Jemma stared between Zadrus, Dragile and Werrimen.

'There is no way of knowing my dear,' replied Werrimen. 'But we will find out. Trustees have gone to Anders Major to start an investigation, and we will work from there. If he is alive, we will find him.'

Jemma leaned back in her chair, her eyes shut, until she felt Werrimen's hand on her shoulder.

'I have some other news to hand. I sent some crews out, with electrometers, to locate Pritchard, and those working with him. They isolated an area where the meters reacted. Pritchard was seen entering a building. As our people were about to advance, a Norellian sphere flew out from behind the structure. It rendezvoused with a larger craft, not ours and not the Zants' but a rebel ship from Anders Major. The electrometers are no longer reactive, so we suspect that Pritchard, and his people were on board, although we cannot be sure.' Zadrus sat closer to her and took her hand. 'He probably is gone, but we cannot let down our guard. You must remain with me now.'

She nodded. 'I understand, but I'm not prepared to hide. The weekly forum meeting is due, and people will be gathering in the square. We need to deal with that.'

Hunt shook his head. 'Jemma, it may be best if you stay here.'

'No, I won't back away. The more support Zadrus has, the better. The community doesn't know about Matt or Dan, and they're going to be shocked and angry.' She wasn't quite sure what to make of the look on Hunt's face. She stood and turned towards the door, but Hunt reached it first and spoke quietly.

'Well done, Colonel,' he said. 'You just confirmed my belief in you.'

She swore as she shook him off and continued to the door only to find herself flanked by him, with Nik on the other side, as she walked out to the transporter. In the square, well over a thousand people waited. Jemma accompanied Zadrus onto the podium and stood beside him as he set himself up to speak.

'Ladies and gentlemen,' he began. 'I have some very grave news to give to you today. Colonel Dan O'Leary and Colonel Matthew Hunt have fallen victim to the Zants.' He waited until the gasps and angry questions subsided. 'The men were taken from Earth. Then, with extraordinary courage, they commandeered the Zant craft and made contact with the IPL. Several Zants were arrested and incarcerated on the IPL ship, but one of them somehow secreted a bomb on board and set it off, disabling the ship. Our people escaped and bravely tracked the Zants to Fitzroy Island where they were tricked again into a Zant craft. It took off with them on board.' He stopped to catch his breath. The crowd remained silent, their eyes fixed on Zadrus.

'Numerous similar crafts around the globe have since flown out, some with residents of Earth on board.'

Tension was rising in the crowd and Jemma was impressed by the way Zadrus maintained his calm long enough to finish what he had to say.

'While the rescue of our people is our most urgent priority, we must also take a broader view regarding the safety of everyone on planet Earth. We must protect ourselves from any such future interference, and I have called an immediate meeting of the leaders of every city on this planet. This will happen in the next twenty-four hours. It is also our intention to activate the Earth Army as soon as possible. I will hand you over to General Hunt to explain his progress.'

Hunt acknowledged the many applications he'd already received and explained that the first training academy would soon commence construction in the East Australian Settlement and training would commence once the complex was completed. He invited questions which he answered succinctly and then closed the meeting.

Taking no chances this time as they left the meeting, Hunt ran with Jemma to the transporter and hurried her inside. The flight back to the bunker was both quick and quiet. Inside, they found Werrimen deep in conversation with the acting Commander.

'Ma'am, we have been tracking them,' said a woman who had a similar skin texture to Dragile. 'We have the coordinates of their entry to the transport zone but, as you know, our craft cannot follow. I notified IPL command on Sidlow. They will alert every sector. There is little more we can do.'

'Keep me informed.' Werrimen shut down her communicator.

'God,' cried Jemma. 'Is she saying they're gone? They could be anywhere by the time those pilots get here.'

Hunt drew Jemma into him. 'Shh, listen to Werrimen.'

'Every transport zone has one exit, and only one,' said Werrimen. 'So long as we have the coordinates to enter, which we do, we must exit at the point that they exited. We can then intensify our search from that point. Zadrus, are you ready for the IEMO meeting tomorrow morning?'

'Yes ma'am,' he replied, smiling.

She smiled in return and, in that brief second, the change of guard was clearly accepted by both. 'Hopefully, the pilots will be here before the meeting, or close enough for us to establish a link. Now General, how are we going with the Army?'

'We have the applications, the building is about to commence, and I have several of my people working on the first course,' Hunt replied. 'You can leave that to me. I'd rather you focussed on the rescue.'

Hunt was so anxious about Sean, Dan and Matt that Jemma thought his answer contained a gentle rebuff, and the smile from Werrimen suggested she'd thought the same.

'Excellent,' said Werrimen. 'I would like to offer some input. We have different skills, and can instruct in weaponry, flight and advanced technology. Sean is my Prehling, but we have many Trustees here, and would be happy to train others who show promise, to become Trustees.'

Zadrus stood beside Werrimen, as Jemma and Hunt turned to leave. Jemma slowed down as she heard him say, 'You said to Jemma, you will be going with *us*, not with *them*.'

She sighed. 'I wanted to tell you, but with everything else happening, I could not find the right moment.'

He didn't seem angry, more hurt. 'I think this is rather important.'

'I know, and I knew you would not be happy. I cannot let Dragile command this mission but, given the situation with his brother, he must go. Your role here is too important for you to leave. I do not have much choice. I have no idea how long we will be gone, or if we will be able to get back at all. But I still believe I must go. I have never shirked my responsibility before, and I do not intend to start now.'

'I understand.' He held her for several minutes. 'You had better find a way to get back. I am not living the rest of my life without you. This will not be the end of us. If something goes wrong, I will search the Universe until I find you.'

'That is a given,' she replied.

'And Jemma,' he said. 'She is my Prehling. I would have preferred you discussed that with me first.'

'I know, and I apologise. It was her request and I will reverse that decision if you wish, but I feel she will not be receptive to her own learning until we find Sean, or she accepts that we will not.'

'Yes, you are right. I pray that it will be the former, but if it is the latter, will you take over her training, at least until you are able to get back?'

'Of course.'

Jemma picked up her speed, relieved that they hadn't decided she shouldn't go, and headed to bed, praying the pilots would arrive early in the morning. As usual since Sean's disappearance, she slept fitfully, worrying about the transport zone craft and the transport zone itself but mostly about Sean. Early in the morning, she gave up and headed to the meeting room. Werrimen was already pressuring the IEMO delegates to be seated so they could get started quickly. At the appointed time, Werrimen mounted the podium and looked out at the crowd. Silence reigned almost immediately.

'Earth,' she began, 'must take a major step forward into a new era. The IPL will not leave you unprotected. We will always help you defend against invaders, and we must also ensure that you, the people of Earth, develop the skills to defend yourselves. We support the development of Earth's new Army. Every city will provide all necessary resources to those involved, as a matter of priority.' She went on to answer a string of questions and to explain the details of the rescue effort before closing the meeting.

As delegates filed out of the room, Werrimen called Jemma and Hunt to join her. 'The Condonan pilots should reach Earth just before dawn tomorrow. You should both use the down time as we wait to get some rest.'

There were small anterooms in the bunker with comfortable sofas that could be closed off to get some sleep and Jemma decided, given she hadn't slept much the night before, to find one of them. Even though it was only the middle of the day, she fell into a deep sleep and as usual, her dreams moved to Sean. It was often more of a nightmare as she imagined he was hurt and calling for help, but this time her dream seemed very real. Sean was trapped in a building. Matt was with him and someone who looked like Dragile. They were talking about how to escape their predicament. She called to him, but he didn't respond so she said, 'We're coming to get you, just sit tight. Don't do anything foolish, we're coming.'

She awoke to find Zadrus leaning over her bunk and trying to soothe her. 'Are you alright? You were calling out. I think you were dreaming about Sean.'

She described her dream and the Dragile-like being to him. Zadrus lost colour, staring at her, his mouth slightly open as though he wanted to say something but couldn't think how to word it.

'Just settle back to sleep,' he said, eventually. 'You need rest.'

*   *   *

Sean jumped off his bed, tore around the room, opened cupboards, stared into dark corners, even looked under the bed. It was so real, she had to be here. He rubbed his eyes. The dream had been so vivid. Jemma and Werrimen were in a craft. They were searching for him and had gone through the transport zone. He fell back on the bed. Just a dream. Perhaps if he believed it, even a little, it'd help him through this hell. Reluctantly, he dressed and left his room to go for breakfast. The tables were again filled with food, but this time Emilrad and the other Sidlowns were there to share it with them. Matt joined him in the hall and looked so worried that Sean decided not to tell him about his dream. He'd wait until Dan turned up.

They hadn't found anything useful the day before, and Sean was acutely aware of the helplessness that infected not just his people, but everyone in the facility from Lena down. They did discover one thing, and if they focussed on that, maybe he could boost himself and the others. Access to the docking bay was quite easy, so hijacking a craft when a Zant crew came in might be something to consider.

There'd be many people able to fly their craft, and given Condona wasn't far away, it wouldn't be difficult to fly it there and set up a rescue. It seemed that every time he came up with an idea though, someone would shoot it down, so if they didn't like the idea of hijacking a craft, he'd just have to identify other things to work on. Doing nothing was the worst possible way to go. If everyone sank into depression, there'd be no hope at all. He leaned across the table.

'Emilrad, have you ever seen outside? I'd hoped to find some way to get out there and check it out.'

'I have. There is a viewing room, but it's a bit hard to get to. If we can distract the guards, we can take you there. But, as we can't breathe outside, I'm not sure it's of much help.'

'No, I think it could be,' said Dan. 'The Zant guards must have protective gear available to them in case they have to go outside to undertake repairs. If we could find their supplies, we may be able to identify their other facilities, and maybe a long-range communicator. Have you ever seen any crafts outside, other than the type that brought us here?'

Emilrad nodded. 'I have seen transporters a few times, and I saw something once which might have been another building. I only caught a glimpse through a break in the fog before it closed over again. But I do not think it helps. The planet surface is inhospitable, there are constant sandstorms, and no trees or plants of any kind to protect you from the elements. Even if you could get hold of suitable protective clothing, and could get out there, it is far too dangerous.

From Sean's perspective, this type of conversation was much more positive. Despite Emilrad's cautions, it gave them something to think about and who would know, Dan's idea might have some merit. If they kept talking and refining their thoughts, he felt sure a sound plan would emerge. 'Are we just assuming we can't breathe out there because the Zants have told us that, or has anyone tried?'

'Good question,' smiled Emilrad. 'I do not recall anyone trying to go outside since I have been here. Maybe we should ask Lena. She has been here longer than anyone else. I cannot think of any way to determine if the air is breathable other than by going out there and suffocating if it is not. I am happy to listen to anyone else's ideas.'

'If we had equipment, we could,' said Matt. 'But without some measuring tools, I can't either. If we open the door and the atmosphere is very different, we'd most likely be sucked out with no way back, so that doesn't help. If we could get into their control room, they might have instruments to measure, probably both internal and external atmospheres and the gradient between them.'

Buoyed by the conversation, Sean was now certain that if there was a way to escape this place, they'd find it. He told Dan to take a team and go with Emilrad to the control room. With Matt, he went in search of Lena while others were to fan out and pick places they hadn't been before, keeping their eyes peeled for any kind of communication equipment.

Lena sat quietly, making notes in a well-used diary when they found her.

'Good morning, Lena,' said Sean. 'We need to talk to you about what's outside the building.'

'Ah, almost every new arrival ends up asking the same question,' she replied. 'We had another group from Earth, five or six years ago. They wouldn't accept they were stuck here either. One of them decided he'd go outside and see for himself. His friends tied some strong rope to him in case he was pulled out. He was able to breathe, but quickly became very short of breath, so clearly there's some oxygen out there, just not enough to breathe properly. The real problem was the acid in the ground surface. It ate through his footwear and into his feet before they managed to drag him back. We had no medical facilities, and no one with much medical knowledge. His legs became infected and he died. It was an awful death.'

Matt suddenly yelled. 'Oh shit. The ground outside. We've got to stop Dan. He might decide to try it out if he can get to a door.'

Lena, although startled by the shout, jumped up. 'Go, go. Don't let him outside.'

Sean tore out, with Matt and Lena on his heels, shouting into his communicator as he ran. There was no response, and he suspected Dan had turned it off. Lena, unable to keep up, called after them with directions to get to the control room. Sean was first through the door.

Dan and Emilrad sat on either side of a table which contained a variety of measuring instruments, engrossed in a friendly conversation with a couple of Zants, and Dan introduced the nearest one. 'This is Ronal. He's a scientist on Ailazant and he's been explaining his equipment to me. The concentration of oxygen is around fifty percent of what we need, so we can't breathe out there for more than a few minutes. They say we mustn't go outside anyway. If there's something wrong, they call for back-up from another building on the other side of the planet. Their back-up attends in a flying craft. Ronal says the planet's surface is very dangerous, so they're not allowed out there, at all.'

Sean, still breathing hard, asked Dan and Emilrad to head

back to the common room with him. When they got there, he slammed the door behind them and whirled around so he was centimetres from Dan's face. 'What the hell did you think you were doing, turning off your communicators? We didn't know if you were in trouble, or worse, if you'd tried to go outside.'

'Sorry, I thought we'd only be a few minutes but, when we got talking, we found out quite a few useful things.'

Sean shook his head. 'Communicators do not get turned off. Ever.'

'Yeah, sorry.'

'I apologise too,' said Emilrad. 'We should have thought more clearly.'

'Okay, what'd you find,' said Sean.

'They've got several transporters. There are other build-ings like this one, wouldn't say how many, but they also have prisoners, and …' He paused, and with a dramatic wave of his arm, went on. 'There's a central building with lots of advanced equipment.'

'Good work,' said Sean. 'Gives us something to focus on, but any idea how to get there?'

'Maybe we can create a problem, so they have to call for back-up,' said Dan. 'Then we could take over their craft.'

'Possibility,' replied Sean. 'And, if they've got long distance communication equipment in the central building, we might be able to send out a distress signal. It might work.'

'If we can force the guards here to send a signal to the other building, we could overpower their pilots and take the craft,' said Dan. 'It's worth a try.'

Although careful not to let it show, Sean felt a surge of excitement. There'd only be one chance at something like this. After that, the Zants would be on their guard. They'd have to plan every move, yet there were so many unknowns that they couldn't possibly factor in every obstacle. Once he gave the go-ahead, they took it in turns to befriend the guards, although some were quite aggressive. Little by little, Sean developed a profile on each guard and their rosters, so he could predict who would be on duty at any time. Guards were rostered to the building for three months at a stretch before changing over. The current batch had been there for almost nine weeks, so there wasn't much time until the next change of guard.

He divided his team into three, the first group to mount a distraction which would separate the guards making it easier to overpower them. He asked Emilrad to lead that group. The second group would take the guards in the control room, and he planned to lead them himself. Dan would lead the third group, given that it was his idea, to lie in wait for the response team coming in from the other building.

Ronal, the friendliest guard, was to be on duty the next day, and all were in agreement that would be the perfect time to strike. No one slept much and when breakfast time came around, the food was untouched, but the coffee pot ran dry multiple times. Emilrad went first and created quite a ruckus, enabling Sean and his team to slip into the room. By the time Dan arrived, the guards were tethered to chairs, smiling and chatting as though nothing was wrong.

With a fixed smile on his face, Sean pulled Dan out of

earshot. 'Ronal's called for help. He's so relaxed you need to be careful he hasn't given them a distress signal.' He'd barely finished speaking, when a soft thud alerted him to someone outside, which left no time to ponder the possibilities.

A Zant craft slid into a small air lock and its crew waited inside, until the entry was secured, before emerging.

As soon as all the Zants had entered the control room, Dan pounced. Their lack of resistance again made Sean uneasy, but it was too late to pull out, so he grabbed their leader and signalled to Dan to move out. 'They've probably left a pilot in the craft. Hopefully they don't take off when they see us.'

The transporter was big enough for three humans, in addition to the two pilots who had stayed in it. Sean followed Dan and Matt into it and ordered the pilot to take them to the other building, surprised when he obliged without any objection. He flew at a low level, just above the planet's surface.

'I'm uncomfortable,' said Sean. 'This has been too bloody easy. I know they're weak and we're getting used to overpowering them, but they've made no attempt at all to stop us. They're up to something.'

The craft gently docked in the other building. As soon as the door opened, Dan tied the two Zant pilots to their seats.

'Careful,' said Sean. 'They could have some of their mates lying in wait, or they might have interfered with the atmospheric controls. Check that we can breathe okay before anyone steps out. He stood in the doorway himself until he was satisfied the air was suitable, then he moved out, watching carefully for any sign of life, but there was nothing. In the centre of the building, they found the control room that Ronal had described, full of advanced communication and monitoring equipment.

'All right, let's get those two out so they can't take off,' said Dan. 'Then we can investigate this building.'

Sean agreed, but as he started back the entry door snapped shut, and although he picked up his speed, it was too late.

'Not much we can do,' said Matt. 'Might as well look around.'

'Yeah,' said Dan, walking back into the corridor. 'Look for another means of transport.'

Sean shook his head. 'Priority is to get that signal out. We'll see if we can make it do what we need first. Then we can look around.' When he reached the door, he pushed and it opened easily, heightening his sense of uneasiness.

Matt shrugged and walked to a chair in front of a large console. 'They probably just don't expect us to be here. If there's no risk of anyone breaking in, why bother with locks? I've used equipment like this before. It's similar to the stuff in the Administration building. I'm pretty sure I can get it working.'

'Alright, give it a try,' said Sean, keeping one eye on the doorway.

Emilrad had described the intergalactic distress signal in detail. It wasn't dramatically different from Earth's SOS signal. It required a series of three separate frequencies, repeated at different pitches for five sequences. Once Matt was sure the communicator was responding as it should, he sent the signal several times.

'Okay, so what do we do now?' said Dan, checking each way in the corridor. 'Should we try to get back into the transporter and back to the other building? I don't think there's anything more we can do. They clearly aren't worried about us being here. I guess they don't think we can do anything that would cause them a problem.'

'No,' said Sean. 'Let's continue through the building. See if we can find any sign of craft capable of long-distance travel.'

'Okay,' said Matt, 'but don't you think it's odd there are no Zants here? We've met at least fifteen guards in their various rosters, so, where are they? If they've got another escape route, we should try to find it.'

'Yeah, good thinking,' said Sean. 'We'll look but be careful. We don't know what they could do if they got one of us alone.'

Several apartments showed signs of recent occupation, unmade beds, half-eaten but still fresh food, an open printed book in a language Sean couldn't understand, even a small reading light. There was also a dining area which appeared to have been evacuated in a hurry. But no Zants.

'It's obvious they knew we were coming,' said Sean. 'Ronal must have given them a signal, and they've run.'

Matt frowned. 'Possibly, but where've they gone? I guess they could've taken off. Visibility out there's so poor we mightn't have seen a craft moving. But if so, where? And what are they up to?'

'Maybe there's a patrolling mother ship up there,' said

Dan, running back towards the small transporter. 'If that's the case we'd better try to get into our craft and head back before they decide to do something to stop us.'

'Shit,' muttered Sean, as the transporter doors opened on their approach. 'The whole thing was a set up. They didn't care that we came over here because they knew we couldn't escape. Probably didn't think we'd know the emergency signal, or maybe they've got something in place to block it. If there was a craft here that we could have hijacked, they've removed it. Maybe they all crowded onto it and took off. That's why there's no one here. Let's go. Be on your guard. They'll be expecting us.' He grudgingly admitted, but only to himself, that Landi had outmanoeuvred them. Now they'd have to face the music and hope that Landi hadn't found a way to interfere with the distress signal they'd sent.

The pilots thanked him as he untied them, then took off and flew back to the main building. Sean took the lead going inside, releasing the remaining Zants on the way, then headed into the building. It was remarkably quiet, and his uneasiness increased as he continued to the common room where they'd last seen Lena. Zants guarding the door stood aside to allow them in. Numerous people were gathered in the room, and Landi stood at the front, apparently waiting to address the gathered crowd.

'Welcome back gentlemen,' he said, smirking. 'I see that you found our other building. I must object to your treatment of my guards. They were bound for quite some time, although I do thank you for releasing them without harm. Perhaps we could have an agreement. I do not wish to harm any of you, but I must insist you do not again attempt to harm any of us if we are to live in harmony. Do you think that a reasonable agreement? I'm sure you see the sense in it.' Again, he smiled with the sneering look that he'd mastered.

Sean felt Matt tense up beside him, relieved when Emilrad moved in front. The last thing they'd need now was for Matt to rush forward and try to attack Landi. He'd be quickly dispatched by the Zants, and most likely injured. Without medical help, who would know what the outcome would be.

Landi went on. 'I'm so glad you can see things my way. This is a very confined situation. We must all try to get along peacefully. For those new male humans here, we will arrange interviews for you this afternoon. I must ask you to cooperate with my guards. We don't wish to hurt you, but of course we will if you misbehave.'

Sean whispered. 'What the hell does that mean, interviews?'

'Do you remember that I told you they would expect you to make a contribution to their slave trade?' said Emilrad. 'When they bring you in, they refer to it as *interviews*. Rather quaint I suppose, but they seem unable to specify what they are doing. I strongly recommend you do not fight them. They will use whatever force it requires and will not care about hurting you in the process. They just want your sperm, please do not be heroes.'

Matt was frozen in place, staring at Landi. Thankfully, Emilrad's grip on his arm stopped him from acting. Sean also found Landi detestable but was worried that Matt's reaction would put him at risk. Matt had stopped him from taking a swing at Landi once before. He'd have to return the favour now.

'Listen to me,' said Sean, stepping in front of Matt and taking hold of his shoulders.

Matt didn't move. He continued to stare at the front of the room.

'Listen to me,' repeated Sean, his voice harder. 'Have you had a problem with Landi that I don't know about?'

'No,' said Matt, sighing. 'I'd never seen him, or any other Zant before the last few weeks, but I'm damned sure they're responsible for all those people who were taken during the original invasion, including Dana. She was seven months pregnant. He's got her, and he's also got our child somewhere out there, wondering who the hell her father is. I pray every day that they left her with her mother. When these bastards smirk and sneer, knowing they have total control over us, my blood boils.'

'Okay mate, I think I understand, but you're going to have to control it. Not only do I not want to see you hurt, but I need you with me in one piece if we're to have any hope of finding a way out of here. And of finding your wife.'

Sean and Dan kept him talking as they waited for the guards, offering calming messages in the hope he would listen. They continued all the way along the corridor until they were shoved roughly into separate rooms and handed a jar that looked like the kind used after a football game for a drug test, but Sean was sure that wasn't what they wanted. They gave him a bizarre demonstration, using a plastic object, but didn't seem able to just say ejaculate and give us some sperm. Like Matt, he didn't want to go along with them, but he intended to stay alive long enough to find a way to escape. Even so, he was apparently too slow. One of the Zants returned and pulled at his penis. He reeled back in horror.

'Give me a chance!' he exclaimed. 'It's not instantaneous.'

'You have five more minutes,' replied the Zant.

He couldn't think of a better way to kill the mood. He'd thought if he dreamed about Jemma, he'd get it, but now, everything was gone. Five minutes wouldn't fix it, and he was right. At exactly five minutes, two Zants returned, both armed with their equalisers. One shackled him to the bed, the other inserted a needle right through his scrotum. This had to be the worst kind of violation. God alone knew how Matt would be coping. He'd fight them all the way. But, for now, he couldn't focus on Matt. He had to get himself through the ordeal first, help others later. As soon as they'd finished, he was pushed back to his room and shoved inside. He staggered to the bathroom, unable to control the vomiting and shaking. After a while he managed to sit on the floor, head down. He had to concentrate on his breathing to stop himself from passing out. The sensation slowly passed, and he manoeuvred himself into the shower, turning the water on as hot as he could make it, directing the scalding water over every part of his body, doing his best at cleansing even the thought of a Zant touching him. He stood there for more than half an hour before he felt strong enough to turn the water off and move out. Aware that he should dress and join the others for dinner, he did, but he wasn't ready to face anyone yet. Dan would be like him, shattered but okay. Hopefully Emilrad and Catarina would look after Matt. For now, he needed a good night's sleep to get back some emotional balance. He headed back to his room, found the photo of Jemma that he always carried and, holding it close, drifted off into a fitful sleep.

When he woke, he knew in his heart that Jemma and Werrimen had started their search for him. Despite feeling devastated by his situation, he felt absolutely confident they'd succeed even though, deep down, he suspected that was irrational. No one knew where they were. But if it got him through his incarceration, he'd hold onto the thought and give himself something to believe in.

He jumped into the shower, this time at a normal temperature, then dressed and headed out to breakfast feeling a little better, knowing that Jemma was coming, even if only in his dreams. Dan was doing his best to calm Matt, who was holding forth about their need to escape from the bastard Zants. It was obvious he'd taken quite a beating. He was covered in bruises and lacerations and his eyes were blackened and swollen. His fury would take time to abate. Sean left Dan to deal with him and took his breakfast to a corner by himself. He drifted into his own world and he imagined the various ways his reunion with Jemma could take place. He was sure of one thing though, if they were reunited, they would never again be separated.

CHAPTER 22

Real sleep eluded Jemma, as it had since Sean had gone missing. Just before dawn, she gave up and sat on the side of her bed. With nothing else to do given that everyone else was asleep, she waited for the day to dawn, doing her best not to think about what might have happened to Sean. Relieved when Werrimen called to say that the Condonan pilots had arrived, she ran to the meeting room. She looked around for the pilots, but everyone in the room was either human or a Sidlown that she already knew well. Werrimen didn't allow her the time to ask questions, directing her to another room to pick up the protective gear she would need for the journey.

Nik was already in the room, trying on an over-suit. She grinned at Jemma. 'You didn't think I'd let you do this by yourself did you?'

'Oh my God. Oh Nik. Thank you. Thank you,' she cried, throwing her arms around her cousin. 'We'll find them. I know we will.'

As with everything else alien, the kits folded easily into a large backpack. The mask which had the capacity to make oxygen from whatever it found in the atmosphere, attached neatly to the front of the pack, along with a small cylinder which, she was assured, contained breathable air should it be needed. She headed back with Nik to the meeting room. Werrimen sent them off again to pack two changes of clothes into their back packs. Knowing she had to be cooperative if she was to remain part of the expedition, she controlled her irritation that she still hadn't met the pilots, and complied. When she returned, Werrimen led her to the front of the meeting room. There were two people there, who stood apart from the rest, and both were human. Smiling, Werrimen introduced them as Cadzine and Warben.

Jemma frowned, although she shook the proffered hands. 'But where are the pilots?' As far as she knew, no humans had been trained to fly these ships.

'We are the pilots,' said Cadzine. 'It's a pleasure to meet you.'

'I'm sorry,' stammered Jemma. 'But you're human. We were expecting someone from another planet.'

'I understand,' said Warben. 'We are humans from the planet Condona. It shocked us, as we travelled around the galaxies, to come across many planets populated by humans.'

Jemma couldn't think of anything to say. She'd known Anders Major had a human population, but it just hadn't occurred to her that there might be other human planets. As she thought about it, she realised that was quite silly. Werrimen had told her there were many inhabited planets, and most planets were friendly, so why not human?

Warben, still smiling, turned to Werrimen. 'Before we

start, I must inform you that we have had communication through from our home galaxy that they have picked up a faint distress signal. The signal is the one used traditionally by members of the IPL and, since we know the Earth humans are in the company of Sidlowns, we are hopeful the signal might be theirs.' He looked at Jemma and Nik. 'Ladies, you must not get your hopes up, we have no evidence that it is them. My people are still trying to pinpoint the signal but, so far, have not succeeded.'

'Indeed, that is encouraging,' Werrimen replied. 'Has there been any sighting of Landi?'

'No, not that I have heard.'

The briefing lasted around an hour, and Jemma became increasingly impatient as each minute ticked by. She wanted to get started. It'd probably be weeks before they had any chance of success but, even so, once the ship took off, they'd at least be on their way. After the briefing, Werrimen took the Earth humans aside to explain the transport zones and how to cope with them. Jemma was buddied with a Sidlown, as was Nik and each of the other Earth humans. For the first time, since demanding to join the mission, the enormity of what she was about to do overwhelmed her, not just facing up to a transport zone, but the fear of failing, and of never seeing Sean again was almost more than she could bear.

'My dear, I can feel your distress,' said Werrimen. 'No one would judge you if were to change your mind and choose not to go.'

Jemma shook her head. 'I have to go. I understand we

might not find them, but I need to know that I've done everything possible.'

'Well then, we must board the craft.'

Jemma followed her through the blue light into the landing bay, then onto a disc which took them up to a lounge section. Werrimen explained it was closest to the centre of gravity of the craft and therefore the safest place to be as they travelled through the transport zone.

Her Sidlown buddy showed her to her seat. Being a Zant ship, it was more basic than those on the IPL ships she knew. He showed her how to fasten a rough harness attached to the arms and back of her seat. As the propulsion system geared up, she reached out to Nik, who was seated beside her, and the women held onto each other's hands as the craft lifted off. As they flew out beyond Earth's atmosphere, and she looked down to see her planet rapidly reducing in size, the stark reality of what she was doing sank in. She was out in space, probably about to cross the Universe, heading for parts unknown, and going into God knows what sort of danger. There was no way off this ship until it landed somewhere. She sat up when an announcement was made that they were close to the coordinates from which the Zant craft had disappeared.

'This is it,' Werrimen said. 'Prepare yourselves. The sooner we get into it, the sooner it will be over.'

Jemma's Sidlown buddy took her free hand as Werrimen headed for the control centre at the front and closed the door behind her.

'Just try and listen to me if things get rough,' he said.

'We'll get through this together. There is food in the servery between your seats. Cold food only. We cannot risk injury from hot items. Ablutions are more difficult. If you should need the bathroom, you must hold onto the rail that runs between the rows of seats. It is safe enough so long as you are careful.'

Jemma smiled in return and hoped she looked at least a bit convincing that her confidence had returned. Although the ride was rough when they were fully into the transport zone, it didn't seem to be much worse than severe turbulence in an aircraft of her day. The difference was that it lasted a lot longer. She had no idea how long it had taken when they were told they were out of the zone. It had to have been at least forty-eight hours.

When Werrimen re-joined them, her face was flushed. She looked happier than she had since the day she'd told Jemma she'd be coming on this trip and had to inform Zadrus that she'd be leaving him behind. 'It seems we are in my galaxy. That means if we can locate our people, we will have plenty of help available.'

'Are you sure?' said Jemma.

'Come with me,' said Werrimen. 'I will show you. We recognised the planet you can see directly ahead of us. It has a distinctive colour and the cloud around it is unusual. There's nothing else like it anywhere in the Universe. It is the outermost planet of our galaxy. Do you see what this means? That signal may well be the men we're looking for.'

Cadzine held up his hand for silence. 'I'd like to try to

contact Condonan control. If I can get a response, they will be able to confirm that we are where we think we are. Would you all please move outside? I'll let you know what's happening.'

Werrimen stayed with him as he used the long-range communicator. Finally, Cadzine emerged to explain that Condonan command had confirmed their location. 'They will now direct both the search and the rescue. We must wait for instructions.'

In her mind, and with so many people dedicated to finding the men, Jemma was sure that it was only a matter of time, although the constant waiting was getting her down. She trusted the people who were running the mission implicitly, but now she'd again have to control the anxiety that pervaded her entire being. All she wanted was to see Sean, hug him, hold him, and know he was safe.

She jumped as she felt Werrimen's arm come around her. 'I believe we are in the right place, and we will find them. Just a little longer.'

'Condonan Command are almost certain they have identified the location of the signal,' said Cadzine. 'An outer planet in our galaxy has three orbiting moons, and the signal appears to have come from the outermost moon. We are to proceed there and enter an orbiting pattern to wait for other crafts to back us up. It will take about a week.'

Deflated, Jemma headed to her room for a rest. Over the next few days, depression set in and she only emerged for meals. On day four, Werrimen sat her down, and told her sharply that she must occupy herself with something useful.

She was given tasks to do and although most seemed point-less, she busied herself with them, and joined in conversations with Nik and others, and slowly came out of the state that had crippled her. She still dreamed about Sean each night, willing him to be safe until they reached him. Finally, Cadzine announced they'd gone into an orbiting pattern around the targeted moon. The craft that had been sent from Condona was still at least a day away, which meant more waiting, but she could see the moon that was their target, and she imag-ined Sean waiting down there for them to arrive and snatch him away from the Zants.

It was two full days before the Condonans finally arrived. They had a team of Trustees from Sidlow on board who'd contacted Condona as soon as they'd learned there was a problem. On receiving the report that Jemma's mission had entered their galaxy, they'd flown directly to Condona. The search for structures on the surface of the moon could now begin in earnest.

Jemma sat with Cadzine in the control room during the agonising wait, attempting to understand his explanation of images that came through, and what they indicated about the surface of the planet. It was masked by a heavy fog which sur-prised her, given he'd said there was no surface water evident. Then it dawned on her. The fog must be some other kind of gas, arising from whatever made up the surface of the moon. The problem was they had no idea what that could be, and wouldn't, until they got down there. But, if it was toxic, the only way people could survive would be if there were suitable, safe dwellings. Now she understood why they were so intent on the search for structures. It wasn't just a look around. No dwellings would mean no survivors.

'We've magnified each small sector,' said Cadzine. 'It is our best chance of finding something. It is time consuming, and I understand that means more waiting, but we have to be careful. When we go down, we must be sure that it is safe to land.'

Jemma did understand. She understood only too well. They had to determine if there was any possibility of finding anyone alive. Her heart slowly sank as minutes became hours in the painstaking search. She thought she might go out of her mind until someone on the Trustee craft yelled, 'Got something!'

She leaned over Cadzine's shoulder as he worked to focus on five separate buildings, the first promising thing they'd found. One of the buildings was in the centre, the other four equidistant from it, forming a square pattern around the outside, but quite a long distance apart. The central building seemed smaller although it was possibly taller, maybe two or three stories. It had a spike rising from the centre, perhaps a radar or comms tower. Jemma and Nik clung to each other but, as time dragged on, Jemma could no longer contain herself. 'Do you think they're in there?'

Cadzine motioned to the women to sit on either side of him as he zoned in on the buildings. 'There is no sign of external movement or of any life outside the buildings.' He shifted to another screen. 'Look here. There are four small black dots in the central building.'

The dots were moving. Jemma's hands shook as she gripped the desk and whispered, 'Are those people?'

'I cannot tell. It's some kind of life form. We think that building might be the command centre. Perhaps it has a few staff there. We're moving to the other buildings now. We'll know soon.'

Her body slumped. 'This is just taking so long.'

'Jemma, I understand,' he said kindly. 'We have teams checking on the atmosphere and the nature of the surface. We don't know yet if we can land safely, and we must have all our facts before we try. Otherwise, we put our people in jeopardy and fail to help the people down there. Try to stay calm. We are close now.'

'I'm sorry. I know you're doing everything you can. This is all just so overwhelming to me.'

Before Cadzine answered, there were loud cheers from the Trustee craft. All but one of the buildings showed signs of life, and in fact, many lives. Arguments then ran back and forth between their Trustees, the Trustee Commander, and the Condonan command for a couple of hours on how to proceed. Dragile wanted to use the craft that had brought them from Earth. It was a Zant craft, and he thought they'd be less suspicious of one of their own approaching them. Condonan command steadfastly disagreed, insisting there were too many people on board. They wanted to send transporters to each building simultaneously with armed Trustees, to assess the situation.

Finally, Jemma could no longer tolerate the procrastination.

She shouted at the Trustee who was attempting to negotiate with Condonan command. 'This is garbage. You're wasting time arguing. Just decide which way to go and get down there.'

After a moment of total silence in both crafts and the command centre, Cadzine was directed to remove Jemma from his control room. She went to respond, but Werrimen who had been standing close behind, leaned down to make sure the she could be clearly seen. Her voice was both hard and firm. 'She will not be leaving this room,' she said. 'You would do well to remember that both she, and I, are here.'

The response was just three words, 'Your servant, madam.' All heads bowed.

Jemma stared at Werrimen. 'What the hell?'

'Do not worry,' she replied. 'They will behave now.'

Turning back to the Trustee Commander on the Condonan craft, Werrimen said, 'I agree this ship cannot go down. Do you have five transporters available, so you can send one to each building?'

'Yes, madam.'

'Then prepare them to go. Make sure all personnel are well armed and have suitable protective clothing. They must all arrive at the same time.'

The Trustee Commander immediately instructed the crew of the five small transporters to go down to each of the buildings. They were to assess the situation, then contact the Condonan Commander who would send whatever was needed to enable a total evacuation.

Jemma stared at Werrimen, stunned by the absolute

compliance with her command.

Werrimen smiled, 'I'm known to be bossy.'

Although Jemma smiled in return, it was more than that, much more. From the moment she'd met Werrimen, as she recovered from the burns that had almost killed her, she'd felt utterly safe in her company, even before she'd understood who Werrimen was, or where she came from. There was something about her that simply engendered trust. If Werrimen said something, Jemma believed her without question.

More hours passed, before reports finally started to come in. The central building was found to be a control facility as they'd thought. It managed the air and water supply to the other buildings, and it had several Zant crafts docked around it. The transporter belonging to the Trustees quickly took control of it.

'Who knows where they'd get water from on this God-forsaken place,' one of the pilots muttered.

Jemma felt ill. If this place was so desolate, could anyone have survived? *Oh please. Please find him.*

She felt a large arm around her shoulder. This time it was Dragile who held her to him. 'I know how you feel, my dear. I really do. I ache for news of my brother.' He held her and Nik close as they waited, each with their own desperation, for any word of survivors.

One of the outside buildings was derelict, appearing to have fallen victim to fire at some time. Transporters docked in each of the other buildings, including the central administration one. Representatives from each of the accommodation buildings were taken into the transporters and asked to report to Condonan command on their situation.

Dragile, Nik and Jemma stayed close together, waiting for information to come through, Werrimen beside them.

'We'll hear very soon,' said Werrimen. 'The news will be good. I am sure of it.'

Finally, someone on one of the transporters spoke. 'I have with me two representatives from each of the buildings.'

Then a strong male voice said, 'Hello Jemma, I believe you've come to find me.' She held on tightly to Dragile whose broad smile was all the support she needed.

'Yes, I have,' she said, happily. She felt Dragile jump as the screen lit up.

'By the stars Emilrad, is that you?'

'Yes brother, it is. I knew you'd come. I never lost hope.'

'Where's Dan?' Jemma looked at Nik as she asked.

'He stayed behind in the facility to help organise. Matt's there too. They're both okay.'

A couple of emotional minutes passed to allow the greetings, until Werrimen interrupted, 'We must get organised. Your conversations must wait. They are not safe until we get them off that place and land on Condona.' She turned back to the screen and to the Trustee who had deferred to her earlier. 'I need a full report. Do we know how many people are in each building? Are there likely to be any injured or infirm people who need to be moved? What about the Zants? Do we know how many are down there? Will they give us a problem getting out of the buildings?'

'There are around 600 people in our building, mostly human,' replied Emilrad. 'There are a few older people, but really no one who is particularly infirm. And the Zant presence is very small.'

'Our building is much the same,' said another. 'There would be a few less people, around 450. We do have a couple of injured people who we've been nursing. A specialised craft to rescue them would be very welcome.'

'We have around 600 people and no serious injuries,' said a woman.

Werrimen directed the Trustee to contact Condonan Command and provide them with the numbers. 'One large ship should be enough. Take transporters to ferry people from each building. It will need several trips, but it is better than risking a large ship.'

'Yes madam,' replied the Trustee. 'The Zants would now know we are here and will probably have commenced their own evacuation.'

'Agreed, but our main priority must be to rescue the prisoners. We may capture some of the Zants, but their leadership is most likely, as you say, already gone. Focus on the rescue for the moment. We will chase them later.'

'Yes madam. Several Condonan and IPL crafts are heading our way. They will be here within a few hours and might be able to intercept any Zants attempting to flee. We will get them in the end.'

'Oh yes, we will,' said Werrimen. 'I do not care how long it takes. We will achieve justice.'

'It's Landi I want,' said Dragile. 'And I will do anything to get him.'

'We absolutely agree with you,' said the Trustee, as Werrimen put a hand on Dragile's shoulder. 'We believe he runs this facility. He could even be down there.'

'I doubt it,' sighed Dragile. 'He is too cunning for that.'

Werrimen rubbed her hand across Dragile's shoulders. 'We will get him.'

'We must.'

She nodded and turned back to the screen. 'I would like to send Jemma over in a transporter to the Condonan craft that has Colonel Bellamy on board. Is that acceptable to you?'

'Most certainly, I'll organise the docking bay to expect her arrival.'

Jemma hugged Werrimen. 'Thank you.'

Nik walked with her to the transporter. 'Hang in there. It's almost over.'

Jemma felt like she floated into the transporter, barely even noticing the vibration as they started to pull out of the docking bay. The two Trustee guards, assigned to protect her, were heavily armed, which always made her nervous even though she understood the need.

As the transporter separated from the large spacecraft, the shadow of a very small figure crossing the pilot's entrance caught her eye. An agonised cry followed, and the control room door suddenly slammed shut. Jemma froze as she watched her guards desperately try to prise it open.

One of the guards yelled into his communicator, 'Hijack, we need help.'

'We're on our way.' Jemma could just recognise Werrimen's voice through the static.

Ipnes, the senior guard, sat beside her. 'There is nothing we can do now,' he said. 'If you look out the window, you will see there are crafts following us. We have to wait until this character decides to land, then we can act. Do your best to stay calm and let us work out how to handle it.'

She flung herself into a chair directly opposite him. 'Stay calm? Do nothing? Why wasn't this transporter checked? How could a Zant be here, and no one saw him? We can't sit tight. We have to do something.' Yes, she could see the crafts following. But how the hell did that help?

Sean heard the distress call and, seconds later, heard Werrimen bellow at her security people.

'How, by all the stars, could this have happened?' Werrimen swore at the communications' officer. 'Get the Trustee Commander, immediately. Tell them I'm following.'

Sean shouted through the communicator. 'What the hell's happening?'

'Werrimen, Colonel Bellamy, stand down both of you,' said a man, presumably the Trustee Commander. His voice was firm and controlled. 'Werrimen, we are both Supreme Trustees, but I am in command here. You will listen to me. My people have orders to ensure that.'

'You threaten me?'

'No. You are angry. I am giving you time to calm yourself. If you agree to accept my orders, you may follow, but you will stay out of the way of the fighter crafts. Is that clear?'

Sean gasped. He'd not heard anyone speak to Werrimen like that before. He didn't understand the Trustee structure, but he knew there were only three above her in the entire IPL organisation. No way was the current commander her equal.

Dragile seemed to be trying to calm her down, too.

'Remember why you made me stand down Werrimen,' said Dragile. 'You are now in the same position.'

There was a long silence and Sean wondered who Werrimen was murdering. 'I will not interfere,' said Werrimen, 'but hear me well. That girl is like a daughter to me. If any harm should come to her, heads will roll. You will withdraw your fighter crafts immediately.'

'All fighter crafts,' said the commander after a prolonged silence. 'Do not engage with the Zant transporter. I repeat, do not engage. Maintain surveillance.'

Sean could no longer contain his anger. 'What the hell is going on? You said she was safe. Why didn't your people check the transporter?'

'We don't know what has happened,' the commander responded quietly. 'Those transporters were thoroughly searched. A Zant has somehow stowed away. The best way to help her now is to stay calm as we dispatch transporters to chase them.'

'Stay calm when God knows what's happening to Jemma. You can't be serious. Get me on one of the transporters,' Sean yelled back.

Emilrad stepped in front of Sean. 'Commander, I will accompany him. Brother, if you can still hear me, take care. I do not plan to lose you, now that we have found each other.'

'I hear you. And I will see you soon,' said Dragile. 'Werrimen, I am coming with you. We have reversed roles in keeping each other calm.'

'You are right, and of course you will come with me.'

Emilrad told Sean to stay close to a Trustee who looked put out to be baby-sitting.

'Right,' came the rather irritated order, 'follow me.'

'Take it easy,' Emilrad said to the Trustee. 'I am with him.'

The Trustee, whose uniform was a deep grey, gave a formal bow, and said, 'Your servant, sir.' He didn't sound subservient, rather it seemed to be a mark of genuine respect.

Surprised by the startled look the young Trustee had given as he'd faced Emilrad, Sean noticed the stars on Emilrad's crest. There were ten. Not as many as Werrimen's but equal to Zadrus. Although not familiar with the grey uniform, he presumed this fellow was junior. He waited until the younger man had gone to speak to the pilots on Emilrad's orders. 'What was that all about?'

Emilrad smiled, 'Nothing to worry about. I am just senior to him.'

'By quite a distance by the look of that.'

Emilrad just smiled again.

Sean sat where he'd been directed. He could see the hijacked craft through the front of his transporter, which reassured him a little, but he couldn't stop himself from thinking about how Jemma must be feeling. After coming all this way to find him, and now this. She had to be terrified. If only they'd chosen a different path for themselves. He should have rejected the security force and the new Army. They could have aimed for a nice house. A garden. A family. Kids running around. He smiled at himself. Could they really live their lives like that? A nice safe mundane suburban family. He shuddered.

He heard the pilot exclaim, 'There's another craft tailing us.'

Emilrad ran to see. 'Too far away to identify. Keep trying to get them on the communicator. Hopefully, it's friendly.'

'The direction of the transporter that has Jemma on board suggests they are heading to Condona,' said the pilot. 'I don't understand why they would do that. Zants aren't welcome there.'

Nothing the Zants ever did made sense to Sean. He rested back and closed his eyes. He felt so helpless. It was less than a couple of years since they'd left early twenty-first century Earth, and here he was eighty years later, in a spacecraft on the other side of the universe attempting to rescue the woman he loved after she'd also traversed the universe to rescue him. And he used to think climbing a mountain was challenging!

'I've got a transmission,' called the pilot. 'The craft following us has Werrimen and Dragile on board. It is the Zant ship that they used to cross the transport zones. They are going to help us with tracking. It will take several hours to get to Condona, so you might as well sit back and relax, we can't do anything more than we are at this stage.'

* * *

Ipnes, and the other guard, continued trying to break into the control room of the Zant transporter, without success. Jemma knew from past experience she'd have to accept they were doing all they could. She followed their directions, but that didn't help her control her fear. She sensed they were heading down just before Ipnes confirmed it, though he wasn't sure where they were heading. The only inhabited planet he knew within this time frame was Condona.

'Does that mean we have some chance of friendly forces to help us?' she asked.

'Probably. Remember the Trustees are following. They will help us, but first this craft must land.'

They flew across the surface of a clearly inhabited planet, and past a large number of small buildings, which appeared to be residential. People, humans, stared up at them as they passed. This had to be Condona, but she still couldn't understand why they would have come here until she saw a silver shed, much like the one through which Sean had been taken at the dam site. Numb with horror, she realised there was little they could do other than sit and watch as they flew to the back of the shed, then turned towards what appeared to be a cliff face, and into a docking bay. She looked helplessly at Ipnes. They were heading towards a Zant ship which was probably powering up even now. Landi would escape yet again, but this time he was going to take them with him.

When they docked, armed Zants entered the transporter from below through a blue light and ordered her guards to drop their weapons. They were pushed out into the open bay, then roughly shoved into another, much larger craft.

'Ah, Dr Anderson.' Landi turned from the controls to smile at her. 'So good to see you again. I do hope Mr. Bellamy is well. I've heard he and his friends evacuated our wonderful facility in a hurry. Such a shame, they seemed happy there. Now, I'm afraid you're going to have to join us for a while. We don't wish to hurt you, but you must help us get out of here without any more nasty behaviour from your IPL friends. They're so rough and uncouth.'

The security guards closed in around her as Landi spoke. 'I'm sure you understand the IPL is following us,' she responded. 'So, I suspect your chances of getting away are really quite poor.'

'No, I don't think so, my dear. Nonetheless, we will take precautions as we depart. Now, to ensure your travel is comfortable, I'll show you to the travel lounge.'

They followed him, as there didn't seem to be any alternative. She sank into a chair as she felt the vibration of the craft powering up. It was only minutes before they left the ground and shot upwards.

Ipnes thought they would most probably head to Ailazant, given it was so close to Condona and, as they entered the atmosphere of another planet, they seemed to be heading down to a populated area. She heard Landi arguing with someone, gesticulating wildly as he tried to make his point. Suddenly the craft shot upwards again. Landi stormed around the control room, yelling at anyone who got in his way. A few minutes later, they began to descend again, this time in an unpopulated area. Several other crafts landed just after them, one of which looked like the ship that had brought her from Earth.

'IPL transporters,' said Ipnes.

Jemma nodded but continued to watch, hoping to see Werrimen or Dragile. Several smaller crafts landed surrounding the one in which she sat and dozens of armed Trustees jumped out. She knew they were there to rescue her, but the amount of weaponry, and the look on their faces, was frightening.

*   *   *

Sean stood when his craft also landed, but Emilrad ordered him to stay put. He'd been informed that the Zant leaders were unhappy with Landi and they'd called a temporary truce with the IPL, to enable them to deal with their problem. Sean knew the situation was volatile and could deteriorate in an instant, and acknowledged that he was emotionally involved, but didn't consider that this made him a liability. He was perfectly capable of controlling himself and following orders, but arguing would be futile, so he sat with Emilrad near a window to watch what was happening outside.

Suddenly a door opened and Dragile rushed in. 'By the stars Emilrad, it really is you.'

'It is so good to see you brother,' said Emilrad, smiling.

After they embraced, Dragile turned to Sean, 'You must stay strong just a little longer. We will get her back.' He bowed his head slightly to his brother, and returned to the door, leaving Sean and Emilrad to watch in silence through the window.

It was several minutes before a door opened in the Zant craft and a set of stairs extended down from the front. Landi emerged, pushing Jemma in front of him, his weapon held high so that he could easily turn it on her.

Werrimen, standing at the base, motioned to her people to move back and wait for Landi's next move.

'Greetings to you, Werrimen, so good to see you again,' said Landi. 'I would like you to move aside and, of course, take your people with you. I don't wish you to be alarmed but should you force me to, I will not hesitate to kill this beautiful young lady.'

It took Werrimen a few seconds to assess the situation, and when she spoke her voice was laced with venom. 'We will do that. Now let Jemma go.'

'No, not quite yet. We have to remove ourselves from this area before we can give up our insurance. Now make sure you stand aside to allow my people out.' Several other Zants emerged, pushing the IPL guards and pilots in front of them.

'We will allow you through,' growled Werrimen.

'I appreciate your cooperation,' said Landi. 'We will head towards the trees on your right. Wait five minutes after we are out of sight, then you may follow. Come any sooner and we will kill your people. I do hope there is no misunderstanding about my instructions.'

'All right Landi, you win for the moment. But don't think for one millisecond you are going to get away with this. I will hunt you down and bring you to justice, no matter how far I have to go, and no matter what I have to do. I hope that is clear.'

'Very clear, but quite inappropriate at this juncture. You

see I have the prize, and I will have no qualms in killing her if you push me too far. The only value she has to me is in eluding you. It is quite simple. If you take away her value to me, you take away my need to keep her living.' Landi stroked Jemma's hair and her look of revulsion was too much for her guards. Ipnes rushed at Landi and was quickly dispatched with an equaliser, leaving him writhing on the ground. Landi used the resulting confusion to move Jemma, and the rest of his people, away. Ipnes pulled himself up and walked with them, although he was clearly in agony.

Sean was shocked by the length of time it took the Zants to get out of the craft and to the line of trees. They really were quite weak. Any of Werrimen's people could overpower him in an instant, yet he understood why they didn't move. He had no doubt Landi would carry out his threat to kill Jemma, and had to hang on to the hope that he would not want to bring the wrath of the entire IPL down on his shoulders, which would happen if he harmed her. Werrimen would see to that. Sean glared at Emilrad, then flew out of his transporter before Jemma disappeared from sight.

Werrimen grabbed him and forced him to wait. 'I know what this fellow is like. He probably does have something set up to watch us, so we will not risk Jemma's life. Stand down until I give the order.' She was too strong for him to break free, and he knew she was right, so he ceased resisting.

After the specified five minutes, she waived her people forward. Sean ran, as fast as he could, barely aware of the Trustees running with him. He pushed through what he could only describe as thick scrub, although it was different from any kind of bush that he knew. The IPL guards were tied to posts, but Jemma was nowhere to be seen. Ipnes, still in pain, shouted as one of the others worked to free him, to follow the path between two larger trees. Werrimen led the way along the path, until they came onto a small hut.

When Sean rushed to the hut, Jemma yelled frantically to stay away from the lock. 'It's got a trigger wired into it. Got to be something explosive there.'

'Out the back,' called a guard. 'There's a door. Can't see anything here.'

Werrimen checked it, then gave the all clear to break it down and help Jemma out.

'Did you see which way he went?' asked Werrimen.

'He kept going along that path,' Jemma said. 'I heard an engine, so I think he's long gone. It didn't sound like an aerial craft. If I was on Earth, I'd say it was an all-terrain vehicle.'

Werrimen took a quick look around, before returning to check on Jemma. 'I suspect you are right. Everyone, return to your transporters.'

Sean supported Jemma as they walked back to the craft. He felt like his heart might just split in two, and once they were clear of the bush, he wrapped his arms around her and held her to him. 'I was so afraid when I heard that Landi had taken your transporter. After all we've been through, I'd thought we were finally safe.'

'Me too. I was terrified I'd lost you forever, then the Condonans told us they'd heard a signal and thought it might be yours. And then I heard your voice. All I could think about was getting to you.'

He raised her face up to his and kissed her, lightly at first, then deeper, forgetting everyone and everything around him. 'We'll never, ever be separated again,' he said, as he eased back.

She smiled up at him. 'You're damn right about that.'

He noticed two guards, standing a discreet distance behind them, and he whispered to her, 'I think we need to let them get organised. They're waiting for us.'

They separated a little but continued to cling to each other.

'It's okay Werrimen,' Sean said. 'We can do whatever you need us to do.'

Werrimen nodded. 'Good, we must leave as soon as possible. Everyone into your vehicles. Pilots prepare to take off. Zant command will not agree to us chasing Landi all over Ailazant, so we are going to have to let him go, for the moment.'

Sean wasn't confident they were safe yet. The Zant leaders would be disappointed Werrimen had lost Landi. They were clearly angry with him and must have been relying on Werrimen to stop him, probably hoped she'd kill him. All Sean wanted was to get the hell off this God-forsaken planet, but he stood, with Jemma, behind Werrimen as a channel was opened with the Zant leader to discuss what had happened.

'I see,' was the response, followed by an extended pause. 'I am glad you retrieved your people.' Then another extended pause. 'Are you ready to leave?'

'Yes,' she replied.

'Then do that.' The channel was abruptly closed.

'Not quite as bad as I expected,' she said to her pilot. 'Do as he says. Take off straight away before they change their mind.'

In Sean's view, the quicker they got to their destination the better. At least they'd be safe then. The Zants had been a pest to Condona and weren't welcome there either, so help would be on hand should they try anything more to interfere. But, before they could complete their take-off preparation, a channel from the Zant leader opened again.

Werrimen growled. 'What now?'

'Kindly step outside your craft and speak to the commander who is waiting there.'

Werrimen did as he demanded and was confronted by a group of armed Zants.

The leader didn't have the sneering attitude of Landi. He spoke in a firm, although cold, voice. 'I'm afraid that we must take control of this vehicle. It has come to our attention you took this from Landi, but it still belongs to Ailazant. We do understand the situation was very difficult, but now we will have to assume you have returned it to us. It is not our intention to keep you stranded here, so we will wait until you can determine if all your people can fit into your own transport craft. If they cannot fit, we will fly you close to Condona, so you can get more transporters to help you. We are not permitted into Condonan airspace any more than they are permitted into ours. You were given permission to land here as you obviously had very good reason, but you must now, of course, leave.

If you have any thought of attempting to evade us and take off, we will shoot you down. Now, I'm sure none of us want that to happen, but if you were to be foolish, we would interpret that as an act of war which would create a very bad precedent.'

A savage look crossed Werrimen's face, but her voice remained firm. 'Give me a moment to work out our capacity.'

Emilrad touched her on the shoulder. 'Calm down. We still have to get off this wretched planet safely.'

She sighed and nodded, as she called over the Trustees, including Sean and Jemma, and asked their advice. Once they realised that the craft in which Jemma had arrived would also have to stay, it quickly became clear that there were too many people to fit into the small number of IPL transporters.

Werrimen turned back to the Zant and said, 'Would you permit us to land some extra Trustee transporters, to help us evacuate?'

'I'm afraid we do not recognise your Trustees here, so no, we cannot do that. If you wish to follow my people, we will fly you as close as we can to your destination and allow your Trustee transporters to dock on our ship, one at a time, and take you off it. I hope you find my solution satisfactory.'

The senior Trustee pilot advised Werrimen it was best to comply, but thought that she, Dragile and Emilrad should go on one of the IPL transporters and leave Condonan guards and Trustees to go with the Zants. He thought they would be less likely to try any games that way.

Werrimen gently reminded him that she, Emilrad and Dragile were also Trustees.

The pilot responded, 'I know madam, but you are our most exulted Trustees and a very handsome prize.'

Werrimen smiled and nodded. 'Understood.'

Sean waited for her to accept the offer, knowing that she wouldn't want to do anything that would jeopardise the lives of any of her people. He headed, with Jemma, to the craft Werrimen indicated, and waited for her to organise as many people as possible onto the Condonan transporters. She told those who were to travel with the Zants to pack up anything they could find that might belong to IPL members and bring it out with them, then gave the order to commence the evacuation.

*   *   *

It was a relief to finally land on friendly ground. Jemma spotted Matt as she descended through the blue light and ran to him. He threw his arms around her and lifted her off the ground, both laughing and crying at the same time and, as he put her down, she saw Dan and Nik in a crushing embrace behind them. About to run to them she was distracted by Dragile who paced back and forth, swearing and punching at the back of chairs.

'What is it, brother?' said Emilrad, frowning.

'That ship was our last hope to get people back to their respective planets,' replied Dragile, sighing. 'The Zants have systematically destroyed all the Condonan transport zone ships, and the Condonan people have not had sufficient resources to enable them to rebuild. The Zants now have the only crafts in the entire universe that can cross the transport zones. We were just lucky there were two Condonan pilots in Earth's sector who could fly the one we confiscated. Without them this rescue could not have taken place.'

Jemma stared at Werrimen, praying he was wrong, but the way Werrimen frowned as she looked at them, was worrisome.

'Are you saying there is no way for us to get back to Earth?' Jemma asked, struggling to comprehend what he'd said.

Werrimen took hold of her hand. 'We must relax now; we've been through a very traumatic time. The people of Condona have welcomed us here and will look after us. And Sidlow is not too far. They will also help us with all our needs.'

'And I'm sure I speak for everyone here when I say we're deeply grateful for everything everyone has done for us,' said Jemma. 'But how do we get back to Earth?'

Werrimen sighed. 'I am afraid, my dear, that, at this time, there is no way back to Earth. We are stranded.'

In Review

I do hope you enjoyed Stranded and, if so, I'd appreciate a
review, eg on Amazon or Kindle.

If you would like to know more about the author,
have a look at her website:
https://almcdonnell.com

www.ingramcontent.com/pod-product-compliance
Lightning Source LLC
Chambersburg PA
CBHW020540120726
47903CB00001B/63